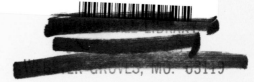

THE SCHOMBURG LIBRARY OF
NINETEENTH-CENTURY BLACK WOMEN WRITERS

General Editor, Henry Louis Gates, Jr.

Titles are listed chronologically; collections that include works published over a span of years are listed according to the publication date of their initial work.

Megda

EMMA DUNHAM KELLEY

With an Introduction by
MOLLY HITE

OXFORD UNIVERSITY PRESS
New York   Oxford

Oxford University Press

Oxford   New York   Toronto
Delhi   Bombay   Calcutta   Madras   Karachi
Petaling Jaya   Singapore   Hong Kong   Tokyo
Nairobi   Dar es Salaam   Cape Town
Melbourne   Auckland

and associated companies in
Berlin   Ibadan

Copyright © 1988 by Oxford University Press, Inc.

First published in 1988 by Oxford University Press, Inc.,
200 Madison Avenue, New York, New York 10016

First issued as an Oxford University Press paperback, 1992

Oxford is a registered trademark of Oxford University Press

Library of Congress Cataloging-in-Publication Data

Kelley, Emma Dunham.
Megda.
(The Schomburg library of nineteenth-century black
women writers)
I. Title.   II. Series.
PS2159.K13M44   1988   813′.4   87-18591
ISBN 0-19-505245-5
ISBN 0-19-505267-6 (set)
ISBN 0-19-507576-5 (PBK.)

2 4 6 8 10 9 7 5 3 1

Printed in the United States of America
on acid-free paper

The
Schomburg Library
of
Nineteenth-Century
Black Women Writers
is
Dedicated
in Memory
of
PAULINE AUGUSTA COLEMAN GATES

1916–1987

PUBLISHER'S NOTE

FOREWORD
In Her Own Write

Henry Louis Gates, Jr.

One muffled strain in the Silent South, a jarring chord and a vague and uncomprehended cadenza has been and still is the Negro. And of that muffled chord, the one mute and voiceless note has been the sadly expectant Black Woman, ...

The "other side" has not been represented by one who "lives there." And not many can more sensibly realize and more accurately tell the weight and the fret of the "long dull pain" than the open-eyed but hitherto voiceless Black Woman of America.

. . . as our Caucasian barristers are not to blame if they cannot *quite* put themselves in the dark man's place, neither should the dark man be wholly expected fully and adequately to reproduce the exact Voice of the Black Woman.

—ANNA JULIA COOPER, *A Voice From the South* (1892)

The birth of the Afro-American literary tradition occurred in 1773, when Phillis Wheatley published a book of poetry. Despite the fact that her book garnered for her a remarkable amount of attention, Wheatley's journey to the printer had been a most arduous one. Sometime in 1772, a young African girl walked demurely into a room in Boston to undergo an oral examination, the results of which would determine the direction of her life and work. Perhaps she was shocked upon entering the appointed room. For there, perhaps gathered in a semicircle, sat eighteen of Boston's most notable citizens. Among them were John Erving, a prominent Boston merchant; the Reverend Charles Chauncy, pastor of the Tenth Congregational Church; and John Hancock, who would later gain fame for his signature on the Declaration of Independence. At the center of this group was His Excellency, Thomas Hutchinson, governor of Massachusetts, with Andrew Oliver, his lieutenant governor, close by his side.

Why had this august group been assembled? Why had it seen fit to summon this young African girl, scarcely eighteen years old, before it? This group of "the most respectable Characters in *Boston*," as it would later define itself, had assembled to question closely the African adolescent on the slender sheaf of poems that she claimed to have "written by herself." We can only speculate on the nature of the questions posed to the fledgling poet. Perhaps they asked her to identify and explain—for all to hear—exactly who were the Greek and Latin gods and poets alluded to so frequently in her work. Perhaps they asked her to conjugate a verb in Latin or even to translate randomly selected passages from the Latin, which she and her master, John Wheatley, claimed that she "had made some Progress in." Or perhaps they asked her to recite from memory key passages from the texts of John Milton and Alexander Pope, the two poets by whom the African claimed to be most directly influenced. We do not know.

We do know, however, that the African poet's responses were more than sufficient to prompt the eighteen august gentlemen to compose, sign, and publish a two-paragraph "Attestation," an open letter "To the Publick" that prefaces Phillis Wheatley's book and that reads in part:

> We whose Names are under-written, do assure the World, that the Poems specified in the following Page, were (as we

verily believe) written by Phillis, a young Negro Girl, who was but a few Years since, brought an uncultivated Barbarian from *Africa,* and has ever since been, and now is, under the Disadvantage of serving as a Slave in a Family in this Town. She has been examined by some of the best Judges, and is thought qualified to write them.

So important was this document in securing a publisher for Wheatley's poems that it forms the signal element in the prefatory matter preceding her *Poems on Various Subjects, Religious and Moral,* published in London in 1773.

Without the published "Attestation," Wheatley's publisher claimed, few would believe that an African could possibly have written poetry all by herself. As the eighteen put the matter clearly in their letter, "Numbers would be ready to suspect they were not really the Writings of Phillis." Wheatley and her master, John Wheatley, had attempted to publish a similar volume in 1772 in Boston, but Boston publishers had been incredulous. One year later, "Attestation" in hand, Phillis Wheatley and her master's son, Nathaniel Wheatley, sailed for England, where they completed arrangements for the publication of a volume of her poems with the aid of the Countess of Huntington and the Earl of Dartmouth.

This curious anecdote, surely one of the oddest oral examinations on record, is only a tiny part of a larger, and even more curious, episode in the Enlightenment. Since the beginning of the sixteenth century, Europeans had wondered aloud whether or not the African "species of men," as they were most commonly called, *could* ever create formal literature, could ever master "the arts and sciences." If they could, the argument ran, then the African variety of humanity was fundamentally related to the European variety. If not, then it seemed clear that the African was destined by nature to be a slave. This was the burden shouldered by Phillis Wheatley when she successfully defended herself and the authorship of her book against counterclaims and doubts.

Indeed, with her successful defense, Wheatley launched two traditions at once—the black American literary tradition *and* the black woman's literary tradition. If it is extraordinary that not just one but both of these traditions were founded simultaneously by a black woman—certainly an event unique in the history of literature—it is also ironic that this important fact of common, coterminous literary origins seems to have escaped most scholars.

That the progenitor of the black literary tradition was a woman means, in the most strictly literal sense, that all subsequent black writers have evolved in a matrilinear line of descent, and that each, consciously or unconsciously, has extended and revised a canon whose foundation was the poetry of a black woman. Early black writers seem to have been keenly aware of Wheatley's founding role, even if most of her white reviewers were more concerned with the implications of her race than her gender. Jupiter Hammon, for example, whose 1760 broadside "An Evening Thought. Salvation by Christ, With Penitential Cries" was the first individual poem published by a black American, acknowledged Wheatley's influence by selecting her as the subject of his second broadside, "An Address to Miss Phillis Wheatly [*sic*], Ethiopian Poetess, in Boston," which was published at Hartford in 1778. And George Moses Horton, the second Afro-American to publish a book of poetry in English (1829), brought out in 1838 an edition of his *Poems By A Slave* bound together with Wheatley's work. Indeed, for fifty-six years, between 1773 and 1829, when Horton published *The Hope of Liberty*, Wheatley was the *only* black person to have published a book of imaginative literature in English. So central was this black woman's role in the shaping of the Afro-American literary tradition that, as one historian has maintained, the history of the reception of Phillis Wheatley's poetry *is* the history of Afro-American literary criticism. Well into the nineteenth century, Wheatley and the black literary tradition were the same entity.

But Wheatley is not the only black woman writer who stands as a pioneering figure in Afro-American literature. Just as Wheatley gave birth to the genre of black poetry, Ann Plato was the first Afro-American to publish a book of essays (1841) and Harriet E. Wilson was the first black person to publish a novel in the United States (1859).

Despite this pioneering role of black women in the tradition, however, many of their contributions before this century have been all but lost or unrecognized. As Hortense Spillers observed as recently as 1983,

> With the exception of a handful of autobiographical narratives from the nineteenth century, the black woman's realities are virtually suppressed until the period of the Harlem Renaissance and later. Essentially the black woman as artist, as intellectual spokesperson for her own cultural apprenticeship, has not existed before, for anyone. At the source of [their] own symbol-making task, [the community of black women writers] confronts, therefore, a tradition of work that is quite recent, its continuities, broken and sporadic.

Until now, it has been extraordinarily difficult to establish the formal connections between early black women's writing and that of the present, precisely because our knowledge of their work has been broken and sporadic. Phillis Wheatley, for example, while certainly the most reprinted and discussed poet in the tradition, is also one of the least understood. Ann Plato's seminal work, *Essays* (which includes biographies and poems), has not been reprinted since it was published a cen-

tury and a half ago. And Harriet Wilson's *Our Nig*, her
compelling novel of a black woman's expanding consciousness in a racist Northern antebellum environment, never received even *one* review or comment at a time when virtually
all works written by black people were heralded by abolition-
ists as salient arguments against the existence of human slavery. Many of the books reprinted in this set experienced a
similar fate, the most dreadful fate for an author: that of
being ignored then relegated to the obscurity of the rare book
section of a university library. We can only wonder how
many other texts in the black woman's tradition have been
lost to this generation of readers or remain unclassified or
uncatalogued and, hence, unread.

This was not always so, however. Black women writers
dominated the final decade of the nineteenth century, perhaps
spurred to publish by an 1886 essay entitled "The Coming
American Novelist," which was published in *Lippincott's
Monthly Magazine* and written by "A Lady From Philadel-
phia." This pseudonymous essay argued that the "Great
American Novel" would be written by a black person. Her
argument is so curious that it deserves to be repeated:

> When we come to formulate our demands of the Coming
> American Novelist, we will agree that he must be native-
> born. His ancestors may come from where they will, but we
> must give him a birthplace and have the raising of him. Still,
> the longer his family has been here the better he will represent
> us. Suppose he should have no country but ours, no traditions
> but those he has learned here, no longings apart from us, no
> future except in our future—the orphan of the world, he
> finds with us his home. And with all this, suppose he refuses
> to be fused into that grand conglomerate we call the "Amer-
> ican type." With us, he is not of us. He is original, he has
> humor, he is tender, he is passive and fiery, he has been

taught what we call justice, and he has his own opinion about it. He has suffered everything a poet, a dramatist, a novelist need suffer before he comes to have his lips anointed. And with it all he is in one sense a spectator, a little out of the race. How would these conditions go towards forming an original development? In a word, suppose the coming novelist is of African origin? When one comes to consider the subject, there is no improbability in it. One thing is certain,—our great novel will not be written by the typical American.

An atypical American, indeed. Not only would the great American novel be written by an African-American, it would be written by an African-American *woman:*

Yet farther: I have used the generic masculine pronoun because it is convenient; but Fate keeps revenge in store. It was a woman who, taking the wrongs of the African as her theme, wrote the novel that awakened the world to their reality, and why should not the coming novelist be a woman as well as an African? She—the woman of that race—has some claims on Fate which are not yet paid up.

It is these claims on fate that we seek to pay by publishing The Schomburg Library of Nineteenth-Century Black Women Writers.

This theme would be repeated by several black women authors, most notably by Anna Julia Cooper, a prototypical black feminist whose 1892 *A Voice From the South* can be considered to be one of the original texts of the black feminist movement. It was Cooper who first analyzed the fallacy of referring to "the Black man" when speaking of black people and who argued that just as white men cannot speak through the consciousness of black men, neither can black *men* "fully and adequately . . . reproduce the exact Voice of the Black Woman." Gender and race, she argues, cannot be conflated, except in the instance of a black woman's voice, and it is this voice which must be uttered and to which we must listen. As Cooper puts the matter so compellingly:

> It is not the intelligent woman vs. the ignorant woman; nor the white woman vs. the black, the brown, and the red,—it is not even the cause of woman vs. man. Nay, 'tis woman's strongest vindication for speaking that *the world needs to hear her voice*. It would be subversive of every human interest that the cry of one-half the human family be stifled. Woman in stepping from the pedestal of statue-like inactivity in the domestic shrine, and daring to think and move and speak,— to undertake to help shape, mold, and direct the thought of her age, is merely completing the circle of the world's vision. Hers is every interest that has lacked an interpreter and a defender. Her cause is linked with that of every agony that has been dumb—every wrong that needs a voice.
>
> It is no fault of man's that he has not been able to see truth from her standpoint. It does credit both to his head and heart that no greater mistakes have been committed or even wrongs perpetrated while she sat making tatting and snipping paper flowers. Man's own innate chivalry and the mutual interdependence of their interests have insured his treating her cause, in the main at least, as his own. And he is pardonably surprised and even a little chagrined, perhaps, to find his legislation not considered "perfectly lovely" in every respect. But in any case his work is only impoverished by her remaining dumb. The world has had to limp along with the wobbling gait and one-sided hesitancy of a man with one eye. Suddenly the bandage is removed from the other eye and the whole body is filled with light. It sees a circle where before it saw a segment. The darkened eye restored, every member rejoices with it.

The myopic sight of the darkened eye can only be restored when the full range of the black woman's voice, with its own special timbres and shadings, remains mute no longer.

Similarly, Victoria Earle Matthews, an author of short stories and essays, and a cofounder in 1896 of the National Association of Colored Women, wrote in her stunning essay, "The Value of Race Literature" (1895), that "when the literature of our race is developed, it will of necessity be different in all essential points of greatness, true heroism and real Christianity from what we may at the present time, for convenience, call American literature." Matthews argued that this great tradition of Afro-American literature would be the textual outlet "for the unnaturally suppressed inner lives which our people have been compelled to lead." Once these "unnaturally suppressed inner lives" of black people are unveiled, no "grander diffusion of mental light" will shine more brightly, she concludes, than that of the articulate Afro-American woman:

> And now comes the question, What part shall we women play in the Race Literature of the future? . . . within the compass of one small journal ["Woman's Era"] we have struck out a new line of departure—a journal, a record of Race interests gathered from all parts of the United States, carefully selected, moistened, winnowed and garnered by the ablest intellects of educated colored women, shrinking at no lofty theme, shirking no serious duty, aiming at every possible excellence, and determined to do their part in the future uplifting of the race.
>
> If twenty women, by their concentrated efforts in one literary movement, can meet with such success as has engendered, planned out, and so successfully consummated this convention, what much more glorious results, what wider spread success, what grander diffusion of mental light will not come forth at the bidding of the enlarged hosts of women writers, already called into being by the stimulus of your efforts?
>
> And here let me speak one word for my journalistic sisters

who have already entered the broad arena of journalism.
Before the "Woman's Era" had come into existence, no one
except themselves can appreciate the bitter experience and
sore disappointments under which they have at all times been
compelled to pursue their chosen vocations.

If their brothers of the press have had their difficulties to
contend with, I am here as a sister journalist to state, from
the fullness of knowledge, that their task has been an easy
one compared with that of the colored woman in journalism.

Woman's part in Race Literature, as in Race building, is
the most important part and has been so in all ages. . . . All
through the most remote epochs she has done her share in
literature. . . .

One of the most important aspects of this set is the repub-
lication of the salient texts from 1890 to 1910, which literary
historians could well call "The Black Woman's Era." In addition to Mary Helen Washington's definitive edition of
Cooper's *A Voice From the South*, we have reprinted two novels by Amelia Johnson, Frances Harper's *Iola Leroy*, two
novels by Emma Dunham Kelley, Alice Dunbar-Nelson's two
impressive collections of short stories, and Pauline Hopkins's
three serialized novels as well as her monumental novel,
Contending Forces—all published between 1890 and 1910. Indeed, black women published more works of fiction in these
two decades than black men had published in the previous
half century. Nevertheless, this great achievement has been
ignored.

Moreover, the writings of nineteenth-century Afro-
American women in general have remained buried in obscurity, accessible only in research libraries or in overpriced and
poorly edited reprints. Many of these books have never been
reprinted at all; in some instances only one or two copies are
extant. In these works of fiction, poetry, autobiography, bi-

ography, essays, and journalism resides the mind of the nineteenth-century Afro-American woman. Until these works are made readily available to teachers and their students, a significant segment of the black tradition will remain silent.

Oxford University Press, in collaboration with the Schomburg Center for Research in Black Culture, is publishing thirty volumes of these compelling works, each of which contains an introduction by an expert in the field. The set includes such rare texts as Johnson's *The Hazeley Family* and *Clarence and Corinne,* Plato's *Essays,* the most complete edition of Phillis Wheatley's poems and letters, Emma Dunham Kelley's pioneering novel *Megda,* several previously unpublished stories and a novel by Alice Dunbar-Nelson, and the first collected volumes of Pauline Hopkins's three serialized novels and Frances Harper's poetry. We also present four volumes of poetry by such women as Mary Eliza Tucker Lambert, Adah Menken, Josephine Heard, and Maggie Johnson. Numerous slave and spiritual narratives, a newly discovered novel—*Four Girls at Cottage City*—by Emma Dunham Kelley (-Hawkins), and the first American edition of *Wonderful Adventures of Mrs. Seacole in Many Lands* are also among the texts included.

In addition to resurrecting the works of black women authors, it is our hope that this set will facilitate the resurrection of the Afro-American woman's literary tradition itself by unearthing its nineteenth-century roots. In the works of Nella Larsen and Jessie Fauset, Zora Neale Hurston and Ann Petry, Lorraine Hansberry and Gwendolyn Brooks, Paule Marshall and Toni Cade Bambara, Audre Lorde and Rita Dove, Toni Morrison and Alice Walker, Gloria Naylor and Jamaica Kincaid, these roots have branched luxuriantly. The eighteenth- and nineteenth-century authors whose works are presented in this set founded and nurtured the black women's literary tradition, which must be revived, explicated, analyzed, and debated before we can understand more completely the formal shaping of this tradition within a tradition, a coded literary universe through which, regrettably, we are only just beginning to navigate our way. As Anna Cooper said nearly one hundred years ago, we have been blinded by the loss of sight in one eye and have therefore been unable to detect the full *shape* of the Afro-American literary tradition.

Literary works configure into a tradition not because of some mystical collective unconscious determined by the biology of race or gender, but because writers read other writers and *ground* their representations of experience in models of language provided largely by other writers to whom they feel akin. It is through this mode of literary revision, amply evident in the *texts* themselves—in formal echoes, recast metaphors, even in parody—that a "tradition" emerges and defines itself.

This is formal bonding, and it is only through formal bonding that we can know a literary tradition. The collective publication of these works by black women now, for the first time, makes it possible for scholars and critics, male and female, black and white, to *demonstrate* that black women writers read, and revised, other black women writers. To demonstrate this set of formal literary relations is to demonstrate that sexuality, race, and gender are both the condition and the basis of *tradition*—but tradition as found in discrete acts of language use.

A word is in order about the history of this set. For the past decade, I have taught a course, first at Yale and then at Cornell, entitled "Black Women and Their Fictions," a course that I inherited from Toni Morrison, who developed it in the mid-1970s for Yale's Program in Afro-American Studies. Although the course was inspired by the remarkable accomplishments of black women novelists since 1970, I gradually extended its beginning date to the late nineteenth century, studying Frances Harper's *Iola Leroy* and Anna Julia Cooper's *A Voice From the South*, both published in 1892. With the discovery of Harriet E. Wilson's seminal novel, *Our Nig* (1859), and Jean Yellin's authentication of Harriet Jacobs's brilliant slave narrative, *Incidents in the Life of a Slave Girl* (1861), a survey course spanning over a century and a quarter emerged.

But the discovery of *Our Nig*, as well as the interest in nineteenth-century black women's writing that this discovery generated, convinced me that even the most curious and diligent scholars knew very little of the extensive history of the creative writings of Afro-American women before 1900. Indeed, most scholars of Afro-American literature had never even read most of the books published by black women, simply because these books—of poetry, novels, short stories, essays, and autobiography—were mostly accessible only in rare book sections of university libraries. For reasons unclear to me even today, few of these marvelous renderings of the Afro-American woman's consciousness were reprinted in the late 1960s and early 1970s, when so many other texts of the Afro-American literary tradition were resurrected from the dark and silent graveyard of the out-of-print and were reissued in facsimile editions aimed at the hungry readership for canonical texts in the nascent field of black studies.

So, with the help of several superb research assistants—including David Curtis, Nicola Shilliam, Wendy Jones, Sam Otter, Janadas Devan, Suvir Kaul, Cynthia Bond, Elizabeth Alexander, and Adele Alexander—and with the expert advice of scholars such as William Robinson, William Andrews, Mary Helen Washington, Maryemma Graham, Jean Yellin, Houston A. Baker, Jr., Richard Yarborough, Hazel Carby, Joan R. Sherman, Frances Foster, and William French, dozens of bibliographies were used to compile a list of books written or narrated by black women mostly before 1910. Without the assistance provided through this shared experience of scholarship, the scholar's true legacy, this project could not have been conceived. As the list grew, I was struck by how very many of these titles that I, for example, had never even heard of, let alone read, such as Ann Plato's *Essays,* Louisa Picquet's slave narrative, or Amelia Johnson's two novels, *Clarence and Corinne* and *The Hazeley Family.* Through our research with the Black Periodical Fiction and Poetry Project (funded by NEH and the Ford Foundation), I also realized that several novels by black women, including three works of fiction by Pauline Hopkins, had been serialized in black periodicals, but had never been collected and published as books. Nor had the several books of poetry published by black women, such as the prolific Frances E. W. Harper, been collected and edited. When I discovered still another "lost" novel by an Afro-American woman (*Four Girls at Cottage City,* published in 1898 by Emma Dunham Kelley-Hawkins), I decided to attempt to edit a collection of reprints of these works and to publish them as a "library" of black women's writings, in part so that I could read them myself.

Convincing university and trade publishers to undertake this project proved to be a difficult task. Despite the commercial success of *Our Nig* and of the several reprint series of women's works (such as Virago, the Beacon Black Women Writers Series, and Rutgers' American Women Writers Series), several presses rejected the project as "too large," "too limited," or as "commercially unviable." Only two publishers recognized the viability and the import of the project and, of these, Oxford's commitment to publish the titles simultaneously as a set made the press's offer irresistible.

While attempting to locate original copies of these exceedingly rare books, I discovered that most of the texts were housed at the Schomburg Center for Research in Black Culture, a branch of The New York Public Library, under the direction of Howard Dodson. Dodson's infectious enthusiasm for the project and his generous collaboration, as well as that of his stellar staff (especially Diana Lachatanere, Sharon Howard, Ellis Haizip, Richard Newman, and Betty Gubert), led to a joint publishing initiative that produced this set as part of the Schomburg's major fund-raising campaign. Without Dodson's foresight and generosity of spirit, the set would not have materialized. Without William P. Sisler's masterful editorship at Oxford and his staff's careful attention to detail, the set would have remained just another grand idea that tends to languish in a scholar's file cabinet.

I would also like to thank Dr. Michael Winston and Dr. Thomas C. Battle, Vice-President of Academic Affairs and the Director of the Moorland-Spingarn Research Center (respectively) at Howard University, for their unending encouragement, support, and collaboration in this project, and Esme E. Bhan at Howard for her meticulous research and bibliographical skills. In addition, I would like to acknowledge the aid of the staff at the libraries of Duke University, Cornell University (especially Tom Weissinger and Donald Eddy), the Boston Public Library, the Western Reserve Historical Society, the Library of Congress, and Yale University. Linda Robbins, Marion Osmun, Sarah Flanagan, and Gerard Case, all members of the staff at Oxford, were extraordinarily effective at coordinating, editing, and producing the various segments of each text in the set. Candy Ruck, Nina de Tar, and Phillis Molock expertly typed reams of correspondence and manuscripts connected to the project.

I would also like to express my gratitude to my colleagues who edited and introduced the individual titles in the set. Without their attention to detail, their willingness to meet strict deadlines, and their sheer enthusiasm for this project, the set could not have been published. But finally and ultimately, I would hope that the publication of the set would help to generate even more scholarly interest in the black women authors whose work is presented here. Struggling against the seemingly insurmountable barriers of racism *and* sexism, while often raising families and fulfilling full-time professional obligations, these women managed nevertheless to record their thoughts and feelings and to *testify* to all who dare read them that the will to harness the power of collective endurance and survival is the will to write.

The Schomburg Library of Nineteenth-Century Black Women Writers is dedicated in memory of Pauline Augusta Coleman Gates, who died in the spring of 1987. It was she who inspired in me the love of learning and the love of literature. I have encountered in the books of this set no will more determined, no courage more noble, no mind more sublime, no self more celebratory of the achievements of all Afro-American women, and indeed of life itself, than her own.

A NOTE FROM
THE SCHOMBURG CENTER

Howard Dodson

The Schomburg Center for Research in Black Culture, The New York Public Library, is pleased to join with Dr. Henry Louis Gates and Oxford University Press in presenting The Schomburg Library of Nineteenth-Century Black Women Writers. This thirty-volume set includes the work of a generation of black women whose writing has only been available previously in rare book collections. The materials reprinted in twenty-four of the thirty volumes are drawn from the unique holdings of the Schomburg Center.

A research unit of The New York Public Library, the Schomburg Center has been in the forefront of those institutions dedicated to collecting, preserving, and providing access to the records of the black past. In the course of its two generations of acquisition and conservation activity, the Center has amassed collections totaling more than 5 million items. They include over 100,000 bound volumes, 85,000 reels and sets of microforms, 300 manuscript collections containing some 3.5 million items, 300,000 photographs and extensive holdings of prints, sound recordings, film and videotape, newspapers, artworks, artifacts, and other book and nonbook materials. Together they vividly document the history and cultural heritages of people of African descent worldwide.

Though established some sixty-two years ago, the Center's book collections date from the sixteenth century. Its oldest item, an Ethiopian Coptic Tunic, dates from the eighth or ninth century. Rare materials, however, are most available

for the nineteenth-century African-American experience. It is
from these holdings that the majority of the titles selected for
inclusion in this set are drawn.

The nineteenth century was a formative period in African-
American literary and cultural history. Prior to the Civil
War, the majority of black Americans living in the United
States were held in bondage. Law and practice forbade teaching them to read or write. Even after the war, many of the
impediments to learning and literary productivity remained.
Nevertheless, black men and women of the nineteenth century
persevered in both areas. Moreover, more African-Americans
than we yet realize turned their observations, feelings, social
viewpoints, and creative impulses into published works. In
time, this nineteenth-century printed record included poetry,
short stories, histories, novels, autobiographies, social criticism, and theology, as well as economic and philosophical
treatises. Unfortunately, much of this body of literature
remained, until very recently, relatively inaccessible to twentieth-
century scholars, teachers, creative artists, and others interested in black life. Prior to the late 1960s, most Americans
(black as well as white) had never heard of these nineteenth-
century authors, much less read their works.

The civil rights and black power movements created un-
precedented interest in the thought, behavior, and achievements of black people. Publishers responded by revising
traditional texts, introducing the American public to a new
generation of African-American writers, publishing a variety
of thematic anthologies, and reprinting a plethora of "classic
texts" in African-American history, literature, and art. The
reprints usually appeared as individual titles or in a series of
bound volumes or microform formats.

The Schomburg Center, which has a long history of supporting publishing that deals with the history and culture of Africans in diaspora, became an active participant in many of the reprint revivals of the 1960s. Since hard copies of original printed works are the preferred formats for producing facsimile reproductions, publishers frequently turned to the Schomburg Center for copies of these original titles. In addition to providing such material, Schomburg Center staff members offered advice and consultation, wrote introductions, and occasionally entered into formal copublishing arrangements in some projects.

Most of the nineteenth-century titles reprinted during the 1960s, however, were by and about black men. A few black women were included in the longer series, but works by lesser known black women were generally overlooked. The Schomburg Library of Nineteenth-Century Black Women Writers is both a corrective to these previous omissions and an important contribution to Afro-American literary history in its own right. Through this collection of volumes, the thoughts, perspectives, and creative abilities of nineteenth-century African-American women, as captured in books and pamphlets published in large part before 1910, are again being made available to the general public. The Schomburg Center is pleased to be a part of this historic endeavor.

I would like to thank Professor Gates for initiating this project. Thanks are due both to him and Mr. William P. Sisler of Oxford University Press for giving the Schomburg Center an opportunity to play such a prominent role in the set. Thanks are also due to my colleagues at The New York Public Library and the Schomburg Center, especially Dr. Vartan Gregorian, Richard De Gennaro, Paul Fasana, Betsy

Pinover, Richard Newman, Diana Lachatanere, Glenderlyn Johnson, and Harold Anderson for their assistance and support. I can think of no better way of demonstrating than in this set the role the Schomburg Center plays in assuring that the black heritage will be available for future generations.

INTRODUCTION

Molly Hite

Although Emma Dunham Kelley's *Megda* proved so popular in 1891 that it was reprinted the following year, it is not a novel that is likely to generate comparable enthusiasm among twentieth-century readers. Parochial in its range of concerns, conservative in its professions of Protestant doctrine, strangely equivocal in its preoccupation with skin color and its studied avoidance of any mention of race, *Megda* also presents a number of problems to anyone trying to place it within the tradition of Afro-American women's fiction that we are now in the process of reconstructing and reconstruing. Unlike the one work that we know precedes it in this tradition, Harriet E. Wilson's 1859 novel *Our Nig,* and unlike the two novels by black women published the year after it appeared, Frances E. W. Harper's *Iola Leroy* and Anna Julia Cooper's *A Voice From the South, Megda* contains no obvious element of social protest. Indeed, the society that it represents seems so stable that protest would be out of place: Megda's sister Elsie at one point quotes an Ella Wheeler Wilcox hymn that concludes with a familiar maxim, "Whatever is, is best" (p. 58), and similar exhortations to quietism recur periodically, reinforcing the implication that personal salvation is the only thing at issue in this Christian *Bildungsroman.*

Yet *Megda* is also a novel by a black woman, and perhaps inevitably it encodes tensions about being black and being female. The genre in which Kelley was working, a genre that

Nina Baym* has termed "girl's fiction" in contradistinction
to the "woman's fiction" that preceded it, was a late and di-
luted version of the sentimental novel. It represented a major
shift in ideology whereby, as Baym observes, a limit-break-
ing form had been transmuted into a limit-enforcing one.
But because the relation of a black woman to the limits pre-
scribed by the dominant culture can never be wholly unprob-
lematic, the aspects of this novel that seem the most ambig-
uous or strained are also the most interesting, suggesting ways
in which social themes have been muted but not entirely si-
lenced in the interests of social policing.

The most immediate question confronting the reader of *Megda*
is also one of the most important: what color are the characters? The photograph of the author in the frontispiece to both
the 1891 and 1892 editions clearly depicts an Afro-American
woman, but the schoolgirls introduced in the first chapter
seem just as clearly to be Caucasian. For example, Megda
responds to the "fair-haired" Ethel's homiletic palm-reading
with the joking disclaimer, "You ought to make a profession
of your talent, and send all the money it brings you out to
the poor heathen; or, better still, give it to some poor heathen
of your own country and color" (p. 15). If the "poor heathen"
who absorbed the attention of mission societies of the period
were by definition nonwhite, a "heathen" like Megda herself,
who by contrast was of Ethel's "own country and color,"
would accordingly be white. Later references to the Lawtons'
"colored footman" (p. 262) and to the " 'son of the South' "
who takes the vacationing girls' bags when they get off the

*Nina Baym, *Woman's Fiction: A Guide to Novels by and about Women in
America, 1820–1870* (Ithaca, N.Y.: Cornell University Press, 1978).

boat at Cottage City (p. 285) likewise appear to indicate that the principal characters are other than "colored" and distinct from low comic "sons of the South"—which is to say, white.

Not only white, but very white: The narrative is so insistent on this point that whiteness emerges as the most overused element of characterization. For example, Megda's three best friends are all blondes, and in some of the descriptive passages they seem almost to be competing for the honor of being—literally—the fairest. The angelic, doomed Ethel is "white as a snowdrop" and her "skin is almost transparent" because of her genetic inheritance: "all her people on her mother's side have very white skin" (p. 108). Dell, "the beauty of the town," has skin that is "dazzling white, without one tinge of pink in it" (p. 36). And Megda's best friend Laurie testifies to her desire for conversion with "her pretty, flower-like face quite white, and the tears standing thickly in her blue eyes" (p. 193); she gets married with her "sweet face . . . as white as the lilies, and as pure" (pp. 356–57). The frequent association of whiteness with virtue tends to support a traditional Western—and of course racist—iconography. Indeed, all three blondes are unequivocally good characters within the moral universe of the novel. Megda herself has dark eyes and "golden-brown" hair, as befits a more ethically mixed protagonist, but her "small, white hands" and "pale cheek" seem consonant in these terms with her fundamental good-heartedness.

By contrast, Maude, the villainess of the story, is the physical antithesis of these characters:

> Maude laughed too, but her large, black eyes glittered angrily. She formed a strong contrast to Ethel and Meg, with her dark, richly-colored face; large, black eyes and raven

hair. It made Ethel's delicate loveliness look almost spiritual,
and Meg's white face look whiter still, and her light-brown
hair almost golden. (p. 171)

Maude begins the book as a hypocrite, thief, and liar and
later becomes ambiguously "dissolute" and "over-excited" as
a result of a bad marriage. Throughout these developments,
her coloring is invariably described as "rich"—although we
are never told *what* color it is. But when she is on her death-
bed and on the verge of repentance, the narrator observes,
"All color was gone from the thin face; it was white enough
now" (p. 388). The implication is that in embracing heaven
at the gates of hell, Maude has finally achieved a condition
of being "white enough" that is at least aligned with, if not
the outward and visible sign of, her conversion to approved
attitudes and behavior. "Being white enough" also recalls
Laurie's comment on Megda's pallor, "The whiter, the better" (p. 157). In many ways, Kelley seems to have used "the
whiter, the better" as the governing premise of her characterization, and insofar as white *is* better in *Megda,* we might
speculate that perhaps Kelley intended her characters to be
seen as Caucasians in order to appeal to a wider circle of
readers.

But there are also tantalizing indications that, on the contrary, *no* one in the world of *Megda* is Caucasian. Henry
Louis Gates, Jr., has noted that the town of Cottage City,
where Megda, Dell, and Laurie spend their vacation, is
modeled on Oak Bluffs, a summer resort of the Massachusetts
black bourgeoisie since the late nineteenth century (Megda's
home town is close to the city of B———, and the novel
itself was published in Boston). This information implies that
the characters may well have been based on Afro-Americans

of Kelley's acquaintance. Certainly the story presents not only bad characters like Maude but also morally good characters who are not "white enough" and perhaps not white at all. For instance, Ruth, the most thoroughly Christian of the schoolgirls (horrifically so by modern standards, inasmuch as she gladly accepts the blame for a theft she never committed), has a "dark face" and "dark, work-worn" hands. To be sure, since Ruth is poorer than the other girls and must work as a servant to earn her tuition, her relative darkness might be read as an index of her social status; this is, after all, a book where gentility is a concern ranking second only to salvation. But Megda's own brother Hal is considerably darker than Megda, a detail emphasized when he takes her white hand "in his own strong, brown one" (p. 32). Differences of color within a family cannot designate differences in class and indeed cannot designate any differences that the community as a whole perceives as socially meaningful. In her *Prologue: The Novels of Black American Women, 1891–1965,* Carole McAlpine Watson terms the characters of *Megda* " 'white' mulattoes," and the near-oxymoron of this phrase suggests that the racial ambiguity of the novel could reflect some of the ambivalence that an upwardly mobile group of mixed-race people might experience when representing themselves to the outside world—or, for that matter, to each other.

Whereas *Megda* never addresses racial issues directly, alluding to them only through the persistent ambiguities of physical characterization, it regularly raises issues about the relations betwen the sexes, most often by making such relations a topic of general discussion. During the first half of the story, the young Megda frequently argues for the equality

and even the superiority of women, and her role as acknowledged leader of a group composed of both boys and girls
lends credence to her assertions. The guardedly feminist tone
of the book's early parts is in fact reminiscent of the sentimental novel at the height of its influence and popularity
some thirty years earlier. As Jane Tompkins has recently
maintained in *Sensational Designs: The Cultural Work of
American Fiction, 1790–1860*, the genre could be very rad-
ical both in its assertion of Christian values embodied in a
community whose exemplary members were women and in
its repudiation of the implicitly masculinist values represented by war, slavery, capitalism, and "worldliness" in general. But the evangelical Christianity of the late nineteenth
century stressed that inequities should be accepted rather than
changed, and it thus stigmatized the aspirations of oppressed
groups as wrong-headed, if not exactly sinful. The shift in
spiritual priorities helped turn the crusading sentimental novel
into the limit-enforcing genre of "girl's fiction," the female
Christian *Bildungsroman*.

The action of *Megda* turns on the conversion experiences
of a group of young middle-class Baptist women and their
subsequent (or even, according to the logic of the narrative,
consequent) marriages. Megda herself serves as a paradigm
of the unruly or willful soul who experiences difficulty arriv-
ing at faith, and most of the plot twists within her story stem
from her missed opportunities to forgive her enemies or to
place her reliance on Jesus rather than on her own perverse
and fallible will. In twentieth-century terms, this emphasis
invariably reduces social questions to personal ones, so that
the novel remains rather claustrophobically centered on the
everyday life of a small, well-to-do community and especially
on the individual quest for salvation.

This quest functions as the structuring principle of the *Bildungsroman* in that it defines the experience of achieving adulthood as an experience of renouncing the self and acknowledging total dependence on God. Within this Christian context, growing up can seem oddly like growing *down*, a diminution, or even a fall. The situation is aggravated by the fact that the self in question is female, for a young woman must grow "up" into one of a very small number of available roles, most of them so constricting that they betray the promise that she displays in her adolescence. For example, despite her elocutionary talents and her detached professional assessment of the Reverend Mr. Stanley's preaching, Megda can never become a minister, and so her "development" must be a process that will shrink her into that nearest available thing, a minister's wife. Her journey toward this goal may well strike twentieth-century readers as a regression, inasmuch as it takes her away from leadership, self-reliance, and personal responsibility for her actions—away, that is, from precisely those qualities that make her attractive as a heroine.

The process is one of sustained humiliation. Megda must come to understand that everything she has assumed about her own competence and integrity has been mistaken, and she must learn to see all the concerns of her happy adolescence as superficial. One by one, her erstwhile followers outstrip her in manifesting a heart prepared, and most unfairly, it is their ability to follow and accept without question that gives them the edge as converts. The specifically Baptist aspect of the conversion experience consists in the renunciation of pleasures that Megda prizes far more than her companions do— card playing, dancing, and especially theater, for which she has a decided talent. But her most debasing experience is a long process of sexual mortification, in which she receives

the attentions of the Reverend Mr. Stanley, construes these
attentions as romantic, learns that on the contrary Mr. Stanley is in love with Ethel, and becomes his wife only after
Ethel has died an erotically charged and triumphantly Christian death in her wedding dress and in her lover's arms.
Although Megda is not technically a second wife, she must
rejoice in accepting her status as second choice: "there was a
corner of his heart where even she could never enter. And
Meg was glad that it was so" (p. 373). The female child of
this marriage is christened Ethel, and Mr. Stanley "loves his
little Ethel with a love that is deep and boundless. Meg often
says, 'her only earthly rival is her own baby' " (p. 377).

Given that the goal of development in the female Christian
Bildungsroman is a Christian marriage, in which the wife is
entirely subordinated to her husband, it would seem that the
feminist speeches in the earlier part of *Megda* exist only to
be exposed as further evidence of Megda's unseemly pride
and self-sufficiency. Certainly Megda seems to be heading
for a fall when she proclaims to Hal, "I do admire character
in a man or woman; I make no distinction between the two
sexes" (p. 60), or when she refuses to stage a scene from
Hamlet because neither she nor Dell would be credible as the
Ophelia who meekly accepts Hamlet's rejection: "I think I
have my share of imagination, but I have not enough to
imagine such an impossibility as that. [Dell] would more
probably send him about his business in double-quick time.
No, girls, I cannot imagine Dell speaking like that to any
man any more than I can imagine myself doing it" (pp. 44–
45). And as far as the marriage goes, Mr. Stanley clearly
has the upper hand: "one look from his dark-blue eyes, one
low, gravely-spoken 'Meg' was enough to banish all signs of
temper, pride and willfullness" (p. 376).

Yet there is no indication that Megda comes to acknowledge her inferiority to men in general and certainly not to the boys she was actually addressing in her youthful feminist speeches. To be sure, the narrator often intrudes to point out Megda's lapses, usually in apostrophes to the reader—"As for Meg, she felt irritably, but unreasonably, angry toward Laurie for refusing to go with them. Does anyone know why?" (p. 292)—or to Megda herself—"Oh, Meg, sincere and earnest in all you say, yet how mistaken!" (p. 237). Nevertheless, there are no narratorial disquisitions on woman's proper place or adjurations to the heroine to demean herself as befits a member of her sex.

Indeed, the narrator intervenes far more frequently on Megda's behalf, as if Kelley were worried that her heroine might not appear sufficiently remarkable and lovable without explicit prodding:

> When I write this, it seems as if I must stop and rest, with my pen in my hand, while my thoughts travel back and dwell upon this part of that night's proceedings. Can anyone imagine—it seems as if everyone must—that crowd of bright-haired girls hovering around the heroine of the hour—their pride and queen? Oh, how the girlish hearts beat, as their eager, loving fingers smoothed a fold here, and fastened a clasp there! If Meg shared their nervousness, she never showed it, except it was a brighter sparkle in the dark eyes, and a firmer setting of the full lips. (pp. 156–57)

Such passages work in opposition to the dynamic of the "girl's fiction" genre, which moves the heroine toward a *telos* of Christian self-abasement. The authorial narrator intrudes here in what might be called a maternal capacity, admiring and cherishing a protagonist who is supposed to be illustrating the sin of self-esteem.

Insofar as she sees her relation to her characters as a maternal one, Kelley is in fact undermining the governing as-
sumptions of the genre in which she is working. Mothers are
the most powerful figures in the woman-centered worlds of
the sentimental novel; in later "girl's fiction" they are com-
mensurately less important and more likely to be agents of
the prevailing tendency to enforce limits. When Megda's
mother waits for her daughter early in the story, for instance,
she is passively watching for signs of conversion: Without
commenting on the fact, she misses in Megda "the inexpressible something in her voice and face, and, looking for it,
[found] it not" (p. 26). Yet mothers in *Megda* are also associated with uncritical acceptance and love of their children,
and in this capacity they carry a potent emotional charge.
Pleading not to be exposed as a thief, Maude cries, "the
disgrace would kill my mother. She is good, if I am not" (p.
94). Megda's mother delivers a disquisition on the necessity
of trusting children that concludes almost mystically, "when
[God] bestows the blessed crown of motherhood upon any
woman he gives with it the power and endurance to keep
each little jewel bright and unsullied" (p. 58). And of course
Kelley herself dedicated the novel "to my widowed mother,
to whose patient love and unwearied devotion during years
of hard struggle and self-sacrifice I owe all that I am and all
that hope holds before me in the future." The maternal figures in *Megda* thus suggest some resistance to the patriarchal
thrust of the female Christian *Bildungsroman*.

In this respect, it is especially interesting that the schoolgirls of *Megda* become not only Christians and wives, but
mothers, and not only mothers, but mothers of daughters.
The denouement that brings the dying Maude back into the
Baptist fold also brings little Maude into the family of little

Ethel, in close proximity to little Megda. The community of schoolgirls that began the novel seems to be replicating itself through motherhood, and the daughters seem to have inherited the powers that their mothers relinquished by growing up. Megda's daughter in particular appears to exist as compensation for her mother's loss of dignity and control:

> The girl, a bright-haired, dark-eyed darling of two summers, is a veritable miniature Meg. She reigns queen over all, even her grave, dignified papa. He obeys her imperious "Tate Ethie, Papa," with a meekness that causes many a laughing, "Oh, Arthur!" from Meg. (p. 377)

In a sense, this doubling of female characters in the subsequent generation recovers a central value of the novel. For if growing up is in many ways a fall in *Megda,* it is a fall from the community of women that is formed within the girls' school, and the narrator looks back on that community with undisguised nostalgia.

Megda is primarily a novel of socialization, and as such it tries to express persuasively the values of the dominant culture. But it also incorporates tensions over issues of race and gender that make it an interesting document from the standpoint of cultural history. If it aspires to be a limit-enforcing instrument, it tends as well to point out ways in which the limits that it espouses are arbitrary and constricting, especially for doubly marginalized people—people who are both black and female.

Yours very truly
Emma Dunham Kelley

MEGDA

By

"FORGET-ME-NOT"

(EMMA DUNHAM KELLEY)

————

BOSTON

JAMES H. EARLE

178 WASHINGTON STREET

1891

CONTENTS

MEGDA.

I.

HAVE you heard the news, Meg?"

"What news?"

"Why, of Ethel Lawton rising for prayers at the meeting last Thursday night."

Meg Randal opened wide a pair of lovely dark eyes, and raised two small, white hands in surprise.

"Do my ears deceive me, or do I hear aright?" she murmured, in hollow tones. "Tell me once again, that there may be no mistake."

Laurie Ray laughed and nodded her sunny head. "Yes, Meg, she did, and so did some one else; guess who."

"Impossible! Keep me not in suspense, but reveal it to me instantly."

"Well, then, prepare yourself for the shock, Meg— Maude Leonard!"

It was really comical to see the mischievous look on Meg's face change to one of astonishment, incredulity, contempt and laughter intermingled. Laurie threw her head back, and a merry peal broke the quiet of the large school-room. A group of girls standing at one of the windows on the opposite side of the room conversing together in low tones, turned their heads for a moment toward the place from which the merry sound came, then looked at each other and smiled.

"Meg is getting off some of her nonsense," said a tall, fair-haired girl, who was none other than Ethel Lawton. "What a happy girl she is, and so lovable."

The other girls murmured assent, and continued their talking.

"I would give considerable for your picture, Meg," said Laurie, still laughing. "Such a combination of expressions was never before seen on a human countenance, I verily believe. One might call it a mixed-pickles expression, if you only looked sour."

Meg shrugged her shoulders and made a little outward motion with her hands — a habit she had when she could not find words to express her feelings.

"You do not mean for me to understand that you are utterly at a loss for words, Meg?" said Laurie. "Such an idea is not conceivable."

"Don't, Laurie," said Meg, the shade of contempt spreading itself over her face, covering over and hiding all the other shades of expression. "The idea of Maude Leonard — well there! I'll say no more; only if she is a specimen of a Christian, all I can say is, deliver me from the misfortune of being one," and Meg gave another shrug of her shapely shoulders and walked up the aisle to her desk.

Laurie hastened after her. "But what do you say of Ethel. Meg?"

"I have nothing to say of Ethel," replied Meg, her voice softening. "She is good enough for all I know; she has never copied definitions in her notebook and gotten a hundred per cent in consequence, or given out ten in deportment when she should have said 'imperfect.' The only thing I wonder at in her case is, that a girl whose parents are as wealthy as hers, and who has only to open her lips, and the world, or a good part of it, is hers, should care about religion. Dear me! only give me all the money I want to spend, and I would be quite well satisfied with a thousand a year, and I would guarantee perfect happiness for myself" — and Meg took up her book of "John Halifax, Gentleman," but started when she felt a light hand laid on her arm. A fair, sweet face bent over her own.

"There is something more than money necessary to true happiness, Girlie," said a low, quiet voice.

Meg's cheek, usually so pale, grew quite pink, but she laughed lightly.

"That is all very well for you to say, Ethel," she replied, clasping the hand that rested on her shoulder. "But methinks you would be of the same opinion as myself, if you were obliged to count every penny and turn it over and over again before making up your mind whether you could spend it or not. I tell you, Ethel, when I get through this school of education I am going to enter the one of matrimony, just about as quickly as I can, and you may be very sure that the all-important man will be a rich one."

Meg's laughing face was lifted to her friend's grave one, but although she was laughing there was a certain earnestness in her voice that convinced Ethel that she meant every word she said — for the time, at least.

"I do not like to hear you talk in this way, Girlie. You are capable of great things. Madam has often told you so, you know, and although you say things a great many times just to hear yourself talk, yet I do not like to hear you say such a thing as that, even in fun."

"Oh, but I am not in fun, Ethel; I am in dead earnest. Ask Laurie."

"Ask Laurie nothing," exclaimed that young lady, elegantly. "I have known this young lady," she continued, pointing her finger at Meg, with a comical look of despair, "for five and ten years, as the old sea-captain says, and I do not know her yet. I would advise you, Ethel, not to undertake the task of reading her, for you will find it a difficult, if not a hopeless one."

Ethel sat down and took one of Meg's perfect little hands in her own. Meg's hand was her one source of pride, and it would almost seem as if she were justified in this pride. Such a delicate, white, slender, dimpled hand as it was! Meg looked on smilingly while Ethel turned it over, palm upward.

"Shall I read your fortune, Girlie?" asked Ethel.

"If it pleases you, fair Sibyl," returned Meg.

Laurie leaned over with a look of deep interest on her pretty face; she always enjoyed anything of this nature. "Don't faint, Laurie," murmured Meg, concernedly.

"I see," began Ethel in a low, earnest voice, that belied the smile on her face, "a happy, merry, laughing girl. She is happy, she is merry, she is laughing; but under all the happiness, all the merriment, all the laughter, runs a vein of deep, earnest feeling; a wish to be good, to be true, to be noble. A vague, undefinable feeling it may be just now when she is so young and light-hearted and careless, but it is there and some day it will make itself known to her and fill her whole being so that she will know no peace and happiness until the longing is satisfied, and she proves herself worthy of the noble feelings and lofty desires that her nature has been endowed with. I see she is a girl beloved by everybody. She is the darling of a widowed mother's heart, the pride of a loving brother and sister, the comfort and never-ending source of delight to all who know her. She has a great capability for making friends; all who know her love her.

"For this reason, and also because it is her nature to be light-hearted and gay, she is apt to forget that the good Father who has endowed her with these blessings — this bright, happy nature, this faculty for making friends, the rare accomplishments of mind and body — will one day demand them all from her hands with the question, 'What have you done with the talents I gave you?' She does not mean to be careless, she is never irreverant, she has great respect for old age. She is only a little thoughtless, a little carried away by her own light-heartedness. She has yet to learn the sad lesson of Life, perhaps she will learn it with many tears and bitter heart-aches; perhaps her soul will be drawn to its Maker through a deep appreciation of His mercies to her. But whether by smiles or by tears, by sorrow or by happiness, this dear heart will be laid at the feet of the crucified One. It must be given to the Father of all mercies."

Ethel stopped and looked up into the girlish faces. Laurie's was very sober and thoughtful. Meg's lips were parted, and there was an earnest, troubled look in her dark eyes; only for a moment, though; the instant she caught Ethel's gaze she laughed and drew away her hand.

"Quite a palmist, Ethel," she said, lightly. "You ought to make a profession of your talent, and send all the money it brings you out to the poor heathen; or, better still, give it to some poor heathen of your own country and color. I would take it and thank you kindly." Then seeing how grave and pained Ethel really looked, she laid her willful head against her friend's shoulder, and patted her cheek with her little hand.

"Don't look so curious, Ethel mine; I am not worth troubling this dear head of yours about."

Before Ethel could answer, the bell rang for lessons, and in a few moments, thoughts both trivial and serious, were swallowed up in the process of translating, transposing and analyzing.

II.

OUT IN THE STORM.

A WINDY, rainy, October night. Meg, hurrying
along on her way home from Laurie's, where
she had been since school closed, now laughed and
now scolded to herself, as the wind blew her umbrella,
first to one side, then to the other.

"Well, I may as well put the poor old thing down,"
she said, at last, half aloud; "the wind proves too
much for it, and my temper, too. How it does blow!
I'll pull my gossamer hood over my hat, and then I'll
bid defiance to both wind and rain. Oh, dear, I suppose I must go down to the hall to-night, if it does
rain pitchforks and blow enough to take one's head
off. Being accomplished may have its advantages,
but it also has its disadvantages. One is expected to
do everything, and go everywhere, and then if one
protests, why, the terrible question is asked, 'For
what were your talents given to you?' I declare,
sometimes I almost feel that I would willingly change

places with old Betty Burnside. She says, 'The women say I don't know nothin', the men say I don't know nothin', but I say I do know nothin'.' Well, if she knows nothing, then nothing can be expected of her; that must be one consolation. I beg your pardon!"

Meg, hurrying along with her head down, the better to fight her way against the wind as well as to protect her face from the heavy drops of rain, ran against somebody as she turned the corner to the street on which she lived.

A pleasant, manly voice answered: "The fault was entirely mine — I beg your pardon. Why, Miss Randal, is it possible you are out on such a night as this!"

The gentleman had stopped in his surprise, and Meg also stood still; that is, as still as she could, considering how hard the wind was trying to propel her onward.

"Good evening, Mr. Stanley. Yes, I am out, but the wind seems to know that it is time I was at home, and is doing its best to send me there."

The gentleman laughed. "Allow me to offer my services in helping you to get the better of this troublesome wind. Will you accept my arm?"

Meg smiled slyly to herself as she tucked her little

hand under his arm. What would the girls say if they could see her thus carefully protected from the storm by their young minister! She almost wished they might meet one of them. It was a merry walk they had down the long, dark street, despite the wind and rain. I am not sure but that the wind and rain made it all the merrier. Mr. Stanley's efforts to keep the umbrella over their heads, and Meg's to keep her gossamer hood from blowing off, filled up the little gaps in the conversation which naturally come when two persons of so slight an acquaintance as Meg and the "young minister" undertake to walk even a street length together. Then Mr. Stanley proved such a merry companion, "not a bit like a minister," thought Meg; he had such a pleasant, genial voice, and when they passed under one of the few lamp-posts with which the street was honored and she looked up into his face with her laughing eyes, the eyes that looked down into her own had such a kind, merry light in them that Meg was really charmed.

"His eyes are dark blue and I thought they were black. He isn't at all handsome, but he has a strong, good face, and I like him — I really do. Somehow or other I feel that I shall never forget this walk. Oh, de–a–r!"

Her foot had caught in her long, wind-blown gossamer, but before she could fall a strong arm around her lifted her safely to her feet again. Then came a terrific gust of wind that seized the umbrella in Mr. Stanley's hand, whirled it madly round and round, blew it up and blew it down, blew it on one side, blew it on the other, and finally blew it inside out. The different expressions that passed over Mr. Stanley's face, while watching and trying to prevent the destruction of his property, can be better imagined than described. He might have saved the umbrella had he had the free use of both hands, but he still held Meg firmly with one arm.

"Oh, Mr. Stanley!" said Meg, stifling her desire to laugh by a strong effort, "how sorry I am; your umbrella is ruined."

·He turned his face, flushed with the exertion but laughing still, to her.

"You need not be sorry, Miss Randal; the umbrella can easily be replaced, and the enjoyment it has afforded both of us more than compensates for its loss. It looks thoroughly beaten, doesn't it?" he asked, laughing and holding up the poor, broken thing.

But just then the wind — and it seemed as if it were the same gust that had worked such destruction and had hovered around and above them to listen to what

they had to say about it, and having heard and been
made angry at the light way in which its work had
been spoken of — now came back with renewed force
to show its displeasure of such treatment.   It seized
Mr. Stanley's "Derby," lifted it lightly from his head,
whirled it provokingly before his face for a moment
as if challenging him for a race, and then sent it on
its way down the street.

Mr. Stanley stood, irresolute, for a moment, then
looked uncertainly at Meg.   She was literally con-
vulsed with laughter, but she pointed with her hand
to the dancing hat and gasped out, "Run after it, do;
never mind me."

Mr. Stanley needed no second bidding, but dropped
his umbrella and ran.   And what a chase that hat
gave him!   Only those who have indulged in the
same exercise can have any idea of the "pleasures of
the chase."   Now on this side of the road, now on
that, now rolling over and over in front of him, making him feel sure that he has but to put his hand
down and the victory, in the shape of the hat, is his,
then suddenly taking a new course and flying along
at a great speed, then changing its mind again and
turning back, at which time Mr. Stanley coming up,
panting, close behind, puts his foot squarely into it
and almost measures his length on the ground.

When he straightens himself and turns "to pick the hat up," lo and behold, it is a dozen yards or so up the street in the direction from which it started. As Mr. Stanley, breathless but eager and determined, turned to pursue the hat, he collided with Meg, who, still laughing convulsively, had also joined in the chase. The result was, they threw each other down, Meg having the added humiliation of knowing that she was sitting squarely on the hat.

Mr. Stanley was upon his feet in an instant, profuse apologies on his lips, his hands stretched out to help her. Alas, proud Meg! not noticing the proffered hands, buried her face in her own and did not move.

Mr. Stanley grew frightened. "Are you hurt, Miss Randal? Have you sprained your ankle?"

"Not my ankle, Mr. Stanley," replied Meg, hysterically; "but I am much afraid — I — have — sprained — your — hat," and she rose slowly to her feet, not daring to lift her face from her hands.

The next moment she was undecided whether to feel indignant, or to join in the hearty burst of laughter that Mr. Stanley, after one hard struggle to control, indulged in; but when she, too, looked at the crushed, misshapen thing which he picked from the ground and held up before them, the comicality of the whole thing burst upon her, and her clear, light laugh, rang out on the air; and so these two very dignified young people stood there in the dark street, with·the rain beating down upon them and the wind howling around them, and laughed until they were both fain to stop for very lack of breath.

That one little mishap did more toward drawing these two young people together, and making them feel indeed like friends, than weeks and months of ordinary intercourse could have done. Mr. Stanley's easy way of making Meg feel that the whole thing had afforded him pleasure, put her completely at her ease and added much to the respect she already had for him; while he on his part, was most favorably impressed with the laughing, light-hearted girl, who, however much she laughed and chattered, never once went beyond the bounds of propriety, but proved herself to be as lady-like in behavior as she was in appearance.

Mr. Stanley poked the hat here and smoothed it there, but for all his efforts, in which he was assisted by brilliant suggestions from Meg, the hat still refused to go back to its former shape, or indeed, to any shape whatever. He put it on his head, but it was determined not to stay there unless it could rest itself on his ear; this of course it could not be allowed to do.

"I think," said Mr. Stanley gravely, "it will have to be tied on. Do you happen to have a ribbon about your neck, Miss Randal? Young ladies do wear ribbon about their necks sometimes," he added confidently.

Meg laughed merrily. "Yes, I have one," she answered, fully alive to the enjoyment of the whole thing, "and I will loan it to you with the greatest of pleasure ; I will even tie it on for you, if you would like to have me."

"Oh, will you? You are very kind. I would like to have you, for I can't tie a bow-knot, and if I tie it in a hard one I might have to appear with it on at the tea-table, and that might cause remarks."

Meg standing on tip-toe, passed the band of delicate pink ribbon over his hat, which Mr. Stanley held on with both hands, and tied it in a very pretty bow under his chin.

"Thank you, Miss Randal."

"You are entirely welcome."

Mr. Stanley gravely offered his arm, Meg as gravely took it, and they commenced their homeward walk once more.

"Suppose we should meet some one," said Meg.

"I must confess I am not desirous of meeting one of my deacons, or indeed, any of my parishioners," replied Mr. Stanley with a laughing gleam in his blue eyes. "If we only had an umbrella."

"Why, we have," exclaimed Meg, holding up her own.

"A very brilliant thought, Miss Randal. Suppose we raise it; it will be some protection if we should happen to meet any one."

The umbrella was raised and they continued their walk without any further interruption. As they entered Meg's gate Mr. Stanley said rather hesitatingly as if fearing that what he was about to ask might be denied him:

"Miss Randal, I am very certain that this enjoyable walk I have had with you will never be forgotten by me, but I would like to have some little souvenir to make the memory of it doubly sure and pleasant. Will you allow me to keep this band of ribbon?"

Meg looked up with laughing eyes. "I should think your hat would be entirely sufficient to keep your memory green," she said slyly.

Mr. Stanley laughed. "I will make a fair exchange with you, Miss Randal. I will give you the hat if you will give me the ribbon."

"Agreed."

"I will send it down to-morrow morning."

"Very well."

"And now, good-night, Miss Randal, and many thanks for a most enjoyable half-hour."

"Good-night, Mr. Stanley. I thank you for your protection."

Mr. Stanley bowed in lieu of raising his hat. Meg turned as if to enter the house, but stopped under the piazza and watched the manly form going down the dimly-lighted street.

"A perfect gentleman," she said to herself, "but then, he is a minister, and therefore must be a gentleman. I like him. He is so kind and pleasant, so full of life and vigor. He is strong, too, and I admire strength in a man — physical strength as well as intellectual. I would almost as soon a man be deficient in one as the other. He had me on my feet that time I stumbled almost before I knew what I had done. But," and Meg's laughing face assumed a most determined expression, "the greatest reason of all why I like him is because he did not ask me, the moment I took his arm, if I had ever given myself to the Saviour, and if I had not, if I would not do so, now, before it was too late. That is the way most ministers begin and some who are not ministers. I am tired of hearing it. Just as if I should not know whether I wanted to join a church or not without being told to do so. Such people may mean well, undoubtedly they do, but it is my private opinion that they are apt, very apt, to do more harm than good." And ending her soliloquy with a little stamp of her umbrella on the floor of the piazza, this girl with the laughing face and light, merry heart, who thought herself sufficient for her own perfect happiness, and who was beloved by man, woman and child for her own lovable, wayward, charming self — this girl, lacking only the one thing to make her one of God's most perfect creations, not because of her beautiful face, for it was not beautiful, only fair and sweet and girl-ish — but because of her great capability of loving and of making all people love her — this girl, I say, opened the door and went into her home with this feeling filling her heart. Did the mother and sister and brother, watching and waiting with impatient, loving hearts for the first sound of the sweet voice, the first sight of the laughing face, miss the inexpressible something in her voice and face, and, looking for it, find it not?

The mother, perhaps, nay surely did; but her love for her darling was so deep that she could not bear to trouble or displease her. To the sister and brother she was all they asked for — their pride and joy.

III.

MEG AT HOME.

MEG'S appearance in the small, cosy kitchen was welcomed in the usual way. The mother had a fond, loving smile for her; Elsie a kiss and soft little pat for each cheek; Hal a boyish hug and pinch of the pretty ear; and Meg received the welcome in her usual way. To the mother an answering smile; to Elsie a loving but careless kiss; to Hal a playful box on the ear and a laughing —

"Now, Tease, behave," then she tossed her gossamer on one chair, her hat and jacket on another, and her umbrella she stood up in the corner; she then accepted Hal's invitation to a seat upon his knee and smoothed his curly hair with her white hand, while she told over to her admiring audience the events of the day, not noticing or, if noticing, not saying anything, that Elsie was going about quietly and putting away the scattered things.

The only reason why she did not say anything

about it was, that she had been so accustomed to
being waited upon that she took it all as a "matter of
course." But Meg would have done anything in the
world for her three dear ones; if it had become necessary for her to work day after day to care for them,
she would have done it, and done it cheerfully, too.

As the family seated themselves around the tea-
table in the long, narrow dining-room Meg suddenly
said:

"Oh, I must tell you of the adventure I had to-
night on my way home from Laurie's!" and then followed a description — such as only Meg could give —
of her rather wild walk with Mr. Stanley. She told
them everything, even the request that Mr. Stanley
had made that she should exchange her ribbon for
his hat; and they laughed at her, as they always
did.

"One would hardly judge Mr. Stanley to be so
lively, from his appearance," observed Elsie in her
quiet way.

"No, indeed," returned Meg. "I was very much
surprised. I have never had any conversation with
him before, you know, and I have heard him preach
but — how many times, Elsie?"

"Three times."

"Yes, three times. He is so very dignified in

appearance and — and — well, *I* called him a very stern-featured young man for one of his tender years, don't you, sister? He can't be more than twenty-four."

"He is twenty-five," said Elsie.

Meg opened her dark eyes. Hal laughed teasingly. "Sister is ahead of you, Girlie; you had better look out."

"How did you know that, Elsie Randal?" asked the astonished Meg.

Elsie laughed softly. "Mrs. Lawton told me on the cars yesterday coming out from the city. He took dinner at their house last Sunday."

"Oh, and that reminds me," said Meg with a carelessness that was a trifle assumed. "Ethel has come out and joined the good ones; she rose for prayers last Thursday night."

Elsie looked up quickly — a glad light shining in her gray eyes, but she did not speak.

Mrs. Randal sighed. "What a happy mother Mrs. Lawton must be," she said.

Meg laughed lightly. "Yes, don't you envy her, mother? And see what a wicked sinner your youngest female is. But I have even still more joyful news for you. The wandering sheep has been brought back to the fold — or else she goes in for the first time — I am not prepared to say which. Guess who else rose for prayers. Hal, you guess."

Hal stopped a piece of cake on its way to his mouth. "Laurie," he said quickly.

Meg laughed. "Laurie! The idea! Why, she would never think of rising unless some one took hold of her and pulled her up by main force. No; you guess, sister."

"Dell."

"No, not Dell. You are almost as brilliant as Hal, sister. Dell Manton will remain Dell Manton to the end of the chapter; that girl is true blue — no deceit about her. She is no angel and doesn't pretend to be one; she would no more pretend to be what she is not than" — here Meg cast about in her mind for a good comparison and lighted upon herself — "than I would."

"Do you call it being 'true blue' to keep from making a profession of religion, Girlie?"

It was Elsie who spoke.

"Yes, I do," answered Meg boldly, "unless you back your profession up with noble actions. I call Dell true blue, myself true blue and everybody else true blue who will not lower themselves in their own or anyone else's estimation, by making false professions of religion."

Meg looked very proud and her lips were curled scornfully.

"But, Girlie," said Elsie, "are such professions necessarily false? Anyone who would make such a false profession would be very wicked indeed; every one must know that. I am certain that there are no truer girls on the earth than you and Dell, but — but" —

Elsie stopped, confused, before the laughing face turned toward her. She had tried so many times before to talk seriously to Meg about religion, and every time she had found herself unable to get only just so far. Meg would turn that laughing face of hers, with the little scornful curve of the red lips, toward her, and she would stop confused, ashamed, and almost ready to beg Meg's pardon for presuming to preach to her.

"But — but — oh, sister, don't you try to assume the role of preacher — it would never suit you. Well, I see you are not going to guess the riddle, so I will tell you. Brace yourself for the shock — Maude Leonard."

Meg spoke the name contemptuously and looked around the table to see what effect the name would have on the three. Hal gave a low whistle, Mrs. Randal looked surprised, and even Elsie, who was always so quick to see one's virtues before she saw their faults, looked incredulous.

Meg was satisfied. "You are not more surprised than I was," she said, rising from the table. "I must confess my nervous system received quite a shock when Laurie told me. Indeed, I am so nervous even now, Hal, that I am not in a fit condition to go to the hall alone; so put on your overcoat and hat and come with me — *do*, that is a dear brother."

Very few could resist Meg when she spoke in that sweet, coaxing way — certainly her brother could not.

"You know how to get around a fellow about as well as anyone I know of," he said, with assumed gruffness. "I don't believe the person has yet been born whom you could not twist around your little finger."

Meg laughed. "I hope you do not mean to insult me, or is that only a figure of speech? My little finger looks scarcely large enough to twist such a tall young giant as you around," and she held up her hand and looked at it thoughtfully. Hal took it in his own strong, brown one.

"Oh, what a hand!" he said, tenderly stroking it.

"What objections have you to that hand," asked Meg, rather conceitedly. "It is generally considered a rather pretty one."

"Pretty is no name for it," returned Hal. "It is a regular little beauty."

"Don't make her any vainer than she is already, brother," said Elsie smilingly, on her way to the sink with a pile of dishes.

"Do you think it is really necessary to go to the hall to-night, Meg?" asked Mrs. Randal. "It is still raining hard and the wind blows badly."

"Oh, dear, mother, what a question for you to ask," replied Meg. "What do you suppose would be accomplished if I didn't go?"

"What an important personage our Megda is," said Hal mischievously. "She'll be supplying the pulpit for Mr. Stanley some Sunday."

"Not much," replied Meg, tossing her head proudly. "I'll leave that for some of our converts to do. But, about to-night's meeting, mother. You know that if I should stay at home there would be nothing done, and we should have to pay two dollars just the same. I really think they might let us have the hall for nothing. I have to play for the singing and be Secretary and Treasurer in one. It may be nice to be accomplished, but it has its drawbacks and this is one of them : being obliged to go out in all kinds of weather."

Although Meg scolded she was proud at the same time to think that she was of so much importance.

"You should not be so capable, my sweet sister," said Hal, taking up the umbrella.

"I'll be at home soon after nine o'clock, mother," said Meg.

"Take good care of her, Hal." And the mother left her dish-washing, and Elsie her dish-wiping, and both went to the door to see them off.

"You may trust me," said Hal pompously; and Meg laughed as she tucked her hand under his arm and went with him out into the dark, wild, stormy night.

They stopped for Laurie on their way; she was ready and waiting for them.

"Take Hal's other arm, Laurie," said Meg.

"I second the motion," said Hal, looking down on Laurie with admiring eyes.

Laurie accepted the proffered arm with a flushing "Thank you." Meg commenced her usual lively chatter, very seldom waiting for any reply to her questions, and not getting any when she did wait, for Hal's head was turned from her and he and Laurie were engaged in "silent conversation." Anyone who has been in their situation will understand what I mean by that rather vague expression.

Meg excused their impoliteness, only saying to herself as she had said a good many times before, that she didn't know what Hal could see in Laurie to like so well; she was very pretty, and a good little thing enough, but there was no depth to her. She never asked herself why she should care so much for her, for she certainly did think a great deal of Laurie; if she had, she would probably have answered the question in her own easy, laughing manner, "Oh, extremes sometimes meet."

Meg was so careless in her conceit that nobody ever thought of finding fault with her for it.

When they reached the hall, Hal excused himself from going in on the plea "that it was important that he should see his barber."

"It won't take you more than five minutes, will it, Hal?" asked Meg, mischievously.

"I'll be through in time to see you home," he retorted. "You may tell Duncan so."

Meg laughed and led the way into the reading-room. A group of young ladies and gentlemen standing around one of the radiators, turned as Meg and Laurie entered, and upon catching sight of their "leader" made a rush for her.

"Just the one we have been waiting for, Miss Randal," said a tall, slender young man, with a compliment in every word.

Meg answered him with a smile and a nod and

turned to a girl who had a mass of golden hair braided loosely and wound round and round her head, large gray eyes and a red, smiling mouth, with small, white teeth. Her skin was dazzling white, without one tinge of pink in it. This was Dell Manton, the beauty of the town.

"I am more than surprised to see you here, Miss Manton," said Meg, ceremoniously. "I had hardly dared to hope for such a pleasure. How did you get here?"

Dell was no adept in witty repartee; she always put plain questions and gave plain answers. "Joe brought me here," she answered.

"Happy Joe," murmured Ed Holmes sentimentally.

Dell acknowledged this compliment with a withering glance, and the young man immediately withdrew.

"But where is Ethel? She isn't here and it is time to begin," said Meg.

No one answered, but each looked at the other. Meg, feeling at once by that fine intuition of hers that something was wrong, drew herself up proudly and surveyed them all with sparkling dark eyes.

IV.

ETHEL'S ABSENCE.

WHO knows why Ethel is not here?" asked Meg. Still no answer. Meg's lip commenced its scornful curve. "Does no one know, or are you afraid to tell?"

This insinuation was too much for Dell. "I think we all know; indeed, I am sure we do, for that was the subject of our conversation when you and Laurie entered the room. Ethel has expressed herself as unwilling to go on with the society unless said society will banish from its entertainments and socials such dissipations as whist, dancing and theatricals."

Dell spoke with her characteristic plainness. For a moment there was silence — all eyes directed toward Meg. There was a slight tinge of pink in her usually pale cheek and her lips were curled scornfully, then a laughing light broke out into her eyes and all over her face, and her voice sounded clear and sweet.

"Ah, well! we might have expected this. I dare

say she will change her mind after a more mature deliberation on the subject; until then we must get along without her as best we can. I only hope she will think better of it before we give that scene from 'Hamlet'; she would make such an ideal 'Ophelia.'

"A better 'Desdemona'," murmured Will Duncan.

That was all Meg said, then she walked proudly up to the front of the room. The rest, ruled and governed by her in this as in everything else, followed her. Had she expressed herself to be of the same mind as Ethel and asked them to give up the things which Dell had mentioned, they would have done it without one murmur of remonstrance — such was her influence over them.

May Bromley ran after Meg and caught her arm. "Maude Leonard has refused to take part in our sociables, too," she whispered.

Meg turned her face toward May and smiled; that was her only answer, but May had seen that smile before and knew what it meant. She laughed merrily and gave the arm she held a squeeze.

"Oh, Meg," she said, in that tone of voice which suggested a high appreciation of Meg's skepticism.

Mr. Duncan, as president of the society, called the meeting to order. Meg seated herself at the piano.

"Suppose we open our meeting by singing that

good old song, 'Forgive and Forget'," said Mr.
Duncan.

Meg smiled as she turned over the leaves quickly
to find the place. "One would think that Will was
fifty-one instead of twenty-one," she said to herself.
"He talks like his grandfather. That is the only
fault I can find with Will — he tries so hard to be
older than he is."

Then she struck the opening chords and the young
voices burst forth in melody, Meg's clear, sweet notes
ringing out above all the others in the chorus:

"Then Forgive and Forget, for this life is too fleeting," etc.

Dell's beautiful, strong alto sounded delightful, and
Dell herself seemed to throw her whole soul into the
words. But that was the way Dell always sang.
Will Duncan's bass and Ed Holmes' tenor added
strength and beauty to the lines, while the others did
their part well. Meg's voice was the pride of the
school; it was so clear and sweet — not particularly
strong as yet, but what it lacked in strength it made
up in expression.

After the song the president said, "The secretary
will please read the report of the last meeting."

Meg was secretary; and an excellent one she

made, too. The minutes were read and approved, and then the meeting was open to the business of the evening.

The president began: "As is doubtless known by all, the society have decided to give an entertainment in the hall above, consisting of music, both vocal and instrumental, readings and a scene from 'Hamlet.' Perhaps the first thing we had better do will be to decide on the evening. Will someone suggest an evening?"

Melvin Pierce moved that they fix on Wednesday evening, Nov. 25.

"Those in favor of this evening," said the president, "please raise the right hand."

Every hand was raised. "Not necessary to call for contrary minds — it is a vote."

The president stopped just here as if not knowing exactly how to proceed. Meg, catching his eye and reading its expression aright, rose to her feet and said:

"Mr. President, I am afraid it will be necessary for us to change the play we were intending to represent. I was not thinking that we would give the entertainment at so early a date. Our 'Ophelia' will probably not have time to change her mind with reference to taking part in our wickedness, and we really have no one else who is so fitted for the part as Miss Lawton. I move that instead of 'Hamlet' we give 'Macbeth'."

"I second the motion," said Ed Holmes quickly.

"The motion has been made and seconded, that we change the play of 'Hamlet' to that of 'Macbeth.' Those in favor of so doing signify in the usual manner. Contrary minds. It is a vote."

The next thing was to choose the Act and assign the characters. Act II, Scene II, was agreed upon, also the latter part of Scene II in Act III. Meg as "Lady Macbeth," Will as "Macbeth."

"We have commenced at the wrong end of the programme," said the president with a smile. "The 'variety' should come first. Miss Randal, will you favor us with two 'Readings'?"

"With pleasure, Mr. President."

"Thank you. Miss Manton, will you contribute toward the success of our entertainment by a contralto solo?"

"I will, Mr. President."

"Thank you. Mr. Holmes, will you oblige us with a tenor solo?"

"Yes, sir."

"Thank you. I presume the members of the quartette will consent to give one or two selections. Are the ladies agreeable?"

Meg and Dell were very "agreeable."

"Mr. Holmes?"

Yes, Mr. Holmes was also agreeable.

"And I am sure Mr. Duncan is," said Will laughingly. "That completes the programme, I believe.
The admission fee must next be decided upon. Has
anyone any suggestions to make?"

Melvin Pierce rose. "Mr. President, I think the
talent we are to have demands a good price for the
tickets. I move the tickets be fifteen, twenty-five
and thirty-five cents respectively."

"You hear the motion; does anyone second it?"

Bert Marston opened his lips to do so when Meg
rose to her feet. "Mr. President, I, for one, object
to having two prices for the whole tickets. The
price (fifteen cents) for the half-tickets is very good,
but I think we shall find it more successful in doing
away with the reserved seats. But comparatively few
of the people here prefer the front seats. I move as
an amendment that we have but one price, twenty-five
cents, thus giving everyone an equal chance."

"I second the amendment," said Dell promptly,
and, as usual, when Meg led there was no resistance.

The ushers were then appointed — Ray Blanding as
head usher, to be assisted by Hal Randal, Bert Marston and Melvin Pierce. Ray declined on a plea of

bashfulness; a burst of laughter greeted this declaration. The president rapped for order and reminded
the bashful young man that "this is a society that
receives no declinations." His objections thus over-
ruled, Ray was forced to withdraw them amid many
smiles and merry glances. The ticket seller and col-
lector were then appointed and the business brought
to a close.

The paper for the evening was then listened to. It
was prepared and read by May Bromley, and its subject was: "Moral culture." Rather a deep subject
for flighty May to undertake to handle, but it contained more sense and more careful knowledge of the
subject than any of the members had given her credit
for having.

"We will have to waive the discussion until some
future meeting, as it is already within ten minutes of
our closing hour," said the president. "For myself,
I can say that the paper has proved most interesting.
I think Miss Bromley should be congratulated upon
her admirable handling of the subject; it certainly
showed both careful thought and study. We will
bring the meeting to a close by singing, 'Merry
hearts'."

"What a splendid 'Lady Macbeth' Meg will make,
won't she?" said faithful little Laurie to May, as

they stood together for a moment, putting on their gossamers.

"Beautiful," answered May. "But come to think of it, Laurie, why didn't Meg go on with 'Hamlet,' and give the part of 'Ophelia' to Dell. She is fair enough, goodness knows."

"Who is taking my name in vain?" asked Meg, coming up.

"I am," answered May. "Why didn't you give the part of 'Ophelia' to Dell?"

Meg smiled a superior smile. "Look at her now and learn my reason."

Both girls looked at Dell, who was standing up very straight and dignified, talking earnestly to Bert Marston. There was a most determined expression on her lovely face; she was evidently "laying the law down" to Bert, and he was listening to her intently.

"Do you see?" asked Meg.

"Yes," answered May, laughing.

"But I don't," said Laurie, a puzzled expression on her flower-like face.

"Oh, little goose," said Meg, with affectionate scorn. "Can you imagine Dell saying to her 'Hamlet' in response to his 'I did love you once,' 'Indeed, my lord, you made me believe so'? I think I have my share of imagination, but I have not enough to imagine such an impossibility as that. She would more probably send him about his business in double-quick time. No, girls, I cannot imagine Dell speaking like that to any man any more than I can imagine myself doing it."

"What part of the scene from 'Macbeth' will you take, Meg?" asked one of the girls.

"That part where 'Lady Macbeth' and her lord are conferring together after the bloody deed has been accomplished. Then I can relieve myself of some of the scorn I feel for my Macbeth," replied Meg with a laugh.

"Oh, Meg, you are too bad," said May.

"Hullo, Randal," suddenly exclaimed Melvin Pierce. "What do you mean by showing yourself at this late hour? The business of the meeting has but just been brought to a close," and he bowed very politely to Hal, who had just entered the room.

"Very fortunate for me," replied Hal. "I have no doubt everything was as satisfactorily settled without me as it would have been with me."

"Thanks to your sister, yes," replied Melvin.

"Does it rain out, Hal?" asked Will, coming up with his umbrella in his hand.

"It doesn't rain in, sure," said Melvin, looking up to the ceiling as if to find confirmation to his words.

Will did not deign to notice this foolish remark, and looked at Hal for a reply.

"Very little," replied Hal; "but enough to warrant the use of an umbrella if a bonnet is in the case."

"Bonnet!" exclaimed Meg, indignantly, before the others had a chance to laugh at Hal's rather suggestive remark. "Hal calls everything a woman puts on her head a bonnet, if it is nothing but an old cloud."

"Well, I do not pretend to know the name of every kind of head-gear a woman wears," replied Hal. "I have too much respect for my brains to even try to remember them. Let him who is a man of leisure undertake that task."

"Amen," said Melvin solemnly.

Meg turned to him with a laugh. "You heathen," she said. "It is well that our young converts do not hear you; you would fill them with horror for your wickedness."

"Meg," said Hal gently.

She turned to him and opened her eyes wide at the look of pain on his face; she opened her lips to ask him if his barber had turned preacher and read him a sermon before coming to the hall, but a feeling of shame that was as new as it was unpleasant, stopped her. She bit her lip and turned to Will, who was at her side asking for the pleasure of seeing her to her home. Instead of answering him with her accustomed sweet graciousness, she surprised him beyond measure by saying curtly:

"Oh, certainly, Mr. Duncan, only I am afraid the pleasure will prove to be a task and a very disagreeable one, too. My! how the wind does blow!"

They had reached the door by this time; Hal, being ahead, opened it and all were greeted by a terrific gust that sent them back into the entry again.

"Can't you keep the umbrella up, Hal?" called Bert Marston.

"I am not going to try," returned Hal, drawing Laurie's hand closely through his arm, and making a determined plunge forward.

They went crowding out after him, laughing and talking all at once. They seemed to be the only people out. The streets looked dark and deserted. The girls gathered their skirts up underneath their gossamers, keeping up their laughing and chattering, and dropping off one at a time with their escorts when they reached the street on which they lived, calling gaily to each other, "See you at school in the morning," until Hal and Laurie, Will and Meg found themselves alone.

Will was even more dignified than ever, and

scarcely spoke a word. Meg, as Hal told her afterward, did talking enough for both, though all the
time she was drawing comparisons between poor Will
and her escort of the earlier part of the evening.

"Dear me! I do believe Will is getting bow-legged;
he does jerk along dreadfully. I am sure it doesn't
blow nearly as hard as it did three hours ago, and Mr.
Stanley didn't bump up against me and pull me
around as he is doing. This is the last time you will
torture me, young man. I ought to have gotten my
life insured before I left home. Oh, here we are at
our gate, thank goodness!"

All this was, of course, said to herself; to Will she
said most sweetly: "Thank you very much, Mr. Duncan. Isn't my prophecy verified?"

"What prophecy?" asked Will, in his most dignified manner, although he was having great difficulty
in keeping on his feet.

"What prophecy! Why, Mr. Duncan, you are growing forgetful. I prophesied before we left the hall,
that the pleasure would prove but a task, and a most
disagreeable one; was I not right?"

Will bowed most gravely and came very near sitting down on the doorstep. "It is always a pleasure
for me to render you any support, however feeble and
ineffectual it may be, Miss Randal. But I beg to

appropriate the pleasure to myself; I have enjoyed the walk home with you very much."

"Oh, what a fib!" said Meg in her mind. Aloud: "You are too kind, Mr. Duncan, but I will not give you occasion to change your mind in regard to the pleasure by keeping you out in the wind and rain. Good-night."

"Good-night, Miss Randal."

Will was spared the trouble of lifting his hat, as the wind lifted it for him, and he had some difficulty in getting it again. The wind, however, was kinder to him than it had been to Mr. Stanley, and after twirling it around once or twice, drove it into a sheltered nook and left it there. Mr. Duncan gravely picked it up, put it on his head, repeated his good-night to Meg and passed out of the gate.

Meg went into the house and entertained her Mother and Elsie in her usual manner by relating everything as it had happened at the reading-room, leaving nothing out, not even that Ethel had decided to withdraw from the society. But she told it all in her own light, laughing way, and neither of them had any idea that she was feeling just the least bit sorry about it. Hal came in, but he appeared rather silent and grave, though no one seemed to notice it except Meg. She did not say anything about it, however, and

after a few minutes they bade each other good-night
and went to their respective rooms.

Meg slept alone — she preferred to. Elsie and the
mother shared the same room, the one off the sitting-
room. Hal used the one off the dining-room, but Meg
scorned alike both rooms and went up stairs alone.
"She wanted to go up high to sleep," she always said.
It seemed to her as if she couldn't breathe when she
slept down stairs. She wanted to be alone, too; with
none but her thoughts and her dreams to bear her
company.

To-night she had plenty of thoughts; they crowded
themselves upon her thick and fast, but after half an
hour's tolerance of them she banished them from her
with the expressive gesture of her hands, and the
words, spoken half aloud:

"Well, I am certain Ethel is slowly losing her
mind. As if there could be anything wrong in private
theatricals! I shall go on with my sinful pleasures
until — well, until I begin to lose my mind, too, and
then I'll stop."

V.

A MEMENTO.

AS Mrs. Randal and her little family were about finishing their evening meal on the day following the events recorded in our last chapter, the door-bell rang. Hal went to the door. In a moment or two he re-entered the dining-room bearing a large paper parcel, much resembling a band-box in shape, in his hand.

"Miss Megda Randal, Presented," he read aloud, and handed the package to Meg with a low bow and the words, "A Jack-in-the-box, Girlie."

Meg received the package with big, dark eyes.

"What can it be?" said Elsie, looking vastly interested. Mrs. Randal was almost as curious as her children and all waited impatiently while Meg undid the fastenings and opened the bundle. When she had broken the string and commenced to take off the paper a laugh began to grow in her eyes and around her mouth, while her pale cheek flushed pink. A suspicion of what was in the parcel had flashed across her mind, and still she was rather doubtful of the suspicion being correct.

"He wouldn't do it — I know he wouldn't, he was only in fun," she said to herself; and then — a burst of laughter from Hal, an exclamation of surprise from the mother and Elsie, and Meg found herself staring at a hat — a gentleman's hat — a battered, misshapen, tipsy-looking hat — in fact, the very hat she had helped to capture, and alas! to ruin the night before.

"You look almost as crushed as the hat, Girlie," said Hal teasingly. "But I don't wonder, I should think you would when you look upon your heartless work."

Meg shook the poor thing at her laughing brother. "Don't you dare, Hal Randal," she said.

"Dare what?"

"Remind me of my dreadful mishap."

"It isn't I who am reminding you of it; it's the hat."

Meg doubled up her little fist and gave the hat a vicious poke.

"Don't, Girlie," groaned Hal. "It has suffered sufficiently from your — your — your fist now. Dear me, little one, how many pounds do you weigh?" Then, very anxiously: "I say, Girlie, has that been sent to you as a gentle hint that a new one would be very acceptable? I really think you ought to have offered to make it good. Let me see — is the number inside?" and Hal left his seat and approached Meg with the liveliest interest expressed on his face.

Meg gave his curly hair a sharp pull as he bent his head over the hat. "Behave, Hal. Haven't you any sense at all? Oh, dear me, mother, whoever would think that Mr. Stanley would do such a silly thing as this!"

"There's a note," said Hal, poking his finger under the lining.

Meg took it and read aloud:

"Mr. Stanley presents his compliments to Miss Randal and begs her to accept this reminder of a most pleasant 'adventure' in the same spirit in which it is given."

Hal groaned. "And he a minister!"

Meg looked up inquiringly. Hal proceeded to explain.

"That hat didn't cost less than two dollars and fifty cents, and he pretends to call it, in its present state, a pleasant reminder. Well, he may be sincere in what he says, but I doubt it. He must have more of a 'cash supply' than I have."

"Oh, you let Laurie sit down on your hat — your silk one, too — and you would keep it in a glass case ever after to feast your eyes upon," retorted Meg, a little flushed.

Elsie took the hat and looked at it thoughtfully.

"Trying to ascertain its original shape, sister?" asked Hal.

Elsie smiled. "No, I was thinking what a strange thing it was for Mr. Stanley to do."

"You mistake," said Hal, gravely. "Mr. Stanley did not do it. Girlie did it."

"Hal!"

Hal caught Meg as she flew at him and drew her down on his knee.

"I did not mean that," said Elsie. "I meant his sending it to Meg. It seems so unlike him; or rather what I had imagined him to be."

"Has he gone down in your estimation, sister?" asked Meg, laughing. "I will confess, although I have not made a very minute study of his character as you have appeared to do, that I am somewhat surprised at his actions. I did think he was too dignified to have such foolish actions," and Meg turned up her nose scornfully.

"I do not see that his doing this is necessarily deteriorating to his dignity," replied Elsie, gently. "It has not made me think any the less of him; it has only surprised me."

"What do you say about it, mother?" asked Meg.

"From what I have seen of Mr. Stanley," said Mrs. Randal, "I have been greatly pleased. He impressed me very favorably the first time I heard him preach. I am quite satisfied as to his perfect gentlemanliness, and am sure that he would do nothing in the least way questionable. He has done this from a pure spirit of fun; you know, Meg, ministers are human as well as the rest of us, and suppose you receive it in the same spirit. Doesn't his note request that?"

Meg's eyes were dancing now. "Yes, mother; but what do you think about his keeping my ribbon? Do you not object to that?"

Mrs. Randal shook her head at Meg. "Oh, you naughty girl, you are going to throw my maxims and theories back to me. I understand you. I have talked to you and sister so many times about what your behavior before young gentlemen should be. I am not going back on my theories at all. My girls know what I wish of them; they know that the desire of their mother's heart is that they shall grow to be good, pure, noble-minded women, respecting themselves and thus commanding respect from all with whom they come in contact. I trust you both, fully, and am more thankful than I can tell, that I am able to do so."

The laugh had faded from Meg's eyes and given place to a serious look, while Elsie's filled with tears as she said earnestly :

"And I think, mother, that that very trust which you place in us, does more toward making us try to become what you would like to have us be than almost anything else would." Elsie wanted to say "except your prayers," but she was afraid Meg would laugh at her.

"Then I am more glad, if possible, than ever that I can and do trust you," replied Mrs. Randal, lovingly. "I pity any mother from the bottom of my heart who cannot put trust in her children. She must be a most unhappy woman."

"But don't you think, mother," said Hal, who had been listening very attentively, "that it is often the mother's fault that she cannot trust her child?"

Meg pulled his ear, and said emphatically, "Not when she is such a mother as ours is."

"I agree with you there," replied Hal heartily. "But our mother is just a little above the average, as you will agree with me. Everybody is not blessed with as good a mother as we are, and that is why I asked the question that I did, and if I am not greatly mistaken our mother agrees with me. How is it, mother?"

"I do agree with you, Hal, to a certain extent. A mother is sometimes so afraid of trusting her child, and that child, unless she is possessed of more than the usual amount of pride, deceives her mother, sometimes unnecessarily so, for the very reason that she has never been taught any better. Her mother has never trusted her, has never encouraged her to go to her and ask her permission in little things as well as great ones, teaching her and proving to her gradually, that whatever is best for her, the mother will surely do. These mothers have their laws and by-laws, so to speak; their children are made acquainted with them early in life, and also with the fact that these laws must be obeyed without any questions being asked; if they are not, then punishment will come quick and sure. Some mothers follow this idea with the very best of intentions; they really think it is the only way in which a child can be virtually brought up. Others do it through sheer ignorance — they do not know any better. But then, it is just as certainly true that some children's natures are such that the "trust method" would be the very worst one for a parent to follow. We cannot judge in a matter of this kind; we do not know what either child or mother has to contend with. Let us be content in knowing that God watches over all with equal love and care; that, when he bestows the blessed crown of motherhood upon any woman he gives with it the power and endurance to keep each little jewel bright and unsullied."

"Mother," said Meg, "don't you think that God sometimes punishes a mother through her child?"

"Yes, Meg, but the punishment is never unjust, it is always deserved. And such cases go to prove to us that, no matter how early in life we commit sin, we shall certainly be punished for it sometime before we die; the punishment may not come until after many years, but it will certainly come."

> " I know that each sinful action,
>   As sure as the night brings shade,
> Is somewhere, sometime punished,
>   Tho' the hour be long delayed."

quoted Meg. "You seem to be of the same opinion as our over-effusive poetess, Ella Wheeler Wilcox, mother."

> "That each sorrow hath its purpose,
>   By the sorrowing oft unguessed;
> But as sure as the sun brings morning
>   Whatever is, is best."

added Elsie, softly. "Why don't you quote the pleasantest part, Girlie?"

"Because there was not so much relation between that and what mother said as the part I gave. But you might know that you would bring in the pleasant-est parts, sister — that seems to be your forte."

"And a most praiseworthy one it is, too," remarked Hal. "I wish there were more of sister's stamp — life would be more enjoyable."

Meg turned and looked closely into Hal's face.

"I mean it, Girlie," he said, smiling a little at her surprised look.

Meg clasped her little hands together with a despairing gesture. "Don't tell me you are growing serious, Hal," she said, entreatingly. "Half of my enjoyment in life will be ruined if you do."

"Why? Can't I be serious and still be pleasant company?"

"No, you can't; I dislike serious people."

"No, you don't, Girlie; I have heard you say many times that you had no respect for gentlemen, or ladies either, who never had a thought above dress and good times, and who couldn't do anything but giggle and talk silly nonsense. You admired character — you respected high ideas and lofty desires and noble pur-suits; you despised weakness" —

"Hal, do stop being ridiculous," interrupted Meg, rising to her feet, for Hal had repeated the words she so often used in a tone of voice that resembled her own very much, holding his head very high and just a little to one side and curling his lips exactly as Meg did. His imitation of her was so good that it made them all laugh.

Meg stood up in the middle of the floor and struck her hands together; this action was always considered a sort of prelude to a speech.

"The curtain rises," said Hal, sotto voice. "Act I, Scene III."

Meg gave him a withering glance and commenced: "You are right, Hal. I do admire character in a man or woman; I make no distinction between the two sexes. There is no reason why a woman should not possess character as well as a man. I hold that there is more real moral character in a woman's little finger than in a man's whole body. But we will waive that question for the present; I will speak of men and women collectively now, not individually, putting woman where she ought always to be put — on a basis with man. I say I admire character and consider no person worthy of my or any other rational being's notice who does not possess it. Right here let me warn you against confounding character with reputation. Reputation is one thing, character is another. The world may take your reputation from you, but it cannot take your character. I despise a person of little mind — one might as well not have any. I would not thank anyone to always think as I do; say 'yea' to my yea and 'nay' to my nay. I do not deny that it is very pleasant to have your own way — never to meet with opposition — but I am quite sure that such an order of things would soon prove monotonous. What is the use of people's living if they do not give an opinion of their own once in a while? They might as well be born deaf-mutes, and be governed entirely by one superior mind — the president, for instance; only I am afraid he would be even a more tortured man than he is now — I have no patience with these people who never give an original expression to an original idea, but who sit calmly down with folded hands and say, 'Oh, it makes no difference to me — do just as you think best and I shall be satisfied.' Satisfied! Do they know what the word means?" Here Meg broke suddenly off to say rather sharply: "What are you grinning at, Hal? What have I said that strikes you as so amusing?"

"I beg your pardon, Girlie," replied Hal, a little disconcerted at the unexpected turn Meg's eloquence had taken. "But I was thinking that the people you were then describing, very much resembled those with whom you associate. So much so, in fact, that I should think them the originals of the thought."

"Yes," parroted Meg, "so much so, that they are the very ones I mean."

Hal opened his eyes. "But surely you have respect for them, Girlie."

Meg made her little outward motion with her hands.

"You mean to say that you have no respect for Dell and Laurie and May and Holmes and Duncan and all the rest of your devoted subjects and humble admirers, Meg Randal?"

Again the outward motion of the hands. Hal leaned back in his chair.

"Then, if you have no respect for them, why are you so intimate with them? I, myself, can scarcely acknowledge a person whom I do not respect, as an acquaintance, much less could I call him friend."

Meg looked quickly at her brother; she could not remember of his ever speaking to her in that way before; then she braced herself for the battle, determined not to be beaten, even if she had to give expression to some ideas which she had not yet been able to make her mind up to, whether they were right or wrong. She would hold her own and still she would do it more in fun than in earnest, just to find out what Hal's ideas really were; he very seldom gave any of them a chance of finding out.

VI.

COMPARING NOTES.

PERHAPS your ideas of respect and mine differ Hal."

"Respect is respect and nothing else.   There can be but one definition to it."

"And that is?"

"To esteem."

"And esteem is?"

"To respect."

Meg laughed.   "Very good, Hal.   I'll originate another definition, one more suited to my own feeling. Respect is tolerance."

"It may be — it must be with you — if you feel toward your — your — what shall I call them? your acquaintances?"

"No, no, friends; my friends."

Hal smiled disdainfully.   "Your friends, then. Give me an analysis of your feelings toward them,

Meg. I must confess you have rather excited my curiosity."

"And your disgust, too, if one is to judge from the expression of your face. Well, Hal, I shall have to take them individually. I'll begin with Laurie."

Hal blushed. Meg, not seeming to notice it, proceeded:

"My 'liking' for my friends will take the three degrees of comparison — positive, comparative and superlative. To begin: I like Laurie; like her very much. I can use no stronger term, for to love any one it is quite necessary for me to find perfect satisfaction in that one. Laurie comes very far from that. She lacks firmness of mind, independence of thought and action; she is too easily led. She depends too much upon the support of others; she does not think for herself. She has no mind. She is more like a pretty, soft, white kitten" —

"You have estimated Laurie's value sufficiently, Meg," interrupted Hal, who had grown quite pale. "For your dearest friend, you rate her rather low. Pass on to Dell, please."

"There is no difference in my liking for Dell and Laurie. I think just as much of one as I do the other; my liking for them both is of the comparative degree. Yet I respect Dell more than I do Laurie.

I admire her spirit; there is 'true grit' there. She is honest to a fault; she scorns deceit and despises a liar as much as I do. She makes no pretensions of being better than she is; she is not ashamed of having done a thing after she has done it, and if she has done wrong she is not ashamed to acknowledge it. In other words, more forcible than elegant, Dell 'never goes back on herself.' She is true blue every time."

The earnestness with which Meg had spoken, brought a flush to her cheek.

"Yes," said Hal. "I admire Dell myself; both for her great beauty and for that quality of truthfulness which she possesses to a remarkable degree; but I do not think she is one who would inspire deeper feelings in anyone."

Meg laughed. "No? She seems to have done so in Ed Holmes."

Hal pushed his chair back impatiently. "Ed Holmes is — a donkey!"

"Amen," replied Meg fervently. "Dell has often expressed her feelings for him in the same complimentary manner."

"How about May?" asked Hal. "Of what degree of comparison is your liking for her?"

"Positive. I care very little for May. She takes

the same part in my group of friends as one of the
background figures did in that Japanese wedding we
had last Winter; she helps 'fill up.' I could get
along without her as far as action is concerned, but
the group would not be complete without her."

Meg noticed a look growing gradually in her
brother's face, deepening as she talked, that she had
never seen there before, and she saw, with her characteristic keenness, that it was a look of pained surprise and bitter disappointment. She was astonished
at her own feelings of regret at seeing it, but what
she had commenced in fun she was determined to
carry out in earnest.

"Of course you have no respect and very little
liking for any of the gentlemen of your acquaintance?" remarked Hal.

"Of course," replied Meg carelessly.

"What of Maude Leonard?"

"Maude Leonard I thoroughly despise."

Hal looked up at the passionate tone. Something
in Meg's face warned him not to question any more in
that quarter.

"And Ethel?" he asked. "Surely you have always
paid her a certain amount of the respect she has
always demanded of every one."

For the first time Meg's eyes fell, and a burning

blush suffused her face. Hal was almost startled at the effect his words had upon her. He did not know what a feeling of shame filled the girlish heart at his innocent thrust. But Meg was honor itself; she would not sully her lips with a lie. What she thought, she would say.

"I honor and respect Ethel Lawton above all my acquaintances. I am proud to think she has called me her friend."

Hal was completely at a loss to understand his sister.

"Then why do you not let her continue to call you friend? She would gladly do it."

Meg's voice was low and full of feeling, but she held up her head proudly and her lips curled themselves scornfully. "Because I am not worthy," she said.

Oh, what a pity that someone — the right someone — had not been there to lead the girl out of the tangled path of doubt and dark uncertainty in which she was walking and place her feet in the narrow, shining way. Elsie longed to, but did not dare, and the mother, with all her grand ideas and lofty principles, shrank from wounding her child's feelings in pointing out to her wherein she was wrong. A mistaken love, too often met with in this beautiful world of ours.

If Hal had only known how Meg's heart was really beating with its burden of unsatisfied longing; how she was yearning for help and guidance in the great solemn question that is sure to confront us, one and all, sometime in our lives, and was even now presenting itself to Meg's heart to be settled by her and her only. But Hal, like so many more, judged only by outward signs and was deceived. He saw only the proudly lifted head, and the scornfully smiling face; he did not see the beating, troubled heart; if he had, his answer would certainly have been different.

"You carry your sarcasm too far, Meg," he said sternly. "You certainly ought to respect religion."

"Oh, Hal! Girlie does respect religion," said Elsie, reproachfully. "No one can say that she does not."

Elsie had seen the shade of pain that had passed over Meg's face at Hal's words, and her gentle, loving heart was filled with pity. Meg knew this, but she resented pity almost as much as insult, and now she crushed down the new, inexpressible feeling that was rising in her heart and answered both brother and sister gaily.

"It seems to me that we are converting the dining-room into a confessional. The subject of confession is proving itself a most tiresome one to me. I move we lay it aside until next prayer-meeting night and let it be brought up and discussed by those more competent to settle it than we; our young converts, for instance, might take it in hand — they would certainly go to work on it with all the ardor of youthful Christianity."

Meg did not mean to say all this, but it seemed as if she had got started and could not stop, urged on as she was by the growing displeasure on Hal's face.

"Suppose we go back to our former subject — there is less danger of our coming to swords points on that. You wonder, Hal, why I can appear to be so friendly with people for whom I have so little respect. I do not see the necessity of my respecting a person in order to like them. I suppose I do respect them in a certain sense of the word — they have qualities that one must respect. What I do not like in them is their utter want of spirit. We will except Dell, for she has spirit enough. They are too dependent; they let other people think for them; they have no settled ideas of their own about anything, or if they have they do not give expression to them."

"Perhaps if they did," remarked Hal with a smile, "you would not like it any better than the present order of things. You could not queen it over them quite so royally as you do now. Would you like that?"

"I might not like it quite so well, but I should respect them a deal more than I do now. I would like to be opposed in something once; there would be the spice of novelty in it, at all events."

"Well, you may meet somebody before many years who will oppose you enough in all conscience," replied Hal with a grimace. "I pity the poor fellow, though, with all my heart. He must be possessed of more spirit than any young gentleman I have the pleasure of knowing."

"Indeed and indeed!" drawled Meg. "Spare your pity, my brother; no poor unfortunate will ever draw upon it through any idiocy of mine — I'll promise you that."

"Girlie," said Hal, rising and putting a hand on each of her shoulders — Elsie and the mother had left the room —"did you mean what you said about" —

"About Laurie?" interrupted Meg, lifting a laughing face to his. "Yes, I did, Hal, every word."

He turned away, disappointed and not a little hurt. Meg ran after him and put an arm around his neck.

"But you know, Hal, you interrupted me before I had finished. May I say the rest of it now?"

He nodded, smiling in spite of himself.

"Well, then, if Laurie is a kitten, she is one of the sweetest, most lovable kittens that ever purred. And it is my firm belief that she is one grand exception in the great family of human kittens; though she may have claws — and I do not deny that she has, there is enough of the human kitten about her for that — yet I have never known her to show them to a living creature; and very few are the kittens you can say that of, Hal."

Hal stooped down and left a kiss on the white forehead. "Spoken like my own generous little Girlie," he said lovingly.

Meg returned the kiss, but in her heart she could not help saying: "Yes, he calls me generous because I have praised Laurie. Are all men alike, I wonder?"

To her mother she said lightly: "What about the ribbon, mother? Shall I allow Mr. Stanley to keep it?"

"If you have promised it to him, Meg."

"Then I suppose he must have it. I shall be more careful in the future about making contracts with young gentlemen."

"It would be as well," said Hal with a laugh.

VII.

THE LOST ESSAY.

"MISS RANDAL, why did you not prepare your essay this week?"

"I did prepare it, madam."

"Then I have overlooked it. I did not find it among those left on my desk."

"It was not there, madam."

Madam de Crando looked very sharply at Meg. "Explain yourself, Miss Randal."

"I prepared my essay, madam, but instead of taking it home last night as I generally do, I left it in my desk, shut up in my folio — and when I looked for it this morning it was gone."

Madam de Crando had no reason to doubt Meg's word; she knew her to be perfectly reliable at all times, but she could not help feeling surprised and showing her surprise in her face.

"That is very strange, Miss Randal; you are perfectly sure you did not take it home?"

"Perfectly, madam."

"What young lady is appointed first monitor this week?"

"Ruth Dean."

"Whom did you leave in the room last night when you went home?"

"No one."

"Was not Ruth there?"

"No, madam; she was in the library, reading."

"Did you see any of the other girls before you left?"

"I passed Maude Leonard in the hall as I went to the dressing-room and Laurie Ray was waiting for me in the 'study'."

Meg could not help noticing how Madam de Crando passed over the mention of Maude's name and seized upon Laurie's.

"I suppose she is sure that such a high-souled creature as Miss Leonard would never think of such a thing as taking what doesn't belong to her; the bare idea would make the pure-minded Maude faint," thought Meg.

"Did Miss Ray remain in the 'study' until you were ready to join her?"

Meg's blood boiled at the question and the insinuation it contained, but she answered calmly, "No, madam."

" Ah ! do you know where she went ? "

" You think you have the culprit now, don't you ? "
thought Meg sarcastically. Aloud she said : " Yes,
madam, she went to the dressing-room with me and
remained there until I was ready ; we passed out of
the building together and Laurie did not leave me
until we reached her own gate. I am quite positive
she did not return to the school again, as my brother
called at her home shortly after tea and found her
with one of her sick headaches. She had been taken
with it a few moments after she had entered the
house and had immediately gone to bed."

Meg gave this very minute explanation with the
most innocent of faces. Madam de Crando looked at
her closely every minute, but could detect nothing
either in Meg's looks or manner that she could object
to, and yet she felt almost sure that the girl was
laughing at her.

" Very well, Miss Randal," she said, somewhat
stiffly. " I will excuse you for the present. I am
very sorry this thing has happened, and if we succeed
in finding your essay, as I trust we shall, I shall be
more glad than I can say. But wait one moment,
please."

She pressed the electric button beside her desk,
and to the girl who responded to the call she said,

"Find Miss Dean and send her to me immediately, please."

In a few moments the door again opened and a small, slight, dark-faced girl entered the room. Her face had no beauty in it except the beauty of expression — which to my mind, is the best kind of beauty — and her dress, though wonderfully neat, was undeniably shabby and bore in every little shining fold and wrinkle the unmistakable fact that "it was an old one made over." As she came into the room her dark eyes, that always wore such a dreamy, far-away look, as if they saw not the things they rested upon, brightened and shone with a pleased light as they fell upon Meg. They were beautiful eyes, though they always had the effect of filling other people's — over-sensitive people's, perhaps — with tears when they looked at them.

Meg smiled brightly back to her and put out her little, white hand under cover of madam's desk. Ruth took it in her own dark, work-worn one, and so they stood before their stern-featured preceptress.

Madam told Ruth in a few words why she had been sent for, and then said, "Can you enlighten us any, Miss Dean?"

Ruth, who had grown quite pale when madam commenced to talk, but had now regained her self-possession — probably encouraged by the warm pressure of those small, white fingers around hers — looked her questioner squarely in the face and said firmly :

"No, madam, I know nothing of the essay."

"You have not seen it at all?"

"No, madam."

"Very strange," murmured madam. "You were the last in the school-room, were you not?"

"Yes, madam, last in the school-room, but not last in the building."

"Indeed! Whom did you leave here?"

"Maude Leonard was in the 'senior's parlor' translating a French exercise."

Madam frowned, then said shortly, "Miss Leonard, of course, knows nothing about it; we will not trouble her by speaking to her of it."

Meg's lip curled, but she said nothing.

"I will excuse you, Miss Randal, but Miss Dean will remain a few moments."

Meg gave Ruth's hand a parting pressure and left the room with a very haughty step. Madam looked after her with an approving smile. She admired and respected Meg more than any other young lady in her school.

Meg collided with some one the instant she opened

the door leading into the hall.   She stepped back into
the room again and said in a ringing voice:

"Did you wish to speak with madam, Maude?"

Madam left her chair and went to the door.   She
saw Meg and Maude standing just outside the door.
Meg looked downright wicked and Maude very much
embarrassed.

"What is it?" asked madam.

Before Maude could speak, Meg said: "When I
opened the door Maude fell against me.   I presume
she was waiting for you to be at liberty that she
might speak with you, probably about the lost
essay."

Not one of the other girls would have dared to say
that.   Madam, indeed, looked a trifle displeased.

"Miss Randal!" she exclaimed in a reproving tone;
but Meg was looking at Maude, who had by this time
regained her self-control and was looking with innocent, surprised eyes, first at Meg, then at madam.
To be sure, the rich color that was always in her dark
cheek was deepened somewhat, and her eyes dwelt
longer on madam's face than on Meg's, but she looked
quite innocent when she said in her low, soft voice:
"I beg your pardon, madam, but I do not understand.
Has some one lost an essay?"

"Miss Randal can not find hers.   I did not mean

to trouble you about it, Miss Leonard. Of course you know nothing of it?"

"No, madam."

"Oh, little Ruth, little Ruth," said Meg to herself, "why could you not have been born rich and wicked, instead of so poor and so good?"

"I was quite sure you did not," continued madam. "Would you like to see me about anything?"

"Not if you are engaged, madam," replied Maude, sweetly. "A little later will do as well."

"Yes, after you find something to come to her for, you—Christian," thought Meg, fiercely.

"I can see you now perfectly well, Miss Leonard," said madam. "Miss Dean, you may go into the reception-room until I send for you. Miss Randal, you are excused."

Meg bowed and passed out, giving Maude the most scornful of all her scornful looks as she did so. Maude, not seeming to notice it, followed madam into her office with her usual soft, sweet smile.

Meg passed through the hall and up the stairs so quickly that she did not hear Laurie's call, and entered the library. She drew hastily back when she saw who was sitting in one of the great easy chairs drawn up before the open grate. The library and senior's parlor both contained an open grate, and a fire was kept burning in them three seasons out of the four. Madam thought they made the rooms look more cheerful and inviting, and I am sure she was right. "Come in, Girlie," cried Ethel, rising from her chair with a glad smile on her fair, delicate face. But Meg called back as she hurried away :

"No, thanks ; I made a mistake."

"And a pretty big mistake, too," she added to herself, as she ran up another flight of stairs that led to the dressing-rooms. "The biggest mistake I ever made in my life."

Poor child ! She was, indeed, making a huge mistake, but it was a different one from the one she had in her mind.

"To think that Ethel Lawton could leave me and the rest of the girls — every one of whom are miles and miles above that — that female Judas down stairs — because her principles will not allow her to keep such bad company as we are; we do things that shock her sense of right; we are not fit for the society of pure-minded, high-souled creatures like her and Maude Leonard. Oh, no, I couldn't think of going into the room where you are, Ethel, for fear my breath would taint the air you breath. Call Maude in when she gets through lying to madam, and her presence will bring peace and happiness to you. Angelic creature !

Noble-minded Christian! Oh, that the world held more like her!"

Meg was growing tragic. She walked the long hall with quick, impatient steps, her hands making violent gestures.

"Oh, dear me, Meg, are you practicing your part of 'Lady Macbeth'? You look savage enough to do murder in earnest. 'Is the deed done? Has Duncan drawn his last?' I'm not sure that those are the precise words, but then I haven't the immortal William at my tongue's end, as you have," and Laurie came panting up the stairs with something white in her hand.

Meg turned impatiently, though not the least "put by" at being caught in her private theatricals.

"No, the deed is not done, though I wish it were. My fingers do itch to do the bloody deed. But seriously, Laurie, I am in a most murderous frame of mind."

Laurie drew back in mock affright. "Where is the dagger?" she whispered fearfully.

"In my bosom," laughed Meg. "Don't you see the handle sticking out?" and she drew a lead pencil from between the buttons of her basque.

"But seriously, Laurie" — for the second time —"I feel downright wicked, and when I tell you the circumstances of the case, you'll see I have good cause. You know I finished my essay yesterday afternoon about half-past two; my subject was: 'Nature and Art.' I put Nature before Art every time. Well, I did not take the essay home as I generally do, for I was afraid I might forget to bring it this morning. I have done so before and had to send Tommie for it, to say nothing of the private lecture from madam on forget-fulness. When I looked for it this noon it was gone. The question is, 'Who has taken it?' Someone beyond a doubt, as it could not walk off by itself. I endeavored to endow it with various superior qualities, but the power of infusing motion into its pages was beyond me."

Here Laurie opened her lips to speak, but Meg stopped her with a wave of the hand, and again began her excited walk up and down the hall, Laurie trotting along beside her to take her chance of saying a word when it should come. She was " Mr. Dick " to Meg's "Dr. Strong."

" Laurie, I know Maude Leonard took that essay! I feel positive of it. She had no motive for doing so — it was done out of pure meanness. She knows I have never missed a week since I have been here in sending in my essay, and I am the only one of our class who can say that. But if she thinks to make madam suspect me of lying she will get mightily disappointed. But affairs have taken a more serious turn than she thought for — or at least, an entirely different one. Madam suspects Ruth Dean of knowing where the essay is. The idea! I would stake my life on Ruth's honor. The poor child is waiting in the reception-room now until madam is ready 'to pass sentence upon her,' and Maude is in the office 'asking madam about some exercise or other.' In reality she is getting off her lies in regular wholesale fashion. Poor little Ruth! If I had known how things were coming out I would have bitten my tongue off rather than have said one word about the essay. I would rather madam would have thought I had not prepared one. Oh, if I could only find it."

Meg was really very much excited. She clenched her little hands together and stamped her foot as Laurie commenced again to say something.

"I tell you, Laurie, it is a deadly shame that such things are allowed. Why are such persons as Maude Leonard allowed to exist? She is a liar, a cheat and a deceiver, and everything else that is bad. She is utterly without principle. This is not the first time by any manner of means that she has done mischief, and every girl in the building knows it. How madam can be so blind passes my understanding; but I think the glitter of Maude's gold dollars is what causes part of the blindness — it is too much for madam's weak eyes — morally weak, you understand. But poor little Ruth has nothing — Laurie, let me alone, I can't stand still, I am too angry."

"Well, then," cried Laurie, grown quite desperate at not getting a chance to say what she wanted to say, "look at it walking, then; it is certainly worth your attention."

"Laurie Damon Ray, where in the world did you find it?" gasped Meg.

Laurie laughed, she could not help it. Meg's face was a study for a sculptor.

"That expression would make your fortune for you if you were only on the stage, Meg," she said. "Well, if you have really decided to let me speak, I will tell you. I found it in the dressing-room back of the blind."

'You darling!" exclaimed Meg, rapturously, giving the delighted Laurie a hug, which was a rare thing for stately Meg to do. "She must have laid it there while she was putting on her things and gone off and forgotten it, or, what is more likely, left it purposely, trusting to luck to keep it there until it was too late to send it in. She was probably intending to take it back to my desk in a day or two, feeling quite sure

that I would take it to madam and say I had found it
where I had left it.   I wouldn't have blamed madam
if she had felt a little doubtful as to the truth of such
a statement.   But it was a careless thing for her to
do, for the janitor might have found it.   She must
have been intending to take it away to-night — Laurie,
come quick."

Meg had been talking more to herself than to
Laurie, and all at once broke off in what she was saying, and went running down the hall dragging the
surprised Laurie with her.   As they ran up the stairs
Meg whispered :

"'Sh, Laurie, don't make a sound.   Stand here at
the door and don't let anyone come in."

Meg went into the library, but soon returned.
"Come back up stairs again," she said.

Laurie obeyed without a word ; she was used to
doing as Meg told her without asking any questions.
Meg seemed to think of this and looked at her with· a
half-smile.

"I wouldn't have you any different now for the
whole world, you dear little kitten," she said to
herself.

In a few moments they heard the library door close,
and voices calling to each other.

"Going my way, Lill ? "

"Yes, if you'll wait a minute, Lu."

"Where are you going?"

"Up to the dressing-room after my reticule."

"Hurry up."

"Yes."

Light feet came tripping up the stairs, the owner humming a gay little song. Laurie and Meg heard her go into the dressing-room, then in a moment come out and run down stairs. They heard Lulu Martin ask carelessly:

"All the girls gone?"

"No," answered Lill. "There are half a dozen 'belongings' up there — Meg's and Laurie's and Ethel's and one or two more."

The two girls passed down into the lower hall, the great door slammed, and all was still again.

Meg and Laurie sat down on the stairs and waited. The library door again opened and a slow, tired step ascended the stairs. Meg knew it was Ethel, but she stood up and peeped over the banisters. There was a sad look on the pale face as Meg caught sight of it for a brief moment, and a little pang shot through her heart, but she said to herself:

"I don't care — she has disappointed me fearfully. I trusted her so and thought her so good and noble. Oh, Ethel, how can you be so blind!"

She waited until Ethel came out and passed down the stairs. She leaned far over the banisters and caught a glimpse of her as she crossed the lower hall, then the door clanged heavily behind her and Meg sat down on the stairs again beside Laurie.

Another fifteen minutes passed, then the sound of footsteps coming up the stairs called Meg up from her seat again.

"Laurie, look," she whispered.

Laurie stood up and looked down the stairs. Ruth came slowly up the hall; her face was pale, her eyes red with weeping. The girls could see how her slight form shook with heavy sobs -even then, and they looked at each other with indignant faces.

"What a shame!" said Laurie, in a low tone, but Meg said never a word.

Ruth ascended the stairs slowly, passed into the dressing-room and presently came out again with her wraps on. She looked so sad and full of trouble that Meg could not bear it, and with a whispered, "Stay here a minute, kitten," she ran down the stairs.

Ruth turned in surprise, but Meg said carelessly: "I am detained to-night; am not going just yet. What is the verdict?"

Ruth's sobs came thick and fast. "I am suspended," she said.

"What!" Meg almost shrieked the word in her surprise and indignation.

"I am suspended. I do not know what Maude said to madam — I do not know as she said anything, but after she had left the office, madam called me in and — I cannot tell what she said, I was so confused and troubled, but she gave me to understand that she was quite sure I had the essay or could tell where it was, and until I was ready to return it to its rightful owner I must remain at home. Oh, Meg, you know I have not gotten it, don't you?"

Meg was so white with anger she could scarcely speak.

"Yes, yes, Ruthie, I know you are innocent, and madam shall know it before many hours. Let me see."

Meg was almost undecided what to do; at last she said: "Ruthie, trust me. That is all I can say now. Trust me," and Ruth answered, "I do trust you, Meg."

Meg leaned over — she was much taller than Ruth — and left a light kiss on Ruth's forehead.

"Thank you, Ruthie. Now run home and put all your trouble away. Leave it all with me."

"I will, and with my Saviour, Meg," and Ruth was gone.

Those words, "and with my Saviour," seemed to strike Meg dumb. Was Ruthie — little, timid, shrinking Ruthie, who always seemed afraid to speak aloud almost, a "professor", too? Meg did not laugh at the idea. The look on the little, patient, dark face, and the tone of the low, earnest voice seemed to fill her with a certain sense of awe.

"And with my Saviour." Meg said it over to herself two or three times.

"Meg," called Laurie, "are you asleep?"

"'And with my Saviour.' What is there about those four words that makes me feel so? It can't be the words themselves; no, it was the way in which they were spoken. I cannot doubt Ruth's goodness, and if she is anything, she is sincere. Both goodness and sincerity will be put to a severe test shortly. Will she prove faithful? If so, my skepticism will receive a blow. In my heart I pray she may."

Meg went back to Laurie, quiet, and for her, subdued.

VIII.

A DISCOVERY.

"HOW much longer are you going to stay here, Meg?" whispered Laurie. "I confess I feel quite like a 'tragedy character,' but at the same time I am human, and like all the rest of humanity, have a stomach. The fact is being pressed upon me in the most ravenous manner."

Meg smiled. "Only a few minutes longer, kitten," she said. "Run into the dressing-room and get my lunch-basket; there are some 'duchesse crackers' in it."

Laurie needed no second bidding, and was soon leaning comfortably back against the wall, munching the crackers.

Fifteen minutes passed, a half hour. It had grown quite dark on the stairs and the two girls felt chilly sitting there. Laurie had finished the crackers and was growing restless, not to say nervous.

"It is quite like a story, Meg," she whispered, giggling a little. "We are like two avenging spirits hiding here, waiting to pounce upon the guilty one when she shall come forth. Dear me! I shall see madam's great-grandmother's ghost walking up the hall if I sit here much longer. Goodness! what is that?"

Laurie came very near screaming. Meg put her hand out and said, "'Sh, she is coming.'"

After that Laurie had all she could do in watching Meg. As she afterward said, "It was as good as any theater she ever went to." I will give what followed as it was seen with Laurie's eyes.

Meg leaned far over the banisters and watched the figure coming up toward them, with stern, dark eyes. Her face was very white and wore a pitiless look. Maude Leonard — for it was she — ascended the stairs with quick, light steps. She put her hand on the knob of the dressing-room door, then stopped and looked down. Meg could see by the light that fell from the large window that she was smiling; then she opened the door and went in.

In a second Meg had glided down the stairs and stood in the open door. Laurie, unknown to Meg, was just behind. Maude crossed the room, little thinking she was not alone, and drew aside the blinds.

A low cry escaped her. "It is gone," she said aloud.

"It is here," said a voice that made her almost jump from the floor, and Meg stood before her, holding out the stolen essay.

"Oh, for some red light!" Laurie could not help thinking.

The two girls stood and looked at each other steadily for a full minute. Maude with a flushed, guilty face; Meg with a white, scornful one. It seemed for a second as if Maude tried to look defiant, but it would have been impossible for one more proficient in deception than she to have met boldly the steady, accusing light of those dark eyes. Meg was brave because she felt sure she was right. A less courageous girl would have trembled at what was before her; not so Meg. If she trembled at all it was with anger. Maude knew she would receive no mercy at Meg's hands. She knew that to appear sorry would but make Meg more pitiless. She therefore dropped her assumed manner and put on her original one.

"Well?" she said haughtily.

"Not quite as well with you as you thought it was," replied Meg curtly. "Your sin has found you out for once, Miss Leonard. You stole this essay from my desk, hid it behind that blind, and have just now been looking for it. You need not deny it — it would be useless."

"I do not intend to deny it." Maude could not help answering as she did — the clear, dark eyes compelled her to.

"What do you intend to do about it?" she asked coolly.

"You will go to Ruth and acknowledge to her that you took the essay."

Maude looked relieved. "Is that all?" she asked.

Meg's lip curled. "No, it is not all. You will also clear Ruth in the eyes of Madam de Crando."

Maude lifted her head haughtily, her face flushed deeply. "I will not do that, Megda Randal; I would die first."

"You will do it."

"I will not."

For just a moment they looked at each other, then Meg said, clearly and firmly: "Very well; as you choose. I will clear her myself."

Maude Leonard laughed scornfully. "Where are your proofs, Miss Randal?"

"Here is one of them," said a timid voice.

Both girls started, and Meg could not repress a joyful little cry as Laurie came forward, and stood before them. Maude covered her face with her hands, and at the sight Laurie's eyes filled. Not so Meg's.

"Laurie," she said, "will you go to madam's sitting-room and ask her to step up here for a few moments?"

Laurie turned to obey from mere force of habit, when Maude, with a low cry, sunk down on the floor at Meg's feet.

"Spare me that, Meg," she cried. "Spare me that for my mother's sake."

Meg looked down on her, her face full of scornful triumph. Somehow it made Laurie's heart ache to see that look on the face she loved so well. For the first time in her life she felt disappointed in Meg, but she did not say anything.

"Meg," said Maude, lifting her face, from which all the rich colors had gone, "I know there is no use in my trying to deceive you. I will tell you the truth. I took the essay from your desk last night, intending to keep it until Monday and then put it back. I was going to do this because I was jealous of your always having a paper prepared at the right time, and of being in such favor with madam. I put it behind the blind, feeling almost sure that no one would find it. Even if there had I should not have cared so very much, as it could not have been proved who put it there. I knew if you made known the loss of your essay to madam that her suspicion would rest upon Ruth Dean, as she is the last girl in the school-room every night for this week. But, as you say, my sin has found me out. I ask forgiveness from you with all my heart, and from Ruth, too, but I cannot humble myself in the way of which you speak. Madam would lose all faith in me, would most likely expel me, and the disgrace would kill my mother. She is good, if I am not."

"Yes," said Meg, "and deserving of a better daughter than you. A pity you did not think of her heart before. What of Ruth's mother? What of her heart? She has none, I suppose; poor people cannot afford such luxuries."

Meg stood still a moment; Laurie gave her an imploring look which made Meg feel as if she should like to shake her.

"Will you go with me to Ruth's at once?" she asked.

Maude lifted her face. "Yes," she said.

"Very well."

They put on their wraps and went down the stairs and out of the building without another word. It was dark and cloudy and they walked fast. As they drew near Ruth's poor home, they saw a light burning in one of the windows; the curtain was up and they could see into the room. The tea-table was spread, the fire was burning brightly and everything looked cheerfully pleasant, if very poor. Ruth was nowhere to be seen. Meg went up to the door and rang the bell. In a few moments it was opened by Ruth herself. Meg stared at her in amazement. She had expected to find her almost sick with grief, and here she was, her little dark face perfectly free from all traces of violent sobbing, her large, dark eyes full of a bright, solemn, and to Meg, indescribable light. She smiled when she saw who was standing on the steps, and invited them in in a pretty, shy way. Meg found her tongue — it was never lost for long — and her easy, graceful manner with it.

"Tea all ready for us, Ruthie? But why do you put the lamp in the window?"

Ruth laughed as she placed chairs for her unexpected callers, and said, "I put it there for mother; she has not returned from Mrs. Lawton's yet."

"She has all the sewing she can do, doesn't she? Is she quite well?"

"Quite well, thank you. I hope she will return early; she would like to see you."

"I don't hope so," thought Meg, and turned to Maude. "Maude is really your visitor, Ruthie;

Laurie and I are only a sort of body-guard," and Meg laughed.

Maude blushed deeply at Meg's little thrust, but Ruth said innocently: "Oh, are you? Maude is to be congratulated on having such an agreeable body-guard. Did you wish to speak with me about anything in particular, Maude?"

Maude was playing nervously with the ends of her rich lace scarf. Meg felt like shaking Ruth for being so gentle with her. "And she knows as well as I what Maude has done," she said to herself.

Maude opened her lips and then the words came almost faster than she could repeat them. Ruth listened to what she said with a startled face. Meg, watching her, was more than astonished to see a look of pain gradually settle upon it, and the large eyes fill with tears. What did Ruth mean by acting as if she were really sorry to hear what Maude said instead of dancing with joy! Ruth herself explained her meaning when Maude had finished by holding out her hand and saying, "I am truly sorry, Ruth; will you believe me and forgive me?" by taking that hand in both her own and saying in a voice that trembled with feeling:

"Forgive you, Maude? To be sure I will, with all **my** heart. And oh, Maude, let us both thank God for giving you the courage to acknowledge your wrong before it was too late, and ask Him to ever increase that courage to resist every temptation that may come to you."

Maude cast down her eyes and was silent. Laurie was crying, but Meg's face wore its most scornful look.

"Why doesn't the coward tell the truth?" she was thinking. "She doesn't say how she was forced to acknowledge it. Well, if she doesn't, I am very sure I shan't."

Ruth went on. "I have been praying ever since I came from school, that Jesus would make it all right, and He has so soon answered my prayer."

"Does that explain the look of peace?" thought Meg.

"Let us all kneel down and thank Him," said Ruth, all her shyness swallowed up in her happy thankfulness.

She drew Maude down beside her, still clasping her hand in hers. Laurie knelt and buried her face in the cushions of her chair. Meg alone remained standing, but she bowed her head. Then Ruth prayed, and oh, how she prayed! Laurie and Maude both sobbed, and Meg felt the tears coming into her own eyes, but she forced them back. Ruth prayed like one inspired, and Meg was forced down upon her knees in spite of herself.

When they rose to their feet Ruth went up to Meg and kissed her. "My friend," she said.

Meg laughed. "Do not think too much of me, Ruthie. I have done nothing."

"You have only made me unspeakably happy," said Ruth simply.

Meg turned to Maude. "Have you anything more to say?" she asked.

"Nothing," replied Maude; but she did not look at Meg.

"Then we may as well go," said Meg shortly.

Ruth looked at Meg sadly. To her, Meg's manner seemed strange. "She has such stern ideas of right and wrong," thought Ruth. "She scorns mean actions; but it seems to me that she is unnecessarily hard with Maude. It is because she has not the love of God in her heart. Dear Meg, how I shall pray for her!"

"Good-night, Ruthie," said Meg. "We'll see you at church on Sunday?"

"Yes, if nothing happens to prevent," replied Ruth. "Good-night."

"Good-night," they answered, and went out of the yard and down the street.

At Maude's house they stopped. It was a handsome dwelling, plainly showing outside the wealth of its owner.

"Meg," said Maude, but still not looking at her, "are you going to tell Madam de Crando?"

The words, "Yes, I am going to tell Madam de Crando," rose to Meg's lips, but she did not speak them.

"Shall I let Ruth get ahead of me in generosity?" she asked herself bitterly. "No, I will be a Christian, too, for once in my life if I never am again, and return good for evil out of the over-abundance of the former quality that is in my heart."

"I have reserved my forgiveness until now, Maude," she said sweetly. "I grant it to you in the same spirit of earnestness in which it is asked. You are quite safe with me. Good-night."

She put her hand through Laurie's arm and led her quickly away. "I spoke the truth at all events, kitten," she said. "We know how much earnestness was wasted in both the plea and the pardon."

"Oh, Meg," said Laurie, "don't you think Maude was really in earnest?"

"Certainly," answered Meg. "As earnest as I was."

Laurie thought it best not to say anything more about that. "What shall you do, Meg?"

"Do?"

"About the essay, I mean. What shall you tell madam?"

"Oh, I shall tell her it was left in the dressing-room and found by you."

Laurie looked at Meg with admiring eyes. Meg laughed lightly. "Well, was it not?" she asked.

"But suppose she does not believe you?"

Meg dropped Laurie's arm, and drew herself up proudly. "Laurie Ray!"

"Oh, I didn't mean that exactly, Meg dear," said frightened Laurie. "I meant, suppose she thinks it a little strange; you know she cannot at least help thinking you were just a little careless."

"Yes, I do not doubt it," replied Meg calmly.

"But you won't want her to think that, Meg?"

"No, but it will be quite necessary. The life of the Christian is often a hard one, Laurie; we have many things to contend with. We are obliged to do things that are hard for us to do, but we shall reap our reward some day."

"Don't, Meg," said Laurie in a pained voice.

"Well, I won't, then, kitten; it isn't nice."

"And you really will not tell of Maude?"

"Laurie Ray!" Again the haughty lifting of the head.

"Oh, I know you won't, Meg," and Laurie stopped in the street and put both arms around Meg's neck. "You are the dearest, noblest, grandest girl that ever walked the earth!"

Meg laughed as she returned the embrace. "What strong language, kitten," she said. "Nobody but a kitten would be guilty of such idiocy. But you are very much mistaken, Laurie. I am a sinner — a wicked, wicked sinner; but I have one consolation in being such — I have plenty of company. Now, good-night. Be at church on Sunday."

"Yes; but are you going in the morning, Meg?"

"Oh, yes. I am anxious to see if Mr. Stanley will give the 'hat adventure' as an illustration to 'He that ruleth his temper,' etc."

"Oh, Meg, you sinner!"

"There! just what I have been trying to impress upon you. Good-night."

"Good-night."

Meg walked more slowly after she left Laurie. She was thinking deeply. It may appear strange to my readers when I tell them that Meg gave no thought to what she had done for both Ruth and Maude. She might do a kind act for anyone every day of her life and not waste a thought upon it, but it was impossible for her to do an unkind act and not be thoroughly ashamed of herself for doing it fifteen minutes after. She was impulsive, and, like most impulsive people, her impulses were not always good ones. Now, as she walked along she felt ashamed of the words she had spoken to Maude at her gate, but almost too proud to acknowledge it even to herself. Pride was Meg's besetting sin; it often kept her from converting noble thoughts into noble actions. She knew she had been wrong in speaking in the way in which she did, but pride kept her from acknowledging her wrong and saying she was sorry for it.

Meg had always prided herself on her independent spirit; she had always found herself to be sufficient for her own comfort and happiness; she had never found it necessary, as the other girls had done, to depend on others — to look to others for help; she had always been proudly independent of everybody; it had made her impatient with others less self-confident. She had laughed at Ethel for saying she would find, some day, that she needed a Saviour's help.

"Religion will do for those who cannot depend on themselves; they are obliged to ask for help from somewhere — but what do I want of it? I am perfectly happy — have always been so — and what reason is there that I shall not always be so? Simple little Laurie thinks me little lower than the angels;

what I have done to-day has increased her admiration for me, if that is possible. Would she rate me so high if she knew the real reason for my doing as she did? The only reason why I promised Maude not to expose her is because I could not bear to think that anyone — especially such a timid, weak little thing as Ruthie — should get ahead of me in generosity. That is my only reason. Can it be that I am as great a coward as Maude? Why didn't I tell her and Laurie what my real feelings were? It can't be it was because I was afraid. No, no, no. I will not think of such a thing. The idea of my being a coward! Besides, Maude understands me perfectly — I meant that she should; but does Laurie? Pshaw! I'll not think of it any longer. But I needn't have lowered myself so much in my own estimation as to pretend what I did not feel, or that is, to allow Laurie to think my motive for doing as I do, was a purely unselfish one. Well, I'll think no more about it now, at any rate. The next question is: 'What shall I say to Madam de Crando on Monday?' That is easily answered. I shall take the essay to her and tell her it was found in the dressing-room behind the blind. She will naturally conclude that I put it there while getting ready for home and forgot all about it. It makes no difference to me what she thinks. And

Maude will be free from all reproach and blame, except that of her conscience, and she will not suffer much from that source; people of her stamp are not troubled with too much conscience. I haven't a doubt but that Ruth will look up to her with the same amount of admiration that Laurie pays to me — as one who has met and wrestled with temptation and come off victorious — and Maude will allow her to think so and be delighted. But, am I not nearly as bad myself in allowing Laurie to think — oh, misery! I'll not be tortured with self-accusations any longer. Here is home, sweet home. The homage paid me here is true and heart-felt, if undeserved, and the dear love showered upon my unworthy head is appreciated and returned with full interest by me. Oh, if mother, sister and brother composed the world, what a queen I should be indeed! Methinks it is as well that they do not, for my conceit would be something terrible; it is well-nigh insufferable now." And for the very first time, probably, in all the eighteen years of her happy, petted life, Meg felt a slight contempt for herself — a strange, unaccountable feeling of dissatisfaction. But her pride kept her from showing in the slightest manner, how she felt. Poor Meg! She was as submissive a victim to the tyrant, pride, as she considered Ethel and Ruth to be to their religion.

IX.

BEHIND THE CHURCH DOORS.

"COME, Girlie, hurry up if you are going to walk to church with me."

"Yes, I'm coming, Hal; wait just a minute."

"Can't you get that crimp to stay in just one particular place? Sister is ready, and has been for five minutes."

"Well, tell her and mother to run ahead, and you wait just a second longer, that is a darling."

"Oh, yes, a dear old darling I am when you want me to wait for you. Well, hurry up or I'll run on ahead, too."

Hal's words were threatening, but he had no idea of carrying the threat into execution. He told his mother and Elsie to start on ahead, and he and Meg would catch up with them — perhaps.

In about five minutes Meg came running down the stairs. Hal heard her coming, and hid behind the parlor door.

"All ready, Hal; you were a darling to wait for me."

Hal, in his place of concealment, laughed softly and peeked through the crack of the door. "Lacing her gloves up now, by all that is truthful," he said to himself.

Meg finished lacing her gloves and looked around. "Hal," she called. No answer.

Meg started for the sitting-room, got as far as the hall glass and stopped to survey herself. She pirou- etted around on her toes, looked over her right shoul- der, over her left, tipped her brown velvet hat a little further back, that more of the bright crimps might show, and then called again. "Hal." Still no answer.

"I'll just see how long she'll stand and admire that new rig of hers," said Hal to himself. "The little darling! She does look fine this morning, and no mis- take. She's a sister for any fellow to be proud of."

But Meg, warned probably by the tolling of the bell, had stopped her examinations for good, and com- menced her search for Hal in earnest. She ran to the door and looked up and down the street, then flew back into the parlor and stood in the middle of the room. "Hal," she called, impatiently, and stamped her little foot upon the floor. Hal stepped softly up behind her and caught her in his arms. What a scream she gave!

"'Sh, Girlie," said Hal; "it is Sunday morning."

"A nice thing for you to remind me of, after teazing me by making me think I had to walk to church alone, and then frightening me half out of my wits, you hateful boy!" retorted Meg, and gave him a kiss to punish him.

"Never mind, Girlie, I've left you wits enough to look as pretty as a pink. That is a lovely rig you have on — dark red is becoming to you."

Meg almost screamed. "Dark red, you simpleton! Why, it is seal brown."

"Oh, well, what is the difference?" said Hal, as he locked the door and put the key in his pocket. "I said it was becoming, and that is the main point, isn't it?"

"Just now it is," replied Meg. "Isn't that Lill Norton and Lulu Martin ahead?"

"It looks like them," replied Hal carelessly. "Yes, it is, and there is May Bromley just coming out of her gate. We'll not be the only ones to go in to slow music."

"May has on her new suit," said Meg. "Her's is a garnet, Hal; now don't you see the difference between dark red and seal brown?"

"Well, there isn't much. Ethel Lawton looked fine this morning, Girlie."

"Did she? Where did you see her?"

"She drove past with her father while I was waiting for you. She had on — I think it was black — anyway it was velvet, and she had on a large hat with ever so many plumes. She was as white as a snow-drop, and her hair shone like gold."

"You must have been very observing, Hal; how did you manage to see all that?"

"They were driving very slowly. Ethel leaned out of the carriage and looked at every window in hopes of seeing you, I suppose. How much she thinks of you, Girlie."

Meg's lip curled.

"But do you think she is strong?" went on Hal, not seeing the curling lip. "She looks very delicate; her skin is almost transparent."

"Oh, yes, she is strong enough," answered Meg hastily. "She inherits her fair skin; all her people on her mother's side have very white skin. But her new suit is green, Hal — an emerald green velvet, and it is perfectly lovely. I was up to the house when it was brought home from the dressmaker's; but no doubt it looked black to you as it shades on the dark. Her hat is imported. There! they have all disappeared inside the church and the bell has stopped. We shall be the last ones."

"All your fault, Girlie. I am going to explain my frequent tardiness to Mr. Stanley when I get better acquainted with him. I'll tell him he will never know what it is to be late at church until he is married. The organist will have to look out and get long voluntaries then. He'll think you came in late purposely to-day, Girlie — to show your new rig."

"Who will — the organist?" asked Meg demurely.

"No, Mr. Stanley."

"I don't care what he thinks," replied Meg, blushing a little. "And don't, for pity's sake, keep calling it a rig, Hal; call it a suit."

"Oh, well, I will if it *suits* you any better."

Meg gave him a withering glance. "Melvin Pierce got here?" she said scornfully.

"Guess what I think, Girlie," asked Hal, as they went up the stairs. Meg looked up, questioningly.

"I think Mr. Stanley is setting his cap for Ethel. Be a good thing for him, wouldn't it? They look fine together, too."

They had stepped inside the vestibule, and Hal had bent his head close to Meg's as he whispered the last question. He was surprised to see how the fair face flushed, but Meg smiled and gave him a little push.

"Yes; now stop whispering and go in before Mr. Lane stops playing."

They went in and took their seats. Heads were turned and every face smiled a welcome on Meg. Meg's face wore an answering smile. She looked in Laurie's seat — so did Hal — and both thought her looking prettier than ever in her new suit of navy-blue cashmere trimmed with chinchilla. All the girls had on their new suits and looked very pretty.

Meg never questioned whether it was right or wrong to think of such things in church. She never turned in her seat to stare at anyone, or did anything else that she considered improper, but she could not keep her thoughts from dwelling, first upon one thing then upon another, instead of keeping them strictly upon the sermon. Elsie always listened attentively to every word that was said, drinking them in eagerly and showing her earnestness and deep interest in her parted lips and softly-shining eyes. But then she was good, dear, quiet little Elsie, thought Meg, and cared for such things.

This morning Meg did not venture to look at Mr. Stanley until Hal touched her foot softly with his. Looking at him to see what he might want and seeing his eyes fastened earnestly on the pulpit, Meg turned her head quickly and looked, too. The thought flashed upon her that Mr. Stanley might possibly have exchanged pulpits, and she should see a stranger occupying the chair. What was her embarrassment to meet Mr. Stanley's dark-blue eyes gazing earnestly at her. There was nothing in that certainly; the look was a very grave, unobtrusive one; but Meg flushed hotly beneath it and dropped her eyes, at the same time feeling deeply angry with herself for doing so. As for Hal, mischievous fellow, he was obliged to turn his head and look out of the window. Laurie, watching him, wondered what he could see in the church-yard to bring such a broad smile on his face. Meg did not venture another look until she was standing with the others singing the "Doxology."

Mr. Stanley did not sing, but he was passionately fond of music. Now he stood with his hands clasped behind him and his eyes raised toward Heaven. His face wore a rapt expression as if he had forgotten all earthly things and was thinking only of things spiritual, as, indeed, he was. Somehow his face, or the expression it wore, fascinated Meg, and she kept her eyes upon it, even after the singing ceased, and the young minister, lifting his hand, said in a deep, solemn voice, "Let us pray."

The prayer was short but tenderly impressive. Then followed the hymn: "Come Near Me, O My

Saviour." Mr. Stanley read the verses through, and
Meg's cultivated ear was charmed with the rare
elocutionary powers he displayed. "Oh, what a
grand 'Macbeth' he would make," she thought. "He
is just the style, too; a handsome face is not necessary, and his form is just perfect — not short and not
tall, but strongly-made and broad-shouldered. And
that voice! deep, thrilling and musical. Oh, if he
would only join us!"

Mr. Stanley little thought the way in which the
beautiful words of the hymn and his manner of rendering them were being received by one fair member
of his congregation. As he finished, he looked at
Meg and noticed the look of deep admiration on her
fair, lifted face, but mistook it for one of reverent
feeling for the words he had read. He was pleased,
and said to himself: "I was not mistaken when I said
there were rare qualities in that girl's nature. She
will make a most lovely woman."

The text Mr. Stanley chose was from the seventh
chapter of St. Matthew, the seventh and eighth
verses. He confined himself quite closely to his
notes. He did not step from behind his desk; he
made few gestures, but those he did make were
easy, graceful and well-appointed. The words came
smoothly from his lips; his articulation was perfect,

every syllable could be distinctly heard in the furthest corner of the large room. His voice in its ordinary tone, was deep, but soft and pleasant. When he said anything in which he wished to be particularly impressive, his voice would ring out strong, clear and thrilling. He caught the attention of the entire congregation at the first word he uttered, and held it to the end. Fastidious Meg was thoroughly charmed, though she could not have told his text five minutes after she heard it, nor could she remember one particular thing that he said. He appealed only to her admiration; he demanded that and received it.

The rare, cultivated voice, the graceful gestures, the pure, simple language and the rapid change of expression, received her deepest attention and admiration, but the beautiful words from God's own book, the grand thoughts he gave expression to, and the solemn, comforting assurances held out to his listeners in his earnest, closing words, were all lost upon Meg; she gave no thought to them.

Mr. Stanley commenced by saying: "Our Heavenly Father loves all His children with infinite love; that is, He loves everyone, even the feeblest and weakest of His children, with the self-same love with which He loves His only begotten Son. On account of this infinite love — knowing how great, how many,

how varied, nay, how numberless would be their
trials, their difficulties, their afflictions, their temptations, while passing through this vale of tears — He,
in His grace, made abundant provision, in giving most
precious and encouraging promises concerning prayer,
so that, if they took their trials, difficulties, afflictions
and temptations to their Heavenly Father, seeking
His strength, His counsel and His guidance, and acting according to the loving counsel and advice given
in the Scripture, 'Casting all your care upon Him,'
the position of most of the children of God would be
very different from what it is.   Then again, our precious Lord Jesus Christ loves us with the self-same
love with which the Father loves Him.   Do we all
believe it ?   The former statement, that the Father
loves His children with the self-same love with which
He loves His only begotten Son, and what I now
state, that the Lord Jesus Christ loves us with the
self-same love — that is, with infinite love — and that
with this love He loves the feeblest and weakest of
His children, possibly may appear strange to some of
you.

"Yet this is the statement of Holy writ as found
in John xv : 9, and in John xvii : 23.   Our precious
Lord Jesus Christ, who loves us with such love,
passed through difficulties, trials and temptations

like unto ours, while He was in the world. He was looked down upon; He was despised; that Blessed One 'had not where to lay His head,' and was, while in the world, 'in all points tempted like as we are, yet without sin.' Knowing the position of His disciples in this world, He has given the precious promise which I have read on the subject of prayer, and if it is made good use of, we may have Him as the burden-bearer, ever ready to help in the time of sorrow, weakness and affliction — in a word, in all the variety of position and circumstances in which we are found here in the body.

"Had it been left to us to make promises regarding prayer, I do not know that you or I could have done more than say, 'Ask, and ye shall receive.' Yet, while the promise is so full, so deep, so broad, so precious in every way, we have here — as becomes us with other parts of the Word of God — to compare Scripture with Scripture, because in other parts additions are made, or conditions given, which, if we neglect, will hinder our getting the full benefit of prayer. I judge we have not to lose sight of the passage in 1 John, v : 13–15. 'These things have I written unto you that believe on the name of the Son of God; that ye may know that ye have eternal life, and that ye may believe on the name of the Son of

God. And this is the confidence that we have in Him, that, if we ask anything according to His will, He heareth us : And if we know that He heareth us, whatsoever we ask, we know that we have the petitions that we desired of Him.'

"Here is the first point specially to be noticed regarding prayer, 'If we ask anything according to His will He heareth us, and if we know that He heareth us, whatsoever we ask, we know that we have the petitions that we desired of Him.' If, therefore, we pray, and desire to have our petitions granted, it becomes us first to see to it that we ask for things according to His mind and will; for our blessing and happiness are intimately connected with the holiness of God. Suppose there were living here, in our town, a person who had long carried on a business, who was known by those intimately acquainted with him to be an idle person, one who shrinks from work; or, whenever he can get out of it, seeks to have an easy time of it. Suppose such a person had heard of the promise about prayer, and should say, 'Now I will try if these things are true, and I will ask God to give me $100,000, and then I can give myself easy days ; I can travel about and enjoy myself.' Suppose he prays every day for this large sum of money, will he obtain it ? Assuredly not ! Why not ? He does not ask for it that he may help the poor abundantly ; that he may contribute to the work of God more liberally, but he asks that he may spend his life in idleness, and in enjoying the pleasures of the world. He is not asking for things according to the mind of God, and therefore, however long or earnestly he may pray, he will not get the answer. We are only warranted in expecting our prayers to be answered when we ask for things according to the mind of God.

"The second point we should notice is, that we do not ask on account of our own goodness and merit, but, as the Scripture expresses it, 'In the name of the Lord Jesus Christ.'   I refer you to John xiv: 13, 14 — 'And whatsoever ye shall ask in My name, that will I do, that the Father may be glorified in the Son.   If ye shall ask anything in My name, I will do it.'   The statement is given twice, in order to show the great importance of this truth ; for whenever a saying is given twice in the Word of God, we may be sure a weighty and important subject is brought before us.   What does this statement, given twice by the Lord Jesus Christ, mean ?   If we desire to go to Heaven, how shall we get there ?   On the ground of our own goodness, merit or worthiness ?   Because we are not so bad as others ?   Because we go regularly to a place of worship ?   Because we give a little to the poor? In this way assuredly no one will get to Heaven. It is quite right to go to a place of worship. It is quite right that, of the abundance God gives, we should contribute to the poor. It is quite right that we should act according to morality. But in this way a poor sinner cannot get to Heaven. We must see our lost and ruined condition by nature, and that we deserve nothing but punishment. The best person in this congregation, in this town, in the United States, or in the whole world, is a sinner deserving punishment. Never since the fall of Adam has a single person, by his own goodness, obtained Heaven. Under the old dispensation, there was need to look forward to the Messiah, and since the old covenant dispensation has ceased, there is need to look back upon the Messiah, who, in our stead, suffered the punishment due to us, while hanging on the cross and shedding His blood. All our guilt was transferred to Him, that His righteousness might be transferred to us. And now a sinner — though the oldest and the vilest wretch under Heaven, as assuredly as he puts his trust in the Lord Jesus Christ, shall be for-given, shall be cleansed, shall be justified; that is, shall be reckoned righteous and just, through this his trust in the Lord Jesus Christ for the salvation of his soul. In this way the sinner gets to Heaven — by faith in Jesus for the salvation of his soul. As by faith — in the Lord Jesus Christ — we shall stand before God at the last, so it is now in approaching unto God in prayer. If we desire to have our petitions answered, we must come to Him, not in our own name, but as sinners who trust in Jesus, who by faith in His name are united to the blessed risen Lord, who have become, through trusting in Him, members of that body of which He is the Head. Let none suppose they are good enough in themselves. I deserve nothing but hell. So precisely with all of you, and the very best and holiest persons that can be found. Therefore on the ground of our goodness we cannot expect to have our prayers answered. But Jesus is worthy, and for His sake we may have our prayers answered. There is nothing too choice, too costly, or too great for God to give to Him. He is worthy. He is the spotless, holy child, who, under all circumstances, acted according to the mind of God. And if we trust in Him, if we bide in Him, if we put Him forward, and ourselves in the background, depend on Him and plead His name, we may expect to have our prayers answered.

"Some one may say, 'I have prayed through long years, for my unconverted children, but they have not yet been converted. I feel I shall not have my prayers answered. I am so unworthy.' Does this mean, 'I live in sin? I go on habitually in an evil course?' If so, the prayer cannot be answered, for in the Sixty-sixth Psalm we read, 'If I regard iniquity in my heart, the Lord will not hear me.' That is, if I live in sin, and go on in a course hateful to God, I may not expect my prayers to be answered. But what is meant is, 'My love is faint, I am ignorant, therefore I am unworthy.' This is a mistake. The promises are particularly for such — for the weak, for the feeble, for the ignorant, for the needy; and all such who ask for Christ's sake are warranted to expect their prayers to be answered.

"A third condition is, that we exercise faith in the power and the willingness of God to answer our prayers. This is deeply important. In Mark, xi: 24, we read, 'What things soever ye desire, when ye pray, believe that ye receive them, and ye shall have them.' 'What things soever ye desire' — of whatever kind — 'believe that ye receive them and ye shall have them.' I would specially lay this on your heart, that you exercise faith in the power and willingness of God to answer your prayers. We must believe that God is able and willing. To see that He is able, you have only to look at the resurrection of the Lord Jesus Christ; for having raised Him from the dead,

He must have almighty power. As to the love of God, you have only to look to the cross of Christ, and see His love in not sparing His Son, in not withholding His only-begotten Son from death. With these proofs of the power and love of God assuredly, if we believe, we shall receive — we shall obtain.

"Suppose now we ask, firstly, for such things as are according to the mind of God, and only such things can be good for us; secondly, that we expect answers on the ground of the merit and righteousness of the Lord Jesus Christ, asking in His name; and thirdly, that we exercise faith in the power and willingness of our Heavenly Father to grant our requests; then, fourthly, we have to continue patiently waiting on God till the blessing we seek is granted. For observe, nothing is said in the text as to the time in which, or the circumstances under which, the prayer is to be answered. 'Ask, and it shall be given you.' There is a positive promise, but nothing as to the time. 'Seek, and ye shall find; knock, and it shall be opened unto you.' We have, therefore, patiently and quietly to continue waiting on God till the blessing is granted. Someone may say, 'Is it necessary I should bring a matter before God, two, three, five or even twenty times; is it not enough I tell Him once?' We might as well say there is no need to tell Him once, for He knows beforehand what our need is. He wants us to prove that we have confidence in Him, that we take our place as creatures toward the Creator. Moreover, we are never to lose sight of the fact that there may be particular reasons why prayer may not at once be answered. For the exercise of our faith, for by exercise faith is strengthened. We all know that if our faith were not exercised it would remain as it was at first. By the trial it is strengthened. Another reason may be that we may glorify God by the manifestation of patience. This is a grace by which God is greatly magnified. Our manifestation of patience glorifies God. There may be another reason. Our heart may not yet be prepared for an answer to our prayer. I will give an illustration :

"Suppose that three weeks ago a lad of sixteen years of age had been brought to a knowledge of the Lord Jesus Christ, and that with his heart full of love to the Lord he wanted to do something for Him. And suppose he goes to the Sunday-school superintendent and says, 'Will you have the kindness to give me a class to teach.' A class of nine children is given him. Now this dear boy, whose heart is full of love to the Lord, begins to pray that God would convert these nine children. He prays in private and before them, and also exhorts them to seek the Lord. After going home from his class he gives himself earnestly to prayer that God would convert these nine children. On Monday he repeats his request before God, and so day by day during the week and on Sunday again particularly; and then he goes to his class and expects that these nine children will be converted. He finds, however, they are not, but that they are just in the same state as before. He again sets the Gospel before them; he exhorts, beseeches and weeps before them. During the second week his prayers are most earnest; but on the following Sunday he finds that none of the nine children are yet converted. Does it mean that God will not answer these prayers? It cannot be that this dear boy will have to go on praying and God not regard it. But one reason is that the heart of this boy is not prepared for the blessing. If these children had been converted the first week, he would take credit to himself; he would think what he had been able to do, and would attribute the conversions to his entreaties, instead of to the power of the Holy Ghost. He would take a goodly measure of credit to himself, though he might not be aware of it. But let him patiently go on, and when his heart is prepared, God will, if possible, give it. Thus it is that the child of God has to wait until the heart is prepared for the blessing.

"Many of the dear children of God stagger, because prayer is not at once answered. And because for weeks, months and years, prayer remains unanswered, they cease to ask God, and thus lose the blessing, which, had they persevered, they would assuredly have obtained. It should be especially noticed that all the children of God, who walk in His ways and wait on Him in prayer, have, more or less frequently, answers to prayer. I will illustrate this :

"All who in any measure walk before God, at the close of the day thank Him for His mercies, and commend themselves to Him for protection during the night. In the morning they find no fire has happened, and no wicked hands have molested them. Here is an answer to prayer, and we have to thank God for it. The more we observe these matters, the more we shall find how we get prayer answered. Many that have suffered from sleeplessness have often, in answer to prayer, had sound, refreshing sleep, and have had in the morning to thank God for it. Now all, on the other hand, have sometimes long to wait for answers to prayers. Many of the dear children of God have long to wait for the conversion of their children. While some receive the blessing very soon, others have to wait for many years. But, beloved brethren and sisters, go on waiting upon God, go on praying; only be sure you ask for things according to the mind of God. The conversion of sinners is according to the mind of God, for He does not desire the death of the sinner. This is the revelation God has made of Himself — 'Not willing that any should perish, but that all should come to repentance.' Go on, therefore, praying; expect an answer, look for it, and in the end you will have to praise God for it.

"There is one point I would especially lay on the hearts of my beloved brethren and sisters, and that is — united prayer. In Matthew xviii: 19, the Lord Jesus says, 'If two of you shall agree on earth as touching anything that they shall ask, it shall be done for them of My Father which is in heaven.' If, therefore, there are brethren and sisters in Christ who have unconverted relatives, and if they could unite with two or more persons, and unitedly ask God to convert their children, oh, what a blessing might not come in this way? They should plead this promise before the Lord, read it out when they meet, and put their finger — so to speak — upon it. If they met once a week for half an hour, or once a fortnight, or as often as they conveniently could, to plead this

promise before the Lord, after a while a father would
have to say, 'My son, who almost broke my heart,
has been converted'; and a mother, 'I have a letter
from my daughter, who fifteen years ago left my
home, and has been living in sin, telling me she has
found the Lord Jesus Christ.' How their faith would
be strengthened by such united prayer and such testimonies! After a while, as their faith was strengthened, they would unitedly pray for their Pastor, that
God would more abundantly bless his labors in the
conversion of sinners, and in blessings on the Church;
and as they were further enlarged, their prayers would
extend to Missions, the circulation of the Scriptures
and tracts. They would know the power and blessedness of prayer more and more abundantly, and would
wait earnestly upon God, asking Him, yet once more,
in these days, to grant a mighty revival in the Church
of Christ at large. If this were generally so, with
what power ministers would set forth the truth of the
Gospel, what blessings would come on our Sunday-
schools, on the circulation of the Scriptures, on open-
air preaching, and other Christian work. God grant
we may more earnestly give ourselves to prayer.

"I find it a great blessing to treasure up in my
memory the answers God graciously gives me. I
keep a record to strengthen the memory. I advise

the keeping of a little memorandum book. On one side — say the left hand side — put down the petition and the date when you began to offer it. Let the opposite page be left blank to put down the answer in each case, and you will soon find how many answers you get, and thus you will be encouraged, more and more your faith will be strengthened; and especially you will see what a lovely, bountiful and gracious being God is; your heart will go out more and more in love to God, and you will say — 'It is my Heavenly Father who has been so kind; I will trust in Him, I will confide in Him.'

"With regard to any who do not yet know Him, let the first prayer be offered to-day, before you leave this place — 'Show me I am a sinner.' When you see this ask the Lord — 'Help me to put my trust in the Lord Jésus Christ,' and you will find how ready God is to give blessing. May we all who are the people of God, receive a blessing, and our dear friends and fellow-sinners be stirred up to seek Him while He is to be found. God grant it for Jesus' sake. Let us pray.

"Oh, God, grant that the words thus spoken may be like seeds dropped upon fertile ground, to spring up and bear fruit to the glory of Thy holy Name. May all these precious souls here this morning, learn what a blessed thing prayer is, if they do not already know it. Teach them to trust Thee; to take all their trials, their sorrows and their perplexities to the throne of Grace, and receive comfort and rest. Bless the words so poorly spoken by Thy servant, dear Lord. Forgive us all our sins, and save us for Thy blessed Son's sake. Amen."

X.

IN THE VESTRY.

WASN'T that a good sermon, Meg?" whispered Laurie, as the two girls stood in the vestibule waiting for the others of their class to join them.

"The delivery of it was perfect," answered Meg.

"Yes, Mr. Stanley has doubtless made the study of elocution a specialty. But weren't his ideas good, and so simply expressed! And how comforting he spoke!"

Meg looked at Laurie in a little surprise. "He makes a remarkably fine appearance in the pulpit," she said slowly. "I would have liked to see him enter the pulpit. Did you see him, Laurie?"

"Yes; his manner was all that even you could desire, Meg."

"Very dignified, but easy, wasn't it, Laurie?"

"Yes."

"Why don't the girls come? It takes them long

enough this morning. Oh, here they are. What have you been doing, girls, to be so long?"

"Been waiting for Ethel, but got tired and came away without her," replied Lill Norton.

"What is she doing," asked Meg, stepping to the swing-door and looking into the church.

"Thanking Mr. Stanley for his excellent sermon," said May Bromley. "She seems to be completely carried away with him. 'Twill be a good thing for the young man if she is, won't it?"

Meg turned around with a frown. "What nonsense, May, for a school-girl to talk!"

May looked ashamed. "Well, it would; she will be quite an heiress, and Mr. Stanley hasn't any money."

Meg looked perfectly scandalized. "Well, May Bromley!" she exclaimed.

Lill and Lulu laughed outright, and May giggled.

"Look at her now," said May, anxious to have Meg's scornful eyes leave her face.

Meg looked. Ethel and Mr. Stanley were standing at the foot of the pulpit steps. Mr. Stanley was holding Ethel's hand tightly in his own as if he had forgotten to release it, and was looking earnestly into her pale, refined face while she talked to him. It seemed to Meg as if she had never seen Ethel look so lovely.   There was a delicate pink flush in her cheek and her gray eyes shone brightly.

"What can she be saying to him!" thought Meg.

Just then another figure left one of the middle pews and swept gracefully down the broad aisle. "Maude Leonard," said Lulu, peeping over Meg's shoulder.   "Isn't that suit she has on too lovely for anything?   Such rich black velvet! and look at those elegant plumes!   Look at me, Meg, and tell me if you cannot see my skin turning green; I feel envious enough."

"Oh, come away, girls," said Meg, turning around with a scornfully smiling face.   "If Maude hasn't gone up to add her congratulations to those of Ethel's!   Why didn't we think to form in line and march down the center aisle to pay homage to our king.   Lill, I am ashamed of you.   Have you no heart, or is it so hard that even Mr. Stanley's elo-quence cannot soften it?   You are a lot of heathen, that is what you are.   Come down to Sunday-school now, and see if you can say the 'Golden Text'," and the girls obeyed the command of their 'leader', laugh-ing softly as they went.

All but Laurie.   There was not even a smile on her pretty, flower-like face.   One time she would have laughed heartily at her "idol's" sarcastic remarks,

but now she could not. She could not tell why they
hurt her, but they did. She did not feel as she used;
somehow an indescribable feeling had crept into her
heart of late — at times she felt almost sad. She
said nothing about it to anyone, except, to Jesus.
Yes, she did tell Him of it, and asked Him "to make
it all right." Poor little Laurie was not blessed with
particularly brilliant conversational powers, and in her
prayers to Him she used the plain, simple language
of a child, vaguely wishing that she could express herself to Him better, and little knowing that she was
going to Him in just the way he liked best to have
His children come. He was even now answering her
prayer for help and filling her heart with a great
peace and happiness that she had never known in all
her happy young life before.

Little did Meg think, as she looked laughingly
down into the little face beside her, what thoughts
were in the girlish heart. What would she have said
if she had known?

Ethel came in shortly after the girls were seated
and leaned over Meg's chair as she passed her.
"Wasn't that a comforting sermon, Girlie?"

"A most finely delivered one," answered Meg, with
her most mischievous smile, and Ethel passed on with
a look of pain.

"Thank you, Miss Randal," said a voice at Meg's side.

Meg started. Mr. Stanley was standing close beside her. "They say listeners never hear any good of themselves," flashed Meg, forgetting herself in her surprise and vexation. "But you can testify to the contrary, can't you?"

Mr. Stanley's face flushed a little, and the smile that had lighted it when he spoke to Meg, vanished. He bowed very gravely.

"I beg your pardon, Miss Randal, but you wrong me. I am not guilty of the charge." Then he turned to the others who had not heard the low-spoken conversation. "Young ladies," he said pleasantly, "your teacher, Mrs. Langley, was taken suddenly ill this morning and I have been requested by your superintendent to supply her place. I fear I shall prove but a poor substitute for so excellent a teacher, but I will do my best."

All the girls smiled and flushed, and altogether looked so pleased that Mr. Stanley could not but see that he was kindly received. There was a little pause after he had spoken, the girls were waiting for their "leader" to respond, but their "leader," for the first time in their remembrance, was dumb, and so Ethel took her place.

"You are very kind, indeed, to take our teacher's place, Mr. Stanley," she said in her sweet, calm, lady-like way; "but please allow us to be the best judges of your ability."

He looked at her admiringly, and made some smiling reply; then he commenced the lesson. He did not look at Meg, except when he asked her a question, and then his eyes rested upon her briefly and carelessly. Meg's proud heart swelled almost to bursting. She was angry with him, with Ethel, with everyone in the class, but most of all, with herself. What had she done? He had told her that she wronged him. She had done worse than that — she had insulted him. The idea of accusing him of listening.

She could not put her mind on the lesson; she answered all the questions asked her, correctly — Meg always had a good lesson — but she felt perfectly miserable. Could Ethel have done what she did, purposely?

"She might have known how I would answer her," thought Meg bitterly. "If she did do it purposely, the act was worthy of Maude Leonard herself, and I can say nothing worse about it. What will he think of me? That I am not a tenth part of a lady, no doubt, and I cannot blame him if he does. How he admires Ethel. And I don't blame him for that, either. She looks all that is to be desired — good, sweet, tender and, above all, a perfect lady."

To look and act like a "perfect lady" was Meg's idea of perfection itself. She wanted to be loved, to be admired, to be considered a perfect lady in every sense of the word, and then she was sure of perfect happiness. Thus far in her life, she had had what she had desired, and was perfectly satisfied with herself; but now — pshaw! she wouldn't trouble her head about it.

After the lesson, Mr. Stanley took the few remaining minutes for a general talk. He spoke so easily, yet so earnestly to them, that all were drawn out to say something, even timid little Laurie; but Meg never opened her lips. Mr. Stanley did not appear to notice her silence — "He is too much taken up with Ethel for that," thought Meg. "How earnest Laurie looks; she will be speaking in prayer-meeting the next thing. Even Lill and Lulu appear interested, and Dell has a pink spot on each cheek for the first time in her life, I verily believe. Am I the only heathen in the class? It seems so. They have all apparently forgotten me — thanks to my reverend friend."

Meg was growing more and more bitter every

moment; the sensation was an entirely new one to her; she, who had always been so happy, so sweet and so friendly toward everybody. I do not know what state of unhappiness she would have reached, had not the superintendent's bell put a stop to all talking and thinking as well. Mr. Stanley took his chair, and with a low "Pardon me," to Meg, placed it by her side and sat down. She drew her dress carelessly away with one hand and bent her head haughtily. He said nothing to her during the remainder of the exercises, but when the closing hymn was given out, he found the place and offered to share his book with her. She thanked him with another haughty bend of the head. The hymn was "Come," in number three. Meg did not intend to sing when she stood up, but it was as natural for her to sing as it was to breathe, and before the first verse was finished, her sweet, clear voice was ringing out high above the others. She stole a glance at Mr. Stanley to see how her singing was impressing him. The expression of his face caused a little smile to play around her lips, and she threw all the beautiful pathos her voice was possessed of into the remainder of the hymn.

When it was finished and she stole another look at the strong, earnest face beside her, the smile changed to a look of startled surprise, for the dark-blue eyes were certainly filled with tears. He turned to her after the short prayer, and held out his hand. "Thank you, Miss Randal," he said simply.

Proud, impulsive Meg put her little hand in his. "Do not thank me, Mr. Stanley; but forgive me for speaking to you as I did."

A smile lighted up his whole face. "I will forgive it when I recall it," he said. Then the girls came crowding out, and Meg found herself walking down the aisle between Dell and Laurie, yet half doubtful as to whether it were really herself and not some one else. When had she ever asked anyone's forgiveness before! Never, to her knowledge. And yet, she did not feel ashamed for having done so, but on the contrary she felt happier than she had felt for a week. Besides, she had only done what was right — what she ought to have done — so, of course, there was nothing to be ashamed of.

The next morning, as Meg was on her way to Madam de Crando's, the "essay affair" burst upon her mind for the first time since Friday night. Her resolution was quickly taken. Immediately after taking off her things in the dressing-room, she went to madam's private office. That lady looked a little surprised at so early a caller, but Meg soon turned the look of surprise into one of pleasure by holding out the lost essay, and saying briefly, "My essay has been found, madam."

Madam took it with a smile. "Indeed, I am glad to hear it. Where was it found?"

"In the dressing-room behind the blind."

"Ah! You laid it there for safe keeping, I presume, and forgot that you did so."

Meg made no reply. Madam seated herself in her arm-chair. "I trust you will learn a lesson in carefulness from this, Miss Randal. Had the essay not been found, an innocent girl would have had to suffer for your carelessness. I am more pleased than I can say, that I shall be able to take Ruth back; it would have been a hard thing for me to lose her, particularly in such a manner."

Still Meg said never a word. "Who found the essay, Miss Randal?"

"Laurie."

"When?"

"Friday afternoon after I had seen you."

"Do you remember of putting it there?"

Passionate words rose to Meg's lips, but she forced them bravely back. "No, madam," she said.

"It is very strange; you have never been guilty of such carelessness before, that I can remember of.

However, I think I may trust to your not being guilty of it again. You are excused."

Meg left the room, angry, but not the least humiliated. As she opened the door, Maude Leonard glided quickly away from it. Meg dashed after her and caught her just as she was disappearing into the library. Sorry am I to relate what Meg then did! She seized Maude by both shoulders and shook her until all her heavy black hair tumbled down her back and the pins flew far and wide.

"There, Jezebel," said Meg, between her shut teeth, and giving her a parting push that almost sent her down upon her knees, Meg ran up stairs to the "senior's parlor," threw herself down upon the lounge, and laughed till she cried.

In this state Ethel found her, coming in five minutes later. She went up to the lounge and bent over her. "Why, Girlie, what have you found to laugh at so early in the day? Tell me, so I may laugh, too."

But the sight of Ethel only made Meg laugh the harder. What would she say if she were to tell her what she had done. The very thought of Ethel's dismay — not to say horror, sent Meg off into a perfect gale, and Ethel was obliged to sink down into **one of the** easy chairs and laugh, too, though she did not know at what. But Meg's laugh was always contageous.

At last Meg sat up on the lounge and dried her eyes with her handkerchief. "Tell me what it was, Girlie," said Ethel, seating herself beside Meg, and passing her arm lovingly around her waist.

"Oh, nothing much, Ethel," gasped Meg. "Nothing that would please you," and then she went off into another gale.

"Try me and see," said Ethel smiling.

"Oh, it was only — well, Ethel, it was nothing, really. I was only indulging in private theatricals, and you don't believe in them, you know."

Ethel brushed back the bright hair from Meg's hot brow. "No, dear, I have no room in my heart for them ; it is already full to overflowing."

Meg drew herself away from the tender hand. "Full to overflowing, Ethel? Well, that is not to be wondered at. You have everything to make you happy. A beautiful home, loving, indulgent parents, all the money you want, and consequently, friends ditto — a happy, untroubled future before you. Whose heart would not be full to overflowing? Mine would, under those circumstances."

"The things you have mentioned, Girlie, are not what make me so happy. I am thankful for them —

deeply and truly thankful; but they are not what fill my heart to overflowing."

"No?" said Meg, lifting her eyebrows. "What is it, then?"

"Jesus."

The low, solemn voice drove the mocking light out of Meg's eyes, and the laughter from her face. She forgot Maude and everything else, in looking at the pale, lovely face before her — lovely, with the sweet, solemn light upon it.

Meg drew nearer and nestled her head against Ethel's shoulder in her old, caressing way, and Ethel's arms quickly encircled her and held her close and sure.

"Open your heart to this great love, Girlie. All you have got to do is to say, 'I am a sinner; dear Jesus, forgive me.' Then your heart will be as full of this great happiness as mine is. Oh, Girlie, give yourself to Him; you will not know what perfect peace and happiness is, until you do."

Meg's eyes were moist, but she still laughed lightly. "But, Ethel, I have never committed any great sin; and I am happy — I have always been so. I scarcely know what it is to feel sad."

Ethel looked wistfully into the fair, girlish face on her shoulder — so bright, so sunny, so laughing.

Would she have to taste of sorrow before she could know of this heavenly joy? Would that be the way in which she would be led to the Saviour? "God grant not," was the earnest prayer of Ethel's heart.

"I know you have always been happy, Girlie, but the happiness of which I speak is entirely different from any you have ever felt. It is a peaceful, restful feeling. It makes you loving and forgiving. You not only love your friends, but you love your enemies. You are young now — trouble has never come to you — but it will come; it must come some day as it comes to all, and then you will need the Father. Oh, Girlie, it is so blessed to know that whenever you call on Him for help, He is ready to give it. When you feel sick, and tired and unhappy, just go to Him and lay your head on His breast, and He will fold His dear loving arms around you, and soothe and comfort you into rest. It is a blessed feeling — a blessed feeling."

Ethel's arms had relaxed their hold of Meg, and she was looking before her with dreamy, happy eyes. Meg was almost afraid to speak, and sat and looked at her.

As she looked, a feeling crept into her heart — a strange, happy, peaceful feeling. It seemed to Meg that her heart must be drawing this feeling from Ethel's face. She had never felt like this before.

"Do you feel this perfect peace and happiness, Ethel?" she whispered.

"Yes, Girlie; and I have felt it ever since I gave my heart to the Saviour."

"Oh, if I could only feel it as you do, Ethel," cried Meg suddenly. "But I don't know what to do. I have always been so happy, and it seems as if I had always felt satisfied; but I don't just now. Why is it?"

Ethel drew Meg to her with a low, happy laugh. "Ah, that is just it, Girlie; you have never stopped to think whether you were satisfied or not. Oh, I hope and pray you may never feel satisfied again, until you make a full and complete surrender of this priceless little heart of yours."

Meg smiled. "But, Ethel, if I do that, then I shall have to surrender other things as well."

"What other things, Girlie?"

"I shall have to give up my social pleasures — dancing, the theater and, oh, Ethel! I do love the world and what it gives me — I cannot help it."

"For all these things He will give you a robe of whiteness and a crown of beauty that fadeth not away."

Meg was clinging to Ethel now. "Oh, Ethel, if I could only feel it; if I did not love the world and its pleasures so!"

"Give yourself to Him, Girlie — that is all. Say —

> "Just as I am without one plea,
> But that Thy blood was shed for me;
> And that thou bidd'st me come to Thee,
> O, Lamb of God, I come";

and He will fill your heart and life with such divine blessings, that it will have no room for these things that make you happy for but a little while, and then leave you restless and dissatisfied."

"I will try it, Ethel — I will begin at once; and will you pray for me?"

Ethel's face was radiant as she answered: "Pray for you, Girlie? Yes, with all my heart and soul and strength; every hour of the day and every minute of the hour. And pray for yourself, Girlie; He will certainly hear and answer your prayers."

One of the doors down stairs closed with a bang, and light feet came running up the stairs. A clear, girlish voice sang:

> "Little Fisher-maiden,
> Skies with storms are laden;
> 'Tempt no more across the sea,.
> Dangers waiting there for thee,"

and in a moment more May Bromley thrust her saucy head into the room.

"Oh, you are here, are you, Megda? Been looking high and low for you. We have just ten minutes before that heartless bell rings; come out here and try the 'Military schottische'; the floor is in fine condition — so is my whistle. Come on, madam will never hear; I'll do it softly."

Meg opened her lips to say "No," but just then May picked her skirts up daintily with both hands, and went skimming down the smooth, polished floor, whistling softly the "Nightingale Schottische."

The sound and the sight made Meg's heart beat quickly. She went to the door and watched May a moment, keeping time to the dance with her hands, then her feet commenced to keep the time, too, and when May came around to where she was standing, Meg slipped her arm around her waist, and down the long hall they went lightly and gracefully.

Ethel looked after them, but there was a smile on her face. "She loves dancing; loves it better than anyone I ever knew, but she will give it up; I feel sure she will step over the line before many days. God will claim her as His own in His own good time. I can trust him."

XI.

TUESDAY evening, November 25, 1889. The evening of the first Grand Entertainment given by the "Young People's Literary Society of ——."

Four weeks of study and practice had brought everything to a successful point; that is, it would prove successful if the young actors and actresses did as well on the evening of the 25th, as they did at the last rehearsal, Nov. 24. Not a word of fault could the exacting young "leader" find with her "troupe"; each one did his and her part perfectly. Perhaps Margaret Mather would have smiled with superior scorn on Meg's personation of the murderous "Lady Macbeth"; and Miles Levick might have looked upon the efforts of Will Duncan in his representation of the unhappy "Macbeth" as infant's work, but the privileged few who witnessed the rehearsal of this tragedy of Shakespeare, were loud in their praises, and Melvin Pierce even went so far as to say that if

Shakespeare had lived to see this hour, his pride would have been so great that it would have killed him.

"If he could only be here for this one night, Miss Randal," he said to Meg, as they stood together behind the "scenes", "I know he would say, with his last breath, 'Thank heaven for permitting me, at last, to see my ideal "Lady Macbeth"!'"

"Thank you, Mr. Pierce," replied Meg gravely. "Then you think it would prove 'sure death' to him?"

"Joy often kiss," said Melvin with admirable quickness of thought.

Meg laughed. "There is no getting ahead of you, Melvin. Just let me take a peep, will you, please? I want to see if we are going to have a full house."

Melvin drew the curtain aside, and Meg peeped out. Yes, the large room was very nearly filled, and it still wanted fifteen minutes to the hour appointed; but the face she looked particularly for was not there. She experienced a feeling of regret not unmixed with anger, as she scanned the audience closely. No, he was not there. "I suppose he would as soon be guilty of going to the 'Musee' as of coming here to-night," she thought bitterly. "He looks upon us as a pack of heathen."

"I say," observed Melvin, craning his neck to look over Meg's head, "we are going to have more than a full house; we'll clear fifty dollars, if we do a cent. There's Judge and Mrs. Lawton, but Ethel isn't with them. I suppose she is having a private prayer-meeting over our sinful actions. Oh, ahem! there comes Miss Maude Leonard alias 'Miss Nippy-Piety.' Did you ever see such a sanctimonious expression on anyone's face in your life, Meg? And see how she nips along, as if the floor was hardly good enough for her to walk on. I bet, if the truth were known, she walks that way because her shoes are so plaguey tight. Well, upon my word! here come Deacons Ray and Fly-Catcher. You've mistaken the evening, my brethren" — this in his most affable tones — "it is Tuesday not Thursday evening."

"Be quiet, Melvin," giggled Meg. "You should respect gray hairs, if nothing more."

"And don't I?"

"No. Why don't you call Deacon Huntly by his right name?"

"I beg the old gent's pardon; but — by jove, Meg, he's at it so soon!"

Meg could not help laughing. The young men had given the pseudonym of "Fly-Catcher" to good old Deacon Huntly, for the reason that he invariably sat with his mouth open. The width of the opening depended altogether on the degree of interest he experienced in whatever was passing before him; the deeper his interest, the wider the opening.

"Dear old chappie," murmured Melvin, affectionately; "he is doing it from mere force of habit. Hallo, here comes Brother Norton, Meg!"

Meg turned hastily at the horrified tone.

"The moths have gotten into his hair and laid the corner-stone for a skating-rink! As true as I'm a sinner!"

Meg came very near betraying herself to the people outside, in the laugh she commenced, but strangled. "You ridiculous boy," she said, choking herself with her handkerchief. "Let me pass; you will disgrace yourself and me, too."

"No, don't go; I haven't had so much fun since I was an infant," pleaded Melvin, holding her by the arm. "See, here comes old lady Bently and her brood of little ones; one, two, three, four, five, six — six fair daughters of Ev(e)il ones to be wooed and won. The man that can look on that sight and not be touched must be wōō(e)d or stone, or something even harder."

Meg turned indignantly. "Melvin Pierce, you make any more of your miserable little puns and I'll leave you."

Melvin's face assumed a frightened expression. "Oh, I won't, Meg, I won't; a — pun (upon) my word I won't."

Meg overlooked this last as being unworthy of notice, and turned to take one more long look. Both were silent for a moment, then Melvin broke the silence by exclaiming, "For the good Lord's sake — beg pardon, Meg, I don't mean to be irreverent — but if here doesn't come our parson. Let us pray."

Sure enough, Mr. Stanley was at that moment entering the room. He was alone. The usher showed him to a seat in the center aisle. Mr. Stanley stooped to place his hat under the seat in front of him. Meg saw him smile and bow, then he arose and stepped across the aisle, and accepted the chair which was graciously offered him by Mrs. Lawton. Meg saw this, and then she turned to Melvin with a look of displeasure on her fair face.

"I must ask you to be more particular in your manner of expression when you are with me, Melvin," she said, coldly. "Your remark sounded irreverent, if you did not mean for it to be," and she swept away from him with the air of an injured queen.

Poor Melvin looked after her in dismay. He was not displeased; no one ever felt displeased with Meg, no matter what she might say or do — but he was more than surprised. He had not meant to be irreverent — he had only said it to make her laugh. "And at one time she would have gone into fits over it," he said to himself, as he went to help Will don his "stage attire." "What in the world has come over the spirit of her dreams, I wonder. Is she turning pious? Come to think of it, she hasn't been quite so lively lately; she has seemed more thoughtful. Well, all I can say is, that if Meg Randal would become a Christian, there isn't a minister living who could do the good that she could. She has done me a little bit of good so soon. Such expressions are not right, although I have never thought about it before, and I'll quit making them. Many thanks, friend Megda."

Meg would have laughed if she had known Melvin's thoughts. The moment after she had spoken, she was almost sorry for what she had said. "Whatever made me say it?" she asked herself. "I am sure he did not mean to be wicked, and I have laughed at worse things than that from him many a time. Poor Melvin! he is so good-natured; he will do anything for me. But somehow, his words sent a chill over me to-night. I could not laugh at them — but I needn't have taken his head off. I'll run back and tell him how sorry I am."

"Oh, Meg, here you are; I've been looking everywhere for you. Do fasten this spray of lilies-of-the-valley in my hair, will you?" and Dell stood in the door of the temporary dressing-room with a beseeching look on her lovely face.

"Well," thought Meg, "I'll tell him later."

Oh, what a laughing, talking, excited group there was in the small room, and how pretty and girlish they looked, too! Meg was the calmest one, and she had more to do than all the rest put together.

Dell looked perfectly lovely in her pale-pink dress with a spray of lilies-of-the-valley on her breast and another in the braids of her golden hair. Laurie wore pale blue and had velvety yellow pansies for her flowers. She looked like a big wax doll. Meg wore her favorite pure white cashmere. A large bunch of exquisite white roses was in her belt. She looked pale, but oh, so girlishly sweet and pure. The girls hovered around her, proud of their queen.

The first selection on the programme was a piano duet by "Miss Manton" and "Miss Randal." A burst of applause greeted the two young pianists as they appeared on the platform, and such remarks as: "Don't they look lovely!" "What a beautiful contrast!" "Don't they look too sweet for anything!" went floating through the room.

Of course Dell and Meg both heard — that is, they

heard the whispers and knew they were of praise and admiration; but no one looking at them would ever suspect it. Dell went forward and took her seat at the piano with her cool, matter-of-fact air. Meg smiled a little and seated herself with the "slow grace" that came so natural to her. Mr. Stanley, looking at her, thought, "How proud her mother must be of her!" and looked to see if she showed her pride in her face.

Ah, did she not? It was impossible for that mother to hide the little, tremulous smile that would hover around her lips as she looked at her darling and heard the murmured words of praise all around her. Elsie, too, forgot everything else, and saw nothing but that girlish, white-robed form, while Hal, from his place behind the "scenes" looked out and smiled proudly to himself. Oh, Meg, what a happy, happy girl, and what a thankful girl you ought to be!

After the duet came a tenor solo by Mr. Edwin Holmes. Dell played his accompaniment, as Meg's reading came next. The song Mr. Holmes had selected was "My Queen," by "Blumenthal." Ed had a good voice, and his rendering of the difficult piece was good — remarkably so; but the effect was somewhat spoiled by his turning his eyes in quite a love-sick fashion on Dell, every time he sang, "Ere I cease to love thee, my Queen, my Queen." Dell was supremely unconscious of his rapturous glances, her mind as well as her eyes, being on her music, but they afforded unbounded amusement to Melvin Pierce, Bert Marston and Hal, who were looking at him through a hole in the curtain. They were obliged to go into a corner where they could slap their knees, bend their bodies, draw up their legs and otherwise contort themselves; while Ed, in happy ignorance, ended his passionate cry of "My Qneen, ah, my Queen!" in one long, lingering wail and a last look at Dell, who struck the closing chords clearly and sharply and then rose to her feet and swept on before him without so much as a glance at him. And there he had been emptying his heart before her and she didn't even dream of it.

Meg's reading came next. She had chosen for her first selection "The Polish Boy," by "Mrs. Ann S. Stephens." I shall not stop to give an explanation of the piece, except to say that it is one of the grandest things of its kind that was ever written. Those who have heard or read it, I am sure will agree with me. Meg's rendering of it, as an amateur, was exceedingly fine, especially in that part where the poor mother in her agony, love, fear and self-forgetfulness, pleads for the life of her boy in the passionate words:

"Take me, and bind these arms, these hands,
With Russia's heaviest iron bands,
And drag me to Siberia's wild,
To perish, if 'twill save my child!"

Meg threw all the force she was capable of in her voice and expression. Her gestures were graceful and natural; the audience showed their appreciation of her effort in that truest praise of all — complete, breathless silence. At the last gasping cry of the dying boy, as he lay his head on his dead mother's breast: "Great God! I thank thee! Mother, I rejoice with thee — and thus — to die!" a long, quivering sob sounded on the deep stillness of the room.

It was from Elsie who, with her eyes fastened on her sister, and her lips parted, utterly forgot where she was.

As Meg bent gracefully before the audience, a storm of applause burst forth; there was scarcely a dry eye in the whole room; people looked at one another in astonishment. Everyone knew that Meg had elocutionary talent, but to-night she had surpassed herself. They gave her a hearty encore; she was not prepared to respond with a recitation, but she came out and acknowledged their compliment with a low, graceful bow. Mr. Stanley smiled at her girlish triumph — or rather at her manner of receiving it. It seemed to him as if she were trying to act as she had seen great actresses, and I truly believe she was myself.

Dell's contralto solo came next. She received her praise in the cool, matter-of-fact way characteristic of her. Her manner amused Mr. Stanley even more than Meg's had. "Not a girl of the period, at all events," he said to himself. "Her great beauty does not spoil her. I like her."

Laurie played a duet with Dell, and almost fainted from sheer fright before it was finished, but she looked so bewitchingly pretty that the audience gave her a hearty applause.

The quartette, "Misses Randal and Manton" and "Messrs. Duncan and Holmes," outdid themselves, and were obliged to respond to two tremendous encores. Meg recited "The Widow's Light," by "Marianne Farmingham," tenderly, and in a subdued manner, which was just what was needed. Dell sang "Calvary," and sung it gloriously. Then came the scene from "Macbeth."

When I write this, it seems as if I must stop and rest, with my pen in my hand, while my thoughts travel back and dwell upon this part of that night's proceedings. Can anyone imagine — it seems as if everyone must — that crowd of bright-haired girls hovering around the heroine of the hour — their pride

and queen? Oh, how the girlish hearts beat, as their
eager, loving fingers smoothed a fold here, and fastened a clasp there! If Meg shared their nervous-
ness, she never showed it, except it was a brighter
sparkle in the dark eyes, and a firmer setting of the
full lips.

"Goodness!" exclaimed Dell, "you are the color of
marble. It must be because your hair is brushed
back from your forehead."

"She looks just as 'Lady Macbeth' should look,"
said Laurie, with quick, jealous fondness. "The
whiter, the better."

"I tell you what, Meg," said May, "you look simply immense."

"You will add another link to the chain you have
bound about poor Will, when he sees you in that costume," said Lill Norton sentimentally. She and
Lulu and May had slipped behind the "scenes," to
see if they could help.

"Don't you feel nervous, Meg?" asked Lulu.

"Hurry up, Meg," commanded Dell. "And you
stop your nonsense, girls. Just one minute of grace
for the 'Lady Macbeth' to admire herself in"; and
she led "my lady" to the mirror.

Meg smiled a satisfied smile at what she saw
reflected therefrom. A tall, slender form robed in

heavy brocaded velvet — both Meg's and Will's costumes were hired. The petticoat was of yellow
quilted satin. The overdress and court-train were of
rich dregs-of-wine velvet, brocaded. Her golden-
brown hair was rolled back from her forehead, and
the head covering of rich, yellow lace, was fastened
to her braids with a large star of brilliants. Broad
bands of dead gold were around her wrists and a
necklace of brilliants were clasped tightly about her
throat. Meg was not beautiful — never would be —
but in that costume she looked like a queen. No
wonder that the girls held their breath as they looked
at her.

"All ready," came in sepulchral tones from behind
the drapery that took the place of a door.

"Wait just a minute, Meg," whispered Lill. "Let
us get out first," and there was an immediate rush for
the audience.

The appearance of the girlish "costumers" was a
signal for all whispering and laughing to stop. A
deep stillness settled upon the room. Then the
green curtain was slowly drawn aside and a very well-
furnished drawing-room met the eye. At the left of
the front of the stage was a writing-table, and a student's chair of yellow plush was drawn up beside it.
A portiere of green damask separated the drawing-

room from a narrow corridor, and as the people looked, a beautiful form came slowly from behind it. In the small, white hands was a sheet of paper, but the queenly head was slightly thrown back, and the large, dark eyes rested not upon the paper, but were gazing earnestly ahead with an anxious, perplexed look in their depths.

Before Meg could open her lips to speak a storm of applause burst forth, the younger part of the company even stamped with their feet and whistled. It was a proud moment to Meg, but, unfortunately, as she bent her head in silent acknowledgment of their praise, her eyes rested full upon Mr. Stanley. He was not smiling, but on the contrary a look of stern displeasure was on his face. For just a second Meg's heart beat quickly, and then she set her lips firmly and determinedly together, resolved to do her best.

When she reached the center of the stage, she commenced to read from the paper she held in her hands, and at the first words every sound ceased. People could hardly believe that that tall, queenly woman before them, was really Meg Randal; they hardly recognized her voice in the full, rich tones in which she read :

"They met me in the day of success; and I have learned by the perfected report, they have more in them than mortal knowledge. When I burned in desire to question them further, they made themselves air into which they vanished. While I stood rapt in the wonder of it, came missives from the king, who all-hailed me, 'Thane of Cawder'; by which title, before, these wierd sisters saluted me, and referred me to the coming on of time with, 'Hail, king that shalt be!' This have I thought good to deliver thee, my dearest partner of greatness, that thou mightest not lose the dues of rejoicing, by being ignorant of what greatness is promised thee. Lay it to thy heart, and farewell."

The parts had been slightly changed. At the conclusion of the reading of the letter, the curtain was drawn together, leaving "Lady Macbeth" leaning wearily back in her chair.

The next scene was from Act II, Scene II. When the curtain was drawn aside, Meg was standing in the center of the stage, her head thrown back, her hands clinched tightly by her side, a look of desperate courage on her fair face. She hurled the words from her, quickly and fiercely:

"That which hath made them drunk, hath made me bold;
　What hath quench'd them, hath given me fire.
　Hark! Peace!
　It was the owl that shrieked, the fatal bellman,
　Which gives the stern'st good-night. He is about it?

The doors are open; and the surfeited grooms
Do mock their charge with snores: I have drugged their possets,
That death and nature do contend about them,
Whether they live or die."

"Who's there? What, ho!" sounded from behind the "scenes."

Meg went on:

"Alack, I am afraid they have awaked,
And 'tis not done. The attempt and not the deed
Confounds us. Hark! I laid their daggers ready;
He could not miss 'em. Had he not resembled
My father as he slept, I had done it."

Meg's expression as she delivered the last sentence, was really something wonderful. The pleased audience were interrupted in their applauding by "Macbeth" rushing wildly upon the stage.

"My husband!" exclaimed Meg.

Some small boys on the front seat were wicked enough to giggle most audibly at this, and Will, forgetting himself as an actor for a moment, turned around and glared at them fiercely. Meg looked as if she would like to shake him — she did pinch him slyly — and the audience laughed unrestrainedly. That was the only unpleasant thing that happened. Will at once came to his senses, and the rest of his part was given in praiseworthy style.

When the curtain was drawn aside for the last act,

Meg, so far from showing any signs of fatigue, seemed as fresh and full of vigor — nay, even more so than she was at the first — and Will, seeming to catch some of her spirit, forgot himself, and everyone else, in his part. Could Booth or Barret have done more?

As the curtain was drawn together for the last time, the audience applauded until it seemed as if the walls shook. What spirit of pride and mischief seized Meg as, hearing the loud calls for her reappearance, she turned to Will with blazing eyes.

"Lead me out before the curtain, Will," she said imperiously.

Will looked at her for a moment in surprise, but her brilliancy overpowered all his discretion — he would have done anything she might have asked him.

He took her hand and did as she commanded. The people fairly rose out of their seats. Truly, Margaret Mather could not have acted her part better than did Meg. As she bowed low for the second time, retreating as she did so, Dell stepped forward and handed her a magnificent bouquet of roses and pinks. It was from the members of the Y. P. L. S. Meg was thoroughly taken by surprise, but she accepted it with a bright smile, raised it daintily to her lips, and disappeared.

But Will, holding her hand, felt the small fingers twitch. Meg, in bowing, had looked at Mr. Stanley again. The look of stern displeasure on his face had deepened into one of sorrow and pain.

"Oh, Meg, you darling!" The bevy of fair girls crowded around their "queen" and almost smothered her with caresses.

"Mary Anderson, herself, could have done no better!"

"You were simply superb!"

"I never, in all my life, saw anyone look so perfectly lovely!"

"You looked just like a queen!"

"Judge Lawton almost made a hole in the floor thumping with his gold-headed cane."

"Yes, and Deacon Huntly actually cried out 'Superb!' The idea! a Deacon of the church! There's a conquest for you, Meg."

"Well, Deacon Norton was pretty well excited, I noticed; eh, Lill?"

Meg listened to all these rhapsodies with a smiling face, but her heart felt strangely heavy. She did not say anything until Dell suddenly exclaimed:

"Our minister looked as if he were composing his own funeral sermon all the time. He, doubtless, does not appreciate fine acting."

There were exclamations of dismay, and blank faces at this.

"I never thought to look at him," said May. "I meant to, but I was so excited all the time that I didn't once think of it."

"Phooh!" said Lulu Martin, contemptuously. "I'd like to know what harm there is in it."

"He'd no business to come if he hadn't approved of it," said Dell dryly.

"That's what I say," said Lill. "What think you, Meg?"

Meg was just then bending her head for Laurie, who had not spoken, to unfasten her vail. The girls could not see her face, but they were satisfied to hear her mocking little laugh. "I say as Dell says," she replied, and then commenced to talk about something else.

When Meg reached home, she received Hal's hearty congratulations, Elsie's loving words of praise and the mother's kiss, with the same smiling face with which she had listened to the girls, and with the same strangely-heavy heart, too; and when she had retired to her room, she blew out the light and sank down in a chair by the window, and looked out at the white-robed earth shining cold and silvery under the rays of the moon.

She sat there a long time, thinking. Was Ethel really right after all? Were the pleasures of the world so fleeting? Did it require something higher and nobler to satisfy? A few weeks ago, and she would have felt perfectly happy and satisfied with to-night's triumph — she would have asked for no greater happiness; but now she felt far from happy — almost like crying. "What is it? oh, what is it?" she cried, covering her face with her hands; but no answer came to her. Then she jumped from her chair, turned down the bed-clothes and sprang into bed. "I know what it will be, if I keep on," she said to herself scornfully. "It will be a case of insanity. I act worse than any of the love-sick maidens, sentimental authors write about in their trashy, five-penny novels. I am disgusted with myself."

And Meg cuddled herself down among her soft pillows, and fell asleep.

XII.

IN SOCIETY.

"I HEAR loud praises from father of your elocutionary powers, Girlie," said Ethel, on the morning
after the entertainment.

The two girls were in the senior's parlor. Meg
was sitting on the rug before the open fire, holding
her hands over the blaze to get them warm. It was
a bitterly cold morning. Ethel was sitting in an easy
chair close by her with her Physiology in her hand.

"Was your father pleased, then, Ethel?" asked
Meg carelessly.

"More than pleased," replied Ethel. "He talked
about nothing at the breakfast table, but your 'wonderful talent.' He was quite carried away. Mother,
too, was very much pleased."

"I shouldn't think you would tell me of it, Ethel,"
said Meg, looking into the fire.

"Why not, Girlie?"

"Oh, you think it is such a deadly sin. I was

much surprised to see your father and mother there. Of course, I knew they had always been theatre-going people, but I supposed you had converted them long before this."

Meg did not say this rudely, and when she had finished, the face she turned to Ethel was rather grave than otherwise. A shadow fell upon Ethel's fair face.

"No, I have not converted them to the only true way yet, Girlie; but I hope to do so before many days, with God's help."

Meg was silent, and Ethel went on. "Mother does not care as much for such things as she used. She is commencing to realize that the pleasures the world can give are not lasting; pleasant they may be for a while, but not worth bartering eternity for, and the unending happiness that eternity will bring."

"But these things are not wicked," said Meg in a low, determined voice, with a faint pink stealing into her face. "Nothing will ever make me believe that they are. They are only little harmless amusements. Your religion is too severe, Ethel; it makes mountains out of mole-hills. Why can not a person be just as good — enjoy his religion just as much, and still enter into the pleasures — the social pleasures of the world? I think one derives many personal advantages from going out into society. That is, if one looks at it from the right point of observation. There is a certain charm about society people, which cannot be explained. They possess certain qualities which non-society people do not even dream of."

"Is it your ambition then, to be a 'society woman,' Girlie?" asked Ethel, leaning forward and looking into the earnest face.

Meg laughed sarcastically. "It would require money, Ethel, and I am not an heiress."

"No, and I am," replied Ethel quietly; then she went on quickly: "You have said right, Girlie; it does require money to join the society of worldly pleasure-seekers; as soon as your money is gone, you can no longer be a member. It is an expensive society to keep up; poor people are not allowed to join. It is a society, Girlie, that supports its own rich, but the poor need not apply — they will not be received. But the society of which I am proud to be a member is one that has no respect of persons; the poor as well as the rich, are gladly welcomed to it. All can come without money and without price. The poorer, the more broken-down, the more helpless one is, the more gladly is he welcomed. It is a society, the most honored members of which are those who have come to it, soul-sick and weary of sin and strife, and have simply cast down their burden at the feet of the great Ruler, and asked Him to take them, poor and needy as they are. No one has ever been turned away, Girlie, but all have been joyfully received."

"What is the pass-word, Ethel?" asked Meg, smiling, but deeply touched. "Tell me, that I may enter if I should so wish."

"The pass-word is Jesus."

Meg bowed her head upon Ethel's knee, and pressed her lips to the fair hand she held. "Tell me what it will bring me, Ethel; what it has brought to you."

"Rest and perfect peace," was the low-spoken answer.

Light feet were heard tripping up the stairs. Meg rose and leaned over Ethel. "Pray for me, Ethel," she said, tremulously, then she crossed the room quickly, took up her algebra which she had tossed on to the lounge when she came in, and when the door opened and Maude Leonard entered, both girls were absorbed in their books.

"Good-morning, girls," said Maude in her sweetest voice. "What a dreadfully cold morning it is, isn't it?"

Meg just raised her eyes from her book and nod-

ded, but Ethel wheeled a chair close to the burning
logs, and said pleasantly: "Yes, indeed, it is a bitterly cold morning.   Did you drive to school?"

"Yes," answered Maude, sinking languidly down in
the depths of the easy chair, and drawing her fur-
trimmed skirts daintily away from the blaze.   "James
put an extra robe in the sleigh, but I was dreadfully
cold, then."

"Why didn't I tell James to put an extra robe in
my sleigh," thought Meg, with grim humor, as she sat
in her remote corner, apparently absorbed in "signs
and quantities."

"Come over here, Girlie," said Ethel.

A curt "No, I thank you," rose to Meg's lips, but,
I am happy to say, did not pass them.   Instead, she
said: "I think I will.   A wood fire is the prettiest
and cosiest thing, but it suits the Spring and Autumn
weather better than the Winter."

"I agree with you there," said Maude, pushing her
chair lazily to one side to make room for Meg; but
Meg preferred to sit beside Ethel.   Maude, seeming
not to notice this, went on:

"You two girls must have left early this morning.
I should have thought you would have been tired
enough to sleep an hour or two longer, Meg.   Allow
me to congratulate you on your success of last even-

ing. You have a most wonderful talent. You fairly took your audience by storm."

"Thank you," said Meg, coldly. To herself she said quite savagely, "Hypocrite!"

"By the way, Meg, where is your shadow this morning?" asked Maude suddenly.

Meg looked around the room in mock surprise. She knew very well that Maude meant Laurie; she had called her that before, with the same veiled sarcasm in her tones.

"I beg pardon," said Meg innocently, bringing her eyes back to rest upon Maude's face; "but you can hardly expect to see it in this room so early in the morning; you know the sun doesn't get around here until about two o'clock in the afternoon."

Ethel laughed softly, she couldn't help it. Maude laughed too, but her large, black eyes glittered angrily. She formed a strong contrast to Ethel and Meg, with her dark, richly-colored face; large, black eyes and raven hair. It made Ethel's delicate loveliness look almost spiritual, and Meg's white face look whiter still, and her light-brown hair almost golden.

"Last night's triumph has made you facetious," said Maude sweetly, "or else you do not really understand. I meant Laurie. Where is she?"

"She went to the library after a book."

"Oh," said Maude indifferently; then, as if just recalling it, she said: "Ethel, how very kind it was of you this morning, to send your carriage for Ruth Dean. The poor girl looks, sometimes, as if she actually suffered with the cold. She has a long walk."

Meg looked at Ethel quickly and gratefully. "Did you send your carriage for her, Ethel?" she asked.

"Yes," answered Ethel, blushing a lovely pink. "But that was nothing. I was only too glad to be able to do it."

"It was exceedingly good of you," murmured Maude. "I doubt if the girl ever rode in a sleigh before. She looked like a cat in a strange garret among all the buffalo robes; all you could see was her big eyes," and Maude laughed immoderately.

Meg's eyes flashed as she looked at her. "If it were not for such Christians as she, there would be more sinners — like me — saved," she thought.

It never entered Meg's head that she was doing a poor, foolish thing in judging all by one, or taking the wrong-doing of one as an excuse for her own "holding back." She would have been very quick to see the foolishness in Laurie or any of the other girls, and would have felt a contempt for their weakness, but — we seldom see our own faults.

"Hullo, girls," cried a merry voice, and May Bromley bounced into the room. "How cozy you look in here. I declare, I am well-nigh frozen — all but my tongue."

"That never freezes, does it, May?" asked Maude, in her pleasantest tone.

"No," answered May, not the least displeased. "Once in a while it becomes paralyzed — that is all."

"When is that?" asked Meg.

"Oh, for instance, when I get up to read an original paper before the Y. P. L. S. But, Queen of the Boards, let me pay my heart-felt homage to you this morning," and May dropped on one knee before Meg, raised her little white hand to her lips, and kissed it.

"What nonsense are you up to now?" said a voice from the door-way. "You ought to be hired out to 'Forepaugh' as, 'a girl born without brains.' Think I'll present the idea to your father for his consideration, May; he would make an immense sum of money," and Dell walked into the room, looking, for all the world, like one of the icicles dressed up — as Meg said to herself — with her white face and glittering hair.

"Don't be insulting, Miss Manton," said May, making a face at her. "You have a lovely mouth, don't make it ugly by saying ugly things."

Dell looked at her with cool amusement. "What a pity it is, May-flower," she said, "that you don't realize your own superior smartness. You have just delivered a whole sermon equal to the divine Talmage. What are you all doing in here — holding a conference?"

"Warming our toes," said Meg dryly. "I wish I could warm my brains as well; they seem literally frozen this morning."

"Frost gotten into them?" asked Dell, leaning on the back of her chair.

"Yes, the frost of stupidity," answered Meg. "I can't get this example right if it is to save my life; tried half an hour on it this morning before breakfast."

"Is there room for me?" asked a soft little voice, and Laurie's golden head poked itself around the door.

"Yes, come right in," they all cried, and drew a little away from each other to make room for her.

Laurie seized an ottoman on her way to the fireplace and threw it at Meg's feet. "Room for two, May," she said, gaily; and the two girls seated themselves on it, and leaned their elbows lightly on Meg's lap. Dell sat on the arm of Meg's chair, with her hand resting lightly on her shoulder. Meg was in her "natural state" now — that of the queen with her subjects around her.

> "Oh, love, dear love, be true;
> This heart is only thine."

sung a voice in the lower hall.

> "When the war is o'er
> We'll part no more."

chimed in another; then a rush of feet up the stair-case, and Lill and Lulu burst into the room.

"Still receiving homage, our Queen?" said Lill. "You deserve it."

"If you don't study for the stage, you will make the one grand mistake of your life," said Lulu.

"Amen," said May.

Meg boxed her ears lightly. "No irreverence, May-flower," she said carelessly, but she did not smile.

"But seriously, Meg," said Lill, squeezing herself in between the ottoman and Maude's chair, "why do you not study for the stage? Why! everyone says that you are most wonderfully gifted, and that you could make your fortune as an actress."

"Yes," chimed in Lulu. "Father says he has seen most of the leading actresses of this country, and of the other country, too, for that matter, and he prophesies a brilliant future for you, if you will only undertake it. Why don't you, Meg?"

"Oh, dear!" sighed May. "What a grand thing it must be to have the world at your feet. Just think! your simple appearance on the stage to be the signal for a mighty burst of applause, and people holding their breath and waiting impatiently for you to open your lips and just speak one word. Oh, it must be delightful!"

Meg listened, and as she did, her breath came quickly, her eyes shone, her cheeks flushed. A thrill went through the girlish heart; the ambitious part of her cried out in loud tones: "Yes, that is the life for me. There is happiness, triumph, power, and, therefore, perfect satisfaction."

Then, all at once, her eyes fell upon Ethel. The pure face, with its clear eyes, and sweet, smiling mouth, seemed a reproach to her. Her own eyes fell beneath the calm, reproachful gaze of the other's; the color left her cheeks, and the loud beating of her heart ceased, and grew quiet. The revulsion of feeling made her cold and trembling; nay, it actually frightened her.

"What is the matter with me?" she thought wildly, and the next moment would have sprang to her feet, but just then the door quietly opened, and a little, dark face looked in to be quickly withdrawn with a low "Oh, excuse me, please."

Dell slid off the arm of Meg's chair, and was at the door before it could be closed.

"Excuse you, Ruthie!" she cried. "And why? Are you not a senior, the same as the rest of us, and have an equal right to the parlor? Come in, immediately."

She drew the timid, blushing Ruth into the room, and closed the door. Maude's lip curled scornfully; the others looked at Meg to receive their "cue." Meg put out both arms, and drew Ruth down on her lap.

"Oh, I am too heavy, Meg," remonstrated Ruth.

"Heavy!" laughed Meg. "So is a kitten."

There was five minutes more of laughing and chattering, and then the loud tones of the bell broke up the pretty, merry group and sent them all to the large hall for prayers.

During the remainder of the week, Meg received many congratulations on her success of Tuesday evening. A month ago, the flattering words would have filled her heart with delight; now, they only made her feel restlessly unhappy. And why? Because the workings of the Spirit were already going on in her heart. The time had come, as Ethel had said it would, and as it comes to all, yet it was coming so gently and gradually that Meg scarcely realized it. She only knew that there was something she wanted that she did not have; a longing for something that she could not name. It did not change her much, only made her a little more thoughtful, a little more subdued in her manner.

No one noticed this except Ethel, whose gentle heart was filled with joy and thanksgiving, as she watched, day by day, the change that was gradually stealing over the fair, young life.

"Oh, what a Christian she will make!" she thought, and felt like proclaiming her glad knowledge from the house-tops.

She didn't, though; she only prayed silently and waited patiently, content to trust to the Father, knowing He would bring all things to pass in His own good time.

Saturday night as Meg was walking home from the post-office, she met Mr. Stanley. She had not seen him since the evening of the entertainment, and then she had not seen him to speak with.

It was a beautiful moonlight evening, although the air was sharp and frosty. Meg was walking quickly, her furs tied closely around her throat, her hands tucked snugly in her muff.   She was so busy with her thoughts, that she did not observe Mr. Stanley until he lifted his hat with a pleasant "Good-evening."

When he turned and walked beside her, Meg did not know whether she were pleased or sorry; but she did think nervously, "Oh, dear, I hope he will not introduce the subject of religion."

Mr. Stanley appeared not to have the least idea of doing so when he started out.   He spoke on ordinary topics — her school, her studies, her music, and lastly, her elocution.   Meg hardly knew how it came about, but all at once she found herself talking freely and eagerly about her "hope", as she had always called it.

"The ambition of my life has always been to be a first-class elocutionist; first-class, of course; I could not be satisfied with anything else.   And why should I not be?" she asked with lifted head.

"I see no reason," said Mr. Stanley, quietly. "You have wonderful powers."

"Thank you," said Meg a little mockingly.   "But — but how gravely you speak; and do you know, Mr. Stanley, you are the only one of my friends who has not congratulated me on my efforts of last Tuesday evening?"

Perhaps Meg ought not to have said that, she was

sorry for it right away. It sounded bold and unmaid-enly to her, and she knew it must to him; as if she were "fishing for compliments." His answer took her completely by surprise, and made her face burn hotly.

"I congratulate you on your fine rendering of 'The Polish Boy' and 'The Widow's Light'; they were both admirably given; but I cannot congratulate you on your 'theatrical attempt'."

Poor Meg was dumb. Figuratively speaking, she did not know whether to laugh or cry. She felt like turning to him and saying, in her coldest, iciest tones, "You insult me, Mr. Stanley," and then leav-ing him to his own remorseful thoughts in the middle of the snow-covered street; but he might think that she was indulging in "open-air theatricals" this time, and be more disgusted than ever; so she did the wis-est thing — said nothing and walked quietly by his side.

Perhaps Mr. Stanley thought he had been a little too abrupt, and had hurt the proud girl's feelings — as, indeed, he had — for he went on to say in a moment or two: "You must pardon me, if what I say is not, perhaps, what you would like to have me. I have always considered myself quite a judge of character, Miss Randal. Will you allow me to give you the result of my observation of yours?"

"Then you have been studying it?" asked Meg with quick resentment.

"Yes, I have," replied he calmly.

Meg almost laughed at his imperturbability, though much vexed. "You have aroused my curiosity," she said, "pray, be so kind as to gratify it, now."

"I will do so with pleasure. You are a girl of noble impulses, although you do not always follow them. Your character is made up of contradictory points. By nature you are trusting, but either because you have come in contact with untruth and deception in one form or another, or because, being of the people of the world, you are determined to do as the people of the world do, you are, at times, suspicious and sarcastic. You are liable to scoff at the wisdom of superior minds; this tendency will grow upon you, unless you check it at once, until the nature that God made so pure and trusting, capable of noble deeds as well as impulses, will become tarnished, degenerated and ruined. You have great decision of character and strength of intellect. You have little patience with your weaker sisters. You have a keen perception; you are quick to see the faults of others, but are most unnaturally blind to your own. You have an idea that your own strength of character is sufficient to keep you from doing any weak thing. You are proud,

you have lofty ideas of right, you have little compas-
sion for wrong-doers, little realizing, that, in your
righteous (?) condemnation of them, you are yourself
committing a great wrong.   You have a lovable
nature, you can make many friends, and, what is still
a harder thing to do, you can keep them.   You receive
their friendship and recognition of your superiority,
much as a queen receives the homage of her subjects.
All the time you are smiling at their simplicity, and
feeling miles above them; seated on a throne, as it
were, and looking down, with smiling pity, upon the
'smaller minds.'   And yet, the time will come, Miss
Randal, when their strength will be your weakness.
Your friend, Miss Ray, for instance.   You look upon
her now, very much as you would look upon a pretty,
little pet kitten; you are fond of her, but, in your
heart, you laugh at her; at times you even pity her
for her lack of moral courage.   She will one day, it
may be near at hand even now, pity you for your lack
of the same quality.   You have talents; some day
God will ask you to give an account of them.   When
a person is rich, we expect more from him, where
money is concerned, than we do from a poor person.
It is just so with God.   He does not bestow His gifts
upon all His children alike.   To one He gives but
one talent; to another two; to another three; to

those He gives the most, He expects the most from."

They had reached Meg's home by this time. As Mr. Stanley opened the gate for her to pass through, he looked into her face. It was very pale, and the lips were pressed closely together. She did not say one word; she could not, if her life had depended on it. Her heart felt ready to burst; it was filled with a deep, passionate anger. Never had she been talked to in this manner before. She felt mortified, humbled in the very dust. Mr. Stanley saw this.

"I have spoken very plainly to you, Miss Randal, but I have done it with the very best of intentions, believe me. One thing more I want to say, and it is this. You are capable of great things; you have rare accomplishments; it is in your power to do a grand work. All you have to do is 'to make yourself worthy of yourself.' You can do this in only one way. Give yourself, just as you are, to the Saviour. Do not try to make yourself better by your own strength — you cannot do it. Take the accomplishments He has given you and consecrate them and yourself all to His glory, and your life will be one of God's most perfect creations."

He lifted his hat, Meg bowed her head — she could not speak — turned and ran into the house.

She went directly to her room, threw herself on the bed, and cried as if her heart would break. And when had light-hearted Meg shed tears before? Not for many a long day. She could hardly tell what she was crying for, either. At first she thought it was because she was so angry; then, because her feelings had been so deeply hurt; then, because what he had said had startled and dismayed her; and lastly, she knew it was because she realized how sinful she really was, how thoughtless and wicked she had been.

"Oh, why could he not have left me alone?" she sobbed. "I was happy, I was contented, and I never shall be so again."

Ah, Meg, if you had only said then, "God be merciful to me, a sinner," the "peace that passeth all understanding" would surely have been yours.

XIII.

THE SENIOR CLASS.

IT would seem as if the members of the senior class of Madam de Crando's excellent establishment, had met by special appointment in the reading-room of the public library, had not each one, as she came in and saw the others sitting there, cried out in a burst of pleased surprise, "What! you here?" At last nearly all the class were there, sitting around one of the long reading-tables covered with views and periodicals. Meg, Laurie, Dell, May, Lulu and Lill. Each one had chosen her book for the ensuing week, and settled herself cosily for a "good look" at it.

"Madam's establishment is well represented," said Meg.

"Yes," replied Lill; "all of the senior class here but three — Ethel, Maude and Ruth."

"Wonder where they are," observed Meg absently. She had just made up her mind to begin "Martin Chuzzlewit"; it was so thick she would not be able to finish it before the next week if she didn't.　Meg was an ardent admirer of Dickens.

"Tuesday night, isn't it?" asked May.

"Of course, goose," laughed Lill, looking up from "Pink and White Tyranny."

"Then of course, also, they are at the 'Young People's Christian Endeavor'."

Down went all the books on the table, with the exception of Meg's; she leaned back in her chair smiling at the others' astonishment.

"Well, if I hadn't forgotten all about it," said Lill. "And it was given out at both services on Sunday, too."

"Meg doesn't look surprised," said May.

"Had you thought of it, Meg?" asked Dell.

"Yes; Elsie was getting ready to go when I left home."

"Ethel is going to lead," said Laurie musingly.

"Of course," said Meg a little sharply.　"She is the one who organized it."

"I wouldn't care to be in her shoes," said May, with a shrug.

"Here comes Ruth; I suppose she is going. Good-evening, Ruth."

"Good-evening, girls."

"Are you going to Ethel's meeting?" asked Lill.

"Yes; won't you all come with me?"

There was a pause. All looked eagerly at Meg — Laurie more eagerly than the rest.

"Will you come, Meg?" asked Ruth softly.

"No, I think not," replied Meg slowly, with her eyes on her book. To herself she said, "I would, if that hypocrite wasn't to be there; she would spoil the meeting for me."

The girls drew back, disappointed; yet they did not once think they could go without their "leader."

"Here come Will Duncan and Ed Holmes," whispered Lulu. "Let's ask them if they are going."

"Will looks solemn enough to be going to some kind of a meeting," said Dell.

The young men approached the table where the girls were sitting. "Good-evening, ladies. Anything special going on this evening, and have you taken the reading-room for your rendezvous?" said Ed, with an admiring glance at Dell, who returned it with the coolest smile imaginable.

Will had bowed gravely to all, and seated himself beside Meg.

"We didn't meet for anything special," explained Dell. "We were talking over the advisability of attending 'Ethel's meeting' in a body."

"And have you decided to go?"

"Meg thinks not."

There was a little pause; then Ed said suddenly, "Why not all go?"

Meg laughed. "People would think Bedlam had broken loose, or madam's establishment, at any rate."

Ruth had risen to leave the room, but at Ed's words had stood still again, trembling and blushing. "I am going," she said; "I wish you would come."

"Well, don't wait for us, Ruthie," said Dell kindly. "You will be late. Perhaps we will decide to come."

"Oh, I hope so," replied Ruth, and with a last wistful, beseeching look at Meg, passed out.

"Where is Hal to-night?" asked Will, turning to Meg.

"I left him at home, deep in the mysteries of stenography."

"Are they going to introduce it into his office?"

"Yes."

"Does he like it?"

"Very much."

"Seen anything of Pierce or Marston to-night?" asked Ed.

The girls shook their heads.

"Here comes Blanding," said Will. "Good-evening, Ray," he said to that young gentleman, as he sauntered up to the table.

Just then Will, happening to look toward the window at the further end of the room, saw a face pressed against the glass. "There is Bert now," he said, and beckoned with his hand for him to come in.

The invitation was accepted, and in a moment there was a low hum of voices around the table, all talking together, with now and then a subdued burst of laughter. Fifteen minutes passed; the hands of the clock pointed to a quarter to eight. In the midst of an animated discussion between the young ladies and gentlemen as to the rights of woman being equal with those of man, the door opened and Hal came hurrying in.

He bowed to all at once, then said, eagerly, "I was on my way to the meeting, and happened to look in here as I passed and saw you all, and thought I would stop and ask you to go with me. Will you come?"

"My faith!" said Ray, tragically. "But there are so many of us."

"Never mind that," replied Hal. "The more, the better. Come, Meg."

Meg rose with a little laugh. She had caught the look in her brother's eye and obeyed it. "Well, we might as well, girls; but we shall be late."

"Not so very," said Hal. "It isn't two minutes walk to the church, and ten minutes isn't so very bad."

"Wait a minute," said Bert. "Let's count heads just for the fun of it. By Jove! there are eleven of us. Now if Melvin were only here we would have the whole clique."

"The idea of Melvin going to a prayer-meeting," said May with a little laugh. "He couldn't keep still long enough."

"He would have time to think up a dozen new puns for our meeting night," said Ray. "What a fellow he is for puns."

"Yes, I don't believe he is capable of one serious thought," said Will severely. "A regular rattle-brain."

"He has one of the kindest hearts that ever beat," flashed out Meg; then the gay party passed out of the door, and hurried to the place of "Ethel's meeting."

They entered the vestibule quietly, and stole on tip-toe to the half-open door. A low, sweet voice — Ethel's voice in prayer — fell on their ears. With one quick glance into each others' faces, they silently bowed their heads. Meg's heart beat loud and quick — every word that Ethel prayed seemed meant for her.

"My Father, bless and take care of every one of Thy children — Thine absent children — to-night.

Watch over them and lead their straying feet into the path that leads to Thee and Heaven," prayed the sweet young voice, and every heart in the listening group at the door was touched.

At the close of the prayer, the hymn, "I Hear Thy Welcome Voice" was given out, and during the singing of the first line, our young people walked quietly into the room and took seats together.

At the sound of so many feet, all heads were turned, and looks of surprise, not unmixed with pleasure, appeared on every face. Ethel's delicate face was fairly radiant. In the singing of the second verse their voices rang out, clear and full. The sound sent a thrill through every heart gathered there, and tears filled the eyes of the older people.

> "I am coming, Lord,
>   Coming now to thee;
>   Wash me, cleanse me in the blood,
>   That flow'd on Calvary."

Meg's glorious soprano, Dell's rich alto, Ed's clear tenor and Will's deep bass — oh, how grand it sounded!" Mr. Stanley, in his chair beside Ethel, bowed his head upon his hand and listened.

"Shall we unite in prayer with our pastor?" said Ethel.

It seemed to Meg as if she had never listened to

such a prayer in her life, as the one that Mr. Stanley offered. It seemed as if he had caught inspiration from the glorious singing of a moment before. His face was fairly quivering with emotion, and his voice was full of deep, solemn feeling. Meg's whole mind was on the prayer, when all at once she received a sharp nudge from May, who was sitting beside her. She raised her head impatiently.

May was looking down into her lap, but she turned her eyes slowly toward the left, and Meg followed their glance with her own. What she saw caused her to give a little start. What was it, or who was it? Only Melvin Pierce, with his head bowed down on his hands and deep reverence expressed in every line of his figure. Meg could not help saying to herself, "Of all astonishing things, this takes the lead!"

After the prayer, Ethel said, in a few simple words, that the meeting was open to all; all were invited to take part by speaking, singing or praying. After this the customary silence reigned for a moment or two, then, to the unbounded astonishment of our young people, Melvin Pierce rose to his feet and said, clearly and firmly:

"I want to serve the Master. I want to begin to lead a truer, better and nobler life. Will you pray for me?"

"We will pray for you, earnestly and gladly," said Ethel, her voice quivering with happiness; then she commenced to sing, "Jesus, Lover of my Soul." The rest joined her on the second line, and the grand old hymn seemed to draw each one nearer to the feet of their Lord.

Meg heard a soft little sob, and almost before she could turn her head, Laurie was standing in her seat, her pretty, flower-like face quite white, and the tears standing thickly in her blue eyes. How the soft voice shook and trembled, as if her heart were in her mouth, but for all that, it did not falter.

"I love my Saviour, and I give myself to Him now, to do with as He will. I can trust Him — I do trust Him — for I know He doeth all things well; but oh, pray for me, that I may not wander from Him, but keep close to Him all the time."

Someone commenced softly, "Nearer, my God, to Thee;" the rest took it up, and in a second the room was filled with the divine melody. As the last word died on the stillness, an old, white-haired man arose. His face was shining with a joy unspeakable — his right hand was raised to Heaven.

"I thank God for this supreme hour of my life," he said, in trembling accents. "My prayer has been answered; the one desire of my heart has been granted. Rejoice with me. My little lamb has at last entered the fold. Glory be to God." It was Laurie's father, Deacon Ray.

Meg thought she was dreaming when she heard Dell's rich contralto voice begin, "There were ninety and nine that safely lay." She tried to join in with her, but the tears came and choked her voice. She swallowed hard, angry with herself for being "so foolish," as she called it. Her heart was filled with a great longing; all the restless, dissatisfied feelings that had been gradually taking possession of it, rose in full force and fairly overflowed it. She felt cold, nervous and frightened; and still, strangely happy. All the time that she was saying to herself, "Oh, why did I come! I never will be so foolish again," she was still glad she was there.

Testimony followed testimony fast now, and Meg was scarcely surprised when she saw Elsie rise in her seat and heard her give herself to the Saviour; ready and willing to consecrate her life to His service. If Dell had gotten up and expressed a desire to become a Christian, it would not have surprised Meg. She was almost feeling as if she would like to do it herself, when Maude Leonard rose and testified for the Master. She said she was trying with all her heart to become more worthy of His love, and she desired an interest in all their prayers that she might prove more faithful.

Not one change of expression that had passed over Meg's face during the evening, had escaped Ethel's watchful eye, and now when she saw the soft look die away, and a hard, scornful one come in its place, she felt like falling on her knees and crying, "Oh, Jesus, press Thy finger upon her heart and blot out all angry feelings, and fill it full of Thy powerful love and mercy."

The evening was spoiled for Meg. There was no music in the singing after that; nothing that was said touched her heart, not even Ruth's pathetic little prayer when she spoke of herself as being "the vilest of those who love Him, and the weakest of those who pray." "And she is as far above that hypocrite as the heavens are above the earth," thought Meg bitterly.

At the end of the meeting, Ethel asked those who wished to be prayed for, to stand. Hal was the first one to rise. Laurie gave a fleeting little glance at Meg, but Meg looked proudly, scornfully back at her. Laurie hesitated, then rose to her feet. Melvin stood up, then Will, then Lill and Lulu. May kept her eyes on Meg's face, and remained seated. Dell did not rise because she did not truly feel as if she wanted to, and Ed, I am sorry to say, did not rise because Dell didn't. "No hypocrite there," thought Meg, looking admiringly at Dell's perfect face. She would not trust herself to meet Ethel's wistful look. Was she growing cowardly?

As soon as Mr. Stanley had pronounced the benediction, Ethel went to Meg, and held out her hand to her. Meg took it. "I am so glad to see you here, Girlie," said Ethel, and then she turned to Laurie, took both her hands in hers, and kissed her. "Welcome to the fold, Laurie," she said.

Meg felt a jealous pang shoot through her heart — the first she had ever known. She turned away as Ethel passed on to the others, and came face to face with Mr. Stanley. He saw the trouble in her face, and Meg knew he saw it and understood it, and the knowledge made her ashamed; it touched her pride. She drew herself up haughtily, bowed coldly and passed out into the aisle to speak with Elsie. Mr. Stanley did not feel hurt; he fully understood the proud girl — understood her better than she did herself.

XIV.

A NEW HAPPINESS.

"MEG, you will go to meeting to-night, will you not?" asked Laurie, one week later.

Meg shut up her Ancient History with a snap. "No, I am not going."

"Oh, Meg, why not?"

"Because I do not care to go."

If Meg had spoken the exact truth, she would have said, "Because I do not dare to go."

Laurie crept closer to her. Meg was sitting in the wide window-sill in the upper hall, trying to study.

"Meg," said Laurie, with a trembling voice, "I must tell you how happy I have been this week. I feel so peaceful, so restful. You know I have always been happy, and I know that you have; both of our lives have been particularly bright; but the old happiness is entirely different from this new. Then I was what I might call restlessly happy, and now I am restfully happy. And, oh, the difference, Meg! As much difference as there is between the flickering, dazzling gaslight, and the clear, bright, pure daylight. Then every little disappointment, no matter how trivial it was, troubled me and made me impatient; but now — Meg, I feel that no matter what comes to me, I shall be able to bear it patiently, knowing that it is His hand that chasteneth, and He only chasteneth whom He loveth."

Could this be little timid Laurie that was talking? Meg looked at her in astonishment, feeling that she should never call her "kitten" again. But what was she saying? Did she really know of what she was talking? She had never known trouble of any kind — she had always had everything she wanted — why could she not have been satisfied as she (Meg) was with what she had? She must have expressed her thoughts very plainly on her face, for Laurie said:

"I know that I have never known any real trouble, Meg, but when I have to face it some day, as I know I shall — for we all do — I want some one to help me meet it and bear it, and Jesus is the only one who can do it." Laurie stopped and looked wistfully at Meg. "If you would only take Him for your Saviour, Meg," she said timidly.

Meg looked out of the window and shook her head slowly. "Not now, Laurie; I am not worthy."

Laurie threw both arms around Meg with a low cry of joy. The answer had been so different from what she had expected. "But it is just the unworthy ones that He wants to come to Him, Meg. Don't you know He says, 'I came not to call the righteous, but sinners to repentance'? Why, Meg, if you really feel that you are not worthy, that is just what He wants of you. Just come to Him in all of your unworthiness, and ask Him to forgive you your sins, and help you to be purer and better, and He will be so glad to do it. And oh, Meg, you would make such a grand Christian!"

Unselfish Laurie! Her pride in Meg would show itself in one way or another. It touched Meg more than anything she could have said. She kissed the eager, loving, little face and said:

"The idea of my kitten preaching to me! Run away now, dear; some day, perhaps, I may think of it, but just now, Ancient History must be attended to."

She opened her book again with a smile, and commenced to read, but after Laurie had left her, she stopped reading, leaned her head on her hand, and looked gravely out of the window. Lill and Lulu came up the stairs, singing softly, "I've found a Friend, oh, such a Friend." They did not see the

bowed form in the window, and went right on to the seniors' parlor, where Laurie and Ruth were, and in a moment Meg heard them talking together.

"They are all leaving me," she thought, and the tears sprang to her eyes. "They seem so happy; oh, if I only could! But I can't, and I'll not say and do things I don't mean. Lill and Lulu, too; the change has come to them."

And, indeed, it had. They went through the halls and up the stairs now, singing as in former days, only now it was some hymn, instead of a light love-ballad. Their faces wore a more thoughtful look, and it had only been one short week.

Meg listened to the low hum of voices until she could bear it no longer. She left her seat, and stole softly to the half-open door.

"Girls, I believe there is only one thing that keeps me from being perfectly happy," Lill was saying.

"What is that?" asked Laurie.

"Meg is not with us."

There was a short pause. Meg held her breath and listened.

"Let us all kneel right down and pray for her," said Ruth. "Each one."

How do you think Meg felt, when she heard her class-mates, one by one, praying for her? "Our precious sister," they called her. She felt like rushing into the room, throwing herself on her knees, and praying for herself with all her heart, but she didn't. "It is only because I am excited," she thought. "I must be sure of myself. I should be sorry for it the next minute, and then be ashamed and make others ashamed of me." She wiped the fast falling tears away, and went softly back to her place in the window-seat, and when Ethel came up a few moments later, she was helping "King Alfred drive the Danes out of England."

"All alone, Girlie?" asked Ethel, pausing beside her. "You look lonely out here. Isn't the 'study' more enticing?"

The girls sometimes called the "senior's parlor" the "study."

"No. Solitude is the thing I crave," answered Meg, with a smile.

"Is that a hint for me to leave you to solitude? Well, I will in just a few moments. Girlie, will you come to the meeting to-night?"

"Just what Laurie has been coaxing me to do."

"And you yielded to her entreaties, I hope?"

"No."

"Oh, Girlie, why not?"

Meg must have been very tired, or very troubled.

I do not doubt but that she was both, to say what she did. She slid from the window seat to her feet, and looked at Ethel with stormy, dark eyes.

"Ethel, I want nothing of a society that harbors such a hypocrite as Maude Leonard."

Poor Meg. Ethel's delicate face flushed crimson. "Meg!" was all she said.

Meg turned wearily away. "I have shocked you now, Ethel; displeased you, perhaps made you dislike me; but I have spoken the truth. You know it is impossible for me to pretend what I do not feel. I am glad that it is. I despise a liar and a deceitful person. If I were to go to your meeting to-night, I should derive no good from it; on the contrary, it would make me feel wicked. I will confess that I do wish I could feel this happiness that you and Laurie tell of. From the bottom of my heart I wish I could do as Laurie has done; but to do that, I must take Maude Leonard by the hand, and call her 'sister,' and I will never do that. She is a liar, a cheat and a deceiver."

"Meg, do you know what you are saying?"

"I know well what I am saying," retorted Meg, fairly roused; and then she did what she would have scorned to do a month ago — told Ethel the whole story of the "stolen essay." "Now you know why

I will not do what you ask, Ethel. Can you blame me?"

Ethel was looking out of the window, grieved and shocked. "What you have told me has surprised and pained me, Meg," she said at last. "But there is one thing that I must say to you. If you had the love of God in your heart, you would not feel in this way toward even the meanest of His creatures. You would not take it upon yourself to do what He only has a right to do — to judge and condemn. He has said, judge not, and ye shall not be judged; condemn not and ye shall not be condemned; forgive, and ye shall be forgiven. If you forgive not others their trespasses, then God will not forgive your trespasses. We are none of us perfect. There are none that do good — no, not one. Maude has done a wicked thing, and she must answer for it one day just as surely as you and I stand here. She may answer for it to you and Ruth and Madam — she will, if she truly repents — but if not, then she must answer for it when she stands before the judgment bar. And Meg, just so surely will you, if you dare to try to usurp the place of the great Judge of all, by judging and condemning as you are doing, be brought to account for it at the last day." Then Ethel turned and left her, and Meg stood there alone — speechless,

remorseful and dismayed, but, thank God! no longer
blind to her own folly and wickedness.

Yes, she had been wicked. Where she had thought
herself so free from all petty sinfulness; so upright
and noble in all her actions; so high-minded and
proud of her own spotless character, she had been
only miserably self-conceited, and — more dreadful
than all — downright wicked. It was a hard blow to
her pride, and she could not just then forgive Ethel
for dealing the blow, although she knew full well that
it had been done out of the deep love that Ethel felt
for her.

"Some day I may thank her for opening my eyes
to my own wretched state," thought Meg, as she sank
down in her seat again, still dazed and dismayed.
"Yes, I have done wrong — I see that I have — but
it is just as Ethel said, I have not the love of God in
my heart. Is that the 'something' I have felt the
need of so much lately? Does it explain the feeling
of longing and unrest? If it does, then why can't I
have it — why doesn't it come to me, as it has to the
others? Is it because my nature is so totally unlike
theirs? Mr. Stanley said the other Sunday evening,
that no two persons' Christian experiences were alike.
I didn't think much of it then, but perhaps" —

"And a lady I'll surely be," sang a voice. "Oh,

dear me, Meg, is that you? I wish some old 'Scotch Laird' would fall in love with me. I'd marry him, if I broke the hearts of a dozen 'Donalds.' Don't you think 'Janet' was foolish?"

"No. Marriage without love, is a failure, May-flower. Hasn't your experience taught you that?"

"He, he," giggled May, throwing her books down on the floor, and her strap after them. "Dell says there's no such thing as love. Now how in the world can she say that, Meg, with such a specimen as Ed Holmes continually before her?"

"Don't get sentimental, May-flower; get religious, that is the latest."

The words were not spoken as lightly as they read. The two girls looked steadily at each other for a moment, then May said:

"Their religion seems to make them very happy, Meg. Do you think it will last?"

At one time Meg would have laughed outright at such a question, and the earnest look on May's chubby face as she asked it, but now she did not even smile.

"Yes, I do think it will last, May, and I think it is a blessed thing to have. I know that Elsie seems so perfectly happy that I almost envy her."

"But, Meg," said May wonderingly, "why do you not take the step, then?"

"I don't know," answered Meg slowly. "Only, I do not feel it in my heart to do so."

"I do," said May suddenly, and with a hot blush.

Meg turned an earnest face toward her. "Then do it, May; do it at once, before it is too late."

"I will, Meg."

"Now, let us go to the 'study'; it is half-past four."

As they crossed the hall, Meg noticed a slip of paper on the floor. She picked it up, and saw it was some poetry. On one side was the name "Ethel" written in pencil. "She must have dropped it from her book," thought Meg, and followed May into the "study."

Laurie, Lill, Lulu, Dell and Ruth were there, preparing next day's lessons, but Ethel was not there.

"Where is Ethel, girls?" asked Meg.

"Just gone," answered Dell briefly, her eyes on her physiology.

"Her father came for her," explained Laurie, making room on the sofa for Meg. "He was going to drive into the city, and wanted Ethel to go with him. How many sentences have you translated, Meg?"

"None, but it won't take me long to do them all — French is so much easier than Latin. I found this piece of poetry on the hall floor; it has Ethel's name on it, so I suppose it is hers; I can give it to her in the morning."

There was silence in the "study" for half an hour, broken only by the rustling of the leaves as the girls turned them. The wood in the deep fire-place crackled and sparkled; the last ray of daylight died lingeringly away as if loth to leave so pretty a picture. One by one the girls dropped their books into their laps, and watched, with dreamy eyes, the shadows, as they came from their hiding places and commenced their twilight dance on ceiling, walls and doors. It was the happiest time of day for them all, only always before, the dusky silence had been broken by spasmodic "talks" and laughter, or little snatches of low song. Before Meg had commenced her translations, she had read Ethel's piece of poetry, and the beautiful words were what she was thinking of now:

> " He leadeth me.
>   In pastures green? Not always; sometimes He
>   Who knoweth best, in kindness leadeth me
>   In weary ways, where heavy shadows lie.

> " Out of the sunshine warm and soft and bright,
>   Out of the sunshine into darkest night,
>   I oft would faint with sorrow and affright —

> " Only for this — I know he holds my hand,
>   So whether in green or desert land
>   I trust, although I may not understand,

"And by still waters?   No, not always so;
  Ofttimes the heavy tempests round me blow,
  And o'er my soul the waves and billows go.

"But when the storms beat loudest, and I cry
  Aloud for help, the Master standeth by,
  And whispers to my soul, 'Lo, it is I.'

"Above the tempests wild I hear him say,
  'Beyond this darkness lies the perfect day,
  In every path of thine I lead the way.'

"So, whether on the hill-tops high and fair
  I dwell, or in the sunless valleys where
  The shadows lie — what matter?   He is there.

"And more than this; where'er the pathway lead,
  He gives to me no helpless, broken reed,
  But His own hand, sufficient for my need.

"So where he leads me I can safely go;
  And in the blest hereafter I shall know
  Why in His wisdom He hath led me so."

"Out of the sunshine into darkest night,"

repeated Meg to herself.   Could it be possible that
there were any dark places in Ethel's life?   Rich,
lovely, accomplished, admired and respected by all,
what more could she ask for?

"I oft would faint with sorrow and affright —
  Only for this — I know he holds my hand."

Oh, blessed assurance of Divine love and guidance!
"Whatever trouble she may have," thought Meg,

"she will be able to bear it for she will have His arm to lean upon. And I may have it if I will. That was a sweet thought that Laurie gave me — " I came not to call the righteous, but sinners to repentance." I am a sinner — I realize it now. But oh, if the light would only come — come as it has to the others!""

"Oh, hum," yawned Dell, stretching her arms up over her head, and sitting up straight in her chair. "Are we here for the night, or what?"

There were long-drawn breaths, and half-smothered sighs at such an abrupt ending of all dreams.

"Oh, Dell, how could you!" said May, reproachfully, as she picked up the book that had slipped from her lap to the floor.

"How could I, May-flower? Haven't you a stomach, child?"

"Haven't I a stomach?" repeated Meg, astonished at such a strange question. "Of course I have — or had this noon, if it hasn't walked off."

"Yours may have walked off, but mine hasn't; it is clamoring for its rights now. Who is going my way?"

"I should hope I wasn't," said Meg, solemnly. "It is the downward road to destruction. Haven't your thoughts of the past half-hour been of a more elevating character than " —

" Haven't had any thoughts," interrupted Dell, beginning on a second yawn.

" Haven't had any thoughts ! You don't mean to say that your mind has been wandering in space, do you ? "

" I have been asleep."

Every one laughed at the confession ; it was so much like Dell.

" I might have given you something to dream about," said Lill slyly.

" What was that ? "

" Ed Holmes begins to study medicine with Dr. Duncan to-morrow."

" Phooh, I knew that weeks ago. That is nothing to dream of."

" I give you up as a bad job," said Lill rather slangily.

" And Will is going to study law with Lawyer Holmes," said Meg. " Doesn't that seem strange? Will studying with Ed's father, and Ed studying with Will's father."

" Well, it would never do for Will to be a doctor," said May. " When he entered the sick-room, the patient would think it was his own tombstone walking in, and would prepare himself for it accordingly."

" I wonder," said Laurie, after the laughter had

somewhat subsided, "why the boys have changed around so."

Meg came very near saying, "Why, goose, I suppose each one has chosen the profession he likes best," but she didn't say it; she felt as if she should never speak contemptuously to Laurie again. Instead she said laughingly:

"Well, I shouldn't think it would do for Will to study law now."

"Why not?" everyone asked.

"Because he has signified his desire to become a Christian, and, of course, he will not like to be too much of a 'lieyar'."

There was a little burst of merriment at this, in the midst of which, Dell walked gravely from the room, saying as she went, "It won't do to stay in here any longer. Another effort like that last, and our Meg would be among the missing."

The rest picked up their books, and followed after. In the dressing-room Lulu said, "Have any of you read Mrs. Humphrey Ward's new book?"

"Do you mean Mrs. 'Ellsmere'?" asked Meg.

"Yes."

"I haven't read it."

"Nor I."

"Nor I."

"And you don't want to read it," said Ruth, very determinedly.

"Why not?" asked Lill. "I have read 'Robert Ellsmere'."

"You have?"

"Yes; but I skipped over the 'theology' part of it, and devoted myself exclusively to the love part. It wasn't much, either. That 'Langham' was an idiot — didn't know his own mind ten minutes at a time. I say that 'Rose' was well rid of him."

"I have not read it," said Ruth. "But I know what it is, and I have no desire to read it."

"I have read it," said Meg. "And I agree with you, Lill, that 'Langham', great scholar and philosopher though he was, was not worthy of one of the tears that 'Rose' shed over him. He was utterly devoid of that organ commonly called the heart; but I suppose if he had ever possessed one it had all run to brains before he met 'Rose'. But why do you think one ought not to read it, Ruth?"

"Because such a book as that could never, by any possibility, do one any good, but might and would do one much harm."

"Well," replied Meg, drawing on her gloves, "it might not do for every one to read it, that is true, especially if one made a study of it. One had better be sure of his strength of mind. It wouldn't do for a weak-minded person to undertake it."

"What kind of a book is 'Mrs. Ellsmere'?" asked May.

"Haven't read it," answered Meg; "but they tell me that Mrs. Ward makes 'Mrs. E——' as strong an unbeliever in the Divine Christ as her deceased husband was when he died, and finally marries her to a skeptic of the first water. Her daughter, too, I believe, marries ditto."

"What folly!" remarks Lulu, with the air of an old theologian. "Hadn't she any more sense than to do that? Such a strong-minded woman as she pretended to be, too! She was dreadfully afraid that Rose, silly, weak-minded Rose, would marry a skeptic, but that is always the way your high-souled, strong-minded women turn out."

"What do you say about it, Dell?" asked May, as that young lady rose to her feet, after a long but silent struggle with a refractory rubber.

"I say," replied Dell, flushed but victorious, "that you are a parcel of idiots; giving your opinion on a subject that you know about as much of as I do — and that is nothing — just as if you were so many veteran theologians. I advise you to let such subjects alone for those who understand them, or pretend they do so, and confine yourselves to matters of every-day life. It would be much more to the purpose."

"So say we all of us," commenced Meg, and the others joined in, and went down stairs and through the halls, singing — but not too loudly, for fear madam would correct them for being noisy and unladylike. As they closed the hall door, and passed down the steps, laughing and talking, a handsome sleigh drawn by a pair of spirited black horses, came up the street. A lady and gentleman were seated in it, and as the sleigh passed the great iron gates and the group of girls on the stone steps, the lady waved her muff, and the gentleman raised his hat, and then the sleigh dashed out of sight.

"Ethel and Mr. Stanley," said Dell.

"Thought she went off with her father," said Lulu.

"So she did," replied Lill. "But Mr. Stanley must have gone, too."

"They drove her father into the city and left him there, I suppose," said Dell.

"Yes, I suppose so," repeated Meg slowly.

XV.

AN ANNOUNCEMENT.

THERE will be a baptism in this place of worship on Sunday evening next, immediately at the close of the service."

The young pastor's deep, firm voice trembled a little, as he gave the announcement, and his grave face was full of a glad, solemn joy.

It was a bright, beautiful, cold morning, the third Sunday in the month of January. Mr. Stanley went on to speak of the joy such a notice gave him. Eleven young hearts had been touched by the Divine Spirit, and filled with pure, unselfish love for Christ and His children, which is one of the first and surest signs that the great change had come to them. He then read the names of the young candidates: Elsie Randal, Ethel Lawton, Laura Ray, Maude Leonard, May Bromley, Ruth Dean, Lilian Norton, Lulu Martin, Harold Randal, William Duncan and Melvin Pierce. Meg and Dell sat side by side and heard Mr.

Stanley read the names of their class-mates and
friends. Dell's lovely face did not change once in its
expression. It was white, cold and perfectly composed. She had never felt the least desire to become
a Christian.

"When the change comes to Dell, it will come suddenly, but it will be for all time. There will be no
wondering and doubting on her part. She will feel it
and understand it, and do what she is commanded to
do, without any questioning and without one look
backward," Ethel had said to Mr. Stanley, and he had
perfectly agreed with her.

He and Ethel had decided that nothing was to be
gained by trying to persuade either Meg or Dell.
Such natures as theirs, were not to be persuaded
against themselves.

"We will leave them to the all-merciful and all-
seeing God, who brings all good things to pass in His
own good time," said Mr. Stanley.

A quiver passed over Meg's face as she listened;
her lips trembled and her eyes filled with tears Meg
wished with all her heart that her name was on that
list of happy ones. She had been hoping and longing for the last week that the light would come to
her, but it had not come. "And I never will pretend
what I do not feel," she had said firmly. No one had

tried to persuade her; a general feeling seemed to prevail that it was best to leave her and Dell alone. Mr. Stanley's sermon that morning was especially good. He preached from Matthew xxviii: 19 — "Go ye therefore, and teach all nations, baptizing them in the name of the Father, and of the Son, and of the Holy Ghost."

There were not many dry eyes among the congregation. Meg sat and looked at Mr. Stanley. She somehow felt a respect for him that she had never felt for another person, and as she listened to the earnest words that came from his lips, she felt her heart throb and beat with a feeling she had never experienced before. Yet, right in the midst of it all — when his voice was ringing out its gladsome words, when his face was expressing his deepest emotions, when the congregation were listening with touched hearts and humid eyes, Meg, all at once, commenced to shake in silent but uncontrollable laughter. Dell looked at her in shocked surprise. Meg felt rather than saw her reproachful eyes upon her, and only shook the more. She laughed until the tears rolled down her cheeks; she felt as if every eye were fastened upon her in stern displeasure; worse than all she felt that she was committing an unpardonable offense in the house of God, and toward the man of

God, yet she could no more help it than she could
help breathing.   And yet, when I tell you the cause
of her strange outburst of merriment, I am very much
afraid that you will blame her greatly for her want of
self-control.

All at once while she had been looking at and listening intently to Mr. Stanley, the "hat adventure"
had flashed across her mind.   She could not account
for it then, nor ever afterward; but she seemed to
see him before her eyes as plainly as she had done on
that night, with the misshapen hat tied on his head
with the broad, pink ribbon, his eyes full of gay laughter, and the broken umbrella turned inside out, in his
hands.   Then the picture of herself and Mr. Stanley
in hot pursuit after the whirling hat, passed before
her mental vision, and she felt that she should be
obliged to get up and leave the church.   She thought
of all the solemn things that had ever happened under
her observation, but it did no good.   Dell did not
help matters any by bestowing a warning and most
unmerciful pressure of her foot on Meg's toes.   At
last the paroxysm passed — "spent itself," as Dell
said afterward, and Meg leaned back in her seat,
exhausted, with her handkerchief pressed against her
eyes.   What the proud girl suffered no one can realize, but enough to extenuate herself from all blame

and reproach. She did not raise her eyes again during the remainder of the service.

Mr. Stanley's voice had not faltered in the least; his face expressed neither pain nor surprise. When he closed his Bible and sat down, there was the same deep joy in his face that had marked it at the opening of the service.

When it came Meg's turn to shake hands with Mr. Stanley at the door she never spoke — did not even lift her eyes to his. She felt as if she could never look into his face again. To her surprise he kept her hand in his firm, warm grasp, as if waiting for her to look at him. Of the two "evils" Meg chose the least. She lifted two large, dark eyes swimming in tears, to his. Meg did not know what a beseeching look there was in their shadowy depths; it really bordered on the pathos. The dark-blue eyes that looked back into hers were full of nothing but kindness and good-feeling. To add to Meg's astonishment and delight, Mr. Stanley said, in a low, thrilling voice, "The happy time can not be far distant for you, my friend."

She looked at him and knew that either he had not seen her laughing, or else he had mistaken the nature of her emotion. She bowed her head in reply, and followed Dell out into the vestibule.

"Dell, did he see me, or — what?" She knew she could trust Dell — she would be sure to tell her right.

"He saw you," said Dell promptly; "but he thought you were crying."

Meg drew a long breath of relief. "And he'll never know the difference," she said emphatically. And he did not, until years after.

"What about the rest, Dell? What do you think they thought?"

"Only those right around us saw you, and I am quite sure they thought the same as Mr. Stanley. But, Meg, what in the world was the matter?"

"Hysterics," replied Meg.

"Well, I advise you to leave them at home when you go to church," said Dell dryly. "You might have to be carried out, you know."

"I wonder why Ethel has waited until now to be baptized," said Dell, thoughtfully, as they waited for the rest of the girls to come out.

"She is not strong, you know," said Meg. "Perhaps that is the reason."

"Well, she is no stronger now than she has been for a year or more; not so strong, in my opinion."

"No? Do you think she looks feeble?" asked Meg.

"Yes, very. Her skin is like wax."

"So is yours."

"There is a great difference between the whiteness of my skin and that of Ethel's," replied Dell, who fully realized how beautiful she was, but didn't consider it necessary to be foolish because she was beautiful; therefore, she accepted the fact as a fact, and nothing more. "Mine is a healthy white, and hers a sickly white."

"Who is sick?" asked May, coming up in time to catch Dell's last words.

"Dell thinks Ethel looks feeble," said Meg, over whose fair face a shadow had fallen. "What do you think about it, May?"

"I think she looks decidedly feeble," replied May. "It is my opinion that if she hasn't consumption, she will have it before many years."

"Don't talk nonsense," said Meg sharply. "She is no more consumptive than you or I. Here come the rest; let us go down stairs."

A vague fear had entered Meg's heart. Could it be possible that Ethel would really be with them for only a little while longer? Perhaps that was the "dark spot" in her life. Perhaps she knew that she had only a little while longer to live, and that was why she was so sad at times.

"Oh, it can't be, it can't be!" thought Meg. "She is too good, too noble. She must live to carry on the grand work she has begun. The world would be so much better for her living. There are others that can be spared a great deal better than she; some who do more evil than good by their lives."

The large church was filled to overflowing at an early hour on the following Sunday evening. The young candidates occupied seats in front. It had been their wish that Meg, Dell, Will and Ed should sing the hymn each one had chosen. That Will might assist, it was understood that he was to be the last to be baptized. There is no denying that Meg felt decidedly nervous — something new for her. "I am so afraid that Elsie will faint, or Laurie cry or May struggle, or something," she whispered to Dell, as Mr. Stanley left the room to prepare for the baptism.

"Nonsense," replied Dell, finding the first hymn with the calmest face imaginable. "I'll shake them out of their shoes to-morrow, if they dare to do such a thing."

The candidates now rose from their seats and passed into the class-room at the left of the pulpit. In a few moments Mr. Stanley came out. "I never thought him handsome before," said Meg, to herself, "but to-night his face is fairly beautiful."

Mr. Stanley stood with the open Bible in his hand.

" As it is written in the prophets, behold, I send my messenger before thy face, which shall prepare thy way before thee. The voice of one crying in the wilderness, Prepare ye the way of the Lord, make his paths straight. John did baptize in the wilderness, and preach the baptism of repentance for the remission of sins."

Perfect stillness settled over the large congregation ; the prayer was short but impressive. Then Mr. Stanley descended the steps, and the beautiful voices of the choir rang out, clear, sweet and soul-thrilling, " Nearer my God, to Thee." At the close of the first verse Elsie came forward from the class-room. Mr. Stanley received her at the top of the steps.

"I hear Thy gentle voice," was the hymn that Elsie had chosen, and very sweetly they sang it ! As Mr. Stanley baptized Elsie, Meg felt like crying out, " Take me with you, sister ; oh, take me with you."

She saw their mother wipe the glad tears away, and thought, "I am glad that two of her children have made her so happy."

May came next, then Maude ; and Meg looked on at Maude's baptism without one contemptuous thought ; the scene was too grandly solemn for that. She only said to herself gravely, "God is her Judge, not I." Surely the seed scattered by Ethel had fallen on fertile ground.

Laurie came next, looking so small, so delicate, so child-like. Laurie had chosen for her hymn, "Take me as I am."

Ruth followed, then Lill, then Lulu, and then Ethel. Ethel had chosen the beautiful hymn, so old and yet ever new, "Jesus, Lover of my Soul." When Meg looked at Ethel as she appeared in the door-way, she looked at her through a mist of tears; when the mist cleared away, it seemed to her as if she were looking on one of God's angels. All the girls had worn white, but somehow or other it seemed as if there was something about Ethel that the others did not have. The slender, fragile form seemed almost spiritualized. Her skin was as white as the driven snow; her eyes large, blue and shining. But lovelier than anything Meg had ever seen was the expression of the delicate face. I cannot paint it; only it was just such an expression as Meg had always imagined the angels of Heaven must wear.

Meg never realized before the grand solemnity of the baptismal service. She thought :

"If such scenes on earth are so beautiful, what must Heaven be!" Her heart was filled with joy inexpressible, when she saw Hal come forward in his turn. He looked so good, so earnest, so noble. Melvin, too, how thoroughly happy he appeared. Will looked, as Meg knew he would, grave, almost stern, and very determined.

At the conclusion of the sermon, Mr. Stanley raised his right hand toward Heaven. "Lord, it has been done as Thou hast commanded, and yet there is room."

CHAPTER XVI.

EASTER.

EASTER, this year, came on the thirteenth of
April. It was a bright, cool, lovely morning.
It seemed as if old Mother Nature had decked her
matronly form in her most beautiful robe, in honor of
the anniversary of our risen Lord. "Our girls," too,
seemed determined not to let the old Dame get ahead
of them in point of dress. Every one, even Ruth,
came out resplendent in new hats and dresses. I do
not intend to give a description of each one individually; collectively, there was nothing that they so much
resembled, sitting together as they did, as a bouquet
of sweet, delicately-tinted flowers. I must tell about
Meg's dress; it was the prettiest one of all, as perhaps
it was the simplest. It was one of those beautiful,
delicate shades of "apple green," made very plainly,
and fitted her slender form to perfection. She wore
a small hat covered entirely with apple blossoms —
delicate pink and white beauties. But I do not think

it was so much the delicate dress, or the dainty hat that made her look so charming, as it was the soft, dreamy expression of her fair face. Her dark eyes looked wistful and tender, and her red lips were curved in a little, dimpled smile. I am not trying to make Meg out a beauty, nor am I indulging in foolish rhapsodies over a new dress and hat, but to me there is nothing as beautiful and altogether pleasing, as a sweet, fair, pure life at the time when "girl-hood is about to pass through the window, and womanhood stands knocking at the door." It is "the time of all times" to them. With the life stretching before them like a vista, and only the bright, happy, cloud-less experiences of their girlhood to teach them how to enter it. Happy they who "remember their Cre-ator in the days of their youth," and early look to Him as their Guide and Protector through all the dark journey of life.

Mr. Stanley's text this morning was: "He is not here, but is risen." Luke xxiv: 6. At the close of the sermon he gave the following illustration: "In one of the gloomy prison cells of dark Siberia, sat a poor, hunted, heart-broken prisoner. His face was lined and seamed with suffering; his eyes were full of a dull, heavy despair. Cruel irons manacled his wrists and ankles. For many weary weeks he had been a prisoner in that dreary cell. Wild thoughts of escape had flashed through his mind again and again, but — the smallest infant in the hands of a strong man was not less helpless than he in the grasp of a merciless, cold-blooded despotism. Escape was an utter impossibility, death a terrible certainty, unless some man would come forward and offer his life for his. Vain hope! The man had not a friend in the whole wide world.

"All at once, as he sat there, the door swung open without a sound, and a man entered the room. He was of a most noble, majestic presence; his face was grand in its calm, noble beauty; the eyes were deep, and full of a tender pity. The wretched prisoner with the irons on wrists and ankles, fell prostrate on the stone floor, and hid his face in his hands as if blinded by the glorified beauty of the gracious presence.

"Words cannot express his unbounded astonishment when he felt himself lifted from the cold floor by arms that were strong and tender, and heard a matchless voice saying, 'Arise and be not afraid, for I have come to save you.'

"'To save me?' The poor lips could scarcely form the words, but the man understood. His smile was infinitely sweet as he answered:

"'Yes, to save you. I will give my life for you, that you may be free. The door is open, pass through, and go forth into the light — a free man.'

"'But who are you?' gasped the bewildered man.

"'I am the Son of your King, and heir to His throne, but I have offered my life that yours might be spared; the decree is passed, it cannot be recalled. I gladly lay down my life that you may be saved. Go forth, and sin no more.' He stooped and unfastened the chains from about the man's wrists and ankles, and he passed through the open door and went out of the terrible place into the pure, glad sunlight of a bright world, saved! But at what a price!"

There was intense silence in the large room as Mr. Stanley closed his Bible and looked about him.

"My friends, the Son of the great King of Heaven, Heir to the great white throne, has laid down His life that you might be saved. Will you not accept the sacrifice so freely given? For you He suffered the shame and agony of the cross. For you that noble head, with its crown of cruel, piercing thorns, was bowed low in the dust. He knew what it was to be hungry and thirsty, and no one offered Him bread to eat or water to drink. He was tired and sick and weary unto death, yet there was no place in which He could lay His head. The agony in the garden — what must it have been for His bleeding, tortured heart to cry out, 'If it be possible, let this cup pass from me,' and the great drops of blood stood out upon His forehead. The agony of the cross — but who can paint it? It is beyond all human power. It is enough that we know it was so great as to wring the despairing cry, 'My God, my God, why hast Thou forsaken me?' from those dear lips.

"And all this He suffered for you and for me — poor, miserable sinners, not worthy of one drop of that precious blood that flowed from the thorn-crowned head and pierced side. Once more I ask you, will you accept of the sacrifice? I pray God that you may before it is too late."

Meg had listened, almost breathlessly; her soul had hung upon every word that came from the preacher's lips, and when he said, "All this He suffered for you and for me," a great wave of sorrow passed over her. She felt it throb through every vein of her body. It quickened the beating of her heart, and filled her eyes to overflowing. She felt like falling upon her knees then and there, and bowing her head before the power of the Omnipotent. She could not do that, but she could and she did prostrate her soul before Him. In her heart she cried out: "I love Thee, my Saviour. Take me just as I am, and make me clean." Then how inexpressibly happy she felt! She could hardly wait for the service to end, she was in such a hurry to go home and go to her room, and thank God on her knees for His wonderful goodness and mercy. She wanted to tell Him how much she loved Him.

For the first time the feeling of longing and unrest was made clear. And all this peace and joy would have been hers months ago if she had only opened her heart to Him, surrendered her will to His and believed on Him as her Saviour. That is all the secret — if secret there is.

Mr. Stanley did not go down to the door that morning. Meg waited a moment to see if he was not coming; but he stepped down from the pulpit, and went up to the seat on which he had thrown his light overcoat and hat. He had gotten one arm in, and had turned to put the other in, when the coat was lifted gently, and drawn up over his shoulders. He turned with a smile, and a "Thank you" on his lips, not knowing who had done him the kindness. He stopped at sight of a fair, girlish face fairly quivering with happiness, and two large, dark eyes overflowing with a light he had never seen in them before, but which he had long prayed that he might see.

Meg held out her little hand, and he grasped it

tightly. "Thank you," was all she said; and, "God bless you," he answered.

At a quarter before eight on the following Thursday evening, the vestry of the church was nearly filled. As the last stroke of the bell died away, the doors were closed. All of our young people were there and, as usual, sitting together. Elsie and Mrs. Randal sat exactly opposite. The meeting opened in the usual manner, but everyone noticed a something about their pastor which they had never observed before. They could not tell what it was. A deeper joy in the dark-blue eyes, a glad, expectant look on the earnest face, and a little nervous trembling of the strong hands which was something very unusual. Even Ethel noticed and slightly wondered.

Many testimonies were given, and several hymns sung. It was a grand meeting. At last there was a brief silence; one of the "periods" that come in a prayer-meeting at times — and, alas! only too often in some. The clock ticked loudly on the wall. One or two pages turned softly as if some one was seeking a hymn. Mr. Stanley sat in his chair, his elbow resting upon the table, his head leaning on his hand. It seemed as if all were quietly waiting for something, but Mr. Stanley was the only one who knew for what.

It seemed to Meg as if her heart were trying to

beat above the ticking of the clock. Surely every one must hear it. She had been fully determined to rise and tell of her happiness, and the resolve she had made. It had seemed a comparatively easy thing to do when she had thought of it at home and at school, but now, when the very moment had arrived, she felt as if it were an utter impossibility. She stole a glance at her mother's face to see if she might find encouragement there. It was calm, serene, and wore its habitual patient smile. She looked at Elsie's beside it. For the first time she noticed how much alike the two faces were in feature and expression. She glanced at Ethel — sweet, pure and full of a heavenly joy. The sight quieted the rapid beating a little. She looked at Mr. Stanley. She could see but little of his face, for it was hidden by his hand, but his whole attitude expressed a quiet expectancy. "Oh, I must get up!" went like a flash through Meg's mind; then all at once she whispered, "Jesus, help me." The next moment she was on her feet, and then she left all the rest with Him. What she said, how she looked and acted, whether she appeared graceful or awkward — all these things which had troubled her a little when she had thought of them, were of no thought to her now. She was before her God, and talking to Him, not to the people there:

"I love my Saviour, and I put myself, my whole life, into His care and keeping, to do with as He will, trusting, knowing that whatever He may do will be all for my good. I love Him with all my heart, because He first loved me and gave His life for me. I am most unworthy of His love and goodness, but I have done just what He has told us all to do. I have asked Him to forgive me all my sins, and I have faithfully promised Him to trust Him in all things, and to love Him and serve Him while life shall last. Pray for me that the light may grow brighter and brighter before me, and I may follow wherever it may lead — through the 'weary ways where heavy shadows lie,' as well as through the 'bright, green meadows where the sunshine is '."

"Amen."

The word came from touched, overflowing hearts — deeply, earnestly, thankfully; then Ethel's sweet, low voice commenced:

> "Just as I am, without one plea,
> But that Thy blood was shed for me,
> And that Thou bidd'st me come to Thee
> O, Lamb of God, I come, I come."

Before she had sung three words, the whole room took it up, Meg's voice ringing out above all the others. It seemed as if the sound must rise to the very vault of Heaven, and that the angels gathered about the great white Throne, strike their harps, and ring out their grand "Allelujah" over "the one sinner that repenteth."

To Meg it seemed as if the room were full of angels, and the heavenly melody. It was the happiest moment of all her happy young life. She received the warm hand-shakes and hearty words of welcome, at the close of the meeting, like one in a dream.

XVII.

MEG'S TROUBLE.

WHEN Laurie broached the subject of "baptism" to Meg the next morning, as they walked to school together arm in arm, Meg answered her gently but firmly:

"No, Laurie, I am not ready to take that step just now, and shall not be for some time to come. I want to be sure of myself first — sure of my own worthiness, I mean. Suppose I should be baptized — say in three week's time — and then should meet with some temptation, and should yield to it! I could never forgive myself. I should be that most contemptible of all contemptible things — a backslider. Now you know, the Church thinks it wrong to dance, and play whist, and go to the theater. I like all these pleasures, and have always indulged in them. Whist I do not care so much about, I can give that up; but oh, Laurie, I do love to dance, and I do love the theater. I cannot help it. It will be hard for me to give them up, and until I feel I can give them up cheerfully and willingly, I shall not unite with the church. If I cannot comply with the requests in every particular — if I cannot obey every law, I will wait. I do not think, myself, that such things as dancing and the theater are wicked, but they are against the laws of the Church, and those laws must be recognized by all members. I am going to test myself, Laurie; in a little while, when I feel that I can withstand the temptations, I am going to put myself in the way of them, and then I shall know if I am worthy or not. If I yield to them then I shall know I am not worthy; but if not, then I shall know my strength is sufficient."

Oh, Meg, sincere and earnest in all you say, yet how mistaken! The first prize in logic was bestowed upon you at the final examination last month, but the logic you are using now is very poor indeed. You have not yet learned that you can do nothing by your own strength, but with Him all things are possible. Yet Meg was doing what it seemed right for her to do. Besides, she had set a hard task for herself to do, and we must pity, not blame.

Laurie's pretty face wore a puzzled look. "What you say sounds all right, Meg; and if it is the way you feel, it must be right. I have never felt in that way; but then, I do not go to the bottom of things as you do. And, any way, I have never felt, somehow or other, like doing either of the things you mention, and it seems now as if I never should, I am so happy."

"But you may, Laurie; and then what will you do?"

The puzzled look deepened, and the blue eyes filled with tears. "Oh, Meg," she said tremulously, "I shall have to leave it all with Jesus."

Dear little Laurie, that is just what He would have you do — all He asks you to do. And yet, Meg actually pitied Laurie even then, for her lack of strength of character.

"She did not wait long enough," said Meg to herself, as they went up the stone steps. "She asked to be forgiven for her sins, and promised to live better in the future, and then she thought she was all ready to join the Church, and take upon herself all its requirements, not asking herself if her strength was sufficient to resist all temptations. She just gave herself up without thinking of all this."

And all of your logic, Meg, will not do for you what Laurie's simple faith has done, and will do for her. You will say that Meg had not read her Bible, or she would have seen the command, "Believe and

be baptized," or perhaps you will say that she did
what so many do in these days, "read her Bible to
suit herself"; but she did read her Bible, and she did
not read it to suit herself.   As I have said before —
she was doing what she thought was right, and, if she
had consulted the highest earthly authority, her duty
or her idea of duty would have remained unchanged
to her.   The only thing that seemed likely to teach
her better was — experience.   It is often so.   The
lesson of obedience is often taught by that stern
teacher.   So, let us not call this an act of foolishness
on Meg's part; we will call it by its right name — a
mistaken sense of duty.

> " O, row me o'er,
>   O, boat me o'er,
>   O, row me o'er wi' Charlie,"

May Bromley sang at the top of her voice, as she flew
along the passages and up three flights of stairs to
the "seniors' parlor."

   "Are you crazy, May-flower?" asked Meg, sitting
upright on the sofa, where she had been lying with
her hands up over her head for the last half-hour.
"Or can't you wait one day longer before leaving this
decorous establishment?   A good thing for you that
you leave of your own accord to-morrow; such a

noise as that is enough to warrant madam presenting you with your walking-ticket."

Dell and Laurie, each lying comfortably back in an easy arm-chair, laughed lazily, while May seated herself in the window-seat, and opened a package of nougattines. "Don't talk slang, Megda," she said severely; "it isn't pretty."

But Meg was looking at May with wide, dark eyes, and a look of surprise on her face. May understood, and smiled airily as she put a nougat deliberately between her teeth, and bit it in two with the most aggravating coolness. Meg lifted the sofa pillow, stern determination in her eyes.

"Your choice, May," she said solemnly.

May laughed and put her arm up to protect her head, while Lill, who had been lying asleep on the sofa at the other end of the room, came walking slowly up, rubbing her sleepy eyes, and sniffing suspiciously.

"Does my nose deceive me," she said in hollow tones, "or is it nougattines?"

"You have named them, they are yours," said May, "or part of them, at least. Put down that feather-bed, Meg, and don't look so wild — you shall have one."

"I am content," murmured Meg, sinking languidly down again.

"Where did you get them, May?" asked Laurie, as she received her "share."

"Why, you know," said May, dividing them generously; "or, 'ef you don't know, den I tells you.' I have had a terrible tooth-ache all day, and so I asked permission of madam to go down to 'Lothrops' for some oil of cloves, and"—she passed Meg's share to her over that young lady's head as she spoke.

"You got the nougattines instead," finished Meg, putting her hands up to receive them. "Very good indeed. I find them an excellent remedy for the tooth-ache myself."

May held the "sweets" just out of reach of the white fingers. "But I eat them with the teeth on the other side of my jaw. Isn't that possible? Answer."

Meg dropped her hands. "She wants me to answer," she said faintly, appealing to the ceiling, "and holds the delicious aroma over my organ of smell at the same time—so near, and yet so far. Have mercy, May, I am but human."

"And very human where nougattines are concerned," laughed May. "Answer me, then."

"Don't be silly, girls," said Dell, beginning on her third one. "Tell her she can chew on one side of her mouth as well as the other, Meg. You don't know what you are missing. These are about the creamiest nougats I ever ate. What did you have to give a pound, May?"

"How you do take the poetry out of anything, Dell," said May laughing, as Meg, in mock desperation at Dell's words, snatched the little package from her hands. "I only gave sixty cents a pound."

"Isn't it about time for the rest of us?" asked Laurie.

"Should think so," answered May. "Their shares are ready for them."

"Here they come now," said Dell, as voices were heard in the hall below.

"Oh, I didn't tell you that madam had gone out to drive, did I?" said May. "I met her. She had Miss Tyler and Miss White with her."

"And Professors Strauss and Weir?" asked Meg.

"No, of course not. It wouldn't have been setting a good example to 'my young ladies'," said May, in such perfect imitation of madam's precise tones that they all laughed.

"Well, I should have thought she might have taken the whole establishment while she was about it," said Lill. "Why don't those girls come up! Call them, Laurie."

"Yes, do, pet," said May, "or there won't be anything left of their shares. Lill has devoured almost all of them with her eyes now."

Meg almost choked herself with a nougat at this. Lill smiled supremely.

"May must say something," she said, not the least displeased.

Laurie went to the head of the stairs, and called: "Girls, come up here. The days of miracles have not passed — May has been treating."

"What ingratitude!" groaned May.

Lulu and Ruth rushed up stairs at this, and entered the room. "All here?" they asked.

"All but Ethel and Maude," replied May, sliding from the window-seat, and placing a chair for each with elaborate politeness. Then she gave them their "share" and went back to her perch.

"Ethel is in the library, but she is coming right up. Don't know where Maude is," said Lulu, beginning on hers.

"I do," said May. "And I was going to tell when I first came in, but those — those cannibals caught sight of my candy, and drove the idea out of my head."

"Poor little head," murmured Meg compassionately. "What a cruel thing to deprive it of its one idea."

"Tell us now, May-flower," said Lill soothingly.

"I will; Meg, please shut your eyes, that you may not hear. Well, I met our fair sister out driving. Her father's coachman was not with her, either."

"Who was?" asked Laurie.

"Mr. Augustus Belmont."

This information was received in complete silence, and May was somewhat disappointed; but she could blame her "treat" for that. The girls were enjoying it too much to become excited over Mr. Augustus Belmont.

"Well, what do you say?" asked May at last, finding that no one had any idea of saying anything voluntarily.

"Wouldn't change places with her," said Dell, with her mouth full.

In the midst of the laugh that followed, Ethel came in. She looked very pale and tired. The easiest chair in the room was immediately wheeled forward, and with a sweet smile and a "Thank you" to May for the candy, Ethel sank down in it.

"How pleasant!" she said, looking around her with pleased eyes. "You don't know what a pretty picture you did make, girls, when I looked at you from the door-way."

"What must it be now, then?" said Meg with loving flattery.

It was, indeed, a beautiful picture. The room was partly in shadow, for May had drawn the blind at the window where the June sun would have shone in. May was curled up in the other window-seat, with her head leaning against the dark wood. Meg lay at full length on one sofa, one arm thrown up over her head, the other lying in her lap where the nougattines would be handy. Lill and Lulu occupied the other sofa together, their arms around each other; when one wanted a nougat the other would feed her with one. Dell was buried in the depths of an easy chair, Ruth in another, while Laurie sat on an ottoman and leaned her head against Meg's sofa. Ethel's easy-chair was drawn up beside the fire-place. That had always been, in Summer and Winter, Ethel's acknowledged place. The dark, gaping mouth of the fire-place was filled with ferns and potted plants, until it looked like a little, cool, green glen.

It was a dear, dear room, whether in Winter, when the firelight gleamed on wainscot and ceiling, or in Summer, when the shadows of the setting sun length-ened on the floor. Dear it was at all times and at all hours, but more especially at the "hour of all hours" to our girls — the twilight hour. And this was the last time they would ever sit here as pupils. Never again would it be the same to them as it was now.

The thought was too sad, and they tried to banish it with light talk and laughter. They were all very careful not to mention "to-morrow". All that talk had been gone over with down in the large hall.

"Well," said Laurie at last, "I wish some one would tell me who this Mr. Augustus Belmont is; I have never been able to find out."

"Who is he, Ethel?" asked May.

"I don't exactly know. A New York gentleman, Maude says, and his father and her father were college chums. That is all I know."

"College fiddle-sticks," said Dell. "I don't believe it. He looks like a rascal to me."

Meg laughed. "What do you know about rascals, Dell? How many have you ever met with in your short life?"

"Well," said Dell, nothing abashed, "he looks like a very dissipated young man to me. His eyes are red, and his skin is flabby."

A burst of laughter at this.

"Maude is engaged to him," said Ruth. "She told me so, and showed me her ring. A large diamond. I hope he is not dissipated."

"So do I," said Ethel slowly.

"Maude Leonard engaged!" exclaimed Dell indig-

nantly. "What can her father and mother be thinking of! Just graduating!"

"My mother was married when she was nineteen,"
said Lill.

"Yes, but people are supposed to be more enlight-
ened now," said Dell dryly.

"Oh, you old maid, you," laughed May; and then
she asked suddenly, "How old is Mr. Stanley,
Ethel?"

"Twenty-six," answered Ethel, and her pale face
flushed pink.

"Who is the oldest one in our class?" continued
May, who seemed to be thirsting for information.

After comparing notes, it was found that Maude
was the oldest, as she had just passed her twentieth
birthday, and the others would not be twenty until
after the Summer. Ethel would be twenty on the
first day of September.

Meg could not think why May asked Ethel how old
Mr. Stanley was. But she explained herself while
they were passing up the stairs to the dressing-room.

"Mr. Stanley is six years older than Ethel, Meg.
That is about right, isn't it?" she whispered, and
Meg looked at her for a moment, and then said
shortly, "Do wait until you get out of school, May,
before you talk such nonsense."

"A remark worthy of our Adella," laughed May.

Silence reigned in the "study" after the question of age had been settled. Try as hard as each one might, she could not keep the great "to-morrow" out of her mind. Yet it was not with any feeling of pride that she looked forward to graduating day, but, on the contrary, with one of deep sadness. To think that nevermore would the dear old halls resound with their light footsteps, and merry talk and laughter. Nevermore would they assemble in careless, loving sisterhood in the beloved "study" to talk over their little "plans," or indulge in a little harmless gossip over no one in particular, but the world in general. Perhaps this last half-hour of quiet thinking was the saddest that had ever come into any of their young lives. At last Ethel broke the silence, and all could but feel glad that she did, it had become so painful.

"I do not want to place myself in the position of speech-maker, girls," she said, with a little laugh; "but I cannot help saying what has been in my heart to say all day. I feel assured that we all experience the same feeling in regard to our leaving the dear old place. No need to dwell upon that."

She stopped and wiped the tears away that had gathered on her lashes, and every girl there might have been seen doing the same thing, surreptitiously. Then Ethel went on:

"Somehow or other, I feel very sad indeed; it is not wholly on account of leaving, but something else which I cannot explain. I have a strange request to make, girls, but you will comply with it, I know. It is this: Let us all gather close together, and clasp hands in a circle, and promise to love and remember each other all our lives long. No matter how far we may stray apart in the years to come, our *hearts* will always be united; and if we never meet again on earth, we will try to meet each other in Heaven, where the wicked cease from troubling, and the weary are at rest."

Silently and tearfully, the girls gathered around Ethel, hand clasping hand, and while they sat thus, Ethel prayed in a low sweet voice, that the band of sisterhood, though broken on earth, might be united again in the better world. Then the Class-Song was sung, in low, sweet, girlish voices, and the last, happy, careless school-day that they would ever know, was at an end:

CLASS-SONG.

One more song, and then we sever,
  One more touch of hands and then
We must part, perhaps forever,
  'Though we hope to meet again·

Life's great school is now before us
  'Though our training here may end;
May the same kind love be o'er us
  Wheresoe'er our ways may tend.

Sweet the mem'ries that shall linger
  'Round this dear, familiar place,
Memories of song and singer,
  Thoughts which time cannot efface;
Faithful friends and dear companions,
  All were known and loved so well;
Now has come the hour of parting,
  We must bid you all " Farewell."

XVIII.

COMMENCEMENT DAY.

LAURIE came over to Meg's house on the morning of the eighteenth, about a week after the events recorded in our last chapter. Meg saw her coming up the street, as she paused in her dusting to take a peep out of the window, at the beauty of the June morning, and ran out of the house and down the garden-path to meet her.

"I can't stop but a few minutes, Meg," said Laurie, as Meg opened the gate for her; "I promised to be back by ten o'clock to make some 'velvet cream' for dinner, and you know what a job that is."

"Yes," answered Meg, dusting the floor of the vine-covered piazza with her duster, and motioning for Laurie to take a seat; "it takes a long time to make it, and then quite a while for it to cool. But isn't it delicious?"

"Yes; I hope mine will be as good as your last was.

I will bring some up so we can have it when we get home to-night."

Laurie took her pretty, flower-trimmed hat off and fanned herself with it. Meg laughed gayly.

"Velvet-cream and sponge-cake at midnight! Do you suppose we shall sleep after that?"

Laurie laughed too — a happy laugh. "What a glorious morning, Meg; if to-night is only half as pleasant!"

"Oh, it will be," said Meg, confidently. "It won't rain to-day; the sun set clear last night, and there is a moon, too."

"Well, I ran up to see if everthing was all right. What time are you going?"

"We shall go at about half-past one. I wish you would drive in with us, Laurie."

"Oh, no," said Laurie, quickly. "I will wait for Hal."

"He can come with the others," said Meg, just to tease her.

"No," said Laurie, putting her lips resolutely together, and blushing a pretty pink; "I will wait for him — he would rather I would."

"You little darling!" said Meg, and gave her a hug. "But it is too bad that Hal could not get away for just a few hours this afternoon; you would enjoy the exercises so much. Though no one is to graduate that we are acquainted with."

"No, so I do not care so much. It was very kind in Mr. Stanley to secure so many tickets for us, wasn't it?"

"Yes, very."

They talked a little longer, and then Laurie said: "Well, I must go. You will be at the depot to meet us to-night?"

"Yes, at half-past seven."

"All right. Good-by, until then."

"Good-by."

Laurie went down the street walking a little more slowly than when she came up, and Meg went back into the house to finish her dusting.

It was Commencement Day at the college of which Mr. Stanley was a graduate, and he had procured tickets for "our girls" and their gentlemen friends. Will and Meg were going to the afternoon exercises with Mr. Stanley and Ethel. They were to drive in Judge Lawton's handsome carriage. Hal and Laurie, Ed and Dell, Bert and Lill, Ray and Lulu, Melvin and May were all going in on the evening train to the Promenade Concert, and the others were to meet them at the depot when their train came in. A splendid time was anticipated by all.

Meg had felt very sorry that Ruth had not been invited to go, and after she had finished her dusting, she took off her big apron, put on her shade hat, took her parasol, and started for Ruth's.

Ruth, herself, met her at the door, and asked her in with her usual sweet smile of welcome. Ruth loved Meg very dearly, and Meg respected and loved Ruth.

Ruth was about to lead Meg into the sitting-room, when Meg said: "O, let us sit out here, Ruthie; your kitchen is always so deliciously cool. Those vines at the window make it look so pretty and shady, too. And you have gotten all your work done up, and have let your fire go out so soon; but you were always a smart little thing."

Meg went rattling on, not noticing that Ruth had tried several times to speak, and that her cheeks were quite red.

"I came to ask a great favor of you, Ruth," Meg continued; "I want you to go with us this afternoon. We will all be so glad if you will. I'll take you under my wing, though I think"— Meg stopped short as the sound of a man's voice came from the sitting-room. She looked at Ruth inquiringly.

"I tried to tell you, Meg," whispered Ruth, for the door was ajar, "but you were so busy talking you did not notice. Mother is sick, and is at home to-day. Mr. Stanley called to see her; he came in about five minutes before you."

Meg looked vexed.

"Never mind, dear," said Ruth, "you did not say anything but what you would as soon he would hear. Let us go in."

Meg shook her head emphatically, but just then Mr. Stanley said — as if he mistrusted, by the sudden silence that Meg had found out he was there — "Good-morning, Miss Randal. Don't let me drive you away."

Meg was obliged to go in then, but she felt very much like a child that had been coaxed not to be afraid.

Mrs. Dean was lying on the lounge. She looked very ill. Mr. Stanley sat on a low rocker by her side. Meg went up to the lounge and held out her hand.

"I heard your kind invitation to Ruthie," said Mrs. Dean, with a grateful smile. "I wish you might prevail upon her to go with you; it would do her good. Mr. Stanley has been trying to persuade her."

Meg said, "Oh!" and looked at him. He had gotten ahead of her. She commenced to wish she hadn't come.

Ruth leaned over her mother, and smoothed back a

lock of hair that had fallen out of place. "I shall not leave you, mother," she said, with gentle determination; and Mrs. Dean kissed the loving brown hand.

"We shall have to try again, Miss Randal," said Mr. Stanley, easily. "And perhaps we shall succeed better next time."

Meg looked at him questioningly.

"In our little attempt at giving pleasure, I mean," he said, and Meg knew that he understood and appreciated her "motive".

She was sorry that he did so; it seemed like being praised for a very little thing.

Meg waited, hoping that Mr. Stanley would go, but as he seemed to be in no hurry, she rose at last, and said:

"I hope you will feel better very soon, Mrs. Dean. Don't work too hard, Ruthie; I'll be down to-morrow afternoon, and tell you all about to-night."

Mr. Stanley rose at the same time. "I think I will say good-morning, too," he said. "I have made quite a long call," and in a moment or two, Meg found herself walking down the white, dusty street beside him.

They talked about commonplace things all the way home, and Meg was very glad that Mr. Stanley did not question her about uniting with the Church;

she was afraid he might. At her gate he said, "You will be ready at half-past one?" and opened the gate for her to pass through.

"Yes, I will try to be," she answered.

He raised his hat, she bowed and went into the house, and before Mr. Stanley reached the corner of the street, he heard her beautiful voice through the open window singing:

> "My God and Father, while I stray
> Far from my home on life's rough way,
> O, teach me from my heart to say,
> Thy will be done."

We will pass over the events of the afternoon, and proceed to that of the evening.

Mr. Stanley had conducted his guests up to the room that had formerly been his while a student at the college. He had ascertained from the janitor that it had been unoccupied for the last three weeks —the young gentleman having been obliged to go home on account of sickness in his family, and Mr. Stanley had received permission from the president to entertain his friends in it. It was a pleasant room, with two large windows facing the front campus. Mr. Stanley procured camp-chairs enough for all, but Meg and May declared they were going to occupy the window-seats. The band-stand was just far enough away for the music to sound delightful, and the electric light flooded the room with its soft, moon-like radiance. Hal, Will, Ed, Melvin, Bert and Ray had brought candy, grapes and nuts enough to make the girls ill for a month afterward, and Mr. Stanley had contributed a can of iced lemonade. Withal, they were as happy a party as ever brightened a dim, musty, dreary old college-room.

The girls wore their graduating dresses — soft, white cashmeres, and a bunch of the class-flowers — white hyacinths. Mr. Stanley thought, as he looked at them, "Surely there was never a fairer rose-garden of girls."

Melvin kept them in a perfect gale of laughter over the most miserable little puns that were ever invented. Then his and Meg's "tongue-fencing" — as Meg called it — delighted them all, especially Mr. Stanley. He sat beside Ethel, attentive to her slightest wish, but he also sat where he could watch Meg's fair, sparkling face, shining pure and white against the dark, old wood of the window-frame, with the soft, moonlike light upon it. She pleased him; she made him feel as if he would give the world, if he had it, if he could have just such a sweet, pure, lovable girl for his sister. He could have taken her to his heart, with all her faults, and cherished her as only a brother can cherish the sister he loves.

He was watching her when the band commenced to play — although he could not have told what it was — "Flowers of St. Petersburg Waltz." The moment that the first notes struck the air, Meg stopped her gay badinage with Melvin, listened for a moment with parted lips, and then, all unconscious that she was being watched, laid her head back against the window-frame, and listened with dreamy eyes, and a happy, contented smile parting her red lips.

"How she loves that kind of music," thought Mr. Stanley, still watching her.

In a few moments he saw her lift her white hands a little from her lap, and commence to keep time with them, slowly and unconsciously. He could not help smiling, yet he sighed at the same time. Then he saw the little foot resting on the floor, commence to go up and down, up and down, in perfect time with the music; then her head commenced to move slowly backward and forward, and from side to side, and before the delicious music had ceased, Meg was performing quite a dance on her own account in the deep, wide window-seat. Mr. Stanley found it hard work to keep from laughing outright. Her utter unconsciousness made it all the more amusing.

When the last notes died lingeringly away, Meg heaved a soft little sigh, and thus, suddenly brought

back to earth, looked with frightened eyes around her
to see if any one had seen her. Mr. Stanley found it
convenient, just then, to offer Ethel a glass of lemonade, and the rest were too busily engaged to have
noticed it, so Meg leaned back in her comfortable seat again, and waited breathlessly for the next
selection.

What a perfectly happy evening that was to all!
An evening they would never forget. The intervals
between the "selections" were filled up with light
talk and happy laughter. Refreshments were passed
around with startling regularity, and if one dared to
refuse them, he or she was warned that they would
never be taken to the Promenade Concert again —
meaning, of course, the one who refused the refreshments, not the refreshments themselves.

And so the time passed. The concert closed with
a beautiful rendering of "Clayton's Grand March",
with variations ; there was a general move of the prom-
enaders toward the great iron gates, and our young
people gathered up their wraps and "debris", and
with many lingering, backward glances, passed out of
the room they had made cheerful for three hours, and
made their way, decorously, to the depot.

Laurie was to stay with Meg all night. After
they had bidden Hal good-night in the sitting-room,

and were mounting the stairs to Meg's room, Meg looked over her shoulder at Laurie and said, gravely, " Would you like some of the velvet-cream, Laurie ? "

" Don't mention it, Meg," was Laurie's answer, accompanied with a shiver of disgust.

How long the two girls would have lain awake " talking over things," I do not know, had not Hal, who slept up stairs that night, knocked sharply on their wall, and called out in beseeching tones, for them to have some mercy on him, if not on themselves. Conversation then ceased, and the girls bade each other good-night.

As Meg turned her bright head on her pillow and settled herself for sleep with a happy smile on her fair face, she little thought that never again would the bright world look quite the same to her as it did that night. Never quite the same.

XIX.

A CALL.

ARTHUR STANLEY walked up the broad, gravelled walk that led to the front entrance of Judge Lawton's handsome residence, on the morning after the "Promenade Concert," went up the marble steps, and pressed the electric button. A colored footman opened the door and upon Mr. Stanley's inquiry if "Judge Lawton were at home", answered in the affirmative, and conducted him to the library.

The judge was seated before his heavy writing table. He rose to his feet as Arthur was announced, and went forward to greet him with a pleasant smile and extended hand. Mr. Stanley proceeded at once to business in a most manly, straightforward way which greatly pleased if greatly surprised the judge. What he said was said briefly but earnestly. "Judge Lawton, I love your daughter, and have come to you to ask your permission to tell her so, and to ask her to be my wife."

Such a request from a young man to a parent must always have a more or less startling effect on the latter, even when, as in Judge Lawton's case, something of the kind had been rather expected.

Judge Lawton had a deep respect for his young pastor, and told him so. He was his ideal of what a young man should be; but — Ethel was his only child, and his life's idol. He told Arthur so, and smiled a little sadly, as the young man said eagerly:

"Do not think of it in the light of losing a daughter, Judge Lawton, but of gaining a son. I will love her and cherish her while life shall last."

"Yes, I know," said the judge, whose stern face was wonderfully softened. "I believe you; but Ethel is so young — not quite twenty."

"I will not take her from you until you are perfectly willing to have her go," said Arthur, tenderly.

"That would never be, then," replied the father, with a smile. "But it isn't for me to say, but for Ethel herself. Does she love you?"

"I do not know."

"Do you *think* she does?"

The young man's cheek flushed, but he answered steadily, "I do not think her wholly indifferent to me."

The judge smiled and held out his hand. "Ethel

is in the garden. Go to her and tell her what you have told to me, and — my best wishes for your success."

Arthur grasped the extended hand in both of his. "Thank you, sir; and may God deal with me as I do with her."

He hastened from the house, and went through beautiful shadowy paths to the place where he knew from past experience, he should find her — a rustic seat underneath the branches of a grand old oak.

She rose to meet him as she saw him coming, and then stood still before the great light on his face. How fair and pure and womanly she looked to the young man, as she stood there in her white dress, with the sunlight flickering through the branches on her sweet, upturned face, and in her truthful, serious eyes.

"The very pearl of womanhood," he thought, and went straight to her and took both her hands in his.

"I love you, Ethel. Will you be my wife?" And Ethel answered simply and gravely, with the lovely wild-rose color dyeing her white cheek, "Yes, Arthur, for I love you with all my heart."

　　*　　　*　　　*　　　*　　　*　　　*

"Oh, dear!" sighed Meg, at the dinner-table that day. "I feel so — so" —

"I pity you, my dear," said Hal, gravely. "I know what it is to feel that way myself. A disagreeable feeling, isn't it?"

Meg smiled, too spiritless to reply.

"Aren't you feeling well, dear?" inquired Elsie anxiously.

"Oh, yes; that is, I do not feel sick, only so"—

"So, so," interrupted Hal. "Well, Girlie, see if that will make you feel any better," and he tossed a dainty cream envelope beside her empty plate.

Meg picked it up listlessly, then gave a little cry of delight. "From Ethel! Oh, I do hope she will want me to come up there this afternoon—I feel just like it. Where did you get it, Hal?"

"I met that young Jake of theirs coming to the house with it, and saved him the trouble of coming any further."

Meg read the note, and looked up, smiling. "Just what I had hoped for," she said. "She *does* want me to come up this afternoon—she has something to tell me, about last night, I suppose," and Meg put the note back into the envelope, with a happy face, and handed it to her mother to read.

"But you know you promised Ruth you would go there this afternoon," said Elsie gently.

"Yes, I know; but I can start early, Ethel's dinner

hour is two, you know; I shan't want to get there until half-past three. I have *felt*, all the morning, just as if something were going to happen, but I must confess I felt as if it were going to be bad instead of good news."

At two o'clock, Meg started for Ruth's house. She wore a pale-blue cheese-cloth dress, and a large black hat with slightly rolling brim, and a wreath of yellow daises around the crown. She had a great sheaf of yellow daises over her left shoulder. A wide band of black velvet was around her white throat. She walked slowly, for the sun was hot. As she was about to enter the gate at Ruth's home, Mr. Stanley came along. He stopped to speak with her.

"How do you feel after last night's dissipation?" he asked, with his hand on the gate.

"Quite well — considering," said Meg laughingly.

"Considering the refreshments?" he added; then he went on, more gravely, "You are faithful to your promise."

"Of telling Ruth all about it? Yes."

"Remember me to Mrs. Dean and to Miss Ruth, please. I shall try to see them some time to-morrow."

Meg bowed and Mr. Stanley walked on.

"How happy he looks," thought Meg, wondering a

little; then she went up the path and knocked at the door.

Ruth opened the door, and Meg stared in astonishment at sight of the radiant eyes.

"Why, Ruthie, what is the matter? Has somebody died, and left you all their money?" she asked, as Ruth threw both arms around her neck, and fairly sobbed for joy.

"Oh, Meg, I am so happy, and so glad that you are the first one to hear of it, for you are my best earthly friend, Meg," and the excited girl hurried Meg into the sitting-room where Mrs. Dean was, and forced her gently down into a rocking-chair.

Mrs. Dean was calmer than her daughter, but Meg could see that she was feeling wonderfully happy over something. She looked from one to the other in bewilderment. Ruth laughed hysterically.

"Yes, I will tell you, dear," she said; then she burst out again. "Oh, Meg, what do you think? Madam de Crando has been here this morning, and — *hired me for next year as assistant to Miss White.*"

Meg put out both hands. *"Ruthie!"*

"Yes, Meg, she has. I am to teach Rhetoric and Language in the very school where I studied them. Doesn't it seem strange? And oh, Meg!" (here Ruth slipped down on her knees before Meg's chair and caught the white hands in hers), "it is you whom I have to thank for this great happiness; you, next to God."

"Me!" exclaimed Meg.

"Yes, you; my best, my dearest friend. I know all about the affair of the lost essay; what you did for me — and oh, everything, Meg."

"You know it all?" interrupted Meg. "How did you know it?"

"Laurie told me."

"Then Laurie did a very wrong thing," cried Meg indignantly; but Ruth stopped her.

"I suspected it, Meg, and asked Laurie if it were not so; I knew it would be of no use for me to ask 'proud Meg', for she would give me no satisfaction, and so I asked Laurie and insisted on her telling me."

"But what had that to do with madam's kindness?" asked Meg, subdued but still bewildered.

Ruth laughed and gave the hand she held a loving shake. "Where is all your wisdom, Meg? Madam must have suspected all the time just how matters were, but she did not want to create a disturbance, so she said nothing at the time, but waited until she could make it up to me in her own way. And Meg, I owe it to you, because if you had not kept silent about it, of course madam would have known who the guilty one was. It would have made her feel very badly, and, so far from being sorry that she had accused me wrongfully, she might have felt very bitterly toward me. Don't you see now, you darling — you darling?" and Ruth covered the white hands with kisses.

"I see now," said Meg smiling. "And I am very glad for you, Ruth. But — has Maude confessed to her?"

Ruth's happy face grew sad. "No," she answered. "But, Meg, I hope you do not feel bitter toward her now."

"No," replied Meg humbly. "It isn't for me to judge her."

Ruth kissed her silently.

A happy half-hour passed, and then Meg left them, her heart lighter for her visit. But as she walked slowly along, she could not help questioning madam's kindness. Would it not have been kinder in madam to have told Ruth, plainly, her motive for doing as she did? Would it not have been acting more honorably toward Ruth? Why should she wish to spare Maude's feelings? She had not considered Ruth's in the least.

"I am very much afraid," thought Meg, as she entered Judge Lawton's beautiful grounds, "that, if I were in Ruth's place, I should be tempted to decline madam's offer with thanks, and tell her that I could not think of entering an establishment as one of the faculty, where I had once been accused by its preceptress of stealing. But it is a grand chance for Ruth; I could almost find it in my heart to envy her if I were not so very glad for her. And Ruth does not look on things as I do. Why is it, I wonder? I think I know. Because she is a Christian, and I am not, though I am trying hard to be. Jesus, help me," and with this prayer on her lips, Meg looked up and saw Ethel coming to meet her. The two girls linked arms, and commenced a slow walk up and down the cool, shadowy garden-paths. Then Ethel happened to think that Meg must be tired after her long walk.

"How thoughtless I am, Girlie!" she said contritely. "Here I am walking you up and down, and you must be so tired. You look pale to-day, too — paler than usual. Aren't you feeling well?"

"Oh yes," answered Meg; "perfectly well, only I am rather tired."

"Of course you are. Come right up to my room; it is about as cool there as it is out here."

"I am always tempted to break the Commandment whenever I enter this room, Ethel," said Meg, as she followed Ethel into her exquisite little boudoir.

Ethel laughed, took Meg's hat, and placed her in the easiest chair the room afforded — a low, deep, willow rocker.

Meg heaved a sigh of deep content as she leaned back and looked around her. She had been in that room many times before; had stayed all night with Ethel on several occasions; but its beauty was ever new to her, and ever appealed to her keen sense of refinement, taste and comfort. And no wonder, for it was a perfect little gem of a room.

It was all white — the paper on the walls, the carpet on the floor, the drapery at the windows, the coverings of the easy-chairs. From where Meg sat, she could look through into a large, airy, beautifully-furnished bed-chamber, also furnished and decorated in white. The pure whiteness was relieved in the boudoir by trailing vines of the delicate-green English ivy. In the wide, deep window which projected out from the walk until it might almost be called a bow-window, Ethel had placed large pots of ferns and potted plants, with myrtle and ivy, until it looked like a veritable green bower. In the corners of the room were large pots, out of which more ivy grew, and clung with its delicate fingers all over the walls, and had even commenced to cover the ceiling. White marble busts of Shakespeare, Dickens, Hawthorne and Irving glistened through the trailing ivy, from the various corners.

"I might almost imagine myself in a grotto," thought Meg, bringing her eyes from their admiring survey of the room, to Ethel, who was watching her with a happy smile on her lips.

Meg could not help thinking, as she looked at Ethel, how perfectly she accorded with the room, with her white dress, fair face and golden hair. She was about to express her thoughts in words, when, to her surprise, Ethel left her chair, and came to her, kneeling on the floor at her side, and wrapping both arms around her.

Now, I had no idea of writing a love-story when I began, nor have I any idea of making it into one now; I am giving the facts of the case, and no more. If I put more sentiment than wisdom in it, pardon me; it is the fault of the age we live in. Yet a little sentiment now and then, has never been known to hurt anybody; it is only when it is carried to extreme that it is objectionable, and then — it but verifies the old adage — "Extremes are dangerous."

"Meg," said Ethel in a low voice, "I believe I am the happiest girl in all the world." And then she told her, softly and tenderly and reverently, as if she were speaking of something sacred, of what Arthur had said to her that morning under the spreading branches of the old oak; and Meg listened with a slowly whitening face, and a great pain gradually creeping into her heart. But Ethel had her head on Meg's shoulder, so her face was turned from hers.

"And see, Girlie," said Ethel at last, "he has given me his mother's ring. He has neither father or mother, you know."

"No, I did not know," said Meg, and she took Ethel's hand in hers, and looked long and wistfully at the pretty gold band with its one pure-white pearl.

"I hope you may be very happy, Ethel," said Meg, and kissed her.

Ethel had ordered a dainty luncheon to be served in the breakfast-room for herself and Meg. Meg sat down to it, and laughed and talked and ate, hardly knowing what she did. After that, they went for a quiet stroll in the garden, and at half-past five, Ethel had the dog-cart brought around to the door, and, despite Meg's assurance that she would just as soon walk, ordered her into it, got in herself, and they were soon rolling along the road toward Meg's home.

When about half the distance had been accomplished, a stylish phæton drawn by a span of prancing bays, passed them. Maude Leonard and a young gentleman were seated in it. Maud looked very hand-

some and stylish, but her bow of recognition was too
full of haughty condescension to suit Meg; she barely
returned it. The gentleman with Maude was fault-
lessly dressed, and the manner in which he lifted his
hat was perfection itself; but there was a dissipated
look about his handsome face that neither girl liked.
As Dell had said, "his eyes were red and his skin
flabby."

"Mr. Augustus Belmont," observed Meg, slightly
scornful.

"Yes," answered Ethel; "I was so full of my own
happiness that I did not think to tell you of Maude's.
Her mother called at our house yesterday afternoon,
and told mother that Maude and Mr. Belmont were
engaged. The wedding is set for some time in
October."

"I hope she may be happy," said Meg carelessly.

"I pray that she may," said Ethel fervently.

When Meg entered the sitting-room at home,
Laurie sprang from behind the door with a little
scream. Meg laughed.

"Laurie Ray, I am surprised! A young lady
of nineteen years, almost twenty, having such childish
actions!"

"Oh, well, Meg, I am so glad to see you; I have
been waiting here one mortal hour."

"That is too bad."

Then Meg looked over her shoulder at Laurie, as she went into the hall to hang her hat up, and said, lightly, "Have you come to tell me that you are engaged?"

The look of astonishment on Laurie's pretty face at such a question, was so comical that Meg laughed until the tears came.

"Don't look so stunned, Laurie," she said, seating herself in a chair. "I didn't know but you had. Engagements seem to be the order of the day."

"What do you mean?" asked Laurie slowly.

"Oh," replied Meg, rocking herself carelessly and smoothing down the ruffles of her dress. "I have heard of two this afternoon. And they are of two of our class-mates, too, Laurie. What do you think of that?"

If Meg had looked at Laurie, she would have been surprised at the look of actual terror on her face.

"Who are they, Meg?"

"Guess."

"I — I can't."

"Well, Maude is one. You are not surprised at that?"

"No. But, the other?" Laurie asked the question in almost a whisper.

"Ethel and Mr. Stanley."

Laurie sprang to her feet with a low cry. "Oh, no, Meg, not that; don't say that!" she cried, and burst into tears.

Meg rose slowly to her feet and looked at her. The look dried Laurie's tears at once. Meg's face was white to the lips, but full of haughty displeasure, and cold, forbidding pride. Just a moment she stood there, tall and straight, and looked at Laurie, then she sat down in her chair again, and said, easily:

"Yes, Ethel and Mr. Stanley are engaged, and I have never seen a girl so happy."

Laurie, almost frightened out of her wits at what she had said and done, answered humbly, "I am glad she is happy."

"So am I," replied Meg. "I am glad for her with all my heart."

But even when she said it, and afterward, when Laurie appeared to be ashamed of her little outburst, as though she realized that she had made a great mistake in supposing that Meg was hurt in any way by Ethel's happiness, her proud heart cried out in an agony of pain and humiliation at the thought that any one, especially little, childish Laurie, should dare to think she needed pity.

And all the time Meg knew that she did.

XX.

A VISIT.

MEG, Dell and Laurie were seated in Mrs. Randal's sitting-room, in earnest discussion. Meg had the chair of state, the large, old-fashioned, softly-cushioned "rocker". Dell sat very upright in a straight-backed chair. Laurie, as usual, on an ottoman, but so excited was she over what they were talking about, that half the time she was on the floor.

One whole hour they sat there, and when Dell and Laurie at last rose to go, Meg followed them out of the house, and even half way down the shady walk; and when she left them it was with the impressive words: "Remember, Saturday morning at ten minutes past eight — rain or shine. Sure!"

"Sure," repeated both the girls, as impressively.

This was on Wednesday afternoon. On Saturday morning, at eight o'clock, precisely, a gurney drove up to Mrs. Randal's door. It was raining, probably as hard as it ever had rained, and looked, as Meg said rather petulantly, as if it might rain forever and the

day afterward.   But for all that she was dressed for
traveling, and waiting when the gurney stopped at
the gate.   Her trunk was taken out by Hal and the
driver, and strapped in its place.   Then Meg, closely
attended by mother and sister, stepped out upon the
piazza.

Meg wore a plain, tight-fitting flannel dress — the
lovliest shade of gray.   A peasant cape of the same
color, and a pretty shirred tennis cap.   She wore a
small white vail over her face, and had her gossamer
on her arm.

"Put your gossamer on, Girlie," said Hal, clearing
the space from the gate to the piazza, in about two
steps.

He took it from her arm and wrapped it, with
loving care, about her.   Then he took her reticule,
opened his umbrella, and escorted her to the gurney
— lifted her in and sprang in after her.   In another
moment, mother and sister were straining their eyes
to catch a last glimpse of the gurney, as it was fast
disappearing from their sight in a mist of driving rain.

"What a long week it will be!" sighed the mother.

"Dreadfully long," echoed the sister.

    *   *   *   *   *   *

"Oh Meg, you darling!   I knew you would come,
but I was so afraid you wouldn't."

Hal laughed outright, and several people standing near, smiled "openly" in spite of themselves, as Laurie gave expression to her joy, fear and relief, in this rather contradictory manner. Meg laughed and returned the kiss heartily. "Let us be thankful that madam is not present, Laurie. Dell, you look most provokingly calm and undisturbed. Doesn't this storm effect you in the least?"

"Well, yes, I can't deny that it does," replied Dell, who always told the strict truth even on the smallest occasion. "I always did dislike wearing a gossamer — they wet the ankles so; but that is all that I complain of. We shan't be out in it much."

"I know it," said Meg, "but it is too bad it isn't pleasant; it will be so dull on the boat."

"Haven't you brought your book?" asked Laurie. "I have, and so has Dell."

"Yes," answered Meg; "I have brought 'John Ward, Preacher.' What have you?"

"I have 'Ester Ried'."

"And you, Dell?"

"Oh, I have 'Johnstown Horrors.' I had not decided what book to take until this morning, and then the weather decided for me. Quite appropriate, isn't it? Didn't know but we might have a flood before it got through."

Both girls laughed at Dell's choice and her reason for making such an one. Then Hal, who had gone to buy Meg's ticket and get her trunk checked, came up and asked them what they were laughing at.

"Dell is in a watery frame of mind," said Meg. "She thinks there is nothing like adaptability."

"She is referring to my choice," explained Dell, holding up her book for Hal to read its title. "Do you not think it an appropriate one?"

"Very. Have you seen hers?"—and Hal took Meg's book from under her arm and held it gravely up. "'John Ward, Preacher.' She is in a theological frame of mind which is almost as bad as that of which she accuses you. I do not know but the book may change her religious views entirely. She may come back to us a thorough Presbyterian."

"Never," said Meg firmly. "Their creed is too — too" —

"Are you quoting Oscar to us?" inquired Hal severely.

"I can't find words to express my opinion of it," finished Meg, not heeding the interruption.

"Then don't try," said Dell dryly. "You ought not to allow yourself to read such books, Meg."

"Why not?"

"Because they do you no good. It is no matter if

you do not understand the different beliefs; what do they amount to? There is but one Bible; take that for your guide and be satisfied. What do you care for different people's different opinions? Reading them up is only liable to throw you into a very undecided and dissatisfied frame of mind, which is much worse than a 'watery' one, I assure you."

"For when you are in the latter, you are supposed to be all right," laughed Meg. "Oh, Dell, you have any amount of logic, but it is all as dry as saw-dust."

"It is very good logic," said Hal seriously; "the very best kind — good, common-sense."

Just then the whistle sounded, and the girls had barely time to gather up their "traps" before the train steamed into the station. Hal kissed Meg tenderly, and said, "Be a good girl, and don't forget the postal". Then he shook hands with Dell, and then fell behind with Laurie to say his good-by to her in a low tone.

Meg and Dell hurried out together, good girls as they were, but Hal was beside them to help them into the car, and when the "all-aboard" was shouted, and the train moved slowly at first, then faster and faster, he stood on the platform and watched it out of sight.

For the first half-hour the girls talked and laughed

very quietly together, but after that they settled back
in their seats, opened their books and began to read.
Meg and Laurie found theirs very interesting, and
were very soon oblivious to everything and everybody
about them. Dell's eyes were constantly wandering
here, there and everywhere. Now she would look
dreamily out of the window at the gray, misty, rain-
drenched country through which they were passing,
an inclination probably derived from the sight of the
book she held open before her, and then she would
allow her eyes to wander carelessly around her at her
fellow-passengers.

During one of these "eye excursions" a young
gentleman, sitting two or three seats in front of her
on the opposite side of the car, happened to look up
from the paper he was reading, just as Dell was looking at him. She was looking at him, and still *not*
looking at him ; that is, she was looking at him without seeing him, for she was thinking deeply of something that had happened at home that morning before
she left, and as she thought a smile curved her lips.
The young man returned the look with interest. He
had never before beheld such a beautiful face. She
did not seem to resent his admiring gaze, but on the
contrary, judging from her continued stare, appeared
to like and encourage it. He laid aside his paper and

proceeded at once to "business". Poor, unconscious Dell was literally miles away. The young gentleman (?) assumed his most fascinating (?) manner; he leaned back in his seat easily and gracefully, and allowed a smile, half pensive, half amused, to steal over his countenance. Presently he took courage to raise his hat, hardly decided as to how the young lady would take that. Eureka! She smiled! Alas, it was to her father that the smile was really given. Without more ado, the young gent rose from his seat and skipped jauntily up the aisle. Her focus being thus abruptly removed, Dell came to herself with a little start. She looked up, surprised, to see a strange young man partly leaning over the arm of her seat, with a smile on his face. The look of surprise was so genuine, that the young man paused, hardly knowing what to do. The smile faded, and he looked — alas for him! downright foolish.

"I beg your pardon," he stammered at last, "but, did — did — I thought — did you not wish me to sit beside you?"

Dell stared at him. But Dell was not entirely ignorant of some of the follies of the age, if she had lived out of the city all her life. She determined to give the young man a little lesson.

"Is there anything the matter with the seat you

have just left?" she asked curiously, as if really thinking there might be.

He smiled a sickly smile as if to say, "Oh, of
course you are only joking."

"Is there?" repeated Dell, with the manner of one
who meant just what she says.

"No — no — not that I am aware of."

"Then I advise you to go back to it," she said,
calmly; and resumed her reading without so much as
a flicker of a smile.

Down went Meg's head into her own book, and she
laughed until the tears came; she could not help it.
Laurie tried hard not to laugh, but it was too much.
As for the young man — the way in which he went
out of that car, and made his way to the "smoker",
was a caution. Dell put the "finishing touch" to it
all, by saying — when the young man had disappeared
— "Time for refreshments," and gravely fished out
from some hidden region a bag of brambles.

When Meg and Laurie had gotten over their laughing, they commended Dell most highly on her "manner of treatment". "It is just what he deserved,"
said Meg indignantly, but always careful to speak in
a low tone. "I never heard of such impudence.
Perhaps he will not be quite so eager to indulge in
such unpardonable conduct at another time. I only

wish all such 'upstarts' would meet with like treatment in like instances."

At New Bedford they took the steamer for Cottage City. The rain still came down in torrents, but they pinned their dresses up underneath their gossamers, took their reticules under their arms, raised their umbrellas, and hurried as fast as they could in the little way they had to go.

I shall not say anything of the "sail down", for after two or three ineffectual attempts to sit on deck under the awning, and view the scenery, our girls made their way to the saloon, settled themselves in easy-chairs, and gave themselves up to the only pleasure that presented itself — reading — while the rain came pouring down, wrapping earth and sky in a thick, gray cloud.

At half-past two they reached Cottage City, the boat being over an hour late. The rain had ceased to a considerable extent, but it was foggy, cold and most disagreeably damp.

"Not much like the second of August," said Meg, as they made their way through the pushing, struggling crowd to a "son of the South," who was proclaiming in stentorian tones "that he carried luggage to all parts of the city."

"He may as well carry ours then," said Dell.

The girls decided to walk to the cottage at which they were to stop. A fifteen-minutes' walk brought them to it. It was a pretty white cottage situated on the corner of Trinity Park and Montgomery Square. Right opposite the front entrance was the Methodist Tabernacle. Around the corner and about two minutes' walk, was the Casino, in which were the Post-Office and free library. But what the girls rejoiced in most, was what they called "the little green pump". Never had water tasted so deliciously pure and cool. They were soon on the most intimate terms with "the little green pump". Three times every day, and often four and five, the three girls might be seen walking, arm in arm, in the direction of their invaluable friend.

The cottage was owned and let by a superannuated preacher and his wife — Rev. and Mrs. ——, of Cambridge — and the people stopping there were all pleasant, educated and refined; though our girls saw little of them, as they spent the evening in their own rooms. On the front and back of the house were wide piazzas, and it was on them that the girls passed some of their pleasantest hours. The street cars passed the front of the house, and there was a great deal of foot-passing. The electric lights on the Tabernacle grounds shone through the branches of the

large trees, and lighted the front piazza and the girls'
room, which opened out on a balcony facing the park
in which the Tabernacle was situated, with its beautiful, soft, moon-like radiance. Withal, it was a most
beautiful place, and our girls daily and hourly congratulated themselves on their good fortune in pro-
curing such a desirable situation. Their meals they
procured at the "B—— House," which was situated
immediately back of the cottage.

But to go back to the "night of arrival". The
girls were glad enough when they found themselves
in their pleasant, comfortable room. I am not going
to enter into details in the least, so I shall say nothing of how the room was furnished, except that there
were two beds in it, and the question as to who
should occupy one bed alone, was at once brought up,
discussed and decided upon in this wise: they would
"take turns". So far so good.

The time between three o'clock and five was given
to the transferring of dresses, etc., from their trunks
to the two clothes-presses in which the room rejoiced,
putting the bottles of camphor, glycerine, bay-rum,
eau de cologne, vaseline, etc., etc., on the wash-stand
and toilet-table. Then Meg threw herself down on
the bed with a sigh of relief.

"I'll sleep in this bed to-night, girls," she said.

"So please do not make any objections to my tossing about on it as much as I please."

"We have no objections," replied Dell, coolly possessing herself of the other. "Come up here, Laurie, and get rested."

So Laurie accordingly "came up".

"Let us map out a plan of action for our week of pleasure," suggested Meg, "beginning with to-morrow morning."

"Map out all the plans of action you please," said Dell, closing her eyes; "I'm going to sleep."

"You lazy thing!" exclaimed Meg, throwing a pillow at her, and hitting the foot-board. "If we don't plan to suit you, don't complain."

"No," murmured Dell, already half asleep; "anything will be agreeable to me."

To give the "plan of action" as it was really carried out: Every morning they arose at sunrise and took a long, pleasant walk along the shore. When they came back Meg and Dell went immediately to breakfast; Laurie went to morning prayers at the church near by. Meg and Dell loitered over their breakfast that Laurie might get back from prayers before they finished. Two or three times during the week they accompanied Laurie. After breakfast they made their beds, set their room in order, took their books or crocheting and sat out on the front piazza. Sometimes they went to the beach and watched the bathers, but never indulged in that pastime themselves. At one they went to dinner, came home and had their siesta, as Meg called it. Between three and four o'clock they took a promenade, sometimes in one place, and sometimes in another. Toward sunset they strolled along the beach again. Between six and seven o'clock they went to supper, and after that, every night, to the band concert. At ten they went to bed, and slept soundly all night.

Meg was changed. Dell did not notice it, but Laurie's loving, watchful eyes saw it, and she grieved in secret over it. Meg was restless and had spasmodic fits of gaiety followed by one of deep depression. At times she would keep Dell and Laurie in a perfect gale of laughter half an hour at a time; then, when she thought herself unobserved, she would sit quietly by herself, looking before her with sad, wistful, dreamy eyes, until, suddenly thinking her silence might be noticed, she would give expression to some ludicrous thought, and jump up and catch one of them around the waist, and waltz her madly around the room.

Thursday morning as they were sitting out on the front piazza, reading, a party of bicycle-riders passed the cottage. The girls looked up from their books, and watched them absently. There were about a dozen of them, and they presented quite a gay appearance in their gray bicycle suits and bright-red sashes.

One of the riders said something to the one beside him in a low tone. The one addressed turned his eyes toward the cottage where our girls were. The look of careless indifference gave place to one of pleased surprise, and murmuring a word or two of apology to his astonished companion, he wheeled his bicycle sharply around, and rode up to the gate.

Exclamations of a very complimentary nature escaped our three girls, as they recognized him, and hastened down the walk to meet him. "Why, Mr. Blanding, is it possible!" "Why, Mr. Blanding, how came you here?" "Why, Mr. Blanding, how glad we are to see you!" And Mr. Blanding laughed, as he raised his cap and shook hands with the girls, as if he were very glad to be there.

"I came down with the Club of which I am a member," he explained. "Did not get here until last night. We rode our machines as far as New Bedford, and then took the boat. Where were you last evening?"

"We were at the concert," answered Dell; while Meg offered him a chair on the piazza.

"Were you?" he said, as he took his seat. "I did not see you. I was riding around there, too."

"We did not walk about any," said Meg.

Then they asked about the folks at home, and he answered, "They are all well."

"I tried to get Will and Ed to run down with me," he added, looking slyly at Meg and Dell; "but they said they couldn't spare the time."

"Where are you stopping?" asked Laurie.

"At the 'Sea View'," he answered.

The girls opened their eyes at this.

"We are not going to stay later than Saturday," Ray hastened to explain with a laugh, "so we can afford to pay high board for that short time. And that reminds me, there is to be a 'Hop' at the 'Sea View' this evening. Would you like to attend? I should be very happy to have the honor of your company."

He looked at all three as he spoke. Meg's eyes shone with pleasure, Dell smiled her assent, and only Laurie looked disturbed.

"I shall be most happy," said Meg. "You are very kind."

"I should like to attend very much, thank you," said Dell.

Ray looked inquiringly at Laurie. Her face was

suffused with blushes, but her blue eyes looked steadily back at him.

"Thank you very much, Mr. Blanding," she said
in a low, trembling voice; "but I do not think I care
to go."

Ray understood and respected her reason. He
only bowed, and said kindly, "I should be very
happy to have you go, Miss Ray, but you know best."

Laurie's grateful look thanked him. As for Meg,
she felt irritably, but unreasonably, angry toward
Laurie for refusing to go with them. Does anyone
know why?

Dell took Laurie's reason calmly, as a "matter of
course". She was not at all surprised, much less
angry. Laurie was doing what she thought was
right; Dell did not consider it any of her business to
question that right. Besides, she fully understood
Laurie, as well as the rest did, and she respected her
for not doing what she thought she ought not. But
then, Dell's conscience was not troubling her, and
Meg's was; had been for the past four weeks. She
determined to drown it to-night if it were a possible
thing.

Poor Meg!

In the afternoon, great clouds came rolling up from
the West, covering the bright-blue of the sky, and

hiding the sun from sight. At six o'clock it commenced to rain — not hard, but in a most provoking,
misty, drizzling way. The girls went to supper and
came back again in their gossamers with the hoods
pulled up over their heads. At quarter past seven
Meg and Dell commenced to dress, Laurie serving as
waiting-maid. Meg spoke sharply to her now and
then — she had been very cross with her all the afternoon — but Laurie bore it meekly and patiently.
She was going to have her revenge on her after they
had gone and she was there alone. She was going to
spend the evening in prayer for Meg; she could
afford to bear with her patiently now.

"Of course we shall go in a carriage," said Meg,
standing in the door of the clothes-press, and looking
at her dresses hanging up inside; "so I shall dress as
I should have done if it had been pleasant."

"And that is?" said Dell, interrogatively, looking
up through the meshes of her long, golden hair which
she was brushing.

"In my white mull."

"Very well; so shall I."

At eight o'clock Ray came for them. The girls
wrapped their peasant-capes about them, put their lace
scarfs over their hair, and glided down the stairs.
Laurie held the lamp over the balcony railing to light

the way from the door to the carriage. Ray helped them in and away they went.

Meg was feeling feverishly unhappy. She was doing what she knew to be a weak thing. Where was all her boasted "strength of character"? Laurie had proved herself worthy, and she — Meg — was fast proving herself most unworthy. So she told herself, bitterly, as she leaned back in the carriage.

"But it is easy for Laurie to be good," she said to herself, in self-defense. "She has everything to encourage her. A lovely home, all the money she wants, a father to take care of her; and then Hal" — Here Meg found her thoughts intolerable. She sat up straight in her seat and commenced to talk vivaciously with Ray.

When Meg went into the large, brilliantly-lighted ball-room, and took her seat, she thought: "If I have been weak enough to come, I need not dance. I will surely be strong enough to resist that temptation."

So she smilingly declined Ray's request that she should dance the Lanciers with him, on the plea that she wanted to watch the others a while. So Dell went off with him instead, and Meg sat and watched the gay crowd. But when the first, clear, beautiful strains of music burst upon the air, Meg felt herself tremble all over. Her cheeks flushed, her eyes shone, her heart beat quickly Before the first figure was finished, she was almost wild to get up and take part in the intricate mazes of the dance. She kept time with the music softly with her hands and feet, and when the dance was over, and Ray led Dell to a seat beside her, Meg greeted them with, "What perfect music!"

"Isn't it?" replied Ray, unfurling Dell's fan and fanning himself and Dell with it. "The next number is a waltz. Surely you will not be content to watch that?" he asked lightly.

Meg smiled — she wasn't quite sure.

The music commenced — soft, dreamy, intoxicating — "Flowers of St. Petersburg." When had Meg ever been proof against her favorite waltz? The music entered her whole being, and took entire possession. She looked up into Ray's face bending over her, with shining eyes. He smiled and held out his hand. The next moment she had risen to her feet, his arm clasped her lightly, but firmly, and together they went swaying down the long, smooth floor.

"You are a perfect waltzer," whispered Ray, but Meg scarcely heard him.

After that until twelve o'clock, Meg did not miss one number. Ray brought up several of his "bicycle acquaintances" — all pleasant, refined, intelligent, but worldly young men — and introduced them. Meg did not have time to think, did not want to think. The gentlemen coaxed and pleaded that they would stay "just one hour longer" — "just one dance more," but the girls were inexorable. At twelve o'clock they bade them good-night, and were driven back to their cottage.

When Meg and Dell entered their room — softly, for fear of waking Laurie — they found the lamp burning dimly on the table, and beside it was Laurie's little Bible with her handkerchief put between the leaves. Meg stood looking at it for a moment, then she opened it slowly to the place where Laurie's handkerchief held it, and her eyes fell upon these words : "The Lord loveth whom He chasteneth."

Meg closed the book and stepped to the bed where Laurie lay, fast asleep. How pure and sweet and untroubled looked the pretty, flower-like face! A smile parted the pretty lips; the whole expression was one of simple trust and perfect peace. Meg turned away with an aching heart. Dell was shaking out the folds of her white dress, with a rueful face.

"We shan't be able to wear these dresses here again, Meg," she said, going into the closet to hang hers up. "They are crushed beyond redemption."

The words were thoughtless, and were thought-lessly spoken, but they went through Meg's heart like a dart. Oh, to be alone once more; to fall upon her knees and ask God to forgive her for all her bitter feelings for the past weeks; her weak, sinful yielding to temptation; her bitter complaining against her Heavenly Father's will, before she was lost "beyond redemption". Her sin looked terrible to her that night. She had dared to question God's goodness; she had dared to rebel against His righteous will.

"Father, forgive me," was the prayer she said that night, and said it many times over, before she fell into a deep, untroubled sleep. She had put herself altogether, in His strong, merciful hands; she had prayed for strength to say from the heart, "Thy will be done." She had simply "gone back" to Him — to the shelter of His dear, loving arms, and He was holding her firm and sure. After that night, the lamp of Faith burned more brightly before Meg in her path through life, driving away the mists and shadows of uncertainty and doubt, and making all clear before her.

Saturday morning found "our girls" all ready to go home. They had had a delightful time, but still they were ready to go home. Ray and his friends had made the remaining time pass very swiftly and pleasantly. They went as far as New Bedford with the girls, and then left them to make the rest of the distance home on their wheels.

The day was beautiful, clear, cool and sunshiny. The young people found comfortable seats on the upper deck and enjoyed the sail home in a degree that made up for the sail down. As the girls settled themselves in their seats in the train after bidding the gentlemen good-by, Meg looked at Laurie's pretty, unconscious face bent over her book with a loving, peaceful smile.

"Darling Laurie," she said to herself. "What a lesson you have taught me! You have taught me the meaning of that prayer, 'Lead us not into temptation.'"

XXI.

A WEDDING.

IT is the evening of the fifth of October — a most beautiful, calm, moonlight evening. The Church is brilliantly illuminated. Carriage after carriage has rolled up before the front entrance, deposited its daintily-dressed burdens, and rolled away again. The hands of the clock point to the hour of eight. Inside the closely-packed church a deep stillness has settled. A look of expectancy is expressed on every face. Fans of all colors flutter lazily to and fro. In two of the front seats sit "our girls". Every member of the "senior class" but one is there, and their dress is the graduating dress with its bunch of hyacinths. It was the wish of the bride that the "class" should attend the wedding in a body, and wearing the dress and flowers that they wore on their graduating day — four months before.

At last the low, sweet notes of the organ rise, fall and tremble on the air; then a louder burst of joyous music, as the organist breaks forth into "Beautiful Bride's Wedding March," then the Rev. Arthur Norman Stanley, accompanied by the Rev. Percy Leon Nordre, of Brooklyn, comes from the room on the left, and the handsome, faultlessly-dressed bridegroom from the room on the right. There is a little flutter, a little stir among the guests, then the doors are swung open, and down the broad aisle move the bridal party.

Maude Leonard, in her beautiful dress of cream satin, with the bridal veil falling in folds to her feet, and the crown of orange blossoms on her dark hair, makes as handsome a bride as any one might wish to see. In her hand she carries a large bouquet of orange blossoms and lilies of the valley. She is leaning on the arm of her father, and behind her walks her "maid of honor", Adele Belmont, sister of the groom. She is dressed in a short costume of white lace over primrose satin, and carries a loose bunch of yellow primroses in her hand. A small cap of white lace caught up at the side with a spray of the same flower rests on her dark curls. On her feet are dainty slippers of primrose satin. She makes a most charming "maid of honor".

The bridal party moved slowly up the aisle; the groom left the chancel and came to meet his bride;

and then, with the low, soft notes of the organ breathing out sweet music, Maude Leonard and Augustus Belmont were made man and wife.

At the beginning of the marriage service, the "class" had risen to their feet, and all through the ceremony, had stood with bowed heads. It was a "whim" of Maude's that they should do so. They had demurred against it at first among themselves, until Meg had said: "Let us do as Maude wishes. It is probably the last favor she will ever ask of any of us, and she is to leave us — in one sense of the word — forever. Let us do as she wishes." And so they had consented, and they were glad now that they had, for as they listened to the solemn words of promise, their young hearts were touched, and all felt nothing but tender love for Maude, and regret that she should so soon leave them. The first link was broken in the golden chain. But Maude had no regretful feelings; and as she moved down the aisle leaning proudly on her husband's arm, her face expressed nothing but joy and happiness.

And so she passed from among them, to enter a life of social pleasure and excitement, and from that night until years after, she was literally lost to them.

The glorious October days passed swiftly along, and glided serenely into those of dark, cloudy, foggy

November. To Meg, the time seemed to go by on wings. She had put herself — her life — entirely into the Father's care and keeping, willing to trust Him in all things, feeling sure that "He doeth all things well". And the peace and the rest that had been promised her, were slowly but surely settling down upon her.

She had one great longing and desire, and that was, "to secure a position as teacher in either a public or private school, that she might continue her study of elocution." But this, too, she had left with Him, knowing that He would make all things come to pass in His own good time. Meg was fast learning the grand lesson of Faith.

One cold, damp, misty night toward the end of November, Meg was sitting in the little kitchen, her feet in the oven, "David Copperfield" in her lap. She was fast becoming acquainted with "David", and liked him immensely well. It was the night for the "Young People's Christian Endeavor Meeting". Meg had a bad cold, and did not feel like venturing out. She played for them at the meetings now, but knew if she were not there that Dell or Lill would play. Just as she was smiling over that amusing portion where David tries to impress upon the mind of his "child-wife" the necessity of his having his meals more regularly, the door opened and Dell walked in. She had her gossamer on, and her face gleamed white under the dark hood.

"Why, Dell!" exclaimed Meg, letting her book fall into her lap, and taking her feet out of the oven. "What good fairy sent you here to-night?"

"Rather a heartless fairy, I am afraid you will think," answered Dell, sitting on the opposite side of the stove, and putting her feet up to warm. "I came to see if I could entice you out. I met Hal down street, and he told me that you were not going on account of having a bad cold, but I wanted you to be there to-night, and I have waded my way up here. It is bad walking."

Meg looked at Dell, surprised. "But why to-night, in particular, Dell?"

"Because I am going to take the first step to-night, Meg," answered Dell in a firm voice. "And I want you to be there."

Meg rose from her seat immediately and went around the stove to Dell. "And I will be there, Dell," she said, in low, glad tones, and she bent and kissed her.

That was enough. Both girls perfectly understood each other. The only thing that was said between them on the subject, was when Meg was putting her jacket on; then Dell said — not boastingly, but as if to strengthen her own determination: "There is one thing that I am sure of, Meg. I am never going to put myself in the way of temptation, as a test to my own strength and worthiness." And Meg replied, "That is where you are wise, Dell, where I was very foolish."

Ah, Meg was learning that with "her own strength she could do nothing, but with Him all things were possible."

Mrs. Randal and Elsie had already gone, so Meg blew the light out, locked the door and put the key in a corner of the back piazza.

That night more than one heart was made glad with the knowledge that three more young lives were placed in the Father's keeping. Meg was surprised when Ed Holmes and Bert Marston confessed themselves ready and anxious to do work for the Master. Mr. Stanley's prayer at the close of the meeting was full of heart felt thanks to the "Giver of all mercies". At its conclusion, he said, "All glory be to Thy Holy Name, O Christ, whose love is infinite, and whose power is unlimited."

It was a glad sight to see the young Christians taking their sisters and brothers by the hand, and welcoming them to the fold. The young pastor's face shone with a light of perfect peace and happiness, as he watched them.

Two weeks later, Mr. Stanley called on Dell. The object of his visit was to see when Dell felt as if she would be ready to unite with the Church. Her reply was — well, it was Dell's answer, and that is saying it all — "I am ready to unite with the Church at any time. I am as ready now as I should be if I waited a year."

"Will Christmas Eve suit you?" asked Mr. Stanley. "Our brothers think that would be a happy time for it."

"It will suit me perfectly well," replied Dell.

Her manner pleased Mr. Stanley exceedingly. "Such a character as hers is as admirable as it is rare," he said to himself, as he left the house, and made his way to Meg's home.

He had not talked with Meg once upon the subject of baptism. He had felt as if it would be better for him not to. He had thought that when she felt ready to unite with the Church, she would tell him so. But it had been seven months now since she had entered into the Christian life, and nothing had been said on either side about her taking the second step. Mr. Stanley had his doubts as to the advisableness of speaking to her upon the subject now, but the young pastor was a very conscientious person. He said to himself, what so many earnest, conscientious pastors say to themselves: "This may be the 'time of all times' for me to speak to her. She may be waiting and longing for it, and if, in the years to come, I were to find it out — perhaps when it is too late — I should never forgive myself for the neglected duty. I will go to her, and if my errand is fruitless, I have only to leave her in the hands of a just and generous God. He will lead her according to His own judgment."

Meg was alone when Mr. Stanley rang the bell. She opened the door for him, looked a little surprised and — did he fancy it? — it seemed that her fair face grew a little pale as she saw who her visitor was, and invited him to walk in. He talked on commonplace things at first, and he noticed for the first time, what a new expression of sweet, grave dignity was settling down on the girlish face. There was a stately, womanly air about her, too, as she moved about the room, which was very attractive.

At last Mr. Stanley introduced the object of his call. He told her that Dell, Ed and Bert were to take the step; they had expressed a desire to be taken into the church — at least, Ed and Bert had, and Dell was glad to do it at the same time. "Do

you not feel ready to come with them, Miss Meg?"
he asked, resting his kind, dark-blue eyes earnestly
upon her.

Meg listened to him silently, a pink flush tinging
her pale cheeks as she did so, and when he asked her
if she did not feel ready, she answered him by asking
him a question.

"They are to be baptized in the church, are they
not?"

"Yes," he answered, looking at her in a little
surprise.

She shook her head. "I would rather not," she
said. "When I am baptized, I want to be baptized
in the river. That seems to me to be the only right
way."

Mr. Stanley looked at her silently for a moment.
What a strange girl she was! And yet, her idea
pleased him, he hardly knew why.

"Do you think it makes any difference where you
are baptized — whether it is in open air or under cover
— so long as you obey the command, and conform to
the rules and ordinances of the church?" he asked.

"It seems to me the only right way," she repeated.
"And it is the way that our Saviour took."

He did not smile; he understood her and respected
her sense of right. He saw she was not talking

merely for the sake of argument, but because she felt
what she said. He would not urge her — he would
not try to change her mind — indeed, he knew how
fruitless such an attempt would be — he only said
as if defending the mode of baptism in his church:
"But it would hardly be prudent to be baptized in
the river at this season of the year. Do you not
think so?"

Still she shook her head with a smile. "Then I
will wait until it is pleasant. Baptism any other way
seems to me not so satisfactory. Not that I think
it is not as true as one in the river would be," she
added quickly, seeing the look of grieved surprise on
his face, "only, I could never be satisfied with it. It
is the way in which I feel, that is all. You do not
blame me?"

He smiled down into the anxious, uplifted face.
"Blame you? far from it. There is nothing to blame
you for, but much for which to respect you. Yet I
shall look forward to the time when we shall have you
safe with us. It will be some day, will it not?"

"Oh, yes," she answered eagerly, "I have fully
decided that question in my own heart. It will not
be long."

"God grant that it may not be," he answered
fervently.

Before Meg realized what she was doing, she was telling Mr. Stanley about her unhappy "test". She did not know what induced her to speak of it, but his manner was so kind and friendly — almost brotherly — that she felt an irresistible desire to tell him, and hear what he thought of it. She was almost sure he would despise her for her egotism (for that is what it looked to her now) but instead, he only laughed — yes, he actually laughed.

He said: "You relied on your own strength. You see the folly of it now?"

"Yes, oh, yes," she answered earnestly.

"Then it was perhaps the best thing for you to do, since the teaching has not been vain," he said, much to her surprise and delight.

"You really think so?"

"Yes, I really think so. If it had not been for the best and for your good, it would not have been at all. You have tested your own strength, and it has failed you. You will be glad now to lean on Him whose strength is all-sufficient."

How the words cheered Meg; she had been regretting her "folly" ever since her eyes had been opened to the light, but now she felt that it had been all for the best.

Mr. Stanley stayed an hour longer, and when he

went away, he said to himself, the same as Ethel had said weeks before, "What a Christian she will make!"

On Christmas evening at six o'clock, was a memorable time. At eight o'clock Judge Lawton's handsome parlors were the scene of friendly intercourse and happy enjoyment. Ethel was holding an informal reception. She stood in the door, dressed in a robe of admiral blue plush, made very plainly, and with a great bunch of drooping white roses against her left side.

"Our girls" were there, and "the young men belonging to us", May said laughingly to Dell. Mr. Stanley, of course, was there. There was music — vocal and instrumental — promenading through the beautiful rooms; laughter, talk and — refreshments. All the evening Meg could not keep her eyes off Ethel. She had never seen such an expression on any face in her life. So tender, so happy, so full of glad delight, yet withal so peaceful and trusting. In all the years that followed Meg only remembered Ethel's face as she saw it that night. When Mr. Stanley spoke to Ethel, or stood near where he could watch her, Meg turned her eyes away; she could not trust herself to watch the proud, tender light in the **dark-blue eyes.**

In the course of the evening, Ruth said to Meg, "Oh, Meg, I have something to tell you."

"Have you? What is it?"

"Come into the conservatory, where no one can hear us."

The two girls went into the green, softly-lighted room, fragrant with the breath of a thousand blossoms, where the fountains were tinkling, and the birds in their gilded cages were drowsily twittering. The girls stood by a deep marble basin where some goldfish were swimming. Judge Lawton's conservatory was his great pride and delight.

"It is good news for you, Meg dear," said Ruth, passing her arm around her. "At least, I think I may safely say it will be good news to you. Madam came to me this afternoon at my home, and told me that she had decided to employ some one as assistant to Prof. Weir for next term, and she wanted to know if you were engaged in any kind of employment; that is all she said, but Meg, I am positive she asked me that in the hope I would tell you, and you would apply for the position."

Ruth stopped and looked at Meg with shining eyes. Meg's fair face flushed and she drew herself up proudly.

"Don't, Meg dear," said Ruth softly.

Meg laughed, a little ashamed. "What is your opinion, Ruthie?" she asked.

"That madam is trying — in her own way, but still she is trying — to make amends to both of us. We ought not to doubt her sincerity, Meg, even if we do not exactly approve of her manner of showing it."

"She should have come to us, Ruth, in both cases," said Meg.

But for all her pride and wounded feelings, Meg felt gratefully happy. And she was trying hard not to judge others.

"Your piece of news is good, Ruthie. I will apply for the position, and if I am so fortunate as to get it, I shall be one of the happiest and most thankful of girls."

And she did apply for it that very night, before she retired to rest. She had little fear that she would not get it, for she had been Prof. Weir's pride, as well as the pride of madam and the whole school, in regard to her rare elocutionary powers. He had told her many times, that she could teach elocution as well as he, after a little experience; and this was just the chance she wanted above all others. She could continue her own lessons now, besides adding her mite to the "family fund". The latter thought was the best of all. She wanted to be able to support herself, and at the same time help her mother, and then she would be quite content. "And I shall consider myself the most ungrateful of all ungrateful mortals, if I complain of my lot then, or refuse to be happy and make others happy around me," she said to herself severely, as she at last laid her head down on her pillow and tried to sleep. But sleep did not come for a long while; not until the gray dawn came up, damp and chill.

For one long week Meg was kept in suspense; necessarily so, as she knew, for madam had gone to the home of her city relatives to spend the Christmas holidays. But almost as soon as she returned and received Meg's letter, she came herself, to answer it in person. She was very kind indeed, and Meg felt very grateful to her.

"You know," said madam, as she rose to leave, and putting both hands on Meg's shoulders, "that you were always one of my favorites, and it will be a great pleasure for me to know that I have you still with me," and she kissed Meg on both cheeks in true French fashion.

That was a great condescension on madam's part, and Meg appreciated it.

"You are very kind to me, madam," she replied earnestly. "I shall do my best to be worthy."

"I am sure that you will. And you know, Meg, that this may be but an opening to you. Who knows but in a few years at the most, you will be 'head teacher of elocution' in some of our fine city schools. I assure you Professor Weir is loud in his praises of you. He has always admired you exceedingly."

Madam looked into the clear, dark eyes as she spoke, but Meg only smiled and answered gravely, "Professor Weir is also very kind."

"He is a perfect gentleman," was madam's somewhat unexpected reply.

Then she went away, and Meg hastened to carry the "good news" to her dear ones. Of course they rejoiced with her, but Hal said rather jealously, "I wish it were possible for me to make any kind of work unnecessary for you, Girlie."

And Meg answered quickly: "I am glad it isn't, brother. It will not be work but pleasure for me, and I could never be satisfied with leading an idle life."

So Meg commenced her duties where the happiest hours of her life had been spent. It seemed very strange to think that she and Ruth, of all the girls, were back among the old scenes; but now they were there as dignified teachers, not merry, laughing pupils. It was quite a while before Meg could bear to go into the senior's parlor, but after she had become somewhat used to the idea of being there in the capacity of teacher, she found herself often going there with Ruth when "off duty", for an hour of quiet talking, studying, reading or thinking.

At these times it seemed to Meg, as she sat in "Ethel's chair" beside the fire-place, that she had suddenly grown very old and grave and dignified; she could almost imagine that the ghosts of departed class-mates entered the room at the quiet twilight hour, hovered around her for a few moments, and then disappeared. But such things could only have happened when she was in a half-somnambulistic state, for she would come to herself with a little start, and seeing Ruth in her chair on the opposite side of the fire-place with her head on her hand, and her great, dreamy eyes gazing steadily ahead of her as if trying to pierce the darkness of the dim, unknown future, Meg would laugh and say — trying to speak lightly — "Come, Ruthie, let us leave the scene of our labors, and make our way homeward — poor, forlorn sisters-in-misery that we are!"

And Ruth would answer, passing her arm around Meg's waist, "Let us rather say, 'blest sisters in happiness that we are'."

XXII.

JOY AND SORROW.

JANUARY and February passed quietly by. Meg was settling down to her "Fate in Life", as she humorously called it, with the meekest of resignations. Once when Hal rallied her on her "old-maid" existence, she drew the corners of her red mouth down, and said very pathetically, "I'm a lone born creetur', Dan'l, and everything goes contrary with me." After that Hal invariably called her "Missis Gummidge".

But Meg was growing to be quietly, contentedly happy; thankful for the goodness and mercy of her Heavenly Father.

One wild, rainy, boisterous March afternoon, Meg started to go home rather earlier than usual. To her surprise Prof. Weir expressed a desire to accompany her, giving as his reason, "that he was afraid the wind would prove too much for her." Meg, at first, thought she would refuse his company, but he seemed so anxious, that she accepted it, rather glad than otherwise to have it.

Prof. Weir was a man of some thirty-five years of age, tall, slight and fair, with kind, gray eyes, and a long, drooping mustache. He was very quiet in company, seldom giving his opinion on any subject unless it was called for, and then, as Hal expressed it, "going ahead of everything". He had been very kind indeed to Meg, making her duties as easy as possible for her, and Meg liked him very much, and respected him highly.

To-night but little was said by either, during the first part of the walk; all their thoughts and energies were given to the boisterous wind. Meg could not help thinking of that other windy, rainy night, when Mr. Stanley had walked from the corner with her. She was smiling over it rather sadly, when she suddenly became aware that her companion was talking to her in a low, earnest voice. When she had collected her thoughts sufficiently to hear what he was saying, she found, to her great astonishment and pain, that he was asking her to be his wife.

"I love you, Miss Randal, with all my heart and soul. I am thirty-five years old, and you are the first woman I have ever said that to. I will be a good husband to you; you shall have everything

it is in my power to give you.   Will you be my
wife?"

Meg's face had flushed painfully while she listened.
She would have given a great deal not to have had
this happen; for, like every good, pure-minded girl,
Meg felt far above tampering with the affections of
any man — trying to win his love, only that she might
throw it away.   Marriage seemed to her almost as
solemn a thing as death.   The idea of marrying where
she did not love with her whole heart, never entered
her head; she gave no thought to the worldly advantages such an alliance as this would bring her; she
only knew that she did not love him, and she would
not wrong him or herself by accepting his proposal.

Meg told him this as kindly and gently as she
could, and he took his disappointment like the gentleman that he was, but Meg knew, by the expression
of his face, how great the disappointment was.

If Meg had any doubts as to the sincerity of his
affection for her, those doubts were rapidly dispelled
during the days that followed.   Prof. Weir never
changed in his kind, thoughtful, gentlemanly behavior
toward her.   He made her feel perfectly at her ease,
and above all, he gave her to understand that he
realized fully how hopeless his love was; he never
troubled her with a repetition of it, and Meg apprecia-

ted his kind courtesy, and respected him with her whole heart.

* * * * * *

"The ordinance of baptism will be administered on the morning of Sunday next — Easter — at nine o'clock."

Such was the announcement made from the pulpit, by the Rev. A. N. Stanley; and as Meg heard it, a thrill of happiness passed over her, and from her heart arose the glad cry, "Praise the Lord, oh, my soul, and all that is within me, praise and bless His holy name."

Thursday evening found the vestry of the church nearly filled. There were fifty-two testimonies given. By every one the Spirit of the Lord was felt. It was a joyful meeting; there was such a blessed feeling of relationship, as if each one realized that they were all brothers and sisters in Christ — children of the same loving, all-merciful Father.

When at the last, Meg rose to give her "experience", it was very quiet. At first the beautiful voice trembled a little, then, as she forgot all else but her one great happiness, it grew strong and firm. She said:

"I think my experience can be given in a very few words. Last April I became convinced that the life

I was leading was not the right one.   I was happy —
at least, I thought I was — but I was not satisfied.
There was a longing for something that I did not
have; a feeling of unrest that I could not explain.   I
listened to a sermon preached in this place on Easter
Sunday morning, and that sermon was just what I
needed.   It explained the feeling of longing and
unrest.   I knew then that it was the Saviour I
wanted.   He had said, 'Come unto me, and I will
give you rest.'   'Though your sins be as scarlet, I
will make them like wool.'   I went to Him, and He
did give me rest.   I asked Him to forgive me my
sins, and He has forgiven them.   The love I have for
Him in my heart for His great mercy, is unspeakable.
If I were to devote all the years of my life to His service, I could not begin to pay Him the debt I owe.
It is impossible for me to express the great happiness
I feel — to know that all my sins have been forgiven,
washed away by the blood of the Lamb.   I have never
felt ready to unite with any church until now.   I
wanted to be sure of myself, I am sure of myself now.
I want to be baptized.   I feel sure that it is not only
my duty to do so, but that I shall not be perfectly
happy until I am.   Then I shall feel as if I am, in
reality, one of His children."

Easter Sunday was one of the most beautiful days

that ever dawned. The morning was perfect. It seemed as if it could not have been pleasanter. The sky was of the lovliest, most delicate shade of blue; not a cloud was to be seen. The sun shone brightly, the air was clear and warm. As Meg was driven through the quiet streets that led to the river, not a sound disturbed the Sabbath stillness, but the singing of the birds in the trees, until the carriage entered the great gate that opened into the beautiful grove; then the low hum of voices was heard from the crowd of people congregated under the trees, and on the banks of the river.

The place of baptism was the most beautiful spot in that section of the country. The river lay between two groves. On one side nothing was to be seen but green banks and giant trees; on the other, the land rose higher, and among the trees, down near the water's edge, were several huge rocks. At one end the river wound itself around shelving banks, and between small, bush-covered islands, as far as the eye could reach; at the other it disappeared under an old, gray, moss-grown arch of stone, which helped to form what was called the " stone-bridge ". People stood on both banks of the river, and on the bridge. Some stood in groups, others stood by themselves, or leaned carelessly against the trunk of a tree, while others sat on the rocks. There was not one thing to mar the beauty of the scene, and all observed perfect order.

The choir, consisting of "our girls", with Will, Ed, Bert and Melvin, were already in their places when the carriage containing Meg, Mrs. Randal, Hal and Mr. Stanley, entered the grove. They took their places at the water's edge, and then a solemn stillness settled over everything. Meg was not dressed in white; she wore one of the baptismal robes. The deep black made her face look like marble. People looked at her anxiously, and asked each other if she were going to faint.

Meg could hardly realize that "our young sister", who was the burden of Mr. Stanley's prayer as he stood at the water's edge, was really herself; it seemed too good to be true. The first hymn that Meg had chosen was, "Just as I am, without one plea." Oh, how they sung it! At first Meg stood with her eyes cast down, but before the second line was finished, she lifted her face to the blue sky, and sang with them out of the very fullness of her heart. At the words, "O, Lamb of God, I come," she threw aside the long cloak that covered her robe, and stepped down to where Mr. Stanley was waiting for her, hardly feeling the strong clasp of Hal's hand on hers as he led her down.

It was the supreme hour of Meg's life. Never could she forget the feeling of joy and happiness, rest and peace, that she realized as she was led out, firmly and tenderly, to a spot underneath an overhanging branch of a huge oak.

> "Just as I am, and waiting not,
> To rid myself of one dark blot."

For months and years afterward, whenever Meg heard that hymn, she seemed to feel again the baptismal waters close over her; the deep, blessed feeling of rest and peace, joy and happiness. She said once, "If I were ever tempted to go astray, and I should hear that hymn — either played or sung — it would save me."

Not for all the wealth of the world, would she have parted with the memory of that hour. It was, verily, "a foretaste of heaven below" to her. The choir of youthful voices seemed to her like the angelic choir of heaven. Oh, no; she would part with anything else, but never with that blessed memory, for she knew then, what was meant by "true happiness".

As it happened, Easter Sunday was also Communion Sunday, so Meg received the right hand of fellowship and partook of the "Sacrament" on the same day.

Ethel was not at the evening service, and Mr. Stanley looked very grave. As Meg gave him her hand on her way out of the church, he said: "Would you mind walking with me to Ethel's? She is not feeling well, and wanted me to bring you to her after service, if you would go."

"Yes, certainly I will go," replied Meg quickly.

She had no time to say anything further to him just then, as Mr. Stanley was obliged to turn to the others, so she stepped inside a pew and waited for him. After all had passed out, Mr. Stanley put on his light overcoat, took his hat, and they went out together.

He was very quiet, and looked very grave. Meg did not ask him any question until they had entered the avenue that led to Judge Lawton's house, and then she said:

"Ethel is not very ill, I hope?"

Mr. Stanley roused himself with a start. "I beg your pardon, Miss Meg," he said. "I have been very thoughtless. I was thinking so deeply, and — I do feel very anxious. Forgive me. No, Ethel is not very ill, but she is very weak and tired."

"She must feel quite badly, or she would have been at church."

"Yes."

Meg felt very anxious. Mr. Stanley seemed so very quiet and grave, and he looked pale.

When they reached the house, Meg did not wait to be announced, but went directly to the family sitting-room. Judge Lawton and his wife were both there, their chairs drawn close up beside the sofa on which Ethel was lying. They greeted Meg kindly — she had always been a favorite there — and made room for her beside Ethel. Meg almost cried when she looked at Ethel.

Ethel's face looked like wax as it lay on the crimson pillow. Her eyes were large and bright, and she breathed quick and short. Meg went up to her, bent over and kissed her. Ethel smiled her usual sweet smile and seemed glad to see her. She held Meg's head down a moment while she whispered, "Thank God for this day, Girlie.

Meg whispered back, "I am so happy, Ethel!"

Mr. Stanley came up and took his betrothed's hand in his. "How are you feeling, Ethel?" he asked.

"Much better, Arthur," she answered, smiling lovingly up into his eyes.

He seated himself beside her, still holding her hand in his. He hardly removed his eyes from her face all the time they were there, and her fingers clung to his like a child's to its father's. She did not talk much, but she listened to the others. Her eyes rested often on Meg's face with a wistful look.

When Meg rose to go, she thought Ethel looking quite well — better than she had seen her for a long while. Her eyes were bright, her lips scarlet, and there was a red spot on each cheek. She said this to Mr. Stanley as they were walking home together. To her surprise he did not share in her relief, but, on the contrary, looked graver than before.

"She is in her Heavenly Father's care, Miss Meg," he said reverently. "I am content to leave her there; I can trust him."

During the days that followed Ethel seemed to grow frailer and weaker. Her loving parents, almost wild with anxiety, took her away with them to some rambling old farm-house in a quiet part of the country. They went on the twenty-fifth of April. The wedding had been already set for the twelfth of June, just one year from Graduating Day, but the preparations had been stopped when Ethel had become too weak to give any attention to them.

Ethel had preferred to have a quiet home-wedding. Only about fifty invitations were to be sent out. Meg was to be "maid of honor", and the dainty white lace dress, furnished by the bride, was already completed, as were also the pretty cap and slippers.

While Ethel was away, Meg went about her daily work with always this prayer in her heart and often on her lips: "Dear Father, spare her; do not take her from us."

It seemed as if she had never loved Ethel half so well as she did now.

Mr. Stanley was with Ethel two days of every week, and he always reported her condition first to Meg on his return.

The family had been away three weeks. It was now the middle of May; Meg had spent an unusually restless day at the school, and immediately after lessons, had put on her things and gone home. It was the day for Mr. Stanley to come from Ethel, but he would not get to L—— until half-past seven, and it was now but little after four. But when at home, Meg could not settle down to any work, but wandered from room to room, taking up a book only to lay it down again; catching up a piece of fancy-work and throwing it again to one side; now looking out of this window, now out of that, until Elsie said:

"Put on your hat, dear, and take a walk to Dell's; the air will do you good."

"I believe I will," replied Meg.

She ran up to her room to smooth her hair. On her way past the window she looked out. A well-

known form was coming quickly up the street. Meg
held her breath as she watched it. It was Mr. Stanley. He was walking rapidly and looking eagerly up
at the windows as he approached. For a moment
Meg stood rooted to the spot; something must have
happened to send him home at that hour. What
could it be?

Meg could not tell how she ever reached the door,
but she turned and ran out of the room, and down the
stairs, opened the front door and ran down the walk
with both hands stretched pityingly out, and a very
white face.

But Mr. Stanley's face was radiant with happiness;
his dark-blue eyes shone with a glad light. He
grasped the extended hand in both of his, and said,
joyously:

"Oh, Meg, our darling is spared to us!"

The revulsion of feeling was so great, that Meg
clung to him, laughing and crying alternately. He
soothed her as if she had been a baby, and when she
was quiet once more, he told her all the glad news.

For the last week Ethel had surprised them all by
growing rapidly better. The doctors had told them
that they need have no further fear for her, only she
must be kept from any violent excitement. This was
a comparatively easy thing for them to do, as Ethel

was not at all of an excitable nature. Mr. Stanley
had left her perfectly happy and very cheerful, and
still determined not to postpone her wedding-day, as
the doctors had at first advised her to.

"She is just a little superstitious about it," said Mr.
Stanley with a fond, loving smile. "She does not like
to postpone our wedding—any more than I do," he
added laughingly.

He was in high spirits, which seemed a strange
thing for him. "They are coming home on Saturday," he continued; "and that will give them about
two weeks in which to finish arrangements! O
Meg," he added earnestly, "how good God is!" Meg
could not answer him; the tears choked her voice;
she only bowed her head silently.

This was on Thursday. On Saturday afternoon at
four o'clock, "our girls" and "young men" were all
assembled at the station to welcome Ethel on her
return. And a hearty welcome indeed it was! They
had time only to press her hand, and bid her "welcome home", before she was assisted into her carriage and driven away; for she was a little tired with
her journey. But the dear face smiled lovingly back
to them from the carriage window, and the white hand
waved to them until the carriage passed out of sight.

"She looks better than I ever remember of seeing

her," observed Melvin, as the young people walked slowly home together.

"She looks better than I have seen her look for a long while," said Dell. "There is a healthier color in her face than I have seen there for a good many weeks."

"Of what are you thinking, Meg?" asked Ruth.

Meg turned an earnest face toward them. "I was thinking of Mr. Stanley's words to me on the day he brought the glad news home. They found an echo in my heart then and it has been there ever since. To-day I feel it more than ever—'Isn't God good!'"

They were silent — their hearts too full to speak; but it seemed to them all, that the burden of every song the birds were singing, of every sigh of the wind among the branches, of every rustle of grass by the roadside, was an echo of the words that Meg had spoken — "Isn't God good."

*   *   *   *   *   *

It is the afternoon before Ethel's wedding-day. All the girls have been to see Ethel, and look at the beautifully-decorated rooms. Ethel wanted to have all her young friends about her on this last day of her happy girlhood — the girls to spend the afternoon with her, and the gentlemen to come in the evening — but her mother was afraid it would tire her too much, and Mr. Stanley, too, objected to it for the same reason; so she had only had the girls there for an hour or so of pleasant talk, and had a nice little tea of strawberries and cream, cake and lemonade served for them on the side piazza, and then they had gone into the parlors and admired the decorations.

Let us look in upon them before they leave, and listen to their talk.

"And this is where you are going to stand, Ethel?" asked May, starting forward as if to pass through the gates of flowers, and take her stand beneath the great marriage-bell; but Meg pulled her back.

"Don't pass through, May," she said. "No one must stand there but Ethel."

Ethel laughed. She was leaning back in an easy-chair, watching her friends with loving eyes.

"Are you superstitious, Girlie?" she asked.

"No," answered Meg, "only fanciful."

The marriage-bell was of solid white clove pinks; the gates — one of which was ajar, the other closed — were of roses, pink and white. Their perfume filled all that part of the large house. In the background was a bank of moss, over which were scattered sprays of lilies of the valley and pink and white hyacinths. It was a beautiful sight.

"And you are going to open the gate for the bride

and groom to pass through, are you, Meg?" asked Dell.

"Let us see you do it now," cried May, "and Laurie and I will represent Mr. Stanley and Ethel," and the merry girl drew Laurie's hand within her arm, and assumed a very solemn expression of countenance, but there was no smile on Meg's face.

"I would rather not, May," she replied, gravely.

"How sober you look, Meg," said Dell, "anybody would think it was to be a funeral instead of a wedding. Ethel, you must order us all out of these rooms, or May will be asking us to go through with the marriage ceremony next."

"Well, and if I should," said May, forlornly, "you wouldn't have the heart to blame me. It is the only way I ever expect to go through with it."

The girls laughed, and Dell said:

"May is quite reconciled to her fate; she has decided in her own mind that she is to be the 'old maid' of the class."

Much laughter and merry talk followed, and then the girls bade Ethel "good-by until to-morrow", kissing her lovingly as they did so.

"What a happy girl I am!" said Ethel, as she returned their caresses. "And fortunate, too, in possessing such friends."

Meg stayed behind, by Ethel's request. At six o'clock Mr. Stanley came for his "last call" until to-morrow, when he would come, never to leave her again until "Death should them part".

"Arthur," said Ethel, "I have been asking Girlie if she would not like to see me in my wedding-dress to-night, and she has positively forbidden me putting it on. What do you say? Wouldn't you like to see us both dressed up in our 'snowy costumes'?"

Never had Meg seen Ethel so merry! And never had she seen her look so well and happy! Somehow it made Meg's heart ache to watch her.

Mr. Stanley sprang to his feet eagerly. "Oh, if you only would, Ethel!" he said.

That was enough. Ethel turned her face, flushed and glowing, to Meg. "Do you hear that, Girlie? Come."

She held out her hand, and Meg rose with a little smile. "You are commencing to spoil her so soon, Mr. Stanley," she said reproachfully.

Mr. Stanley laughed — such a happy laugh — and took up a book to read while he was waiting for them.

In half an hour they came back. Meg's dress was white lace over pink silk. Her flowers were pink hyacinths. She looked lovely, and Mr. Stanley told

her so, openly and heartily; then he turned to look
at his bride.

Ethel's dress was an ivory white silk.   Her wreath
was of orange blossoms, her bouquet of orange blossoms and white hyacinths.   Her fair hair gleamed
like gold underneath the misty bridal veil of costly
lace; her blue eyes shone softly; her lips were like a
scarlet line; a lovely pink color was in her cheeks.
Mr. Stanley looked at her long and earnestly, and
then, oblivious of Meg's presence, he took her in his
arms, and held her close to him.

"My wife," he whispered.

*   *   *   *   *   *

At nine o'clock the next morning, as Meg was
dusting her room, her mother called to her from the
foot of the stairs, "Meg, come down."

Meg dropped her duster, and ran down the stairs;
something in her mother's voice had startled her.
When she entered the sitting-room, Hal came to meet
her with a white face.   Elsie was crying.

"Oh, Girlie," said Hal, with a great sob in his
voice, "Ethel is"—

"Not dead!" screamed Meg.

"No, not dead, dear, but dying."

Meg pushed him away from her with both hands.
"What do you mean, Hal?" she cried.   "Ethel can-

not be dying — she isn't dying. How wicked in you to try to frighten me so."

"I am not trying to frighten you, dear," said Hal. "It is true; and she has sent for you to come to her."

Meg stood still and looked first at one and then at the other. Ethel dying! Impossible! She had never seemed so well as she had last night when Meg had left her.

Hal went up to his sister, and touched her gently. "Don't look like that, dear. It is all for the best."

"How was it, Hal? Tell me," she asked him pitifully.

"She was taken suddenly ill this morning with hemorrhage; there is no hope for her. But she is conscious, and wants to see you. Won't you come, Girlie?"

Meg shivered. "Yes, I will come. But," she added with a little passionate cry, "don't call me that, brother. I cannot bear to hear it. Oh, Ethel, my darling, my darling!"

At the avenue gates Hal stooped and looked anxiously at Meg. "I think I will not go in, dear," he said.

He was going to ask her if she felt that she was sufficiently self-controlled to see Ethel, but the expression of her face answered him better than words could have done. It was as white as snow, but perfectly calm.

Hal kissed her tenderly and left her. Meg entered the great, silent house alone. Oh, what a difference from yesterday !

As she passed the parlor doors, a sweet, delicate perfume floated past her. It was the scent of the roses, pinks and hyacinths. Meg ran through the hall and up the stairs ; she could not bear the sweet, heavy perfume.

At Ethel's door she stopped, for she heard Ethel's voice, weak but clear. She was pleading with some one, tenderly and earnestly. Meg heard her say, "Promise me," then a heavy sob, and she knew it was with her father that Ethel was pleading.

Meg turned away, and leaned her head against the wall. In a few moments the door was opened and Judge Lawton came out, sobbing like a child, and leaning heavily on his wife's shoulder. Neither of them saw Meg — their eyes were blinded by their tears.

They passed down the stairs, and entered the library, and then a large, stout man came out of Ethel's room, whom Meg at once recognized as the great Dr. L—— of B——. He was wiping his eyes on his handkerchief, but he caught sight of Meg and went to her at once.

"Are you Miss Randal?" he asked.

Meg bowed.

"She is waiting for you. You had better go right in."

He opened the door as he spoke, and Meg passed into the room.

Ethel was lying on the bed, her face as white as the pillow on which it rested, her fair hair surrounding it like a golden cloud. She smiled when she saw Meg and held out a white hand. Meg had to bend her head to hear what she said.

"Girlie, I have only a few words to say to you: I am very tired, and it — is — almost — time — for — me — to — go; but never — forget — what — I — say, will — you?"

"I never will, Ethel."

"Thank you, dear; I have always loved you very dearly, Girlie. You have seemed like a sister to me, I am going away from you all, but it will only be for a little while. We shall meet again. Girlie, will you promise me one thing?"

"I will promise you anything, Ethel."

"Will you take up my work where I leave off, and go on with it for me — my religious work, I mean?"

Meg did not falter for a second.   "I will do what I can, Ethel, I promise you."

"Thank you, Girlie."

Ethel was quiet for a few moments, then she said: "Kiss me now, Girlie, but do not leave me.   Give my last love to the girls — and tell — them — we — shall — meet — again — up — there."

Meg kissed the white face lingeringly and lovingly, and when she raised her head Mr. Stanley had entered the room, and was standing at the bedside.   His face was white and drawn with suffering, and his blue eyes dark with pain.   He bent over Ethel in speechless grief, and Meg slipped from her place beside the pillow and stole softly to the window.   She would have left the room, but Ethel asked her not to.

Meg never forgot that scene.   It didn't seem as if Ethel were dying; she and Arthur talked together as if it were a parting for a few days or weeks at most.   Meg did not know what a restraint Arthur was putting upon his feelings, that he might talk to Ethel quietly and calmly.   A feeling of awe stole over Meg as she listened to the low voices.   Ethel put up her hand now and then, and brushed the heavy, dark hair away from Arthur's forehead, and he smiled down into the large, blue eyes tenderly and lovingly.

"I am going, Arthur, but — it — won't — be — for

—long; only—just a little—while—before. I will—wait—for—you—and—watch for you. You—will—come—soon, Arthur?"

"Yes, my darling; when I have finished the work He has set for me to do here."

She gazed up into his face with yearning eyes, and the first cry broke from her lips. "Oh, Arthur, how can I leave you!"

Meg crept from the room, unable longer to bare the sight. Ethel did not see her go; she saw only the face bending over her, unutterable love and anguish in the dark-blue eyes. It was his turn to soothe her.

"It is only for a little while, my darling—my wife."

A look of ineffable joy passed over her face as he called her by that dear name; then her face grew suddenly gray—the shade of death was passing quickly over it. Arthur saw it, and clasped his arms tightly around her as if to hold her from the cruel grasp of Death, but she only smiled sweetly up at him. Ethel was dying the death, as she had lived the life, of a Christian.

"Only—a little—while—before," she whispered dreamily. "Then—no—more—parting,—Ar"—

The word died on her lips. She turned her head

slowly until her cheek rested against his; and thus, lying upon his breast, she fell asleep.

* * * * * *

Meg was lying on her bed. She had cried until she could cry no more. It was early twilight of the day on which she had looked for the last time here below on Ethel's fair, lovely face. It seemed so sad, so sad! Sadder than anything she had ever heard or even read of. To die on her wedding-day, and just one year from the day on which they had all sat together in the dear "study", the day before graduating day, and talked together lovingly and earnestly, and sung the "Class Song" with clasped hands.

The second link in the golden chain was broken. The "class" had stood together around the open casket at the grave, and as they sang sadly and tearfully, "Asleep in Jesus, blessed sleep," dropped each a white hyacinth (Ethel's favorite flower) on the lovely form.

How beautiful Ethel had looked! She was dressed in her wedding-dress — veil, wreath and all. During the service at the house, the casket had stood between the rose-covered gates, through which she should have passed, a breathing, happy bride.

Mr. Stanley's grief had been something terrible in its speechless, unnatural calm, but no one had dared

to offer a word of comfort. They knew he was seeking and would find comfort from the only true source,
that of the all-seeing, all-wise and all-merciful Father.
With Him let us leave him, trying to say with submissive resignation, "The Lord gave and the Lord
taketh away. Blessed be the name of the Lord."

> "Asleep in Jesus, blessed sleep!
> From which none ever wake to weep.
> A calm and undisturbed repose
> Unbroken by the least of woes."

XXIII.

AT REST.

ONE year later.   The Randal family are gathered
around   their   tea-table — Mrs.   Randal,   Elsie,
Hal and Meg.   One other is there, too; a small,
slender, black-robed form — a pretty, pale face from
which all the roses are fled, leaving only lilies there —
and fluffy, golden hair.   The large blue eyes are sad
and wistful, but the expression of the sweet face is
one of patient suffering and undying trust.

Laurie, doubly orphaned, has found a peaceful
home here.

Six months before on the twenty-seventh of Decem-
ber, Mr. and Mrs. Ray had started on a trip to Boston, to visit a sister of Mrs. Ray's who had been taken
suddenly ill.   Laurie was to stay with Meg while
they were gone, and a happy time they had planned
to have.   Laurie will never forget how she stood on
the old stone porch and kissed her father and mother
good-by.   Ah, not one of them thought it was the
last "good-by" on earth.

Mrs. Ray had been very loth to leave her one "little ewe lamb" for even so short a time as two weeks, and she had held her to her closely and lovingly while she gave her her last injunctions with a kiss between every word. But father Ray had patted Laurie's golden head, and said soothingly :

"It won't be for long, mother, that we will leave her, and we know she is safe at all times. We have no need to fear."

And Laurie had sent them away with laughing promises "to be a good girl, and not drive Mrs. Randal quite crazy".

"If you *have* her *son*," interposed father Ray slyly ; whereat Laurie had gathered up some snow in her hands and thrown it at him, and he had dodged it, and so, laughing and looking at their darling over their shoulder, the father and mother had gone away ; gone away from her, never to return.

Laurie attended to the few duties that remained for her to do, then put on her wraps, locked up the house, and went to Meg's. It was the Christmas holidays, so Meg would be at home during the two weeks that Laurie was with them.

The two weeks passed rapidly and gaily by. Then came a letter from Laurie's father and mother, telling Laurie that she might expect them home on Thursday. This was on Wednesday morning. That afternoon Laurie and Meg went to the old stone house, made fires, dusted rooms, and did some really fine cooking.

Thursday just before lamplight, they sat in the large, dusky kitchen, each one at a window, and waited for the sound of the sleigh-bells that would announce the dear ones coming. It had commenced to snow — great, white flakes that floated lazily and noiselessly down from the gray clouds. Laurie got up and went to the mantle for a lamp.

"I'll put a light in the window, Meg," she said, "and they'll see it way down the road."

Ah, Laurie, even then their eyes were being dazzled by a light brighter than the noon-day.

The two girls sat and waited, hardly realizing how swiftly the time was passing. The table stood ready, the fire burned brightly on the hearth, the tea-kettle sang cheerily on the hob; eight o'clock sounded — muffled and made indistinct by the rising storm. Both girls started to their feet.

"Eight o'clock! What can be the matter, Meg."

"I don't know," replied Meg with a pale face.

She had had one of her "presentiments of coming misfortune" that forenoon, but she had said nothing about it, partly because she did not want to cause

Laurie any uneasiness, and partly because she had determined in her own mind, not to have any further faith in these "presentiments"; but now she could not help thinking of it, and her heart sank as she did so.

"I haven't heard the train come in, have you, Meg?" said Laurie, pressing her face against the window-pane, and putting her hands up that she might see out.

"No," answered Meg, doing the same thing, though hardly realizing what she did. "But it may have come, and we not have heard it."

"Yes; but it is due at half-past six, and here it is after eight."

"But, Laurie," said Meg soothingly, "it may have been delayed at the other end of the line. We might take a walk to the station; I suppose John would stay there with the sleigh until the train came, if he waited all night."

Laurie smiled feebly at the jest.

"Come, dear," continued Meg cheerfully, "we are not afraid of a little snow, and any kind of truth is better than suspense."

Laurie turned away from the window, and went obediently to the entry for her hat and jacket. Just **then the sound** of bells, close to the house, fell on their ears. Meg started for the door, but before she could get there, Laurie had run swiftly past her, and when Meg reached the porch, was half way to the gate — a small, slender figure with the snow-flakes falling upon it.

There were two persons in the sleigh — two men. One of them sprang from it before it stopped, and reached the small figure at a bound. It was Hal. He put his arm around her, and half led, half carried her into the house. He did not speak until all three stood in the kitchen. Meg looked into his face anxiously, as the light of the lamp fell upon it, and her heart beat quickly at the whiteness of it — the look of tender love and pity in the blue eyes as they rested upon Laurie.

Hal was hoping to have seen Meg alone first, but Laurie was there, and must be told. After all, perhaps it was better for her to hear it from him. She looked up into his face — her own was as white as the snow falling outside, but Meg's eyes could not have been raised more bravely, more courageously.

"What is it, Hal?" she asked, her voice low but firm. "Tell me; do not be afraid."

Hal's eyes filled as he looked at her. "Oh, my darling, if I could only bear it for you!" That was all he said.

"Is it papa?" she asked quietly.

Meg looked at her in surprise; she had expected a storm of tears.

Hal nodded. "Poor mama!" she said pityingly. "Where is she, Hal?"

Oh, how could he tell her!

"Where is mama, Hal?" she repeated.

"She is with him, darling."

"Yes, of course, but — where are they?"

"They are both in heaven, dear Laurie; don't "—

Both Hal and Meg sprang forward to catch the swaying little form, but she steadied herself in a moment, and held them back. Oh, how white the small face was! How full of terror the large, blue eyes! The watching eyes filled, and the loving hearts ached for her.

"It is God's will, Laurie," said Hal, longing to comfort her and hardly knowing how.

"Yes, I know. Tell me all about it, I am strong."

Not one word could Meg say. She could only hold one of the small hands closely in hers, and keep her eyes on the white face.

There had been an accident half way up the line to Boston. The accident had occurred about half-past five, an hour before the train was due. Hal had heard of it while at his office, and gone directly to the

station. He had taken the seven o'clock train out
to make sure of everything before alarming Laurie.
The train had stopped a few yards away from the
place of accident. The engine to the ill-fated train
lay over on its side like a huge, tired-out monster;
the first and second cars were a mass of ruins; people
were hurrying to and fro, lifting a timber here, mov-
ing a seat there, the lanterns they carried gleaming
through the falling snow like great fire-flies. Groans
and screams were heard as bodies were tenderly
lifted and carried to some place of shelter; but
alas, from some carefully-lifted bodies no screams or
groans came — they were far beyond all such signs of
suffering.

Hal went to work at once, helping to remove the
debris, and to carry the dead and wounded, and all the
time he was looking keenly about him. Before looking into each face he turned to the light of the lantern,
he closed his eyes and murmured this prayer: "Oh,
God, be merciful. Spare my darling."

But at last he came to two forms lying still and
motionless under one of the heavy iron seats — their
faces pressed close together, hand clasped in hand.
When Hal saw them thus, he knew who they were
before looking into their faces. He sank on his knees
and buried his face in his hands. "God help her,"

he moaned. But when he turned the faces toward him, he could not find it in his heart to grieve for them; so peaceful, so restful, so supremely happy they looked. "Gone home together," he thought. "What a blessed thing for them, but what a terrible thing for her!"

Hal and Meg looked with wondering eyes at Laurie, as she listened to what Hal told her. No violent burst of weeping, no cries, no lamentations, only a deathly face and large, wide-open eyes. When he finished, she bowed her head, and they knew she was praying.

Meg longed to comfort her, but she could find no words to say to her. All that long night she held her in her arms, but not one word passed between them.

The next morning the bodies were brought to the old stone house, and laid side by side in the large, dim, dusky parlor. Laurie crept in after them, the people closed the door and left her there, alone with her dead, and with her God.

Meg stayed away from her a whole hour, and then could bear it no longer. She started to go to the parlor and met Laurie on the threshold coming out. An expression of peace rested on the small, pale face, looking so wan and drawn after the night's suffering, and the blue eyes were filled with a tranquil light. The loving words of pity on Meg's lips died away as she looked.   Laurie put her hand in hers.

"Whom He loveth, He chasteneth, Meg," was all she said; but at the words, all Meg's pride and self-esteem passed away like mist before the sun — passed away, never to return, and gave place to a sense of unworthiness and deep humility, which she had never felt before.   She had murmured against the will of Almighty God, and what had her suffering been compared with Laurie's?   Mr. Stanley's words of prophecy had come true.   Laurie had proven herself the stronger of the two.   Meg felt humbled and ashamed. She felt that between herself and Laurie there could be no comparison.   Hereafter Laurie was the one to be "looked up" to, not herself.

After the funeral Meg had taken Laurie home with her, and there she had remained ever since.   Her father had left her with money enough to make her independent all her life; she need never be obliged to do any kind of work.   The old stone house, with its handsome, heavy furniture, was her own.   At first she had thought of having some good, middle-aged woman to live with her as a companion and house-keeper, but she could not bear, just now, to stay in the house where all her happy, careless, untroubled girlhood had been spent. Many homes were open to her. Judge Lawton and his wife entreated her to make her home with them, but she refused them all, gently and gratefully, and went home with Meg. But, on one condition only, would she live with them: "that they would accept a remuneration from her." In vain Meg proudly refused it. Laurie was proud, too, and remained firm.

"But you are the same as my sister, Laurie. I love you as I do Elsie; and you will be my sister in reality some day," Meg said, as a last argumentation.

Laurie had smiled and blushed, but still remained firm, and Meg was obliged to succomb.

She had been with them now six months, and Meg loved and respected her more and more every day. She was learning from her — Meg was learning from Laurie — the grand lesson of faith and submission to His will; learning to bear with patience the little trials and cares and disappointments of every-day life.

To-night as they sit around the tea-table, each face reflects the peaceful happiness that each one feels. Laurie has never troubled them with any outward display of grief. Sad she has looked many times, but never sullen and fretful; never has complained of "the hard way in which God had dealt with her".

"It seems a long time to look forward to," Meg is saying, "but it will soon pass. You must not be so selfish, Hal; we cannot spare her yet."

Hal looked across the table at the pretty, blushing face of his "fianceè". To Hal, Laurie seemed but little lower than the angels. He had always loved her — ever since she was a little child — but her life, as he had seen it daily for the last six months, had deepened his love into almost adoration.

"And I cannot live without her any longer," he replied to Meg's last remark.

"What a boy! Aren't you living with her now?" asked Meg a little scornfully.

"Yes, but I want her all to myself."

Meg looked at him pityingly for a moment, then said, sententiously: "You cannot help it, poor thing! It is the nature of your sex."

"What is?" asked Hal.

"Selfishness," replied Meg dryly.

Laurie laughed. "You shall not call my boy names, Meg," she said.

Meg dropped her fork and leaned back in her chair. "Enough," she said. "You are both beyond any help from me."

"After all," said Elsie in her low, quiet voice, "it is just as Laurie says."

Hal looked at her with a bright smile. "Rightly said, sister. It shall be as Laurie says."

Laurie looked down on her plate, and did not speak. The discussion was upon her marriage with Hal. Hal was urging her to be married in October. Although it would only be nine months since her parent's death, yet he, as well as his mother and Elsie — yes, and Laurie too — did not think that need make any difference. She was alone; she was engaged to Hal; her parents had long looked on him as their son, and the husband of their child. They had given their consent to the engagement freely and gladly. Laurie knew that if they were there to tell her what to do, they would tell her to comply with Hal's request; to do what she, herself, had really decided upon doing.

Mrs. Randal and Elsie approved of it, fully, though they were in no hurry to lose Laurie. Meg, alone, opposed it; but the only reason why she did so, as they all knew, was because she could not bear the thought of having Laurie go from them. She loved her with her whole heart; loved her for her own invaluable little self, and for the many lessons that she had been unconsciously teaching her. And Laurie returned her love in full — when had she ever done anything else but love her? — and dreaded to leave her as much as Meg dreaded to have her go. She hesitated to answer Hal now, because she knew that in so doing, she would pain Meg.

"Well, Laurie?"

It was Hal who spoke. He was smiling, but his tone was a little impatient — he wanted her to answer him.

Laurie raised her eyes and looked wistfully at Meg. Meg read the answer in them, and it sent a pang through her heart, but she said, gaily:

"Oh, never mind me, Laurie. I will withdraw all opposition. Be merciful to Hal and shorten his agony. Don't you see how suspense is torturing him?"

Laurie gave her a swift, grateful smile, then looked at Hal. "It shall be as you wish, Hal," she said.

The Summer months passed swiftly away — July, August, September — and brought beautiful October, the best month of all the twelve. The wedding was to be on the twenty-second. It was to be very quiet; they were not even going away. The ceremony was to be performed at Laurie's own home, in the presence only of relatives, and the "class". The hour was eight o'clock in the evening. There would be no reception, only a short half-hour for pleasant talk, and then the guests would go away, and leave the young, newly-married couple in their large, rambling old stone house.

As the wedding-day approached, Meg felt a feeling of sadness creeping over her. She could not help thinking of that other wedding that "was to have been" eighteen months before. Meg missed Ethel more and more every day. She had taken up the "good work" that had been begun by her, and had done her best in filling the empty place. Her efforts had even thus early proved most successful. There had been a growing interest in the Y. P. C. E. meetings from the time of her support of them, and much praise was given to her for the result of her earnest efforts. When she felt any feeling of pride arising in her heart over these expressions, she would whisper to herself: "All to the glory of God. All to the glory of God."

Mr. Stanley had changed scarcely any. During the first twelve months after Ethel's death, his face had worn the marks of a great sorrow, and a great struggle. It seemed as if he had grown ten years older, but he was kind and pleasant with everyone, as he had always been. That he had suffered intensely was plainly apparent to everyone, but he had never complained to a single person. During the past Summer months he had seemed more cheerful, never gay, for that was not his nature, but several times, lately, when he had been talking with Meg, and she had made one of her bright, witty remarks, she had seen him glance at her as if in appreciation of her laughing jest with the merry sparkle in his dark, blue eyes that she had seen in the days before Ethel's death. He did not make any open preference for Meg's society, and still he showed her plainly in a hundred little ways when with her, that he enjoyed being with her very much. For her — she loved him with her whole heart, respected him above anyone she had ever known, and trusted him fully.

The day of the wedding dawned. It was a perfect day. Meg went around the house with a smiling face when Laurie was near, but with a very sober one when by herself. She dressed the pretty, fair bride herself. Laurie's dress was very simple, but rich. When she was dressed, Meg gave her the very best compliment anyone could, under the circumstances.

"You make an ideal bride, Laurie," she said, and spoke truly.

Laurie's dress was soft, white mull of the finest quality, made entraine. Her veil was of rich lace and fell in folds to the floor. Her wreath was of orange blossoms; her bouquet of the same and lilies of the valley. Her sweet face was as white as the lilies, and

as pure; her blue eyes shone brightly through her
veil, and the pretty, soft, fluffy "bangs" glistened like
golden threads. No wonder Hal looked as if (as Meg
said) "he could eat her".

Meg wore nile-green with pink tea-roses. The
other girls looked very fair and winsome in their
pretty, softly-colored dresses.

Meg looked at Mr. Stanley with wistful, pitying
eyes, as he took his place before the young couple.
His face was so pale and grave, and there was such
a sad look in his blue eyes.

"How he must suffer!" thought Meg, her heart
aching for him. "Laurie looks as lovely as a dream,
but not as Ethel looked. Oh, no; there will never be
so lovely a bride as our darling made. Oh, why could
she not have lived!"

Meg had asked that question many times; it
seemed to her whenever she looked at Mr. Stanley's
pale, sad face, that she would gladly have given her
life for Ethel's if she could have done so.

After the ceremony there was an hour of pleasant
talk, and then the guests went away and left the
young husband and wife together.

"What a very pleasant time!" said Dell to Meg, as
they stood in the guest chamber putting on their
wraps.

Meg smiled assent.

"Mr. Stanley was very pale," continued Dell. "I suppose he was thinking of Ethel, don't you?"

"Yes," answered Meg.

"What a sad thing that was," murmured Dell musingly; and Meg cried passionately:

"I hope I may never realize a sadder!"

XXIV.

MRS. STANLEY.

THREE years later, and once more, the twelfth of June. Just four years from the day of Ethel's wedding-day and death.

Meg, Dell, Laurie and May, are gathered in Laurie's large, cool, shady parlor. The long windows leading out upon the verandah, are open, and a gentle breeze is swaying the lace curtains to and fro, and lifting the soft, fluffy "bangs" from Meg's white forehead, as she half sits, half lies upon the floor, bending over a tiny, white-robed form with a small, white face, large blue eyes, and little rings of golden hair — Laurie's six months' baby-girl — little Meg.

She is lying upon a handsome, brightly-colored silk quilt of "crazy" work, one of Auntie Meg's numerous gifts to her dear little namesake, and made by Auntie Meg's own loving hands. Laurie, looking very little like a "mother", sits in a low rocking-chair, with some dainty lace-work (for one of "baby's" dresses, of course) in her hands, and looks at the pretty picture on the floor before her, every now and then. Dell, lovely as ever, is lying back in the easiest chair the room affords — a large, deep, roomy stationary-rocker of old-gold plush. May, as may be supposed, is sitting in the window, holding the lace curtain back with one hand, while she grasps the window-sill with the other. She, too, is looking at the picture on the floor, and after a little while, says :

"I can't get used to the idea at all."

Meg looks up with laughing eyes. "What idea, May-flower — that of being an 'old maid'?"

May put on one of her most comical faces, and says : "No, I didn't mean that just then. It is cruel of you to remind me of my misfortune, Meg; I never do you."

Meg laughed. "Pretty good, May-flower; you paid me back in my own coin. But what idea did you mean?"

May left her seat, crossed over to where Baby Meg was kicking up her little pink toes in the air, and touched her. "This," she said.

Meg and Laurie laughed. "Nevertheless," quoth Dell from her chair, "it is a very substantial idea."

May went back to her seat in the window. "Meg," she said solemnly, "are you reconciled?"

Meg looked at her, and then at Dell and Laurie. "What ails our sister to-day?" she asked. "Her mind seems to be wandering."

"It is," returned May. "I am *wondering* if it is to be my lot to walk alone through life; to have no strong arm around me upon which to lean."

"You deserve such a lot as that if you can't make a better pun," said Dell. "May, why didn't you keep a firmer hold upon Melvin? You and he would have made such a splendid span. You might have gone through the world getting a fine living by making puns. Why didn't you keep him?"

May looked at her with scornful eyes. "Why didn't I keep him," she repeated. "That is just what I want to know. It wasn't my fault — I did my best. But please do not speak of us as a span, Dell; we are not horses."

"Tell Dell the truth, May-flower," said Meg with a loving look.

"The truth, my queen? And isn't that just what I have told her?"

"No. Tell her, or I shall."

"I have told her, Meg."

"You refuse?" asked Meg, lifting herself up on her elbow. "Then I shall tell her."

"Meg," said May imploringly, and put her hands over her ears.

"This is the reason, Dell," began Meg relentlessly. "She did not try to keep Melvin, because those bright eyes of hers saw that he, unconscious to himself, very much admired our little Ruth; also, that Ruth was experiencing a deeper feeling even than admiration, for Melvin. I did not know it — you did not know it — no one knew of it. Melvin, himself, did not realize how much he really liked and admired Ruth; but this little match-maker here had a keener penetration than any of us, and from talking of Melvin to Ruth, and of Ruth to Melvin, soon found out the true state of affairs. I do believe Melvin would have gone right on — all his life, perhaps — feeling vaguely the want of some one thing, and never knowing what that one thing was, had not May — figuratively speaking — opened his eyes for him. The best of it is, he does not know how his eyes were opened. He only knows that he loves Ruth, and that Ruth loves him, and that is all he wants to know. He and May are sworn friends, as ever, and she will never be the one to tell him how he knew his own heart."

Meg nestled down again beside baby. May took her hands down from her ears, and Dell said:

"Quite like a heroine in a romance, aren't you, May-flower? Only the romance lacks one thing."

"What is that?" asked May; and Dell said, not seeing Meg's warning shake of the head, "Sacrifice of love".

May turned her head quickly, and looked out into the shadowy garden.

"You should have worshipped the very ground he walked upon, May; but, knowing that your friend also loved him, and that he, all unconsciously, returned her love, you nobly sacrificed your own love and happiness to theirs. That would have been much more romantic." And Dell smiled as she leaned her lovely head back against the old-gold plush, and closed her eyes.

"May has made something infinitely better than a romance out of it," said Meg softly. "She has made for herself a monument that will last forever in the hearts of those she has made happy, and in others as well."

Dell opened her gray eyes, but before she could express her surprise at the seriousness of the turn Meg's words had given to the conversation, May had turned her head again and said gaily:

"And May has also made of herself an 'old maid'. What a fate! It seems to me that those words should be set to the music of a dirge — never to be spoken, but always to be chanted."

"You'll be married some day, May, never fear," said Dell encouragingly.

"Bless you for those words," murmured May fervently. "Bless you. They infuse new life into my veins, and you know 'while there's life, there's hope'."

"How good it is that we know you, May," laughed Laurie. "For we know just how much you mean what you say."

"Thank you," said May bowing low.

"But doesn't it seem strange that Melvin and Ruth should fancy each other?" said Dell. "They are so entirely different."

"Extremes meet," said May sententiously; and Meg asked, "Have you forgotten all your lessons in 'Natural Science,' Dell, about the 'Laws of Contrast', etc., etc.?"

Dell passed over this question and went on:

"Another thing seems strange to me, and that is: that Will is to be your brother, instead of your husband, Meg."

The three girls laughed heartily at this — it was so much like plain-spoken Dell.

"You needn't think it strange, Dell," said Meg. "I much prefer him in that relation."

"Yes, of course," said Dell; "only it seems strange. Isn't Elsie older than he?"

"Only six months."

"She looks six years younger, instead of six months older," returned Dell. "But Will always did look older than he was. How long will she have to wait for him?"

"Two years," replied Meg. "Will says he wants to make a home worthy of her."

"That sounds just like him," said Dell. "Well, he will get one good girl."

"That he will," replied Meg emphatically. "Elsie would be willing to help make the home, but Will won't hear of it. He knows that he is as sure of her as if they were already married. She would be true to him twenty years, instead of two, and wait for him, if it were necessary."

"I believe it," said Dell.

"I have one consolation in being an old maid," said May suddenly.

"You keep to that subject with a persistency that almost makes me doubt, May-flower," remarked Dell laughing."

"What is your consolation?" asked Meg.

"That I shall have plenty of time to devote to the care of all the little Eddies and Dells that this earth will be blessed with," replied May.

Meg and Laurie applauded. Dell's white face flushed pink.

"Whoever thought five years ago," continued May mercilessly, "that in one year from now, you will be Mrs. Dr. Holmes. Oh, Dell, thy name is not consistency."

"I have to marry him to get rid of him," said Dell; and that is all she would say.

"And to think," said Laurie, "that Lill and Lulu should marry Ray and Bert."

"Lill would not marry Ray until he joined the church," said Dell. "Should you think she could be sure of his sincerity?"

"I am as sure of Ray's sincerity as I am of my own," said Meg. "Ray has been ready to come forward for a long while, but he kept putting it off and putting it off. Lill did well in refusing to become his wife, for if she had married him who knows how far away he might have wandered. He is most sincere, and what a help in our 'Christian Endeavor'!"

"What a pretty wedding it was!" remarked Dell, thoughtfully.

"Double weddings are always pretty," said Laurie.

"You and I will have to have one, Meg," said May drolly.

Meg laughed. "I think we will when we have any," she replied. "I am thinking, May-flower, that you and I may as well make up our minds to a life of 'single blessedness'. The 'girls' will keep us busy taking care of their little ones. Just think! Elsie, Laurie, Dell, Lill, Lulu and Ruth — three of them married, and the other three as good as married."

"And Maude," said Laurie softly.

"Yes, and Maude," repeated Meg slowly. "I wonder if she has any little ones."

"Let us hope not, for the little ones' sakes," said Dell gravely. "The report from the city is, that she is leading a life of continual excitement, and, as I presume she would call it — pleasure."

"How can she feel like going into society again so soon after her mother's death?" said May. "And her father is in feeble health."

"She may be doing it to drown some secret sorrow of her own," said Meg gravely. "Her life cannot be a very happy one, according to the reports we hear of her husband's life and character."

"Omit that last word, Meg," said Dell; "Augustus Belmont has no character."

"Poor Maude!" said Laurie with a sigh. "I am afraid we were none of us as patient with her as we should have been."

"No, we were not," said May. "We are all quick to condemn."

"All except Ethel," said Meg softly.

The girls were silent. They always were at the mention of that beloved name. Laurie looked across at Meg with wistful, loving eyes. If she could see her happy in the way in which she was herself — happy in the love of a good, true man — she would ask for nothing more. Would it ever be?

The gate-latch clicked, and a man's figure came slowly up the shady garden-path. Laurie glanced out.

"Mr. Stanley, girls," she said warningly.

May almost rolled out of the window, Meg sprang to her feet, catching up baby as she did so, and seated herself in a willow rocker. Dell drew herself up into a little more dignified position, and Laurie rose to meet the visitor as the "girl" opened the door to admit him. He came in, smiling.

"Have I disturbed the meeting?" he asked, looking at Meg with baby in her arms. Laurie drew a chair forward. "You could never do that," she answered kindly.

Mr. Stanley turned to Meg. "I called at your house, and your mother told me you were here. I waited for you a little while, and then grew impatient, and came after you. Are you displeased?"

Was she displeased! Her blushing face and drooping eyes answered him even better than her words did. "Oh, no; far from it."

May looked out through the open window, into the softly-coming twilight. "Methinks my fate is sealed," she said to herself, half humorously, half sadly. "I am to be the 'old maid' of the 'class'. May God bless her and make her happy."

Half an hour later, Dell and May, declining Laurie's invitation to stay to tea, kissed Baby, now lying fast asleep in Meg's lap, and took their departure. Meg carried Baby to Laurie's room, undressed her, and put her in her little white crib, then went down stairs to the parlor.

Laurie had gone to the kitchen to see about tea. Mr. Stanley was standing at one of the long windows, gazing out into the dusky garden. Meg could not see his face, but his attitude betokened deep thought.

"He is thinking of Ethel," said Meg to herself, and turned softly to leave the room.

He looked at her over his shoulder, and crossed the room quickly. "Don't go," he said.

Something in his voice made Meg's heart beat quickly for a moment, then almost stand still. She gave one fleeting glance into his face and drooped her eyes. He smiled and drew her gently to the open window. Then he stood and looked down into her face for a moment. Perhaps he was thinking how changed its expression was. The face was as fair as ever — the eyes as dark and bright; the long lashes rested on the soft cheeks, the lips were red and smiling; but the proud, haughty look had gone, or else deepened and softened into one of sweet, grave womanliness and tender pity. Mr. Stanley gazed a moment. His face was very pale and grave, but his dark-blue eyes were full of a loving, tender light. Then he spoke.

I shall not tell what he said, but half an hour later when innocent little Laurie stepped softly to the open door to tell them "that Hal had come" and "tea was ready", what she saw made her give a little gasp of delight, and fly back to the dining-room with flushed cheeks and sparkling eyes.

Hal was standing by the mantel, leaning one arm upon it. His little wife rushed up to him, and clung to the other arm, almost sobbing in her joy. After she had succeeded in making Hal understand, he looked down into her pretty face with laughing eyes.

"And what you saw made you feel as if you would like to do the same thing; is that it, wee wifie? So you had to fly out to your old husband, and hug him. Well, that is doing pretty well for an old married woman."

Laurie boxed his ears, and then kissed him.

"Just the same, wifie," said Hal, taking out his watch, "they must be brought back to earth before long, or I shall eat up all the strawberries. They may be able to live on love now — I was, once — but when they have been married three years, they will want more substantial food," and Hal laughed teasingly.

"For shame, Hal! Have you forgotten when you were young?"

Five, ten — fifteen minutes passed. Hal had commenced to walk the room. "It's no use, Laurie — they must be brought back. I'll run up to our room, and you come to the foot of the stairs and cry, 'Tea is ready, Hal.' If that doesn't start them — him, at any rate — I shall think there is something the matter with his anatomy. Will you do it, wifie?"

Laurie laughed, but shook her head. "Of course not, you rude boy."

"Then I shall call to you and ask you if it isn't about time for refreshments," and Hal started to go.

Laurie clung to him, trying to coax him back. When nearly to the parlor door, Hal said, loudly enough for Mr. Stanley and Meg to hear, "I'll be back by the time tea is poured, wifie," and ran up stairs, two steps at a time, leaving Laurie to beat a hasty retreat to the dining-room.

She had hardly found her breath, when Mr. Stanley and Meg came slowly from the parlor through the hall, followed by Hal, who had stopped on the upper landing and peeped over the banisters to see what effect his words might have had. The sight of him, walking gravely behind the happy couple, and looking triumphantly at her over their heads, upset Laurie's gravity. She was obliged to step to the door and tell the "girl" to bring in the tea-urn. When she turned again all three were in the room.

Mr. Stanley, passing his arm about Meg, and taking her hand in his, walked with her straight up to Hal, and said :

"Will you give your sister into my keeping, Hal?"

As Hal told Laurie afterward, if it had been anyone else but Mr. Stanley, and it had not seemed too solemn a thing to joke upon, he would have put a hand upon each of their heads, and said : "Bless ye, my children." But the expression of the two pale faces before him checked all words of levity that may have been on his lips.

What had passed between them Hal did not know. He had not heard the solemn words of promise made, nor the low, softly-spoken name of "Ethel", as the two who had loved her best on earth, talked about her, tenderly and freely, each to the other.

Meg knew how much Ethel had been to Mr. Stanley, and Mr. Stanley knew that Meg knew it, and although he loved Meg deeply and tenderly now, he knew and she knew, that there was a corner of his heart where even she could never enter. And Meg was glad that it was so. Had he forgotten thus early and easily, he would not — to Meg — have seemed worthy of either her love or Ethel's.

Hal put out his hand, and took Mr. Stanley's proffered one in a strong, close grasp. "I give her to you, gladly, for I like and respect you above any man, and — she loves you."

It looked a solemn thing to see a brother — and he so young a man — giving his precious sister into another's keeping. And it was a touching as well as a solemn sight. Laurie's tender little heart filled, and so did her blue eyes, as she went up and kissed her "more than sister".

But after they were seated at the table and were

doing full justice to Laurie's delicious little repast, their tongues were loosened, and the happy half-hour slipped quickly by.

At nine o'clock Meg went up to Laurie's room to put on her wraps. Laurie flew up after her, leaving Hal and Arthur talking in the hall. Both the young men looked after them with a smile.

Laurie closed the door and went up to Meg, and then what did these silly girls do but fall into each other's arms and cry, softly, but never were happier tears shed than those they wept together.

When Meg lifted her face from Laurie's shoulder, the first words she said were, "Oh, Laurie, I am so unworthy!"

"Unworthy, Meg?" said Laurie with jealous resentment. "Unworthy of — of Arthur? You are never that, my darling."

Meg smiled. "No, I did not mean Arthur, though I am unworthy of him, too, Laurie; oh, yes, I am — but I meant then, that I am so unworthy of my Father's love and mercy."

Laurie kissed her. "We are all unworthy there, Meg," she said solemnly.

Mr. Stanley, much to everybody's surprise, made a most impatient lover. According to his earnest request, the wedding was set for October. To Mrs.

Randal and Elsie, the time flew by on wings. They both felt that the hardest trial of their lives had come. It was hard for them to give her up, and, had she not been going to reside in the same place with them, it would have been difficult, indeed, for Mr. Stanley to gain the mother's consent for so early a day.

At last the day came, the hour, the minute, when Meg stood in her mother's parlor beside the man whom she loved with all the strength of her deep, pure, true heart, and promised to love, honor and obey him till death should them part.

Meg's dress was white silk. A fine white lace veil enveloped her from head to foot. She carried a large bouquet of white tearoses; her wreath was of the same flower. Immediately after the ceremony, the dainty dress was exchanged for a neat traveling costume, and amid a shower of rice and slippers which the "girls" threw after the carriage, Rev. and Mrs. Arthur Norman Stanley were driven rapidly to the station to catch the express to the city. From there they were to take the boat to New York, where two weeks were to be spent with a cousin of Mr. Stanley's — Dr. John Stanley.

There let us leave them, and not return to them until five years of their married life have passed away.

XXV.

AFTER YEARS.

THEY have been five happy, peaceful years. To Meg it has seemed as if every day has been brighter than the one before it. To Mr. Stanley, his fair, lovable wife has been a source of constant light and happiness.

Even after five years of constant companionship with such a man as Mr. Stanley, Meg is yet far from being perfect. Yet her husband loves every little fault in her — the little flashes of temper, the spirit of pride that shows itself now and then, the natural willfulness of her disposition — he loves them all; for, as he once laughingly said to Elsie, "Meg would not be Meg without them." And then one look from his dark-blue eyes, one low, gravely-spoken "Meg" was enough to banish all signs of temper, pride and willfulness.

Two children — a boy and girl — have blessed their union. The boy, a dark-haired, blue-eyed child of four years, is the very picture of his father. He is a quiet, grave, thoughtful-looking child. Every time Meg looks at him, she sees his father reflected in the dark-blue eyes, and upon every small feature. The girl, a bright-haired, dark-eyed darling of two summers, is a veritable miniature Meg. She reigns queen over all, even her grave, dignified papa. He obeys her imperious "Tate Ethie, Papa," with a meekness that causes many a laughing, "Oh, Arthur!" from Meg.

He loves his little Ethel with a love that is deep and boundless. Meg often says, "her only earthly rival is her own baby.

Meg loves both her children with an equal love. If Mr. Stanley sometimes says, half laughing, half serious, that he is jealous of little Arthur, it is when he has seen his wife hold her boy close to her and cover his grave little face with passionate kisses.

Their home is a perfect little nest of beauty and comfort. It was planned by Arthur himself and built for him as a wedding present by Judge Lawton, and furnished according to Meg's taste by Judge Lawton's wife. The childless couple would have it so, and Arthur and Meg put all false pride away, and accepted their generous gifts. They were constant and ever welcome visitors at the pretty parsonage.

Arthur was to them like a son, and Meg, more than ever, beloved by them.

It was known only by Arthur and Meg, that baby Ethel would one day be heiress to Judge Lawton's wealth. Perhaps that was the reason of Meg's passionate kisses on her boy's face.

One warm, sunny afternoon late in June, Meg was sitting in her little sewing-room. Her work had fallen idly in her lap, her hands were loosely clasped, and her eyes were looking through the vine-covered window, at her darlings playing on the smooth, velvety lawn.

Little Arthur had helped Ethel on to his voloci-pede, and she was laughing, half-tearfully, half joy-fully, not knowing whether to be frightened or not. Meg laughed softly to see her. Just then Ethel threw up her little hands with a glad cry of "Papa", and Arthur came through the gate, crossed the lawn quickly, lifted each child up in his arms, kissed them, and set them down again. Ethel clung to him with imperative cries of, "Tate Ethie, Papa; tate Ethie," but he put her gently but firmly away, and Meg could see that he was trying to reason with her. In vain. The small queen stamped her little foot, and struck at her papa with her tiny clenched hand. Meg could not help laughing when she saw Arthur look about him as if seeking some help out of his difficulty, then, not finding any, put his hand into his pocket, take out something and offer it to Ethel. She stopped her crying long enough to look at the thing he offered, then expressed her contempt for it by striking it out of his hand. Little Arthur quietly picked it up, and handed it back to his father.

Mr. Stanley offered the remaining contents of his pocket to Ethel, but they all received the same contemptuous rejection. At last, in a state of desperation, he took out a set of dainty ivory tablets, with a pretty tiny gold pencil attached. At sight of this long-coveted, but heretofore denied article, baby Ethel's eyes shone with something brighter than tears. Her little face wreathed itself in smiles ; she showed her little "pearls" in a happy laugh, nodded her sunny head with condescending approval, took the tablets from her father's hand, seated herself on the grass, and commenced "operations". Arthur turned away with a smile of relief, but alas ! the smile was premature. Away flew both tablet and pencil, and sharp, wild cries of "papa, papa, tum — an' — tate — Ethie," rang on the air.

Arthur looked up at the window, and caught sight of Meg's laughing face. He laughed too, then, and made an imploring gesture for her to come out. She stepped through the long window and crossed the lawn to him. "Oh, Arthur," she said, "to be ruled by such a sprite!"

Baby Ethel always obeyed her mother. Arthur had a most profound respect for his wife's capability of managing the small "sovereign". It was not that she spoke sharply to her, for she never did. Her voice was always low, sweet, but very firm. Baby Ethel seemed to feel instinctively that when her mama spoke in that way, she must obey her. Arthur could control almost anyone by a glance or a word, but here he was "the weakest of the weak".

After Meg had restored order, she and Arthur turned and walked slowly, arm in arm, to the house. Generally he complimented her laughingly upon her "secret power", but to-day he was unusually grave.

They passed through the window, and Meg seated herself in her low rocker, and waited for him to tell her what was troubling him. She knew there was something — she could always tell — but she never wearied him with questions. He always told her everything of his own accord, sure of her love and sympathy in the merest trifle.

To-day he seated himself on a low couch that was in the room, and motioned for her to sit beside him.

She did so, and he put his arm around her and said, "Feel in the letter-pocket, Meg."

Whenever he had been to the post-office and received letters, he always put them in his breast-pocket after reading them, and then let Meg take them out herself and read them — he looking over her shoulder as she did so. Sometimes, I must confess, she read them sitting upon his knee, but that was always his fault, of course; he would insist upon her doing it.

Meg put her little white hand in his pocket, and drew out a thick cream envelope. The writing was in a lady's hand and addressed to "Rev. A. N. Stanley". The hand-writing looked familiar to Meg, and still she could not name it. Too impatient to read it through before knowing by whom it had been written, she turned the page and looked at the signature.

Maude Belmont!

Meg turned her face to Arthur's. He was looking very grave, but he could not help smiling at her big eyes. "Read it through, dear," he said gently.

Meg turned the leaf back and read:

"*To Rev. A. N. Stanley:*

"DEAR SIR: — I will not insult you by calling you 'dear friend'. Once, years ago, I should have called you so, and you would have been glad to have me, but things are different now from what they were then. Then I was happy, at all events, if not as good as I might have been, and I was respected by most people (your wife was not included among those people), if not deserving of their respect. Now I am wretchedly unhappy. My unhappiness is too great to express. I am sick and discouraged, and oh, so tired! I have lived a life of constant excitement and selfish pleasure, and am now reaping the whirlwind. You may know that I have sunken to the very depths of shame and degradation, when I will thus make my wretchedness known to anyone. If my sin has been great, my punishment has been greater. Let me tell you all the shameful truth at once.

"My husband never cared for me; he admired and was proud of my beauty, but it was my money he loved, not me. He has always led a life of dissipation, but his life of former years was an honorable one beside the one he has lived for the past five years. I will not disgust you by repeating it to you. Enough to say that for the last two years he has never come into my presence in a sober condition; has never spoken aught to me but the vilest curses; and has never left me without cruel blows. I have borne it all until now, for the sake of one who is dearer than life itself — my precious baby girl.

"Oh, tell Meg that; it will make her heart tender toward me where nothing else can. Meg was never deceived by me — she knew me well. She despised me, and she had full reason to. She was proud, perhaps she is now — I cannot tell; but I know she has a little girl of her own, and I can imagine what a mother she will be to her. So tell her of my baby girl, and oh, how I love her. I cannot write more now — I am too weak. What I want to ask of you both, is this: Will you come to me? I have only a very little while longer to stay here, and I want to see Meg. Meg was always true, if proud; she would never deceive a living person. I know she will not deceive a dying one. I have written to you instead of to Meg, because I thought that if she would not come to me for baby's sake, she might if you asked her."

The address was given at the bottom of the page. Meg looked up into her husband's face. "Shall I go, Arthur?"

"How do you feel about it?" he asked gently.

"I would like to go very much."

He kissed her lips. "We will go," was all he said; but Meg knew he was greatly pleased.

They left little Arthur with his grandmother and Ethel with Mrs. Lawton, and took the seven o'clock train that night for the city. The New York boat left at eight o'clock. Arthur had telephoned for a state-room immediately after the decision to go had been made, and they were fortunate enough to secure a good one.

Maude's summer home was at Yonkers, and it was from there that she had written to Arthur.

As Arthur and Meg stepped upon the platform, they were greatly surprised to see Mr. Leonard, Maude's father, there, waiting for them. He looked old and bent and feeble, but he thanked them brokenly for their kindness in coming to his child, and conducted them to a hack that was in waiting. Meg hardly noticed that it was not a private carriage into which she was assisted; her thoughts were too busy with Maude and her suffering, but when the carriage stopped, and she saw, through the window, that it was before an old, dilapidated house, her astonishment was great, and she looked with large eyes at Mr. Leonard, but he did not seem to see her. Arthur touched her arm warningly, and she controlled her surprise.

A pretty, neatly-dressed English girl opened the door for them, and conducted them to a small chamber, where she left them for a few moments. Meg sat down on the edge of the bed and looked at Arthur.

"It is even worse than we thought for, Meg," he said. "But you must really control the expression of your face, or you will make Maude feel badly."

"Oh, Arthur! Poor Maude! Poor Maude!"

It was all that Meg could say. She laid aside her hat, bathed her face and brushed her hair. Then came a low knock at the door, and Arthur opened it. The pretty English girl stood on the threshold.

"Mrs. Belmont's compliments to Mr. and Mrs. Stanley, and she would be happy to see them as soon as possible."

"We are ready now," said Meg.

Everywhere it looked very neat, but very, very poor. As the girl pushed open a chamber door, a low, hollow sound fell on Meg's ear, and made her heart beat quickly; then she stepped inside the room, the girl went out and closed the door, and Meg found herself standing in the middle of a small, scantily-furnished chamber, looking at a wasted form upon the bed, a thin, flushed face, with two large, glittering eyes upon the pillow, and then she saw two poor, white hands stretched yearningly out to her, and heard a weak voice cry, "For my baby's sake, Meg."

In an instant Meg was on her knees beside the bed, her arms around the wasted form, the poor, aching head upon her breast. "For your own sake, Maude," she cried, and pressed a kiss upon the dry lips.

Arthur slipped quietly from the room, and left the two together.

Forgiveness was brokenly asked and granted on both sides, then Maude sobbed out her miserable story on Meg's breast. Her husband's money and her own independent fortune was all gone — swallowed up in a life of endless excitement and sinful pleasure. What they had not spent to defray their manifold expenses, her husband had spent for drink, and at the gaming-table. He had even ruined her poor old father; not only taking from him every cent of his vast fortune, but even his home.

"And he gave it all to him for my sake, Meg. My poor old father! I would not leave my husband, and father would not see me suffer."

Maude's suffering, both mental and bodily, was intense. She cried out in agony that she could not die; that she was not fit to die; she was afraid.

"It is so dark, Meg," she moaned. "The river is wide and deep, and I am so cold. Give me your hand, do not let me go. Oh, Meg, tell me something; say something to me from the Bible. I have been wicked, but I am sorry. I do truly repent and ask forgiveness. Oh, Meg! Meg! Pray for me — say something — oh!" —

"Let me call Arthur, Maude, dear," said Meg, trembling in every limb.

She felt frightened. She had never seen anyone

die but Ethel, but alas! Maude's death-bed was vastly different from what Ethel's had been.

But Maude clung to her with the strength of despair. "No, no, do not leave me, Meg, I shall die before you get back. Pray for me. Oh, Meg," and Maude sat up straight in bed, and grasped Meg's arm with both hands, while her eyes seemed to be on fire. "You never deceived anybody — you always told the truth; tell it now, for Heaven's sake! Am I to be eternally lost, or is there yet time for repentance? Tell me quick!"

Poor Meg was almost fainting. What should she do? She had never prayed aloud in her life. She glanced at the door. Oh, if Arthur would only come in! Maude's grasp grew looser; her head fell back upon the pillow. "Quick — Meg — for — Jesus' — sake."

"For Jesus sake." The words were an inspiration to Meg. All fear left her. She knelt by the bed and clasping Maude's hands in hers, told over to her the story of the dying thief upon the cross. "There yet is time for you, Maude. Just say, 'God have mercy upon me, a sinner', and He will surely hear and answer your prayer. Say it, Maude."

"God have mercy upon me, a sinner," repeated the poor lips.

Then Meg prayed; what she prayed, she did not know — but she felt Maude's hands grow quiet in hers; her quick, heavy breathing grew soft and slow, and when Meg lifted up her head, Maude lay asleep, with a smile upon her lips.

She lay thus a long while. The sun went to rest behind a bank of heavy, dark clouds. With night, came rain, accompanied by a low, sobbing wind. One by one the lights gleamed out, and lighted up the wet, dreary streets. Mr. Leonard and Arthur came into the room; the night-lamp was lighted. Meg still held Maude in her arms; she would not leave her. Her arms ached, and sharp pains shot through her head, but she would not leave her post. She took food and drink from Arthur's hands, but her arms never loosened their hold of their burden.

And thus the long night wore away. Mr. Leonard had sunk down in an easy chair; his head rested on his hands; he neither spoke nor stirred. Arthur sat in a chair at the foot of the bed. The rain fell drearily, the wind moaned sobbingly, and the night-lamp burned dimly all night.

As midnight struck Meg felt the form she held, move softly in her arms. The great, black eyes opened slowly, and looked up in her face. All color was gone from the thin face; it was white enough now.

"Meg."

Meg bent her head.

"My baby-girl."

"She wants her baby, Arthur."

Arthur went from the room, and returned with the child in his arms. It was the first time that Meg had seen her. She was three years old, and had her mother's rich, dark beauty, except her eyes, which were large and bright, but a deep blue, and the lashes were long and curly ; but Meg could see even then that there was pride and temper in every line and feature.

The poor mother's arms were held hungrily out, and Arthur placed the child in them. Oh, what passionate cries rose up from the young mother's heart as she pressed her dying lips on the beautiful little face ! Arthur and Meg turned their heads away from the sight.

"My baby ! My baby ! Oh, God, let me take my baby. I will have her — I must have her. Oh, I cannot go without her ! "

So she cried, holding her child close to her, until, strengthless and voiceless, she lay gasping on her pillow. But never will Meg forget the agonized look of entreaty in the large eyes as Maude raised them to her face.

"What is it, Maude?" she whispered.

"B — a — b — y." The white lips scarcely moved.

Arthur took the child and held it in his arms. "You want us to take baby?" he asked clearly, yet gently.

A rapturous look of joy was his answer

"To take her for our own; to love and care for all her life?" he continued.

Another of the rapturous looks was his answer. He looked at his young wife.

"Yes, Arthur, I will be a mother to her," Meg said.

"And I a father."

Oh, how the poor hands tried to clasp theirs! How the dying eyes grew dim with thankful tears! How the white lips tried to thank them, and failed!

"We will call her Maude?" asked Arthur.

The lips smiled.

"Maude Leonard Belmont?"

The dark brows were drawn together as if in pain.

Arthur tried again. "Maude Leonard Stanley?"

The lips parted in a smile again.

"We will love her and cherish her like our own," said Arthur. "We will let no one take her from us." Then he put the child down for it to receive its last kiss, and then carried her from the room.

After that Maude lay very quiet. They saw her lips move twice or thrice as if in prayer, but no sound came from them. Her eyes were closed, her breath came softly and slowly; then yet more slowly and more slowly still, until it died away altogether, and Maude was safe in her Father's house, away from the fever and unrest of this life.

Arthur bent over Mr. Leonard, as he still sat, crouched down in his chair, and touched him gently. He did not move or look up. Arthur touched him again, and yet again. He neither moved or spoke. And when they lifted up his face, they found the reason written upon it. Maude and her father had gone home together.

*　　*　　*　　*　　*　　*

Arthur ordered the removal of the bodies to L—— for burial. Nothing had been seen or heard of Maude's husband. On the fourth day after Arthur and Meg had left their home to go to Maude, the funeral took place. The services were held in the home Church, the pastor officiating.

Side by side with her father, in the very place where she had stood, ten years before, a proud, beautiful bride, Maude now lay in her white casket, pale and cold and lifeless, a mere wreck of former beauty.

"Restless we walk in Life's rich garments drest,
    Death brings a robe of plainness, filled with rest."

As the funeral cortege moved slowly through the beautiful, tree-lined avenue that led to the Leonard family burying-ground, a miserable, repulsive-looking man, greatly under the influence of liquor, staggered along by the side of the hearse, and kept beside it until it stopped at the open vault. Mr. Stanley stepped from his carriage, and the man reeled up to him.

"Look here," he began, with a miserable attempt at a swagger, when Arthur put his hand out and took hold of his arm.

He knew him in a moment, changed as he was from the elegant Mr. Agustus Belmont of ten years ago.

"Do not try to talk with me here," said Arthur in a low, firm voice, which the man instinctively felt was to be obeyed. "I will take you home with me in a few moments, but I will have nothing to say to you now. Get into the carriage and be quiet."

Arthur felt that it would be better to keep the man out of sight; it would do no good to try to explain to him any of the circumstances; the poor wretch would only deepen the disgrace still more, that he had brought upon his dead wife.

Arthur opened the carriage door, and thrust the

man in.   He made no attempt to get out, and when
Arthur entered the carriage, after the last sad rites
had been performed, he saw the reason.

He lay asleep with his head on one of the seats, his
feet on the other.   Arthur could scarcely repress
a shiver of disgust as he took his seat beside the
man.

The disgust deepened into something worse, when,
after an hour's serious talk with the man in his study,
during which he showed not the faintest sign of grief
over his wife's death, Arthur put the question of his
child's welfare to him.   With an oath the unnatural
father said : "I don't care for the brat so long as it is
kept out of my sight.   You may have her, and welcome," he said coarsely.   "Only you'll have to give
me money enough to keep me for a while, at any
rate."

"How much do you want?" asked Arthur, wholly
unable to keep the contempt he felt out of his face
and voice.

"Oh, fifty dollars will do.   She's not worth it, but
I may as well get what I can out of her."

Without another word, Arthur drew up the papers,
and sent for Elsie's husband, now Lawyer Duncan, as
witness to the contract.

Grasping the bills greedily with one hand, Augustus

Belmont with the other, signed away his motherless child.

They let him go from them with scarcely a feeling of regret.

In her adopted home, with a loving father and mother, dear little sister and brother, let us leave the child Maude, nor look upon her again until years have passed over her head.

And now let me say, that, having made her peace with Maude, and returning good for evil indeed, Meg felt more satisfied with herself than she had ever felt before in her life. There had always been a feeling of something undone, that should be done; she could never tell what it was, but now she knew. It taught her a good lesson, for she never knew before the blessedness of "returning good for evil". God surely rewarded her in the years that followed. Her life was filled up with work — noble work — in her home and in the world outside. Beloved by everybody, with a tender, loving husband to guide and protect her, Meg's heart was filled full of gratitude to her Heavenly Father, and with tender pity for all His suffering children.

Verily, He doeth all things well, and maketh all things to come right in His own good time.